Maisey Yates is a *New York Times* bestselling author of over one hundred romance novels. Whether she's writing stories about strong, hard-working cowboys, dissolute princes or multigenerational families, she loves getting lost in fictional worlds. An avid knitter, with a dangerous yarn addiction and an aversion to housework, Maisey lives with her husband and three kids in rural Oregon. Check out her website: maiseyyates.com.

Jackie Ashenden writes dark, emotional stories, with alpha heroes who've just got the world to their liking only to have it blown wide apart by their kick-ass heroines. She lives in Auckland, New Zealand, with her husband, the inimitable Dr Jax, two kids and two rats. When she's not torturing alpha males and their gutsy heroines she can be found drinking chocolate martinis, reading anything she can lay her hands on, wasting time on social media or being forced to go mountain biking with her husband. To keep up to date with Jackie's new releases and other news sign up to her newsletter at jackieashenden.com.

Also by Maisey Yates

The Secret That Shocked Cinderella

Pregnant Princesses collection

Crowned for His Christmas Baby

The Heirs of Liri miniseries

His Majesty's Forbidden Temptation
A Bride for the Lost King

The Royal Desert Legacy miniseries

Forbidden to the Desert Prince

Also by Jackie Ashenden

The Maid the Greek Married

Rival Billionaire Tycoons miniseries

A Diamond for My Forbidden Bride
Stolen for My Spanish Scandal

Three Ruthless Kings miniseries

Wed for Their Royal Heir
Her Vow to Be His Desert Queen

Discover more at millsandboon.co.uk.

A VIRGIN FOR THE DESERT KING

MAISEY YATES

PREGNANT WITH HER ROYAL BOSS'S BABY

JACKIE ASHENDEN

MILLS & BOON

First published in Great Britain 2023
by Mills & Boon, an imprint of HarperCollins*Publishers* Ltd,
1 London Bridge Street, London, SE1 9GF

www.harpercollins.co.uk

HarperCollins*Publishers*, Macken House, 39/40 Mayor Street Upper, Dublin 1, D01 C9W8, Ireland

A Virgin for the Desert King © 2023 Maisey Yates

Pregnant with Her Royal Boss's Baby © 2023 Jackie Ashenden

ISBN: 978-0-263-30694-1

09/23

This book is produced from independently certified FSC™ paper to ensure responsible forest management.
For more information visit: www.harpercollins.co.uk/green.

Printed and Bound in the UK using 100% Renewable Electricity at CPI Group (UK) Ltd, Croydon, CR0 4YY

A VIRGIN FOR THE DESERT KING

MAISEY YATES

MILLS & BOON

To Nic, for being amazing.

CHAPTER ONE

THE FIRST TIME Sheikh Riyaz al Hadid saw the sunlight in sixteen years, she was standing in it.

Her red hair seemed lit on fire by the pool of golden warmth she stood in, her skin glowing. Her lips were like cherries, her body a fever dream.

It had been as many years since he'd seen a woman as it had been since he'd seen the sun. And now, here they both were.

"This is Brianna Whitman."

Riyaz turned toward his brother, Cairo, who gestured to the woman. The way his brother touched her arm, as if there was a physical familiarity between them, made a monster in Riyaz growl.

Apparently, not just within, for both Cairo and Brianna reacted to the sound.

Thoughts, words, feelings, sounds. All of it was the same to him.

Riyaz had been in the dungeon for sixteen years.

One week ago, Cairo and his men had stormed the palace and freed him, taken down the interlopers who had stolen the throne from their father all those years ago.

It had taken a week for Riyaz to go to the upper floors. Freedom was also a strange and elastic concept to him. He had been free in his mind all this time, but now his body was also free. And there was wide-open space, harsh light, too many sounds. He'd stayed where he could control some of what he saw and heard and felt.

But Cairo had come to see him, every day.

As had doctors. Psychiatrists. And now…this woman.

This woman who Cairo had said would not be seeing him in the dungeon, but Riyaz would have to greet in the throne room.

It was a strange thing, being told what to do. Yes, Riyaz had been a prisoner for many years. But it was strange how he had found ways to forget. The dungeon had become his world. He was not told what to do. He had free run of that world. He was brought food. And there was a guard who took pity on him and brought books. A rotation of them. They did not speak. They did not… Get to know one another, but there was no animosity either. And he would read each new book at least three times before the man traded them out.

He had created a workout facility, found ways to keep his body in shape, so that he would not atrophy during his time in captivity. And yet, there had been long stretches of time when he had forgotten why he was doing anything. There was no future to plan for. There was nothing.

He had never known for sure if Cairo had survived the attack on the palace.

When Cairo had returned, and set Riyaz free, he had asked that his brother show mercy to the guard who had brought him the books.

Time had a new meaning now. And there were tasks. He had spent the first sixteen years of his life in such a fashion. His days had been tightly scheduled. There had been expectations of him. He had learned other languages, had learned about other cultures. He had kept his language skills sharp through reading. He read in Arabic, English, French. Consuming information, stories, had kept him from losing his mind.

At least, entirely.

And now here he was, in the sun. Looking at the most beautiful woman he had ever seen.

That was something that had not been supplied for him.

Women.

Appetites were an interesting thing. One could learn to suppress them. He had done so while living in the dungeon. He had gone from living on a diet of rich, elaborately prepared foods, to eating nothing but the bland, boring foods of a prisoner. The same every day. Just enough to keep him going. Enough to keep him fit. They fed him quantity, especially as he added mass to his body, but variety was not the order of the day.

He had learned not to care. And then there were days when he would be overcome with the desire to eat a cheeseburger. He did not know why a cheeseburger specifically. It was not common fare in his family's household. It was not traditional at all. And yet he had tried it before, and it was something that had stuck with him. And it was the thing that haunted him.

So too with sex.

He had been a teenage boy when he had been thrown in the dungeon, after all. His hormones had been in a heightened state.

At sixteen, he had not yet lain with a woman, but he'd thought about it often.

He had been promised to wed a girl who was often in the palace, though he had imagined he would take lovers prior to that marriage. He had thought of her, when

Cairo had come to the dungeon. It was her father that had betrayed them. Dominic Hart.

The first thing he'd said when Cairo had come to collect him was that he wanted Ariel Hart. She would complete the contract that her father had broken. Would restore what had been destroyed.

He had decided that during those nights when he had gone over and over the way that things had fallen apart.

But he did not desire her.

His desire took a generic, lush form, much like the woman in front of him.

And there would be stretches of months where he did not think of his deprivation.

And then there would be nights… Nights when he was so hard it was physical pain. Where he raged at the state of denial he lived in. Denial he had not chosen.

He could respect men who chose to live their lives as monks. Denial of self was not a bad thing, he supposed.

But he had lived in *forced* denial of self for years.

And sometimes he… Sometimes the fury of it all was too much to handle. Though there were other times that there was something glorious in the deprivation. For it made moments others would take for granted sharp. Acute.

This woman was a moment of pure, aching need.

What he wanted to do was send everyone out of the room and pull her into his arms.

But he was very aware of his own strength. Of the fact that he had no finesse. Of the fact that he had nothing but fury and need. And that his brother was touching her.

That his brother made love to this woman.

His brother who'd had all this freedom these many years.

Riyaz was the Sheikh. He had been raised to be all-powerful. He had been raised to be in command.

And had spent sixteen years in command of nothing much more than what he did in the dark.

He was back in power now. And yet… Cairo was the one with the knowledge, the means, to rule.

It was a strange reality.

But then, his reality had been strange from the beginning.

"Brianna," he said, tasting her name.

It was sunshine. Lemon and raspberry. Somehow.

It had been years since he had met new people. And then in this last week he had met many.

She was the one who shone above all else.

"It's nice to meet you, Sheikh," she said. "Cairo has told me about your… Your experiences."

She was sweet. Hesitant to say anything that might hurt him. As if there was any way he could be hurt.

"Do not be careful with me," he said. "I despise that. I'm not simple. And I am not fragile. In any regard."

The woman looked at him with something like pity, and it filled him with a blackened rage.

"And what is it you are here to do?" he asked. "Are you here to fix me?"

"I am here to help you… I'm here to help you with manners. Etiquette, and… What I do is complicated. But I'm not a therapist. However, I have had some experiences with being shut away from the world. And having to learn how to fit in. What I found is that many people want help with that. And need it. It is not as unusual as you would think. I help people. I helped him figure out how to change their behavior to get the promotion. To figure out how to have a relationship. To ascend the throne. After years in a dungeon, though, I will confess this is a first."

"What job title is that?"

"I don't really have a title. When people need me they find me."

He suddenly wanted to know everything about her. And he didn't see why he shouldn't.

"How old are you?"

"Oh. I'm… I'm twenty-five."

"Where do you live?"

"New York."

"In a penthouse?"

"It's a… It's a town house."

"How did you afford it?" New York was expensive. He knew that from reading. Unless it wasn't true now. But he imagined that it was. He'd read books spanning many time periods. Many of them were older. So it was difficult to say what was a more modern truth sometimes. He did try to look at and remember the copyright dates. For context.

"It is expensive. I… Cairo bought my home."

He looked at Cairo. "And what is she to you?"

"She's the woman that's going to help you," said Cairo. "That's all you need to know."

"It is not all I need to know," he said. "I wish to know everything."

"I am going to begin to see about your other business," said Cairo. "Brianna is going to care for you. While I'm away."

"You're going to get Ariel Hart."

"Soon. But I'm not quite prepared for her."

"She will pay for what her father did."

"Do you think that is… Productive?" Cairo asked, and

yet his brother was not neutral. He could see that. And if *Riyaz* could see that—with his long years lacking in social interaction—then it was painfully obvious.

"I don't care about what is *productive*. I'm not even certain what that means. People use that word to talk about all that they accomplish in a day. Days... Nights... What do they matter when you live in a dungeon with no sunlight? What did they matter when you live in a dungeon without other people? You just survive. In the waves of time."

"Yes. But out here there is the sun. Also people. And there are schedules. Which is where Brianna comes in. And we don't have a lot of time. We need to see you ascended to the throne. We need to let the people know that they are free. I would love to give you endless time to adjust to the world around you, but even if you are acting primarily as a figurehead, we need you in figurehead shape."

It was such a strange thing. His brother moved at an entirely different pace than he did. He wore expensive suits. His hair was cut ruthlessly short. His movements were quick and precise.

Riyaz sometimes did not move at all. He watched. He observed. He could be fast if the moment demanded it. But he did not see the point of wasting energy. Everything he did had a purpose. That was why he had set up ways to work out in the dungeon. If he was going to move, he was going to build muscle. Strength.

That seemed a reasonable aim. Riyaz had lived a life where he had little. So he had learned to economize.

Clearly, Cairo did not approach life with the same ethos. His brother was excess personified.

Was Brianna one of his excesses?

He growled again.

"What?" Cairo asked.

"I had a thought I did not like."

"You're going to have to not growl."

"Why?"

"People don't expect it."

He looked around, at the glittering opulence of the throne room. At Brianna, who was being given to him as... Some sort of guide. At his brother, who was now leaving. "I have not expected any of the things that have occurred in this last eight days. Why should I make others comfortable by giving them what they expect?"

"Because you're a sheikh. You have to be somewhat expected."

"What is your plan?" Riyaz asked. "Give me something to expect."

"In a month's time I wish to present you to our people. Riyaz... They have been in captivity as well. Even if not quite so literally. But until we can show you, physically to the public, I don't want to disclose what has occurred. We must move carefully. We must not ever allow anyone to think that we are weak. We cannot invite more unrest. Not after what we have already endured."

"I could fight. If we were attacked."

Cairo looked at him. "I know. But I would rather not have to fight."

Cairo turned to go. "I will be back next week. After which I will be going to Europe to secure Ariel. As instructed."

"Good."

"My wish is only to serve."

His brother gave a small bow, then turned and walked out of the room, leaving him alone with Brianna Whitman. And now he would ask her whatever he wanted. Because Cairo was not here to tell him that he couldn't.

"Is my brother your lover?"

Her face turned a startling shade of pink. "Excuse me?"

"He touches you as a man familiar with your body would."

"Cairo is not… He is not familiar with my body."

But he could see by the way she said his name, and by the way that her cheeks colored even darker, that the idea was not an unpleasant one to her.

This time he made sure to keep the growl inside. "But you would like him to be."

"We're friends. We do not have that sort of relationship."

"Do you have a lover?"

Her lips went tight. "What we're doing is not about me," she said. "It is about you. Shall we go take lunch?"

"I cannot eat this food," he said. "Not every day. It is… Too much. I cannot even fathom it. All day every day, changes in texture, flavor. In addition to all these other things going on. How does one even have a thought with so much…?" He waved a hand. "Everything?"

"Is there something specific I can ask the kitchen to prepare you?"

"Porridge," he said. "And bread. Toasted."

The day that he had been set free from the dungeon he'd had a cheeseburger. After that, he had wanted to return to what he knew. He could manage at least one different thing every day, but the relentlessness of it all… He did not care for it.

"Then that is what you will have."

"And then what?"

"And then… Your training begins."

CHAPTER TWO

BRIANNA TRIED TO catch her breath while she waited for Riyaz to join her in the dining room.

She hadn't been prepared for him. Of course she had come here because Cairo had asked her to. And she would do anything that Cairo asked. And disturbingly, Riyaz seem to have identified that immediately.

Was he her *lover*?

No, Riyaz, but I have spent years fantasizing about it. While he has slept with everything except for me.

Her untouched state was directly down to her feelings about Cairo.

He had rescued her. From her father's crime syndicate when she was fifteen. She had been a near captive. Rapunzel, locked in a tower. And then her father had decided to sell her. To a rival crime lord. He was intent on selling his only daughter into what was essentially human trafficking, and Cairo had been... Somehow adjacent to all of it, which she understood now was part of his working undercover to gain access to the palace in Nazul again. He had rescued her from her father's house one night at a party, after he'd overhead his father talking to a group of men about his plans to essentially sell her to a man he wanted to make his ally. He had gone in search of her, and she could still remember that first time he'd spoken to her.

He wasn't too much older than her, tall and handsome, and she'd thought he had to be a fallen angel.

Your father is planning on selling you.

I know.

She had known, and she'd been…afraid. Desperate to get away. Because she knew what it meant. That she would be losing her freedom, her choice over…everything. She'd been making plans to run away but she hadn't known what she would do when she did.

Come with me.

She'd known it was a risk. That it could be out of the frying pan and into the fire. But she had grown up in a world where she could never trust the adults around her, and in the end, she'd decided it was a risk she'd be willing to take.

The risk had paid off. He had helped her create a new identity, a new life. Had sent her to boarding school, had…

And of course she had fallen in love with him. Over the past decade, it had been unavoidable.

He wasn't what she wanted, though, not really. He was a man who lived on the edge, a man who traveled all over and who took lovers whenever he wanted. She wanted a simpler life. Something normal. Something like the town house he'd bought her, which she'd always loved because it reminded her of her favorite family sitcoms growing up. Homey wallpaper, a clock in the kitchen, some ivy on the cabinets.

He wasn't the sort of man to want ivy on the kitchen cabinets.

So she loved him, even knowing they would never be together. It wasn't a reasonable love. But it occupied her heart, whether she was a realist about him or not.

He was her friend. He'd bought her house. He'd facilitated her business.

He brought her others to help. Because he dealt in people who were refugees from their old lives.

And she had so successfully navigated that transition herself that it seemed only right that she begin to help others to do the same thing.

What she hadn't counted on, when she had agreed to this, was Riyaz.

When he had walked into the throne room, her heart had jumped up into her throat.

He was terrifying. Broad and bronzed, and well-muscled. His jet-black hair was shoulder length, his gaze piercing. His nose was straight, his mouth grim. He had a dark beard that had been expertly trimmed, allowing her to guess at just how sharp and square his jaw was.

He resembled Cairo in some ways. But Cairo held himself with ruthless sophistication, his wardrobe expertly cut, his body honed with lean muscle.

Riyaz looked like a warrior from another time. He was tall, and broad. He looked like he would be at home holding a sword. And maybe in his other hand, the head of one of his enemies.

There was something feral about him, and why wouldn't there be? He had been captive all these years. How could he not be?

And it was her job to help him. Not… Tremble at the sight of him. And certainly not feel embarrassed that he had so quickly zeroed in on her connection to Cairo. The connection that only ran one way.

"How strange to eat at a table," he said when he walked in and pulled his chair out, sitting down heavily at the head of the table. He was pushed away from it, the chair angled, his legs spread wide. There was something so… Blatant about it. It made her feel jittery.

She had never seen someone who just… Wasn't bound by any sort of rule or sense of manners.

He simply was, and expected the world to shift around him.

"Well, it is sort of difficult to try and hold your food and your utensils and a drink without a table."

"Not impossible."

"Well. We are aiming for a little bit better than not impossible."

She had decided that she ought to have the same thing he did. But she regretted it when the bowl of porridge was brought to her. A small plate with dried fruit and sugar was brought out as well, but Riyaz ignored it. Picking up a triangle of toast and dipping it into the bland meal.

She wrinkled her nose and began to put dates on top of hers.

"You said you came from a similar background to mine. Tell me," he said.

"Part of being in society is to learn to observe the agreements that we all make without ever speaking of them," she said. "One such agreement is that we do not ask terribly personal questions of people we do not know. Particularly not in environments like this. If we were at a dinner of state, you could not ask someone about their trauma. And they would not ask you about your time spent in the dungeon."

"Why not? It is the only thing I've done for the last sixteen years. Therefore it is the only thing I have to comment on."

"Right. But... Many other people do not wish to comment upon things that cause them pain."

"You know what causes me pain? The memories of my parents dying. That is particularly painful. Losing sight of my brother in the throne room, wondering if he had also been cut down, while I was dragged away by ten men. Ten men, that's how many it took to restrain me, even when I was sixteen. I raged for a time. But eventually you learn... You learn that you cannot rage always, even at the things that are not fair, because you must bide your time. You must wait. That's what I've been doing all these years. I made sure my body did not die. I made sure my mind didn't... Well. I cannot say that I am the same man that I was who entered that dungeon. But I did not lose myself entirely."

"I see."

He tilted his head to the side. There was an amusement in his gaze, and she wondered if he might've smiled if he was a different sort of man. "You are curious now. And you want to ask. But you have just chastised me for asking questions, so you won't."

"Fine. How exactly did you do those things?"

"Exercise is very good for the mind and the body. Movement. I made sure that I moved. Also... Reading. I have read hundreds of books. Thousands. There was a guard who would bring them to me. You know what I like about people in books? You see their thoughts. It is all plain. Written out before you. When I look at you, I cannot read your thoughts. So I ask you what they are. I should like to read you. As if you were a book. I should like to see the paragraphs between the words you speak. For I think there are many."

"Maybe," she said. "A fair few. But that is very interesting. What were your favorite books?"

"It depends. I love reading for information, because I could not go outside and see things for myself. But then... Reading stories of action. Espionage. That was good as well."

"Romance?"

He had a strange look on his face. "Sometimes I found that difficult."

Of course. Books about human connection. Human touch. She understood that. She liked the occasional romance novel, but sometimes they were too painful.

Because, according to those books, by all rights, the man who rescued you when you were a child should eventually begin to see you as a woman. Eventually, didn't the guardian want his ward? Lies books had told her.

It hurt her to read about people connecting in a way that she hadn't experienced. Being alone like he was... She imagined it was even worse.

"All right. Well, that is good to know. You like to read. That will give you a lot to talk about. Books make fantastic small talk."

"And the weather," he said. "Which I can see now. So... That will also give me something to talk about."

Except he didn't seem like the kind of man who wanted to talk about the weather, and for a moment, she almost mourned what she was trying to do.

She liked him as he was. He was forthright, and different. Part of the problem with her job was that so much of it involved taking someone different and turning them into something the same.

It was what the people who hired her wanted, or what they needed for a variety of reasons. And Cairo had impressed upon her the importance of the situation. The severity of it all.

She understood.

She was going to do what she was asked.

"We should probably begin to discuss table manners."

"I know them," he said, his expression getting dark.

"Rather than trying to remember what happened in the past, I'm happy to begin with a fresh slate here and now. Sometimes... Sometimes when there are memories that are painful, or a time in your life that is painful, it's difficult to try and think back. I should think that maybe it would be easier for you to simply begin again."

He looked at her skeptically. "All right."

She stood, and moved to the side of her chair. "Why don't you stand. And we'll try having you sit again."

"Why?"

"What you did before was a bit jarring."

He stood, and she was unbearably aware of how small she was next to him. She only came just to his shoulder, and he was so... Broad and imposing. He could end her with one hand if he chose to.

He didn't seem volatile in that way, though. At least, she hoped he wasn't.

She took a step toward him, and his body made a strange sort of motion that reminded her of a horse. A great stallion that you had to approach with care. It made her want to extend her hand slowly and let him get her scent. Maybe offer him a sugar cube.

He's not an animal. He's a man.

And yet she looked at him, and could clearly see both, and she had to wonder how much that was true of every human. And just how much they had all learned to suppress it.

That more elemental side of them.

Because in these few moments she had spent with Riyaz, what she had learned was that he was almost entirely elemental.

"You pull your chair back slowly," she instructed, "and don't try to make a sound with it."

"I do not understand. Why people are always trying to… Silence themselves."

"You're used to being by yourself. And… Well, here there are always many people. So if we all made all the noise we wanted… It might be a problem."

"But I'm the Sheikh. Surely I can have as much of the noise as I want."

"All right. That's… Fair. However. Why don't we learn and then…?"

"You know what I do remember when I look at you? My teacher when I was in the nursery. I am not in the nursery." He took a step toward her. "I am not a boy. You do not need to speak to me as if you are teaching me shapes and colors." He was so close that she could smell the scent of him. Soap and skin. And something wild beneath that. Her hands were shaking, her heart throbbing, and she couldn't seem to make either one stop.

"You're beautiful," he said, in the same way that he had just said all those other things. The same tone. It was not soft, it was not said to flatter. It was an observation, like the many that he had made since they'd met, and somehow, that made it almost more... Flattering. Because he didn't lie. And he didn't say things to get a response. At least, not that she'd observed.

"Thank you," she said.

She couldn't remember the last time someone had called her beautiful. If they ever had.

"Do you know how many years I went without seeing anything beautiful? Not a flower. Not the sun, not the desert. Not a woman. Just gray stone walls, wrought-iron bars. Men in uniform. Perhaps they were beautiful to someone, but not to me. The same food. The same space. Everything is different out here."

"Right. Well. Let's... You sit. But... Softer."

This time, his lips did curve. "I do not know that I possess the ability to do anything softer. But perhaps with more care."

"Maybe," she said.

And she watched as he took his seat. This time, much better.

"You can square your chair up to the table, so that you are sitting facing those who are sitting with you."

"Why did you get the same meal I did?" he asked, taking another bite.

"It seemed polite," she said.

"Why?"

"Because I feel as if you... Did not choose to have porridge so much as you are transitioning into the space. And I thought maybe it would make you feel like I recognize that."

"You worry too much about other people. It doesn't matter to me what you eat."

"Now I know that for next time."

"Will we be taking all of our meals together?"

"For a time, yes."

"And what other lessons will there be?" he pressed.

"It's not really like that. There isn't a lesson plan. I want to make things easier for you. So if there is anything that feels especially difficult, you tell me."

And then he laughed. He looked as surprised by it as she did, but the laughter continued. "You wish for me to tell you if I am uncomfortable?"

"Why is that funny?" she asked.

"I no longer know how to recognize discomfort. Or perhaps… Everything around me makes me uncomfortable. I was comfortable in the dungeon, Brianna." He paused then. And she could see him direct the shift in topics. Watch the change in his expression before he did it, marked and clear. "I like the way your name feels to say. *Brianna*. It is an interesting name."

"Well, I know for certain no one has ever said that to me before."

"I have never said that name."

"Well, I have never said the name Riyaz before being prepared to meet you. So I suppose that is… Something we have in common."

"I do not think that comfort matters here," he said. Abruptly switching back. "How can it? The aim of this is not to make me comfortable, but to restore order to the country. So I do not think we should talk of my comfort."

"You had a plan," she said, trying again. "To keep yourself while you were in the dungeon. You had a way of keeping your mind about you. You had a way of making sure that your body didn't fail you. This is not unlike that. There is a mission here. And it is to get you back on the throne. That is as far as we will go now. It doesn't need to be about all the rest of your years. Just about this moment. About presenting you to the people."

"I'm to be married," he said.

"Right," she said. They had spoken of a woman. While she was standing there, but she supposed she hadn't entirely taken the meaning on board.

"Does this woman know you?" she asked.

"She is a woman who was promised to me back when we were children. My brother knows where she is. She will honor the agreement."

She fought against the strange feeling. One of being left behind. Cairo was going to come back here and help his brother. If she understood correctly, maybe even be in charge of the military. He wasn't going to continue his life in Europe or the United States. He wasn't going to continue to be part of her life in the way that he always had been. There was a place for him here. There was a place for Riyaz.

And for this woman that was going to marry Riyaz.

Brianna didn't have a place.

She should be used to that. But even so, she fought against the strange feeling of loneliness that threatened to overwhelm her.

"Well, I will prepare you for your marriage also."

CHAPTER THREE

HE WOKE UP the next morning when the cold from the concrete he slept on became too intrusive for him to ignore.

The aches and pains in his body were, for him, the equivalent of a sunrise. It was the way that he greeted the day. It was… It was how he knew he was alive.

He dragged his fingertips along the hash marks he had carved into the wall, part of marking his days, part of keeping control. When he had been thrown into the dungeon, he'd had a choice. Surrender to captivity, or turn the dungeon into a kingdom of one, which he ruled.

He had opted for the latter. Within the walls of his prison, he had been master of all.

Being able to leave when he chose was still a surprise.

He began to walk up the stairs, his body automatically bracing itself. Tensing. For the intensity of the light and the sound.

But what he was not prepared for was the side of Brianna. Standing very near the top of the stairs, facing away from him. She was wearing a cream-colored dress that fell just above her knee. Her ankles were slim and were a most fascinating shape. Her calves creamy and compelling.

And then there was the way the dress hugged itself

over her rear end. Which was a craving that surpassed any for food he'd yet had.

She turned, and that was like the sunrise. "Oh," she said. "Where were you?"

"Sleeping," he said.

"Right. Only... The servant said that you were not in your room."

"I was," he said.

"Oh. I..."

"I was there," he said, gesturing down the stairs.

"That is not your room," she said, "that is a dungeon."

He shrugged. "It was the only place that I slept or did anything for sixteen years. I find that too much change is uncomfortable. I prefer to sleep in a familiar place."

He realized that the expression on her face was one of... Pity.

"Don't look at me like that," he said. "I'm not a small animal that you need to rescue. I have been rescued, in fact."

For a great many years he had fantasized about saving himself. Building up enough strength to rise up against the guards all on his own.

But the issue remained of what he would find past the guards that surrounded the cell. And he knew that would not be so simple.

He had continued to build up strength, but for his own benefit, and not really for a longer-term plan. That was the lesson he had eventually learned. That he had to find a way to live as best he could within an existence he would never have chosen, and not make his will to survive dependent on what might happen in the future. He had learned to take it day by day. And it was how he was taking things now. Even though he had the sense that the people around him were impatient.

"I don't pity you," she said.

But he could see that she was lying. "Don't you?"

"No," she said. "I might have some concerns. Why punish yourself?"

"Imagine having to try and exist in a world…" He changed tactics. "Imagine trying to live in the desert. Out there. Very different, I would think, to New York. To a town house there. Imagine living there. Nothing to shelter you from the elements. Everything is brighter and hotter than what you're used to. Nothing feels the same. That isn't what it's like for me. I have lived here before. I have lived in the world.

"But it has been a very long time. And these things that you seem to think are reasonable and comfortable, they are not reasonable and comfortable to me. I need to take shelter from them. In much the same that you might do if you were out in the desert. You would need to get away from the elements."

"Right. I'm sorry. I realize that what you're doing is for your own comfort. And that it makes sense to you. But we just… What we are working on is appearances."

"Right. So you should not care what I do when no one can see me."

"I find that I do, though. Because I don't want you to be sleeping on a stone floor when there is a perfectly good bed upstairs."

Flames licked at his gut. Lust that took him by surprise.

A bed sounded appealing. If she was in it.

He wondered what she looked like naked. How her body would look uncovered.

Was she pale like that all over?

His references for female nudity were classical art-work. And she reminded him a bit of Renaissance paint-ings. All red hair and pale skin. He could imagine her being curved in just that way. But would she look at him with need or with pity if he touched her?

He could not stand the latter.

"What is the lesson today?"

"I had thought that we would take breakfast, and then that we might spend some time in the library. There is a very expensive library here."

"Still?" It was one thing that he had not thought to explore, but then... He wondered. Had the palace guard been bringing him books from the palace library all this time? He had been afraid... Afraid that his father's ex-tensive collection of literature had been destroyed. Books were so much his companion that the idea of it had... Had been like another death.

And so even upon his freedom he had not asked about it.

He had not wanted to know the truth.

"Yes," she said. "It's wonderful. I've taken some books from it myself."

"I like this plan."

"Maybe later we'll graduate to watching a movie."

He had not seen a movie since he was a teenager. "I would enjoy that," he said.

"All right. We'll plan that. I can talk to you about some of the movies that have been made since you went into the dungeon."

She wrinkled her nose. "I'm sorry. I feel that that sounded flippant."

"You are all much more upset about my feelings than I am."

"I just don't want to make it sound as if I'm making light of what you've been through."

"I cannot erase those years. They have made me into what I am, for better or worse. I'm not angry about it. I'm not wounded," he said.

"How?"

"Because what I learned was to exist in the moment. Not the past or the future. Or to exist in… Someone else's moment. And that is where books came in."

"I see. Well. Shall we go to breakfast?"

"Yes."

"I hope you don't mind, but I had the chef replace your porridge this morning. I had thought that we could start with something slightly different."

"What is this?" he said when he walked into the dining room. There was a bowl on the table, and it did resemble the porridge he was accustomed to. But it was different. There was fruit on it. And sugar. And there was something like bread next to it, but it was not toast.

"It's oatmeal," she said. "Which is very much like porridge. It's just a different consistency. It has fruit and brown sugar, which is how I like it. And I have given you an American biscuit."

"A biscuit," he said, frowning. "Is that not dessert?"

"No. It is a little bit like a scone. Except also not. I found a recipe, and the staff was all too willing to make this for you."

"I'm not sure I'll like it."

"Neither am I. But you can get toast if you don't like it. Because you are not a prisoner. And this is not a dungeon. And you don't have to take whatever you're served. You are the Sheikh."

She was looking at him expectantly. Hopefully. And so he took his seat, as she had instructed yesterday, and he saw a little flare of pleasure in her eyes.

He wished to make her look like that as often as possible. He took a bite of the oatmeal, and he found it was not dissimilar, though the textures and flavors were stronger because of the addition of the sugar and fruit. But she seemed to be enjoying herself, and even though he wasn't certain if he was, he didn't wish to impact on her happiness.

He decided he liked the biscuit very much. And he did not need to enjoy it just to make her feel better.

"Let us finish this in the library," he said. He had the urge, suddenly, to be in that room, where he had not been since his release.

They left the dining room, and they went down the corridor. One he had not been to since he was a boy. It was very strange. Visiting these rooms.

He had been to the throne room. He had been to the bedroom that he had been given. He had been to the dining room. He had not yet been outside.

He had not gone to explore broadly.

It didn't seem to be the smartest thing.

He had a strange sensation, like he was walking in two different timelines. This present moment, and one years before, when he had been a boy. He had not appreciated books then.

But he had learned to. They had been his only escape. His only window into any other part of the world.

And even though he had told her he did not enjoy

romance... It was only that it had made him ache. For companionship, at times. But especially when there was explicit description of physical acts between lovers...

He had read in great detail how a man might please a woman in those books. And how a woman might please a man.

But sometimes it was too easy for him to picture such things. And it overtook him. If there was one thing that made him miserable in captivity, it was longing for the touch of a woman and being denied it.

But long for it he did. And being in proximity to Brianna only made it... That much more keen.

For the first time he stood near a woman whose hands he wanted on his body. And that was a need that surpassed any he had experienced before.

But then she pushed the doors open to the library, and for a moment his thoughts were interrupted. By memory. And by the grandeur of it. Books from floor to ceiling. Their colorful spines turned outward. Ladders were positioned around the room, on tracks so that you could explore all the shelves.

His father had spent hours in here.

And Riyaz had not understood the importance of it. He did now.

"I cannot believe they didn't destroy it. It seems the sort of thing they might had out of spite."

"I don't know very much about the people who occupied the palace before your brother... Before he took power back. But I have the impression it was a dark time here."

"As funny as it sounds, since I am the one that has lived here all this time, not even I know very much about them. Only the palace guards. I've never even truly un-

derstood why the dictator kept me. Unless it was simply...
He got something out of keeping me like a dog. Perhaps
that's it. Perhaps it is simply that chaining me was even
more gratifying than killing me.

"Perhaps it made him feel secure in his power. Or
maybe I was being held over someone's head. I don't
know. I think Cairo had everyone killed. Not the guard
who brought me books, though. I asked for him to spare
his life."

"Oh," she said, looking pale.

"Did you think that this was bloodless? A coup never
is. And the initial one certainly wasn't."

Tension rose in his chest as he fought against the images of those last moments that he had spent in the palace before being taken to the dungeon.

He didn't wish to think of it.

Of course he didn't. He did not wish to imagine his
mother's dying moments. And perhaps this was why he
had not explored the palace before.

It brought the past too close to him.

He had not spent all these years living in the past. He
had spent his days in the present. Because it was endurable.

These halls were filled with ghosts. He was not accustomed to managing them.

He walked to the first shelf, and took out a book. *"Little Women,"* he said. "I have read this."

"Have you? It's one of my favorites."

"Yes," he agreed. "It is good." He traced his hands over
the letters on the cover. It had been years since he'd read
it. It was one of the first ones the guard had brought him.
He moved over to another place on the shelf. *"Swiss Family Robinson.* I have also read that. *Pride and Prejudice."*

He paused in front of another title. "I do not think my father would've kept this one in his library." He touched the spine. It had been an extremely explicit book about a young woman and a billionaire embarking on a sexual relationship. He had found it instructive. And torturous. He was surprised to see it in the library.

She lifted a brow. "I think everyone read that when it came out."

"Did you?"

She laughed and shook her head. "No. I didn't have any interest. But really, a guard brought that to you?"

"Yes," he said. "It was informative if nothing else."

She laughed. And he had a feeling she only laughed because she hadn't read it, so she didn't actually know what he was talking about.

"Here's one I haven't read," he said. He pulled out a battered copy of a book that had a man with a gun on the cover. One of those spy novels, he imagined. He did not mind those.

It looked like a series, and he took several of them, because he read very quickly, and now there were all these books. And he could choose whatever he liked. He was not bound to whatever he was brought.

He could choose whatever he wanted to, change his mind on a whim. For the first time, the excess of choice seemed like a good thing.

Next to him, Brianna began to climb up the ladder.

He watched her, and he could not deny that he… Felt slightly compelled to look and see if he could catch more of a sight of her legs as she went up.

But then the doors to the library opened with a loud slam, and Brianna gasped, her foot slipping. She tumbled down, and he grabbed hold of her, catching her in his arms as she fell.

She looked up at him, her eyes wide with terror. Frozen. And suddenly, he wasn't there anymore.

Suddenly, it wasn't Brianna's terrified face that he saw. It was his mother.

He pushed her behind him, and rounded on the threat.

His heart was hammering. There was a man there in the doorway. And he growled. Moving forward with extreme swiftness and violence.

"Sheikh Riyaz," the man said, holding his hands up in terror, but Riyaz was not moved.

"How dare you?" he asked.

"My Sheikh," the man said.

He heard another noise, and turned. He saw nothing there.

When he turned again, the cowardly man who had startled… Who had… He had done something. People were dying. It was pandemonium. It was the end of everything. That man had done it. And there were more of them.

Raging, he grabbed a piece of furniture and flung it to the side. Grabbed a chair and smashed it against the wall.

There would be nowhere for them left to hide when he was through.

He couldn't see clearly. His vision blocked by fury.

He saw a chair, and turned it over. There was no one under there. There was a table, and he flipped that as well.

"Riyaz."

Dimly, he heard a voice. A woman's voice. And he turned toward it, taking her into his arms once more and shielding her. "Riyaz," she said. Slowly. Calmly. "It's me.

It's Brianna. And I'm okay. I was startled. But it was an accident."

He growled.

"No," she said. "It's okay. It's okay. This is the library. And you are safe."

"You…"

"I'm safe," she said. "I'm safe."

She put her hands flat on his chest, and it was as if it was a movie, and she had attempted to bring his heart back into motion with a defibrillator. Like he had been electrocuted.

It was Brianna. And he could see her face. Her eyes wide with fear…

She was afraid of him.

"I thought… I saw…"

"I know," she said. "I'm sorry. I was startled, and I fell. I should've held on to the ladder."

"No," he said. He touched her face, and found that her skin was as soft as he'd imagined. "You're okay?"

"Yes."

He moved away from her, conscious of the ever-growing desire inside of him, and of the fact that he… He had lost himself. That had never happened before.

Yes, it has.

Only in sleep. Night terrors, yes. He had those. They had to make sure he had nothing loose in his cell during those times, because he threw things. Because he was dangerous. To himself and anyone who was standing outside the cell, but it was easy for him to understand why that happened. He was lost in those moments between sleep and wakefulness, and it made sense that he didn't have a firm grasp on reality.

But this…

This was something else altogether. If he could do this during the day…

No one would ever be safe around him. There was no question, he had to take Brianna's help, or he would not be safe for those in the palace.

There was also no question, he had to protect her. From him.

"Where's the man?"

"He left," she said softly. "Don't worry about it. Don't worry, we…"

"I could've hurt you."

"But you didn't," she said.

"No," he agreed. But the possibility still remained, and he did not know how she could be so… Sanguine about it.

And he realized… He was just one of the many monsters that she had helped reform. By her own account.

So perhaps there was nothing about this that surprised her at all.

Perhaps they all lost themselves and had moments of insanity. Perhaps she had been held in all of their arms.

He growled.

"Now what?"

"I must make amends," he said, deciding not to tell her the real reason that he had growled.

"You don't need to make amends, Riyaz."

"I should go back to the dungeon for a while."

"You don't need to do that…"

But his decision was made. So he turned and left her standing there. And when he got down into the dungeon, he realized that he had forgotten to bring the books.

CHAPTER FOUR

WELL, THAT HAD been a disaster.

She was still trembling. His fury had been awe-inspiring and terrible to see. It had been so frightening. Pretending that she hadn't been scared had been one of the most difficult things she'd ever done.

But she could see the horror on his face. She hadn't wanted to add to it by showing him he'd scared her.

She took a breath and looked around the destroyed library. And only then did she put her palm to her chest and feel the raging of her heartbeat.

And then…

She thought of how it felt to rest her palms on his chest.

He was so muscular. So strong that she had the feeling he could have dismembered that poor man with his bare hands.

He had certainly looked like he intended to.

The way he had held her against his hot, hard body… He had not intended to hurt her. That much she knew. He wanted to protect her. But she didn't know what he had thought was happening. Or whom he had thought she was.

He's traumatized.

She certainly understood that.

She had grown up in a household filled with criminals. And they certainly hadn't treated others with care.

She had been largely shielded from violence and other unsavory things. But when her father had told her that he was selling her to one of his enemies, that man had told her what he intended to do to her in no uncertain terms. It had been explicit, and tinged with violence.

She had always known that she didn't live in a normal family. In a normal house. And like Riyaz, she had books. Books had told her that there were other kinds of families. But the way that her father cared for her was not love. Books had told her there was something more out there.

And then, like it was a story, a fairy tale, Cairo had rescued her.

All she had wanted, ever since then, was to find a normal life.

Instead, what had she done? She had spent the last decade in love with a man who refused to touch her.

You already know it isn't worth the risk.

She did. She'd decided that a long time ago. She wouldn't ever make a move on him, she kept her fantasies as tame as possible. He was her friend, and they were too different and…

Her phone buzzed in her pocket.

And she had a feeling it was that very man.

She answered. "Yes?"

"I would like a progress report," Cairo said.

"He sleeps in the dungeon and he just destroyed the library."

"Oh. Well, that is not acceptable."

"I'm sorry, Cairo. But he isn't just going to be fine overnight. He's deeply traumatized."

"The psychiatrist said there was nothing wrong with him."

"I think he's remarkably well all things considered. But to say that he isn't affected… That would be ignorant. Foolish. Of course he is." She thought of the way he ate. The way that he limited any sort of sensory input.

"He's very careful with himself. He's quite smart. He knows there's a limit to how far he can push himself. I saw that limit today. Something happened. It triggered… I think it was probably a flashback. He thought that I was in danger and he…"

"He what?" Cairo asked.

"Well, I wouldn't have been surprised if he'd picked me up like he was King Kong and climbed to the top of the library ladder with me. He was ready to kill what he perceived to be a threat to me."

"Were you in any danger?" Cairo's voice sounded sharp.

"No," she said. "I don't need you to rescue me. Riyaz was trying to do just that. I don't think he's dangerous." Intentionally. "I just need time. And I really wouldn't… That woman that you intend to bring back? I wouldn't. Not yet."

"I've nearly arrived at her apartment."

"Stall. Do not bring her back here immediately. Anything could… Disrupt him. For God's sake, wait until he can at least eat something more adventurous than oatmeal."

"If you say so."

"I *do* say so. I absolutely say so."

"All right."

She thought back to just a few days ago. Before she had come here. When Cairo had called her and asked this favor of her. The way that his voice had made her feel. The way that she'd anticipated seeing him.

For some reason, she didn't feel quite that way now.

It was probably because she was still getting over that rush of adrenaline.

Her body couldn't withstand the rush of adrenaline she usually got from speaking to Cairo on top of it.

"I need to go find him. I have to distract him," she said.

"You don't need to do that. Don't push him anymore for the day." But she didn't want to push him. She wanted to check in with him.

"Trust me. You hired me for a reason."

"Because I needed someone who could keep a secret."

"Yes. But also, I assume, because you know that I can help?"

"That too."

"Then trust me."

Now she was going to have to try and get Riyaz out of the dungeon.

She made a decision. Then she realized it was one he might not understand. Given his statements about food. But she wondered. She wondered if he was just still with-holding things from himself. She knew that he slept in the dungeon. What was the real reason for that? She knew that the transition from a life as a prisoner to a real life must be very difficult. She understood it, at least in a limited way.

But she decided to go to the kitchen and get cupcakes. There were some made with spice cake and cream cheese frosting. And some that were chocolate with chocolate frosting.

She grabbed both, and went straight to the dungeon. He wasn't there.

She began to hunt around the palace.

The last place she looked was the throne room. And there he was, standing in the back of the room. Just looking.

"Hello," she said.

"What are you doing here?"

"I was going to ask you the same thing. I didn't expect to see you here."

"You do not know everything, Brianna. I hope you are now humbled."

"Mm. Sadly not." She stared hard at him, daring him to smile. He didn't. "I just gave your brother an update on the situation. And I thought that maybe we should talk."

"Why would you want to talk to me?"

"Well, it's my job to talk to you, Riyaz. Also, you're the only person in the palace that I really know. So if I'm going to talk to somebody, it's all the better that it's you."

The look he gave her was nothing if not suspicious. And she lifted the tray she was holding in her hands aloft. "I have brought you something nice."

"What is it?"

"Cake," she said.

"I don't know that I want it."

"I think you should try it," she said. He was looking at her like she had done something strange, and it suddenly made her feel very silly. She took the opportunity to spin it into a lesson, because then it wouldn't feel quite so... personal. "I think that you should try it because it would be good for you to try something new. I think that you should try it because you might enjoy it. Why are you so afraid of enjoying things?"

His lip curled. "I'm not afraid of anything."

"Of course not. You're a warrior. A mighty king."

"I wasn't *afraid*. In the library. I thought I needed to fight, and I was ready. I am always ready to fight."

"I believe you. I didn't say that you were afraid."

She thought he might be afraid of living life without the parameters of the dungeon. That maybe he was reluctant to believe that he was truly free.

"This is where you... Sit? Or... I guess I don't fully understand the concept of throne rooms. What did your father do in here?"

He looked around the room. "This is where my father would entertain dignitaries. Listen to the plights of our people. Decide on new laws. It was ceremonial, mostly. He enjoyed spending more of his time in the library. He was different than the kings that came before him. More modern. Sometimes I wonder if that is why he was killed."

"In what way?"

"He believed in women's rights. He taught Cairo and I that women were equal. He changed many laws allowing them freedoms. He was ahead of much of the world in human rights in general, as it happens. There was pushback against that. People... People the world over are inherently set in their ways. And they do not like things to change. Yes, there are always agitators looking to progress, but that kind of progress scares the masses."

"And yet, he was happy to make a deal with a man to choose a wife for you."

"Yes. There were still political marriages. My parents' marriage was a political one. But they came to care for each other very much. I think my father saw that as diplomacy, rather than treating a woman as if she were an object."

"Good of him."

"My father was a good man. But he was also a man of his particular station. And that is going to be different to your experience."

"My father was not a good man."

"I have some sense of that."

"My prison was very different from yours. In fact, I didn't fully realize that it was one. I lived in a beautiful house. An estate, really. There were so many beautiful places to play on the grounds. In the gardens. I didn't find it strange that we didn't have children over. That I didn't go to school, rather I had a tutor at home."

"You said my brother rescued you. Sent you to school."

"Yes. He did. He sent me to boarding school. Which was a different experience entirely. I had to learn…"

"Was it difficult to learn?"

"Yes and no. I was immersed in it. Thrown into the deep end of society. As far as a teenage girl went. I was happy in many ways, but intimidated in others. I didn't know how to interact with large groups of children my own age. And we weren't children. So there were politics. I learned to navigate those. Through trial and error. I became very popular."

"Why do you think that is?" he asked.

"Because I'm delightful?"

He pushed away from the wall and began to walk toward her. Caged panther. "No. Why do you think that was? *Really*. Because many people wish they were popular. Many people would love to be. And they spend their entire lives in society observing other human beings, and yet can't fit in. But you did."

"I suppose it's because when you live in a home with a man who has a vile temper, reading the room, the situation, can be a matter of survival."

His expression turned fierce. "Did your father hurt you?"

"Not routinely. But occasionally, I would take a backhand blow to the face. Or just get yelled at. Screamed at. Neither was fun. I learned. I learned because I had to. I learned because it is imperative to learn when you're in those sorts of situations. And so, I guess I transferred that need to read the room into my school experience. And from that, I learned to help other people. People like you and me."

"How many people like you and me are there?"

"More than you would think. People who have lived in abusive homes. Or cults. A person who has been in a controlling marriage for a number of years. There are many reasons that someone might struggle in the world. You're not alone."

"I wouldn't care if I was," he said.

"Of course not. Why should you want connection? Or cake? Have some cake, Riyaz."

He looked at her skeptically.

"Riyaz," she said. "You are skeptical of a treat?"

"In my position, wouldn't you be?"

"Maybe," she said, her heart clenching.

He took a step toward her, moving into a shaft of light. He was beautiful. He had high cheekbones, and the hollows of his cheeks were sharp. Even with his dark beard covering his jaw she could see that.

He was muscled, extraordinarily so.

All that working out he'd done had paid off.

"We've talked about your books. Tell me about your body."

He lifted a dark brow, and her face went hot. "I mean, tell me about how you work to stay... Oh, come on, you're in amazing shape."

He surprised her. Because all at once, he stopped, and he grinned. Then, he chuckled. "You enjoy my body?"

"I would have to be blind not to notice the sort of shape you're in," she said, feeling properly warm now.

"I see. Well. Pull-ups, sit-ups. There was a stone bench down in the dungeon, and I would lay on my back and lift it with my feet. Plus there are many bodyweight workouts that a person can do. I also lifted the bench. I didn't wish to lose my body *or* my mind. There were many things I had no choice but to let go of. My fitness in either of those arenas was not going to be theirs. Not ever."

"I admire that. Very few people would have the presence of mind to make that determination."

He lifted a brow. "Cake and flattery?"

"I'm hoping that you'll take at least one of them," she said.

"I will consider it."

"I have spice cake. And chocolate."

She could see interest flare in his dark eyes.

"You want chocolate," she said.

"I have not had chocolate in sixteen years."

"Riyaz, you must have chocolate. You absolutely must."

She lifted it up from the tray, and held it out to him.

He took it from her, and she watched as he took a bite. And she was more gratified than she should have been by the growl.

"You aren't supposed to do that, remember?"

"You don't mind," he said.

"No," she said softly. "I don't. I quite enjoy it. But don't tell anyone I said that, because I am supposed to be civilizing you, and you do need to learn to not growl in public spaces."

He finished the cupcake quickly.

And then eyed the tray.

"Have another. They're for you."

He did take another. "Maybe you should consider sleeping in your bed also," she said sweetly.

That was met with another growl. "No. I don't think that I could."

"Why not?"

"How would I know when to wake up?"

"What does that have to do with when you wake up?"

"I know when to wake up when I'm too cold. When my body hurts too badly. That's how I know."

"There are alarm clocks, you know. You don't have to count on being uncomfortable."

"Still. I'm not certain."

"Well, that's the beauty of freedom, Riyaz," she said. "The door will be unlocked. So if you decide that you do not wish to sleep in your bedroom anymore you can always go to the dungeon. Because you're not a prisoner. Not now."

"I appreciate that," he said.

"Good."

"I am prepared to sit here." He looked around the room. "I'm not afraid of those who might oppose me."

"Do you think people will?"

"It is always a possibility. Always. But what can be done to me that has not been already done? I have been a prisoner. And I suppose they could choose to kill me. But it does not frighten me. I had to make my peace with death after the first coup."

"You should never have had to do that."

"Maybe not. But it is the way of things."

"Tell me. Tell me what it was like when you and Cairo were children. Before this happened."

This beautiful woman was plying him with cupcakes after he had treated her appallingly. He had wanted to protect her, but he could see that he had frightened her. And he did not care for that. And he could not quite figure out if she actually wanted to hear about his childhood, or if this was some exercise of hers. But he found he wanted to tell her either way. Because he had spoken to no one about this, not even Cairo. And there was something tantalizing about it. He did his best not to remember when he was in the dungeon. It was as if he had no past or future when he was in there. Nothing but the present, because it was the only way to get through any of it. If he remembered how happy he had once been, he might go mad. If he thought about how much better life would be if he were out, he would surely go mad.

And so now, as a man with a future that did not include the walls of the dungeon, he decided to allow himself to be a man with the past. With her.

"We had a good life as children. We had lessons. For

most of the day. Five days a week. Our father was strict. He did not wish for us to grow up to be entitled or spoiled. He was quite concerned about that. He said many kings fall because they love themselves more than they love their people. He said many kings became corrupt trying to protect only their own interests. He did not wish for that to be so for us. So he taught us, not only the sorts of subjects you expect to learn in school, but to give ourselves over to the service of others. To prize philanthropy. Do not take ourselves so seriously. He was a good father."

"And your mother?"

He tried to picture his mother. Tried to picture her when she was not screaming for help. Looking at him with dark, pleading eyes as they...

"I loved her," he said. He could not bring himself to say more.

She seemed to understand. "What kind of a brother was Cairo? I know him as a... A friend."

"A friend you are in love with."

"Nothing has ever happened between us. And it won't. I know that."

"Do you really know that? Or is that why you're here? Do you hold out hope?"

She began to look uncomfortable.

"No. I'm actually not. I decided that this... This would have to be the last thing that I did for him. Because I can't love him, not like that, not for real. I can't. Not when... Not when I want something else."

"What else?"

"This isn't about me. This is about you."

"And Cairo. Admit that you are curious about him for your own benefit."

"Fine. I am. But after this, I won't be as close to him anymore. He's planning on taking over as the head of your military, after all. It matters to him. A great deal. Your health, your happiness…"

"He got along with my intended much better than I did," said Riyaz. "We used to fight about that a bit. He was my very best friend, until summer, when Ariel would come to visit. She was afraid of me. I can't say that I really blame her. She's two years younger than I am. The same age as Cairo. They got along immediately, and he would abandon me for large portions of the day to run wild with her. My parents thought they would make companionable in-laws. Keep each other occupied while I ruled. I always wondered…"

He had always wondered if Cairo loved her. But they had been boys. Children, and Riyaz had never questioned a dictate of his father's. If his father said that he was supposed to marry Ariel, then he was supposed to marry her.

His father could not be wrong.

He gritted his teeth.

What a harsh blow it had been to find out that his father could be wrong. That he could trust the wrong man.

What a harsh thing to realize that in the final moments of his father's life. It made him no less Riyaz's hero. But it did teach him that his father was human. Very, very human.

And he had died like one.

"Cairo," he said, redirecting his own thoughts. Trying to turn off the images in his head of the bloody throne room. The very room they stood in now.

He could not afford to lose himself. Not with her. Not again.

"He was always a big personality. Always brilliant. Always in trouble."

"And you weren't?"

"No. I was the heir. The heir could not afford that sort of behavior."

"And you just... Knew that. Accepted it?"

"Like I said. I wanted to be like my father. And that was the manner of man he was."

He looked at the tray of cupcakes. He wanted another chocolate one. Except... Looking at her, what he really wanted. What he wanted with all of himself, was her. He might not have tasted chocolate in sixteen years, but he had not tasted her either. And he wondered if she tasted like he thought her name did. Like lemon and raspberries and sunshine.

So he took another cupcake.

Because she had offered it. And that was really why it mattered.

Because of her.

"You should have one," he said.

She looked down at the tray. "I don't have a free hand."

He took the tray from her swiftly, and set it on the throne.

"I imagine that's against some kind of tradition."

"If it is," he said, "then I have forgotten the tradition. Therefore it no longer exists. I am the Sheikh, after all."

"Right."

"Have one," he said.

She didn't make a move. So he set his cupcake down, and selected one for her, holding it out.

She came forward slowly, and she surprised him, not by taking the cupcake from his hand, but by tilting her head and taking a small bite off of it.

The proximity to her mouth caused him to feel an electrified sensation that shot down his spine and radiated out toward his groin.

Desire nearly overwhelmed him. He wished to pull her in his arms and have her on the floor. He wished to...

He saw a spark of something in her eyes. And he remembered what she said about being sensitive. To changes in mood. About the way it had been a survival necessity for her.

And he wondered if she felt this. The change in him. The depth of his desire. His arousal.

Or maybe...

Maybe she just felt her own.

"It's delicious," she whispered.

"Yes," he agreed.

"Thank you."

"You are going to eat the whole thing."

"Well. Not out of your hand."

"Take it," he commanded.

And the way that she obeyed him so beautifully only tightened the desire within him yet more.

She licked the frosting off the top, and he was held rapt to the movement of her slick pink tongue. She was so beautiful.

It was easy for him to forget about Ariel, even though they were talking about his past. Even though his memories of Cairo were tangled up in memories of her.

He had never wanted her.

He had certainly never loved her.

A good thing. For if he had... She would not know what to do with the man he was now. Because he was not a man who could offer those feelings.

He once had been. He might've even come to love
Ariel. Like his parents had come to love one another.

But that part of him had been so neatly excised when
the light had gone out from his mother's eyes.

That moment had robbed him of a great many things.
Then his captivity even more. But that ability to love. To
care. To feel anything half so intensely… It was gone. In
many ways, he was grateful, for it had ensured his survival. If he had been left a wailing, grieving boy down
in that cell, how would he have ever come out of it? How
would he have ever survived? It would not have been
possible.

But he did not know what the years had done to Ariel.
Her father had betrayed him.

"Ariel's father betrayed mine," he said. Because now
that the thought was in his head he wished to speak of it.

"Cairo did explain some of the things to me… He was
supposed to be seeking an alliance with us. Through the
marriage. But instead he was paid off by the men who
wished to take over the country. Who killed my family. He traded us for money." He paused for a moment.
"Some might say she should be punished for the sins of
her father."

"And you?"

"I don't know. I haven't decided what I will do when
she gets here."

Anger burned in his chest. He wondered if she had
known. But then, she had only been fifteen. Perhaps it
was foolish to blame her for any of it.

And yet… He found it difficult not to.

"Well. I think… I think you shouldn't consider things

like revenge. Not now. Your father was a modern leader. He didn't keep those sorts of blood scores, I imagine."

"A blood score?" he asked.

"I made it up. I thought it sounded somewhat medieval, and a bit intimidating."

"Well. Definitely that."

"Just focus on yourself. Finding herself. That is actually what I'm trying to help you do. I'm not trying to turn you into the leader you never would've been. But the one you would've been if not for all of this. The one you wish to be."

"Thank you."

"Sleep in the bed tonight, Riyaz."

He nodded slowly. Perhaps it was time.

The roar woke her out of a deep sleep.

It did not sound like a man. It sounded like an animal. And when she began to hear the crashing of furniture, she leaped out of bed without thinking.

Riyaz. She knew that it was him. She knew it was Riyaz having another one of those episodes. PTSD. Flashbacks. Whatever they were.

And she knew that she needed to be the one to go to him. She knew it as sure as she knew anything.

She threw the covers off of her bed, and began to run down the hall.

No one else was coming. They all feared him. She had heard them whispering earlier in the day about the mad Sheikh. Referencing what had happened in the library.

Nobody was confident in his ability to hold it together.

But this… This didn't mean that there was something

wrong with him. And she knew that. She knew that. Even if he didn't.

Even if no one else did.

He was traumatized. And that was understandable.

All she needed...

She opened the door to the bedchamber, and found a dresser on its face.

Curtains torn down. The room was in a state, and Riyaz was standing at the center of it, a hollow-eyed warrior who looked remote. Unreachable.

Gone was the man who read books. This was the man who lifted stone benches. This was the man at his most elemental.

This was what he had tried to prevent himself from becoming.

Tonight, the beast had won.

"Riyaz," she said slowly.

He breathed out hard, and reminded her of a spooked stallion, his eyes wild.

And she knew that he still didn't see. Not really.

"Brianna," he said.

He shocked her. He *did* know that it was her.

But then he crossed the space and wrapped his arm around her, drawing her into the room. "They will not touch you," he said.

"There's no one here," she said.

"There was," he said, insistent.

"No," she said. "No one is here. You're safe."

But what she said was lost as he growled. And dragged her deeper into the room, throwing his body in front of hers as he pinned her to the wall.

She wrapped her arms around him, her hands on his

chest, and she could feel his heart raging beneath her hands. "Riyaz," she said softly. "Riyaz come back."

She moved her hand slowly over his chest, down to his stomach.

Then moved her hands back up. And gradually, she felt his heart rate begin to slow. "It's okay," she said softly. "It's okay."

And then he turned suddenly, hands bracketed on either side of her face against the wall. She could scarcely breathe.

Her heart was thundering radically. His face was so close to hers. And then she reached up and touched him. "Riyaz."

It was like the fog cleared. Suddenly.

And he came back. And then tension of a different kind began to move between them. He moved one hand around her waist, stroking her up and down the way that she had just done him. He was back now, but he was more feral. More himself in some ways, she thought.

He moved closer, and her eyes fluttered closed, and she forced them open. She wanted to watch this. Whatever might happen next.

You're an idiot. He's a sheikh. He's supposed to marry somebody else. You're supposed to be in love with his brother.

Yes. All great reasons to move away.

This is not what you want. You want a normal life. This could never be normal.

Still. She didn't move away from him. Still. She stood there. At his command. Or maybe it was a different command. One that they were both subject to. One that neither of them could deny.

She didn't know what she expected. Perhaps for him to lean in. Close the distance between them. To claim her mouth with his own. Instead, he touched her face. Dragging calloused fingers along her jawline, his thumb moving over her lip. And then he dropped his hand and stepped back.

"This won't stop," he said.

"I..." For a moment she was confused. For a moment, she didn't understand what he meant. But of course he meant the flashback. But right in that second she had thought that perhaps he'd admitted to the thing between them. The pulse that arced there.

"It will. It'll get better. It will..."

He growled. She flattened herself against the wall. Not because she was afraid of him. But because she was afraid of what she might do.

"No. It will not. There is something broken in me. If Cairo needs me to be a figurehead, then that is well enough. But as to whether or not I can rule..."

"Don't let them take it from you," she said, the words coming out fiercely.

She was shocked by it. By the intensity of what she felt. But it wasn't fair. He was a strong man. A proud man. One who would do everything possible to protect those in his life.

Those that he cared for.

He would do the same for his country, she knew it.

"It's PTSD, Riyaz. Soldiers get it when they go to war. Many people have it after they've experienced abuse."

"I read, remember? I'm familiar. But whatever you call it, it is unacceptable for a man like me. For a man in my position. I must be what they need me to be."

"It's you," she said. "They need you. They need you to have survived. And you did. That's what you did for them. That's what you did for the country. You don't have to be perfect. No one would expect that."

"It would be nice if I wasn't a danger to others."

"You didn't hurt me. Did you?"

"You know what I want to do to you?" he said, his voice a low growl. "I want to strip you naked and have you on that bed."

Heat rose up inside of her, and her heartbeat sped up. She could see it. That gruff declaration. His body over hers as he...

She swallowed hard. "That's the adrenaline."

"It isn't."

"You need to go to sleep, Riyaz."

"It will not be here."

"You don't need to punish yourself for perceived trans-gression..."

"You don't know what I need. If you did, then this wouldn't have happened."

And then he turned and stormed out of the room, leaving her standing there surrounded by the shattered remains of all of the furniture. She was going to have to give Cairo an update.

And if she left out the fact that Riyaz made her pulse race, the fact that his dark, sensual promise did not scare her, but rather ignited in her a need that she could scarcely explain...

That was understandable.

The dungeon was dark. And it was familiar. And after all of that it was... The right place for him to be.

His pulse was still racing. His mind filled with images of what he'd seen.

His mother.

Always his mother.

Fear and blood and death.

He growled, and he picked up the stone bench, lifting it, and then, he did something he had not done before. He threw it. And it cracked into pieces. The sound of it deafening. Good. He wanted to destroy everything. And that was the worst of it. Coming back to the present moment hadn't stopped that. What he wasn't certain was how he had prevented himself from…

All he had wanted to do was to rip the clothes away from her body and satisfy himself. As if the only way that he could possibly be free of the beast growling through his body was to claim her. Take her. Slake his lust on her.

No.

He lay down in the corner of the dungeon. And he welcomed the bite of the rocks against his skin.

He deserved to be punished for just that thought alone.

And he knew that it didn't matter what she had said. But the door was open.

A part of him would always be locked in here.

CHAPTER FIVE

"No. THERE HASN'T really been more progress. I wish that I could say there was. I wish… I'm sorry. But I'm still not entirely sure what he thinks he's going to do with Ariel. He doesn't seem to know."

"I'm keeping her. Until you do know."

She thought of the way that Riyaz had talked about Ariel, and Cairo's relationship with her. "She's your friend. Isn't she?"

"I… Yes," said Cairo.

"Riyaz was talking to me a little bit about your childhood. About your connection with her."

"I didn't realize he noticed."

"I think he was jealous," she said.

"Really?"

"Of her. Not of you. He said you were always his best friend until she came to visit."

"That's not how I remember it. I remember him being very busy with matters of the state."

"Well, maybe that's something you should talk to him about."

There was a slight pause. "You seem to get a lot out of him. Considering you've made it sound as if he's barely civilized."

"He *is* only barely civilized," she said. "That doesn't mean you can't talk to him. You can. He likes to talk. When you think about it, it makes sense. He hasn't had anyone to talk to for quite some time."

"I guess not. But then… I'm not sure I have either."

Well, you had me.

But she didn't say that.

"I'll keep you posted. I haven't seen him today. I think he's gone back to the dungeon. Regression is somewhat expected. Two steps forward, one step back."

It was expected, but she didn't like it. And she was trying to figure out a way to… To fix it. But she was still turning over everything that had happened. The way it had made her feel. She wasn't afraid of him. That was the thing.

If anything, she was afraid of herself.

She hung up the phone, and took a sharp breath. If Riyaz was down in the dungeon. Then she would meet him there. And she wasn't going to let fear stop her.

She traversed the corridor, and took the spiral staircase down to the dungeon.

She had a blanket. And her tablet. And she had a feeling that what she was doing was possibly foolish. She also had his stack of books.

A picnic basket with food.

When she got down there, she heard a noise. Movement. Masculine grunting.

She froze for a moment, but then continued to walk forward. She went into the cell, but she didn't see him.

Then she continued deeper, and stopped. He was hanging, suspended from a bar at the middle of the low-ceilinged room.

Pulling himself up, then dropping slowly, exhibiting an intense amount of control.

He had taken his shirt off, and was wearing only a pair of black shorts. She was struck absolutely motionless by the sight of all those muscles at play.

He was a work of art. He transcended the strength of any normal human man.

The dark hair on his chest captured her attention, as did the ripple of his muscles.

And she felt something shamefully feminine begin to rise up inside of her. Need. Desire.

What was wrong with her? She was supposed to be helping him. She was... She was supposed to be in love with Cairo. Was she simply transferring her affection because she was near his brother?

She looked at Riyaz, at the way his dark hair fell into his face, and his animalistic movements.

He was nothing like Cairo.

She couldn't hide behind that. Couldn't use it as an excuse.

And suddenly, he looked up and saw her, dark, furious eyes meeting with hers.

He released his hold on the bar, and dropped back down to earth. "What are you doing here?"

His body glistened, sweat rolling down his pectoral muscles, down over his abs. He looked at her, his gaze moving slowly over her body, and she felt a pulse between her thighs begin to quicken. What was wrong with her?

She had been in love with Cairo for a decade, but she hadn't felt it... *There*. Not like this.

"I brought you food. And a blanket. And a movie. And your books."

"You shouldn't have come here."

"You didn't tell me not to."

"And if I had, Brianna?"

"I would've come anyway. Because somebody needed to check on you."

"I've spent sixteen years by myself. Nobody *checked* on me. I'm not a child. And I am not a dog."

"I know," she said. "I didn't say you were. I'm… I'm sorry I…"

"What movie?"

"Well, it's a… It's an adaptation of *Little Women*. I thought you might enjoy it."

"Maybe," he said.

He was looking at her out of the corner of his dark eyes. The suspicion there pronounced. It would've almost been funny if any of this were funny.

All she had ever wanted was to be normal. She just wasn't.

This was not normal.

She carefully set her items down, grabbed the blanket, and spread it out on the square stones. She took her tablet, and set it up. "Have a seat," she said.

He growled. "You growl too much," she said.

"You *make* me growl too much." But he sat down beside her.

He was sweaty, and she felt like she should object. But he smelled… Something was wrong with her. Because she wanted to bury her face in his chest and get even more of the scent of him.

Pheromones.

She dimly remembered hearing people talk about that before. That's what this was. Perhaps this wasn't specific at all. Maybe it was simply that she had left the whole virginity thing too late.

That was Cairo's fault.

She'd been so wrapped up in him that she had sort of forgotten to pursue other relationships. And maybe now she had hit some kind of wall with her sexual dry spell.

It had been fine up until this point, and now it was too much.

So a sweaty, shirtless, muscular man tested the bonds of her better judgment.

Nothing was going to happen. She was *helping* Riyaz. That was all.

She leaned forward, pushing a few buttons on her tablet, and getting the film started while she began to unpack the food. She really wished that she had gone to change. Sitting on the blanket in this dress, which had ridden up mid-thigh, while he sat there half-naked... It was too much.

And she was going to do her level best to pretend that it was not too much, because the whole thing was just...

"Cheese," she said. "And fruit."

"No cheeseburger?" he asked.

"Sorry. I can make sure that there is one for your dinner."

"You act like my nanny," he said.

"I assure you, I do not feel like your nanny."

She wish she hadn't have said that. Not quite the way she had. But then, maybe she just wished that he didn't make her feel... All of this.

He certainly didn't seem to have a problem eating what she had brought, cheeseburger or not, and she could feel him beginning to settle beside her.

And she just... Found that she enjoyed sitting next to him.

Especially as some of his tension began to resolve.

"I saw my mother," he said.

"What?"

"In the library. I caught you, and you looked so terrified... And it made me think of her. My mother. The way that she looked just as..."

"I'm sorry," she said.

"There is no need to be sorry. I was just explaining."

"But I am sorry. You've seen horrible things."

"The world can be horrible. This is a nice movie about a nice family. And Beth still dies."

It was such a pragmatic thing to say, and it almost made her laugh. Because he was right. Even being a good, normal family didn't protect you from tragedy.

Not that either of them would know. He'd had a good family, but they hadn't been normal, and it made them a target. And she'd had a very, very bad family.

"That's a grim outlook," she said.

"I don't think so," he said. "But then, it is entirely possible that my own viewpoint of the world is not... Entirely normal."

She had forgotten that there was kissing in this movie. It was incredibly mild. And yet... The tension between the characters, two people coming together at all, touching, felt fraught in the positions that she and Riyaz sat in.

He was half-naked.

And she...

She didn't have any experience with men. Her mind wandered. To the books that he'd read. But it also wandered to... The simple truth was he had been in a dungeon for sixteen years. She wondered if he'd had a lover before then.

She wondered…

Was it possible that he was actually…? Also a virgin? The thought made her feel hot.

With her lack of experience, it made sense for her to moon after a man like Cairo. He would know exactly how to touch a woman.

And yet, as soon as she thought of that, she thought of the way it had felt to be held in Riyaz's strong arms.

She had never felt so… Protected. Even while she had been afraid, the way that he had encircled her in his strength had been…

What she knew was that he had protected her. Utterly and completely. Whatever threat he had seen… His intent had been to keep her safe.

The movie was ending, and there was another passionate kiss on-screen.

And in spite of herself, she looked between them. Their fingertips were close to touching, with the way they were seated on the blanket.

And then she looked up, her eyes meeting his.

She saw heat there, even in the darkness.

She looked away quickly.

He was bringing a woman here to marry. And he would need…

What he needed was to learn how to be around a woman. How to be softer.

She didn't need him to be soft with her. She didn't need him to be anything other than what he was.

She didn't know anything about the woman who would be coming to marry him.

But it would be different for her than it was for Brianna.

Brianna was trying to meet him where he was at and coach him. Help him.

Brianna had come from a background that was so far from normal that Riyaz didn't put her off at all.

Whatever woman married him... It was different. He needed to learn how to be *with* someone. He didn't even know how to compromise with the necessities of the world around him. Much less another person.

"I hope you enjoyed the movie," she said.

"Yes," he said.

"I'll leave you. But I hope that..."

"I don't want you to leave me," he said.

"Oh."

"I wish to go to the pool beneath the palace. Come with me."

"Why?" Her heart froze in her chest.

"Because I asked you to."

This was part of her job. Socializing with him.

Except she sort of wanted a break from him. She *needed* one.

She also wanted to be closer to him, and that was not her job.

Cairo was getting that woman right now.

And it was her job to prepare him for it. "Okay... I suppose I might need... A bathing suit?"

"Yes," he said. But there was something dark in his tone. And she wished that it didn't make her feel like he had touched her. But it did.

She let out a shuddering breath, and stood. "I'll clean all of this up..."

"Someone else will do it," he said. "I will meet you. At the top of the stairs."

"Okay. I'll meet you then."

He knew what he was doing. And he knew that it was unfair. But he also recognized that… She wanted him. The way that she had looked at him during the movie made it obvious. Even to him.

Because he could sense this thing between them. Like fire. Something electric.

He could feel it in the tightening of his body, and the answering look in her eyes.

He wanted her.

And he didn't see why he shouldn't have her.

He did not love Ariel. He was hardly saving himself for her.

He had not saved himself for anything. He had been… He had been manipulated. Controlled. And the first moment that he had seen the sun, he had seen Brianna, and it seemed a sign.

That she was his. And meant to be.

He wished to touch her. Taste her.

His brother had ensured that he was given a new wardrobe when he was set free. Along with that wardrobe had been a pair of black shorts that were supposed to be for swimming.

He put them on now, and went to the top of the dungeon stairs.

Several minutes later, Brianna appeared. She was wearing a fluffy pink robe over the top of whatever she had on beneath.

She attempted to look anywhere but his chest, and

he was amused when her eyes couldn't quite stay away from his body.

Yes. He was right.

One thing he had learned was to be certain in all things. The dungeon had been his kingdom for many years. And everything within it in his control. How much he moved, how much he didn't. How much he slept. What he read, at least within the array of five books he had at any given time.

It made him very certain. Even outside of it.

And he did not need experience to know what the two of them wanted from each other.

Could they not just make each other feel good? That was all he wanted. It wasn't even about his own needs, though they were ferocious.

But about her desire.

How he longed to see her flush with it.

"Down this way," he said.

He still remembered. Of course he did. He hadn't thought much about his real life, not once he'd gone into the dungeon. He had read.

When he wasn't firmly in the present, he kept his thoughts on fictional worlds. Fictional people. There he could read about love, desire, sex, anger, revenge, all while keeping distance between himself and those things. For they were contained in books, along with places he had not been, and foods he could not eat.

He had not wanted his entire world to be shrunk down to those stone walls.

He had not wanted them to be the only thing that he could see in front of him.

And reading had kept those pictures in his mind sharp.

Still, he had not thought about the walls immediately beyond the dungeon. The palace. His home. A home he was still in yet could not visit. So he had tried to erase it from his mind. Had done his best to simply…let it fade.

Yet he remembered it all now.

He remembered the underground pool area. All mosaic and pillars. A glimmering sort of underground cave of wonder. They had many happy times there as a family. A place where they could all relax and simply be themselves.

He was certain he would remember how to swim. That, he thought, had to be something buried into your muscle memory. It was a survival instinct, after all.

They walked down to the end of the corridor, down a spiral staircase and into the magnificent room, which was every bit as glorious as he remembered.

And he could remember laughing here. Playing here.

The memories were so sharp, but unlike that moment in the library, it did not intrude on reality. Didn't block out the moment.

"This is incredible," she said.

"Yes. It is."

He began to step down into the water. And then slid forward, slicing through like a knife.

And he found that he could swim. Expertly still.

"Come on," he said.

She looked at him, and he could see color mounted in her cheeks. Then she let the rope slide from her shoulders. Revealing a bright yellow bikini beneath.

And his body went hard like iron.

The body that she revealed surpassed his wildest dreams.

Her breasts were full, spilling from the yellow cups, her stomach soft, her waist small. Her hips were lush, and the way the bottom of the swimsuit caused her hips to dent inward, forced him to imagine what it would look like if he gripped them with his hands and held on tight.

She looked away from him, but she began to walk to the edge of the pool. "It is very nice-looking," she said, her voice suddenly stilted. Stiff.

"Well, it is much nicer than I even remembered. But I think perhaps my memories were blunted by design. Sometimes being able to remember good things felt like a gift. In other times it felt more like a curse."

She didn't say anything, but nodded, getting into the water, the surface lapping up over her hips. She shivered.

"You are lovely," he said.

Her skin went scarlet all over. "You shouldn't..."

"Should I pretend that I'm not looking at you? That I'm not taking careful inventory of each dip and swell of your body? Of the way your breasts look. Firm and glorious. Of your hips, how full and lush they are, and how I wish to grab hold of them."

"Riyaz..."

Her voice was breathless, but not a warning. He swam over to her. "Come," he said, extending his arm.

She hesitated for a moment, and then she reached out, taking his hand, and he pulled her toward him, swimming her out with him, her body pressed against his, and he groaned. "Brianna," he said. "You are... A temptation too many for me."

"Riyaz," she said. "This is not... We aren't..."

He reached up and moved his thumb over her lips. "What?"

"I can't help you with this. This isn't why I'm here. This isn't what Cairo wanted me to do."

"I see. Do you love my brother?"

"Yes," she said.

She looked away from him, clearly ashamed at the admission.

That was something he could not understand. The shame people felt around their feelings.

It was easy for him to talk about how beautiful she was. To admit that he wanted her. It felt absurd to deny such an obvious thing. He was hard, and he wanted to look his fill. He could hide neither of those things if she chose to see them.

And why should he be ashamed of them? She was a beautiful woman. And he was a man who had long been denied the sight and touch of a beautiful woman. Why would he not enjoy her?

And if she loved Cairo... He did not care for it. But he didn't see why she should be embarrassed. He gripped her chin and directed her face toward him. "Why?"

"He saved me," she said. "And has taken care of me ever since. And I'm in love with him. I... He is my friend. But..."

"Are you in love with him, or do you feel bound to him for what he did?"

"I love him," she said.

"And yet it doesn't prevent you from feeling attraction to me."

"I'm human. I said I loved your brother. I didn't say anything had ever happened between us."

"So you're saying you're hungry for the touch of the one you love, but as he has not put his hands on you...

Your overall hunger for touch is greater than your need for him?" He moved his hands down her back, stopping just above the waistband of her bikini bottoms. How badly he wished to cup her luscious derrière. And yet he wished to wait. Until he had more explicit evidence of her desire.

"I just think... It is entirely possible to appreciate the looks of a person while loving another, isn't it? If it weren't, then people wouldn't have affairs."

"But this would not be an affair. You said yourself. My brother has never touched you."

"You are to be married."

"To a woman I don't love. To a woman I owe nothing to."

She wiggled in his hold, and he allowed her to extricate herself. He growled.

"Don't growl at me," she said.

"I wish to touch you," he said.

"We aren't touching. We're talking. I'm here to help you, and it isn't fair of me to take advantage of you."

He laughed, the sound echoing off the walls in the pool. "Take advantage of me? You are tiny. I could force you to do whatever I wished if I were that sort of man. You could not force me to do anything."

"Maybe not. But you have been in captivity for all these years. And how many women have you even been exposed to? Perhaps you only want me because of proximity. It would be taking advantage of you."

"That sounds like an excuse."

"It isn't. You're engaged. You've made that decision."

"Unless I imprison her."

"Her father betrayed you. Not her," she said, frowning.

He did not want her to frown.

"I know. But just as I am a symbol of hope to the people, whether I am fully within my right mind or not, Ariel will serve as recompense. Though, not in prison, but as my wife. Whether it was her sin or not. We cannot help what we symbolize. I am only sheikh because of who my father is. How is it any different that she is to be sheikha because of who her father is?"

She sank deeper into the water, swimming on her back. Away from him. "I know very well what it's like to suffer because of who your father is. To be used as a pawn. It isn't fair."

He swam to her, closing the distance between them, and wrapped his arm around her waist, pulling her to him. He groaned as her breasts made contact with his chest. She looked away, but he could see her pulse beating faster at the base of her throat. He lowered his head, and kissed her there.

The press of his mouth against that soft skin electrified him.

On impulse, he licked her neck, dragging his tongue slowly up, capturing the water droplets that lingered there.

She shook in his arms, a small cry escaping her lips.

"Riyaz," she said. "That's not... We can't."

"You like it."

"I'm talking about something serious," she said, pressing her hands against his chest and pushing herself away from him.

"Tell me," he commanded. "Your serious thing. Though I don't understand why I cannot hold you in my arms while you do."

"Because you *licked* me."

"Yes. You taste delicious."

"That isn't fair."

"I never said that I was fair."

"You're very frank," she said. "You're going to have to work on that. People don't just say whatever they think."

"And why not? It seems to me that it is the duplicity in the world that creates problems. Not honesty. Not frankness. I don't understand why these different things are issues. Why should you not love Cairo and also want me? Why should you be ashamed of either of those things? Why should I hide the fact that I find you beautiful? None of it makes sense to me. It is duplicity that killed my family. Honesty harms no one. You loving Cairo... It harms no one. Who does not wish to be loved? He should be pleased."

"It is embarrassing," she said. "Because when you love someone, and they do not return the feeling, it is painful. Because you feel foolish and exposed to want someone when they had never demonstrated that they want you."

"He would have to be an idiot not to want you."

"I should say... With Cairo... I'm not sure that him *wanting* me would feel especially flattering. He is not discriminate when it comes to sexual partners. It's a hobby to him. Some people run every morning when they wake up. I think your brother takes a new lover. He's not particular."

He chuckled. "How nice for him. When I tell you that I think you're beautiful, I mean I have never looked at another woman and had the same feelings. Or the same thoughts."

"You also haven't seen very many women. I'm just guessing."

"No. But then, it sounds to me as if you're just choosing not to be flattered. Because it is easier."

"How is it easier?"

"You're afraid of what would happen if you believed me. That you were beautiful."

She looked away from him. "Being beautiful has never given me anything. My father…" She looked back up at him. "None of this is about me. None of this is about my life. We are supposed to be talking about you. It's you that I'm supposed to be concerned about."

"How long has it been since anyone concerned themselves with you? Who came alongside you? Cairo rescued you, but did he do this for you? Did he speak to you? Did he try to teach you how to live in the world? Eat the same breakfast as you, and watch movies with you?"

She looked away. "No. He didn't. But I was fifteen, and he was nineteen. And we would not have… It's simply not how that relationship would've worked. He sent me to school. He was establishing his business, his fortune. He didn't need a girl hanging on to him and…"

"Perhaps you should let me listen to you. Perhaps it would be a good thing."

"My father wanted to sell me. What do you think of that? To pay his debts. I was pretty enough. His rival wanted to buy me, and then sell me continually. To whatever men might want to pay for an evening. Or few moments. That is what being pretty meant when I was fifteen. And maybe part of why I love Cairo so much as he didn't treat me like being pretty was all I was. And he certainly didn't use it as an excuse to touch me or ask for payment for what he did for me. Maybe that is why I cared for him so much."

Fury rushed through him. Fury. That any man could

think to put their hands on her when she did not wish them to. That her own father would treat her so.

He had tasted betrayal. A man his father trusted had ultimately led to his death. Had led to Riyaz's imprisonment. But his own father had fought to the death to save him. To save his wife, to save his sons.

He had never known the betrayal of family.

His family had loved them.

"Does your father still live?"

"As far as I know," she said.

"He will not for long. I will find him. And I will have him killed."

"You can't just...do that," she said.

"Yes, I can. I command entire armies. I can certainly command a small group of assassins to take out the human garbage that would dare do such a thing to you."

"This isn't *listening*, Riyaz."

"I have heard everything that I need to. The world would be better off if he was not wasting its oxygen."

It was the strangest thing, he could tell that he frightened her, and yet he could also see a small amount of pleasure reflected in her eyes. She was glad that he wished to protect her.

"I will always protect you," he said. "Brianna, you never have need to fear for your safety."

"Riyaz, that is very kind of you. It is... I'm not your responsibility. You're mine. You're a job that I have to do. Your brother has asked me to and... You and I have known each other for two days."

Was that all? Time had so little meaning to him. And he had very much not met many people in these past years, so there was something about this time that he had spent with her that felt deep. That felt timeless.

This moment in the baths could've been weeks.

This revelation of looking at her, of having a few stolen moments of holding her in his arms.

Though he would not grab hold of her. Not again. Not after what she had said about her father. Not after hearing that her father had wanted to sell her.

She would need to come to him. She would need to be the one to draw her body against his, and then he would hold her, move his hands over her.

He wished to do that.

To touch her everywhere. To kiss her.

He had to be certain it was what she wanted.

He was certain of many things. Not the least of which being that she was attracted to him.

But the reality of what she had been through... He didn't know what else her father might have subjected her to.

He did not know enough about her. And he was hungry for more, and yet she did not seem to wish to share. She seemed to only want to throw her trauma out as a weapon.

"I will protect you," he said. "I pledge myself to you."

"How can you do that?"

"Life has been simple for me, these past sixteen years. It is a funny thing. Because while I might resent that Cairo had access to certain things. Certain freedoms. He also had to do all this work. And he lived a life of complexity. Apparently that has included an endless string of lovers, which, I will not deny I am slightly envious of. I had to *survive* every day. And that is all. I had to care for my body. The day that lay before me from the time I woke to the time I slept was incredibly simple. There was very little in the way of decision-making to be done. I was in control, for all that I was not in charge of whether or not I left the dungeon. That has actually made me incredibly certain in moments like these.

"You think that I've not known you long enough, and yet to me, this is the deepest I have known someone in sixteen years. Deeper even than Cairo, who has not been around. I have shared things with you that I have not shared with anyone else, and now you have shared things with me. It is the simplest thing in the world to pledge you my allegiance. That I promise you."

"Riyaz…" She looked away for a moment, then took a breath and met his gaze. "I appreciate that. But this is a job for me. Nothing more. And when it's over I'm going to go back to my life. I'm going to have a normal life. Someday. This has been somewhat clarifying for me. I am too attached to Cairo, and that needs to stop. I can't afford it. This… This attachment. I need to make my own life. And this is the beginning of me stepping away from him. My feelings for him. All of that. I want to find a normal man, and I want to have a normal family. I want to live in a normal neighborhood. Not some town house that there's no way I could ever afford. I've never had normal. I've never even seen it outside of a book. But can you imagine that? A little house in a neighborhood. Where kids can ride their bikes. My kids. That's what I want. That's what I want more than anything. Normal."

"I see," he said. "I know the normal that you're talking about. I've read about it. But we talked about this earlier, and the truth remains. Normal will never protect you. I will."

"Thank you. I will keep that in mind."

He felt her withdraw before she physically began to do so.

"Were you hurt?"

She was halfway out of the water and stopped. "I'm sorry, what?"

"Had your father sold you before?"

A crease appeared between her brows. "Are you asking if I was assaulted?"

"Yes. Either way, I owe you an apology. I held you because I thought you were beautiful. And I wanted to touch you. I assumed that you wanted the same thing, but I did not make sure. And now that you've told me these things…"

"I wasn't," she said. "But I appreciate you asking. I… I did want you to hold me. It's only that I thought better of it."

"I can't understand that either." The empty cavern of misunderstanding in him seemed endless.

"What? Thinking better of something?"

"I was denied a great many things being locked away. I don't understand why you would deny yourself, with all the freedom that you have."

"Says the man who is opting to eat the same porridge every day? Sometimes you deny yourself because you know that something is too much for you to handle, Riyaz. That's why. Can you not understand that? Can you not see that I have to…? I have to protect myself."

"Then you had best go. I wish to protect you from me. But if you stay… I will find it harder and harder to do so, particularly now that I have confirmed that you enjoyed being held."

She finished getting out of the pool, and went to collect her robe. She hesitated for a moment, and then pulled it on. Then she looked back at him one more time before walking away.

She had no idea what had just happened. Her body and all the rest of her was still buzzing the next day at breakfast.

Riyaz didn't come to breakfast, and she didn't go looking for him. He was probably in the dungeon. Instead, she sat there over a plate of waffles—they had stocked the palace with American foods for her, one of Cairo's thoughtful gestures, damn him for being so good—reflecting on what it had felt like to be held against Riyaz's strong body. On why she had shared anything about her past with him and why... Why she had admitted that she liked him touching her.

Maybe because she couldn't stand him feeling guilty.

He was so blunt and strange, and he asked all kinds of things that he shouldn't. That polite, normal people would know not to ask. But he was neither polite nor normal. So he had just gone and asked after her potential trauma as if it was as easy as yes or no.

But then he made it very clear why. He hadn't wanted to be part of taking away her choice. And she couldn't help but marvel at the sensitivity, for all that the man didn't seem to have an excess of it.

And she had felt like she couldn't lie to him. Of course she had enjoyed him touching her. The press of his lips against her neck... It had kept her awake.

She wondered why he had kissed her there. She wondered why any of it. Why had she told him that she loved Cairo? And why had she confessed her deepest dreams... Being normal. Living in a regular house.

She was supposed to be taking care of him. She was supposed to be helping him. And yet she had ended up… Talking to him as if he was her therapist or something and… It was all just wrong.

She had never gotten attached to somebody that she was working with like this.

And they had only known each other for two days. The way that he had dismissed that, as if it was so obvious that the two days they had spent together were more significant than the time suggested.

And it was. She couldn't explain why. She only knew that it was.

When she was halfway through her waffles, he strode into the room. "My brother has collected Ariel."

"Oh," she said, her heart slamming against her breastbone. "She is not amenable to the marriage. Which is unfortunate. But he said he cannot bring her here now."

"Right. Well…" She knew that was because of her. Because of the report that she had given back to Cairo, but she hesitated to admit it to Riyaz.

She needed him to be able to focus and not have distractions, that much was true. So maybe she could express that without admitting that she had actually told Cairo that she feared slightly for Ariel's safety. She wasn't sure that was true anymore. She didn't think Riyaz was dangerous. Not in that way.

"What is this?" he said, gesturing to the plate that was in his spot.

"Belgian waffles. I thought you would probably like them."

"Are you going to lecture me on self-denial?"

"I was thinking about it. Since you had so much to say about mine."

"All right. I will try the waffles."

"Why don't you try having three adventurous meals with me today."

"All right. Will you let me hold you again?"

"To what end?"

"I don't understand. *To what end*. Did you not enjoy being held?"

"Yes. But men don't typically wish to *hold* women unless there is an end point."

"By which you mean sex."

"Yes," she said, heat rushing through her body. "By which I mean sex."

"I would not be opposed to sex."

"No. I can't."

"Then you will have to come to me when you decide to change your mind."

That simple. And yet, she felt like her body was burning. Boiling with need and anticipation. And somehow she felt... Disappointed at his proclamation that he wouldn't push her. Part of her, she found, wished that he would.

"Why do you think I'll change my mind?" she asked.

"I may not have a lot of practical experience in the world. But I have read what the greatest minds have to say about love. About attraction. About rage and revenge. Desire. Heartbreak. I have read enough to know that there is a certain amount of inevitability to desire. In part because I think when people desire someone, they will come up with whatever excuses possible to give in to that desire. We resist because..."

"Why do we resist?" she asked.

Her heart was thundering so hard she was sure that he would be able to hear it. She knew that she was being provocative and asking him. Implying that what he thought, what he *wanted*, was not valid because he had never lived out among people.

It was mean.

"I have read about these things," he said, his confidence absolute. "I think people resist because they are afraid. There are many foolish reasons to be afraid. Afraid of what other people think. I'm not certain that I could ever find it in me to care about what someone thinks. Afraid of their own responses, that I can understand. Not for myself personally. Only some people have experiences that make them afraid. That they would grow too attached to the partner."

"I see. And which do you think I am?"

The way that he smiled, slow and seductive, made her stomach clench tight. "I'm afraid that you would fall in love with me."

She couldn't help it. She laughed. "You're afraid that I would fall in love with you? That is quite the ego you have."

"Let me rephrase. I think you are *afraid* that you might fall in love with me. That is what holds you back. Because otherwise, what do you care? Cairo never has to know. No one ever has to know."

"I can't live like that. I could not keep something like that from a man that I consider to be one of my closest friends."

"You are required to divulge intimate details from your life to him? I find that very strange."

"Well, it isn't up to you to find it strange or not. I didn't ask."

"Does he let you know every time he takes a lover?"

"I don't have that kind of time."

"Yes, so frequent is the act for my brother," he said, the disdain in his voice almost amusing.

"I don't want to talk about this," she said. "I'm here to help you."

"You can imagine why I might not find that appealing. I feel that I have a connection with you, *habibti*." He had never called her that before. She knew that it was an endearment, but she wasn't sure quite what it meant. "I have not met many people. Cairo might be your friend, but you are the closest that I have to such a thing. Do you not see why it might be... Problematic, for you to act as if you are here to serve me, and nothing more?"

She was angry. Because she *liked* him. Because he wasn't just a job. She had sat and talked to him, she had been held in his arms, and she felt connection to him.

She just didn't *want* to. Couldn't afford to.

"It isn't like that. It isn't that I don't... Find you interesting. But this is a job I'm supposed to do before I go back to my life. And *this* is your life. I'm going to leave it."

"So what would be the problem in indulging your desire?"

Again, the words were so seductive. So...

"Because, Riyaz, that isn't how I'm wired. I don't just have flings with men. If I did... Well, I had plenty of opportunity. But for me, desire can't be separated from feelings."

He looked smug. "So you *are* afraid, then, that you will fall in love with me."

"I am not afraid of any such thing."

No, what scared her the most was the way that she felt

so drawn to him. So attracted, in spite of it being Cairo who theoretically held her heart.

She had to let go of Cairo. She truly did. When she had talked to him last night to give him an update, all she had been able to tell him was that he needed to keep Ariel away.

She hadn't seen the other woman. She wondered how beautiful she was.

Why did it matter if she was beautiful? Riyaz had nothing to do with her.

Maybe she was just jealous because Cairo was off with another woman. Except that was basically a day ending in Y.

Cairo had any number of partners at any given time. None of them seemed to affect him emotionally. And because it didn't affect him she wasn't all that jealous, not really. Anyway, she had somewhat accepted that he would always be out of her reach. That she would always be pining, with absolutely no chance of ever being anything else.

But her feelings for him were still there. Though maybe they were just a shield. Something safe. Something that kept her separate from other people. From other men.

And her attraction to Riyaz… It just kept on growing. And the way that he wanted to talk about it, the way that he just openly acknowledged it…

"Do you know, I have been in love with your brother for sixteen years. And at no point have we ever discussed those feelings. Or my attraction to him. That just isn't something people do. Because it *is* embarrassing, whether you understand it or not. You're supposed to leave those kinds of things unspoken. Because they're intimate. And out of respect for the other person's feelings..."

"Why do you leave these things unspoken? So that you can sit and long with no hope of ever having your feelings returned? So that you can wonder? Is that it? Is it to live in a space of magic, where you can convince yourself that perhaps it could be real? Do you wish to have a story that you tell yourself? Is that it? And if you were to confess your feelings to him, he might say *no*. And then your hope would die. You would have no more stories left to tell yourself."

It was such an unflattering, bracing truth. And she didn't like it. She also had to acknowledge that it was probably true.

"It's the truth. For all of humanity," she bit out.

"I had no choice but to live lives that were not mine," he said. "I had no choice but to live lives that were stories. I have read about how incendiary the touch between two lovers can be. And if I'd had my choice, I would have made that touch real. Reading is magic, but it is not life. You have had all these opportunities, but you haven't taken them. I can understand in some small part why you might wish to protect yourself from the truth, but the reality is, it does nothing for you. It does nothing for anyone. You might live, and let you save all that you desire for imagination. No. That I cannot understand."

"You are about to take over the throne. To rule this country. And you're worried about my... Honesty."

"That I will rule Nazul is a fact. A reality of the birth order in my family, and my lineage. It is not an achievement. And yes, I must work to be... To be seen as fit to do these things. I understand that. But it does not inspire my passion. It does not intrigue me. My life has been about small details, and the small details have… Expanded. The possibilities."

"Eat your waffles. Consider those an infinite sensual possibility."

"I'm not certain that waffles can be called sensual."

"Well, that's because you didn't eat them fresh. Believe me when I tell you, they are probably better than sex."

She shouldn't have said that. And she realized that when she felt the sharp, keen stare coming from him.

"And would you know that for certain?"

"What exactly are you asking me?"

"I think you know. Would you know for certain if the waffles were better than sex?"

"I have a very rich fantasy life," she said.

"So you are a virgin."

"I don't think of myself that way. I'm not defined by whether or not a man has touched me."

"I did not suggest that you were."

And it burned. Her desire to ask him if he was the same. She was too embarrassed. Tongue-tied.

"The waffles are fine," he said. And then he strode over to where she sat at the end of the table, took her hand in his and lifted her into a standing position. "Do you know what I need help with?"

Her heart was thundering radically, and for a moment, she thought he was going to do something like… Press her hand to the front of his pants and allow her to feel his hardness there. The evidence of his desire. Or perhaps he would lower his head and kiss her.

"Teach me to dance."

CHAPTER SIX

THE CONVERSATION AT breakfast had him aching. He wanted an excuse to touch her again. To hold her.

She was such a strange woman. Or maybe she wasn't. He didn't have much experience of women. Or of any human. Maybe all people were like this. Denying what they wanted so that they could live in fantasy land.

He did not see the point of it. It was so... They were all prisoners. People.

Prisoners to all of these made-up prisons.

You still sleep in the dungeon.

Yes. He did. It was called the transition. There was hardly a handbook on how to escape the dungeon. If there were, he would've read it. Though, if it existed, his captors never would've brought it to him, so maybe that was untrue. But either way, he felt that he was handling it as well as anyone could. And even then, what did it matter? What did any of it matter?

There was no grade being given out.

And yet, she was so careful. Brianna.

Sunshine and raspberries and Brianna.

He half expected her to deny the request. But instead, she squared her shoulders and looked at him, her expression defiant. "Of course. Is there a room where you would prefer to conduct the lessons?"

"The library. I imagine it is cleaned up."

"Yes. The staff saw to that quickly. They thought that it might be upsetting to you to see the aftermath."

"It's not upsetting to me."

"Maybe there is something to the way that you spent the last sixteen years, because you don't seem particularly concerned or guilty about anything. You don't seem to harbor a whole lot of bad feelings." She looked away. "I'm sorry. Of course that isn't true. The issue that you had yesterday, it obviously speaks to some deeper things…"

"I don't need you to validate me. I'm fine. And you are correct. Living the way that I did, I could not afford to indulge these sorts of concerns. Why would they matter? These are abstract things. The thing that frustrated me the most about being in captivity was what I could not do for others. For my country. I had to accept the fact that my existence needed to be all about my survival. That is different than enjoying life or living for others, serving others. But when you have no other people to worry about, when the only people who you are in view of are your enemies, your captives, then what opinions have you to be concerned about? Also guilt… I have no guilt or shame. That is also connected to the expectations of others."

"Well, you are a singular person. Because most of us worry an awful lot about what other people think."

"Who do you worry about?" He extended his hand, giving her time to decide if she was going to take it. She did, and he led her toward the library. The touch of her hand to his was a spark. And he reveled in it. It was entirely possible that this was the only contact he would ever have with her. Their palms touching. Her body pressed against his in the pool. Her pulse beneath his lips.

That might be all there was. It was more than he'd ever had.

And yet, the idea of not claiming her fully felt wrong. The beast within him roared, but he did not growl out loud. Which was for her. Only for her. Because he didn't care whether he did or not.

They opened the doors to the library, and closed them behind them.

"I can play some music on my phone. Maybe there's something traditional…"

"Yes. Because there is a wedding dance, you know, and I will have to be in practice for that."

She did not look pleased about that. And he found that it ignited a spark of pleasure in his gut.

"I will have to hold you in my arms."

"That's okay," she said, the words hushed.

He went forward and took her in his arms, held her against his body as they began to move in time to the music. And it was the strangest thing, because he didn't remember. As if he was in another place, another time. But not in that dark way he had gone to it yesterday. It was something different. And so was he.

As if the weight of the past wasn't pressing down on him. As if perhaps he was different. And maybe she was too.

"Brianna Whitman," he said. "Your father was a bad man. Was all of your childhood bad?"

She shook her head. "No. Because I didn't know that we weren't normal. I didn't know… I didn't realize my father wasn't like other fathers. I thought that I was happy enough. I really did. I thought that perhaps… I thought that perhaps we were maybe only a little bit different to other families. We had a very big house. And it was behind a large gate. My father was rarely around. My mother… My mother left when I was about eleven. But I'll never know if that's actually what happened. Because that's when it began to become clear to me that my father wasn't a good man. My father in fact is a very bad man. I don't know if he hurt my mother. I don't know if she ran away and had to hide, couldn't take us because of the danger that it would represent. And I may never know. Cairo has tried to locate her before, but he's never been able to. Whatever happens, I'm not angry with her. I know that my father would never have shown her mercy. If she had taken us… He would've chased her down for the rest of her life. Because we were nothing but collateral for him. Property. My oldest sister, he married her off to his right-hand man. And that just left me. But it wasn't marriage that he wanted for me. It was something elsc. To appease a rival. And that is when I really knew. That's when I really knew he didn't love me. He never had. It was broken, and it could never be anything else."

"What did you do to find joy in those times? Because we all find joy. I grew up a spoiled prince. The heir to the throne. Very little was ever denied me. The one bit of freedom that I knew I would never have is the ability to choose my own bride. But… My behavior, my actions were never going to be hindered by that. I knew it. So they had chosen this pretty American girl for me, but if I did not wish to bed her every night for the rest of my life I didn't have to. I could take mistresses. Other wives.

It was not popular in modern society, but it didn't mean I couldn't. *Nothing* was off-limits to me. At sixteen, the world stretched before me, mine entirely. One thing I could have never imagined was what it would be like to lose that. And yet I did. In a moment." He released hold on her for a moment and snapped his finger. "In a moment, I lost it. Do you know what that's like? That change. So abrupt. But I was not miserable for the entirety of those sixteen years. If I had been, I would have surely descended into madness. Part of what we do is find ways to survive. In ways to make that survival bearable. What did you do to make your survival bearable?"

He found that he wanted to know. Desperately. More than anything, in fact. She was the most fascinating creature he had ever seen. Ever known. And maybe the list of creatures he had seen and known was short, but it did not matter. It was still true.

"Like you, I enjoyed reading. I also loved movies. Movies about families. Who sat around the dinner table every night. And I loved sitcoms. Where there was always a lesson, and everyone was safe. At home every night, in a house with parents who loved them. I loved it, because it gave me hope that those things existed."

"As you said, you want normal."

"Yes. I want what I saw then. I want that thing I saw in all of those homes. I crave it. And I've never been able to have it. Maybe some of that's my fault. My situation with Cairo is hardly normal. And that is of my own making."

She looked down, and a lock of silky red hair fell into her face. He reached up and touched it, pushing it back off of her forehead. She looked up at him.

"Maybe the thing is you are not normal. And that is not

a bad thing. I think that you are singular, Brianna. Why should you contort yourself to fit this ideal?"

She looked desolate. "I want to be happy. I really want to be happy."

"Not in the way that we have made ourselves happy in the past."

She shook her head. "No. Not in that way. Not in that way where we have to take just moments of joy and hope for the best. Hope that someday we get to feel it again."

"What do you feel now?"

Her face went red. "Tell me. Because you do not have to pretend with me. I despise pretense, as you are now well aware. Tell me what you feel. You do not need to make stories for me."

"You are very warm," she said. "And a surprisingly good dancer."

"It shocked me that I remembered. But like swimming, I guess it does not go away."

"You make me… You make my heart beat faster." She couldn't look at him, he noticed. "You make my body feel like it's too sensitive."

"Too sensitive for what?" Desire gathered at the base of his spine, tightened within him. "Or is it something that I could help with?"

Then she did something unexpected. She reached up and touched his face, her fingertips dragging down his cheek, along his jawbone. "I keep thinking about those moments of joy. Taking moments, even though you know they won't sustain you forever. Even though you know they can't last. I… Maybe there's something to that."

Without thought, he turned his head and pressed his mouth to her palm.

He was hard now. His desire a raging beast, and he knew that if he actually did take her to bed he would have to find a way to take it slow. He would have to put her pleasure first.

And he would give thanks for all the times that he read books that left him hard and unsatisfied in the end, because they were lessons. Because they had taught him about female pleasure, and the way that it had to be treated. Because he had learned that a woman could reach her peak over and over again, even if a man could only reach it once in a prescribed amount of time. He had learned all the ways to make a woman wet. To make her desperate.

That was what he wanted if he was going to take Brianna as a lover.

It was not about his own needs, not simply. For his needs were linked with hers.

He wanted her to desire him.

He *needed* her to.

Her eyelids fluttered closed, and a small, tortured sound escaped her lips.

"Do you want me?"

"What would either of us know about it?" she whispered.

He chuckled. Finally, she was saying what was on her mind rather than holding back.

"I know that what I wish is to kiss you until you are begging for more. I know that I should take it slowly, teasing your nipples over your clothes, putting my hand between your thighs and stroking. Touch you until you are arching against me, until you are asking for more. And only then should I give it to you. Or maybe not.

Maybe I should keep it back. Keep more to myself, until you are willing to *beg*. Then, and only then, will I begin to kiss you down your neck, reveal your body slowly to my gaze, expose your breasts. So that I can taste them. I crave that. Your skin. The sensation of sucking your nipples deep into my mouth. And then, I would kiss my way down your body. You have the most beautiful body. The sight of you in that bikini nearly sent me to hell. Or heaven. I'm not certain which it is. I would kiss my way down your soft stomach. Part your legs. And I have no shame, as you know. So I would look my fill until you turned bright red. Until you were begging for me to either let you close your legs and walk away, or feast upon you. And then... I would not. I wouldn't do either, because when I take you, Brianna, you will surrender your control to me. You will trust that I will listen to the cues of your body and give you the pleasure that you want. That you need. You have had any number of years to find the keys to your own desire. But when I have you like that, willing, beneath me, you will surrender to my will. I will kiss your thigh. I will not touch my tongue to that bundle of nerves that's crying out for my attention. I will make you quiver. Press a kiss low to your stomach, until you are begging me, and only then will I please us both by allowing myself a taste of your honey."

"Riyaz," she said, her voice trembling.

"Do you not wish to hear more?"

"It's a little bit like reading ahead in a book, isn't it?" she whispered.

Yes. She was seduced. He was certain of that. She had not said no.

She was choosing this. Him. She was choosing him.

And the need between them. The short moment of joy that they might find in one another's arms.

"No spoilers?" he asked.

"Where did you even hear that?"

"I read it."

She shook her head. "You are astonishing."

"Thank you. But I haven't even touched you yet."

"Riyaz... Kiss me. Please."

And he did not need to be asked twice.

He lowered his head, and Brianna bracketed his face with her palms. Felt the roughness of his whiskers against her skin.

And she wanted to weep.

And then his mouth was on hers, over hers. And it was... It was all that she could have ever fantasized about and more.

She didn't know what would happen after this. He was marrying another woman. And even if he weren't, he was the heir to the throne of this desert kingdom, and that had nothing to do with that sitcom family life that she wanted.

And they were... They could never be together. Not really. His reference point for everything was books. Hers TV. They were pretend people, playing the part of being real. But not with each other.

They had found honesty, *real* honesty here. And she wanted it. More than anything. And maybe this was the gift. Just the moment. And whatever happened after didn't actually matter.

Maybe the gift was these few days, weeks, however long it was, of honesty.

He was the first person that she really felt like might understand her. And she had never thought she needed that. But she had put on a mask and a veneer from the moment that she had left her father's compound, and she had operated in the world with that mask. She had taught other people to do the same. She was teaching him to do it now, and for the first time, she felt some misgivings about that.

Maybe the problem with sitcoms was they were all on a set. Was that they were inherently *not* real.

And neither was she.

Except right now, she felt real. His lips parted, and his tongue swept deep into her mouth. She was shocked by the precision and skill present in that kiss. The way that he called need up from within her body without even trying.

He was a quick study, was Riyaz. And apparently, very good at getting information just by reading.

He reached around, his hand cupping the back of her head, as he kissed her deeper. His other arm was wrapped tightly around her body, holding her to him, and she wrapped her arms around his neck, her breasts pressed flat against his hard chest. Her heart was raging. Her whole body felt like it was on fire. And everything up until this moment had only ever been a pale promise of this sort of passion.

For her, desire was so rooted in the unimaginable. In the thwarted desire that she felt for Cairo. But that was all hazy, and he was right. Riyaz was right. It was just a story. And the story was never anything more than images that you painted in your own mind. Or set pieces for a show.

But it wasn't substantial.

It wasn't real.

This was real. It was hard and sharp. There was nothing gauzy or easy about it. It was the rage of her own heartbeat, the warmth of his mouth, the slick friction of his tongue. The hard hold of his hand in her hair, the steel band of his arm.

It was need and fire. Temptation.

And when he swept her up off the floor, holding her in his arms like a warrior with a conquest, she knew that he didn't care who saw.

And it made her not care either.

This was their moment. Their pleasure. Their freedom.

He opened the doors to the library, and walked down the corridor. There was no ceremony, no concern that there were other people wandering around the palace. He did not pause for any questioning gazes, nor did he offer any explanations.

And she loved it. She truly did love it.

Maybe, maybe later, there would be cause for regret. Maybe she would be sorry that she did this. But she would've made a mistake. One that was her own.

That was normal. Trying things. Seizing the moment. The good feelings. The desire.

She could have this. Why not? Why not take what she wanted?

She had been frozen all this time. Wanting a man she couldn't have.

She wanted Riyaz, so who cared what came in the future? It was her choice. And there was something powerful in that.

He opened the door to his bedchamber, which she had personally never seen him anywhere near, and brought her inside, closing the door behind them and turning the lock.

Her heart thundered erratically as he stepped away from her, and removed his shirt.

She had seen him half-naked before, but this was different. Because he was looking at her with intent, and she knew that it wasn't going to simply be a look. She knew that it would be more. His hands on her body. Her hands on his.

She knew that it would be everything.

And it felt right. To give this to him. To be part of what he was giving himself. Because who else would ever understand? Who else would ever know?

Who else?

He moved forward, reached behind her and took hold of the zipper of her dress, and dragged it down, the fabric falling away from her body, and unceremoniously dropping to the floor.

She hadn't given a lot of thought to the underwear that she had on today, and now she wished she had. Since she was standing before him in nothing more than plain, serviceable white underwear.

But he did not seem to mind. Not at all. His gaze was hungry as it roamed over her curves, and she had never felt more beautiful than she did in that moment.

He moved toward her, taking her in his arms again, and kissing her. "I have a promise to keep," he whispered against her skin. And then he turned his attention back to her mouth. Kissing her and kissing her until she was dizzy with it. With her own need. With the desperation of her desire for him. Until she was trembling, until she was ready to beg, just as he had promised her she would be.

His touch was almost unbearable, she was so hypersensitive. She wanted his hands directly on her bare skin, but she also didn't know if she could endure it.

But then his eyes locked with hers, dark and hungry, and she knew that whatever was ahead... She wanted it. She wanted this. She wanted him.

And somewhere in there, she felt powerful. That this was a choice she was making—good or bad—like a very normal girl.

Except how many normal girls got to experience sex for the first time with a man who looked like him?

He was incredible. There was something raw about him. Something feral. It was always a strange thing when he opened his mouth and began to talk about books. He didn't have the look of a cerebral man.

And then he growled, that growl that he did, and she was reminded. That while he might possess the ability to reason, to be rational. That while he might discuss books and philosophize about why people behaved the way they did...

There was an elemental quality to him. And when he receded to that place—as he had done in the library that day when he had nearly killed a man with his bare hands—he was all in it. Just as he was now.

Right now, she had the beast.

And somehow, she felt safe even still.

He stroked her cheek, then tore her bra away from her body, the movement abrupt and unexpected.

And she gasped. Not because it was unpleasant. Not at all. It was what she wanted. He was what she wanted. And there she was, naked before him, and she reveled in it. Gloried in it. In this moment of ecstasy. Of raw, unbridled feeling.

The truth of it was, people like them… They had to learn to hide their feelings. It was a matter of survival.

She knew that, and she imagined that he did too.

"Give me all of it," she whispered, not meaning to speak, but not being able to control it either.

"All of what?"

"Your fury. Your feelings. Everything that you've always kept back. Because you had to, didn't you? To survive. Even if it wasn't out of fear of your captor, you couldn't allow yourself to go to dark places, or how would you live?"

He looked at her body, his expression on fire. "Do you want to talk?"

"No. I don't. I want to feel. Everything that I never let myself feel. But I want you to come with me. I don't want you to go easy on me. I don't want you to be gentle. I don't want you to treat me like I might break."

"You may regret saying that."

"But I said it. So now you know. It's my choice."

"Good."

He grabbed her waist, lifted her up off the ground, and licked one breast, then another. She shuddered, and he carried her over to the bed, holding her as if she was insubstantial. As if she weighed nothing.

And then he laid her out on the large, sumptuously appointed bed, his eyes roaming over her curves hungrily.

"And now," he said. "I can see the point and purpose to a bed."

He pressed his knee into the mattress, moved up to her body and cupped her breast with his hand. He watched, with rapt attention as he slid his thumb over her nipple.

She felt it pucker. An arrow of pleasure hitting sharp and true between her legs.

"Riyaz," she said.

"Is it good?"

"Yes," she said. "It's good. Please. More. Please."

"It is amazing," he said. "You would not even tell my brother that you desired him, but you will beg me for my touch. Openly. Always be so honest with me," he said. "There is no room for embarrassment or shame. Not with us."

She shook her head, biting her lip as he pinched her nipple. As he moved his hand to her other breast and transferred his attentions there.

He moved his hands down her body, the strong, calloused fingers making her shiver as they trailed over her skin.

He hooked his thumbs into the sides of her panties and dragged them down her legs. And she didn't feel shame. As if his words had been an incantation. A magic spell. As if he had caused it to be so simply with his intonations.

He was magic. Or maybe they were.

"I thought of this, for all those years. Sixteen years, I thought of a woman's body. Various pieces of my imagination put together with images I had seen. Something to make an erotic slideshow in my head. But it was nothing. Nothing compared to you. Compared to the reality of your beauty. You are every promise fulfilled, Brianna. You are all that I desire. And how I desire you." He leaned forward, sucked her nipple deep into his mouth, the growl that rose in his throat gratifying her. She was becoming so fond of that growl.

Her back arched up off the mattress, and he sucked her deep until she was crying out his name.

Then he kissed his way down her stomach. And he did exactly as he promised. He pressed his lips to her inner thigh, beat a path to where she was slick with her need for him.

But that was when he lost his restraint. He reached around and took a handful of her rear, lifting her up off the bed and bringing her to his mouth as he began to feast upon her as if she was all that he had been denied. As if she was everything that he could ever want.

He lapped at her, concentrating on that sensitized bundle of nerves there, finding it unerringly. She gripped his hair, forked her fingers through it. Held him there. He moved his head, penetrating her with his tongue before sliding back up to where she was greedy for him. Could she even tell where she was greedy for him? She was greedy all over. She was desperate for him. For all that they could find together.

She was an expert at trying to find pure joy in moments. And this moment was perfect. She didn't want to see the end of it. She didn't want to see anything but this room. But them. His glorious, bronze skin, the play of his muscles. The intensity of his need for her as he pleasured her.

Desire tightened low in her stomach. Twisting, deeper, deeper. He licked her, then penetrated her with two fingers, and she cursed, shouting out his name and an obscenity all at once.

He growled again.

And again. He worked his fingers in and out of her body, his tongue relentless, and finally she shattered. Need pouring over her like a relentless storm. Then he moved away from her, his eyes never leaving her body as he moved his hands to the closure of his pants and solemnly divested himself of them. Leaving his body exposed to her.

He was thick and proud and she was shocked by how utterly glorious she found him.

There was a woman that she had coached once, trying to help her with some situations at work. She had told her that penises were fine, but she wouldn't be hanging up any art of them in her home.

She thought that she might actually want art of Riyaz in all his glory. Yes, she thought she might want that quite a lot.

She rose up on her knees and pressed her palms to his chest, watched as they slid down over his muscles, rippled over the glorious definition there. "You're beautiful," she said. "How dare they? How dare they hide you away."

He grabbed her wrist, lifted her palm to his mouth and kissed it. Then her wrist, the inside of her elbow, and she shivered. "Riyaz," she whispered.

"Brianna. I do like saying your name."

"I love to hear you say it."

She reached out and wrapped her hand around his arousal, as if she had all the confidence of a woman who had done this before, when she very much did not.

But he felt good in her hand, and his expression was like ecstasy when he let his head fall back as she stroked him.

And then, it was like something jolted in him, a bolt of electricity, and he opened his eyes, watching her as she stroked him.

"I don't want to miss it," he said. "Because you look so beautiful like that."

And she had the thought that she knew how she might look even more beautiful to him. And again, she led with intuition rather than experience. She flicked her tongue over the head of his arousal, and then took part of him in. His growl was a whole force, as he canted his hips forward and drove himself deeper.

She took him in as deep as she could, but he was so large. She used her hand to help as she bobbed her head up and down, glorying in the taste of him. In the way she made him shake.

He was a man who had survived the unimaginable. And she made him tremble.

There was something glorious in that.

Who needed normal when she had this? Who needed normal, when there was all this power?

She pleasured him like that until she could feel the edges of his control begin to fray. "Enough," he said. "Not like this. I need to be inside of you. I need you."

He kissed her mouth, positioning his body over her as he laid her back on the bed, pressing himself between her legs and guiding himself inside of her.

She cried out as he filled her slowly, taking care with her innocence as he did.

He froze, the tendons in his neck standing out. His teeth clenched.

And she looked at him, this man who was trying so hard to exhibit restraint. This man who was hers and hers alone.

And the joy of that nearly burst inside her like fireworks.

He was hers. He was hers. No other woman had ever had him like this. He was inside of her. The only man she had ever been with.

What they were giving each other was beautiful, and in that moment, she thought of the woman. The woman that Cairo was bringing back here. That woman would not have this. Only she did.

She would own him forever in this way.

She shuddered as he thrust in the rest of the way, as pleasure replaced the slight pain that she felt at the invasion. As need began to ripple through her once more.

He thrust hard and fast into her, and stopped when both of them came close to their peak. He let them come down, before pushing them to the edge again. And again and again. Until she was shaking. Begging yet again. "Finish it," she said.

"I don't ever want it to end," he said.

"Please." She lifted her head up from the pillow and she kissed his mouth.

He growled, his hips pistoning forward, thrusting into her over and over again as he cried out her name, his grip bruising on her hips. "Riyaz," she shouted out his name, while his own release was a wordless exultation, another feral growl that echoed in the chamber.

And then she held him, against her body, until he reversed their positions and cradled her to his chest. "Mine," he said.

He stroked her hair, and she snuggled into his chest. And she felt the profound sense of peace like she had never felt before.

"Mine," she whispered.

Even though she knew that once this moment ended, those proclamations would be nothing more than lies.

CHAPTER SEVEN

WHEN HE WOKE in the dark, everything was soft. There was a soft mattress beneath him, and a soft woman lying against him.

His body did not hurt. He was not cold.

And he woke all the same. Yet wholly different too.

It was quite unlike anything he had ever experienced before. And for a moment, he resisted opening his eyes. Resisted rousing at all. He had never even dreamed anything this nice.

But soon, the sunshine beckoned, and when he opened his eyes, it was Brianna.

"Good morning," he said. "That was fantastic sex."

She opened her eyes, and looked at him. "That's quite a greeting."

"I do not see the point in denying what it was."

"Yes. But maybe you should work on your poetry."

"I can do that," he said, taking himself back to books he had read. To romance. To the way that men talked to women in those books. "The heat of your body warmed me in ways nothing else ever could. But that should not surprise me. You are the sun, after all."

"I'm what?"

"The first time I saw the sun... You were standing in it."

She shifted, and he looked into her lovely face.

"What?"

"That day in the palace. I had not come upstairs yet. I had not seen the sun. It was only with you that I saw it for the first time."

"Oh. Well. That is adjacent to poetry. I am impressed."

"I do try. Or maybe not."

"Riyaz," she said. "I want to ask you something."

"And so you have to tell me you want to ask? Can you just ask?" He moved his hand over her bare arm. But he found he would rather touch her bare breast, so he did just that.

"I can't concentrate when you do that."

"Well, the question is important to you, but I did not say that it was important to me."

"Do you want any of this? Do you want to be king? Do you want to rule this country?"

"I don't understand."

"Has anyone ever asked what you wanted? Do you want to marry Ariel Hart, or is it just...? Is it just something that you were told you would do? And now that you're back on the path..."

"You must understand, that when you are royalty... What you want is not part of the conversation. Not in the same way it is in these normal houses. I read about them too. Where they ask children what they want to be when they grow up. It is a thing that you choose. That is not true when you are a royal. When you are a royal, then it is all decided for you. Before your birth. There is a line that carries back thousands of years. In many ways, it made being a prisoner easier. My job is to endure. That is all. And so I did."

"What about your happiness?"

"I have never thought about my happiness one way or the other. My appetites, certainly. But not my happiness. My job was to survive to take the throne. It is not about what I want. It never has been."

"That is very... It's very grim."

"You have accused me of this before. Perhaps it is. And yet there are far worse things in the world than being born into a purpose that you are sure of. I have never had to question anything. All that mattered was the throne. It is about the symbolism, not who I am."

"Is that how you managed to feel no... Embarrassment or shame? You're so deeply rooted in who you are. And nothing that you say or do is ever going to take that away."

"Exactly. I might have been in a dungeon, *habibti*, but I was not the imposter. I never could be. My family's blood is in the stones of this palace. And I was always the Sheikh whether I was beneath the ground or on the throne. So asking me now...do I want to sit on the throne...? It is not really a question. I am the throne."

"But there are moments, right?" she asked softly. "Moments of happiness. Happiness matters."

"I will carry this one with me," he said, touching her face. "I will remember this."

She tightened her hold on him, clung to him rather fiercely, and he could not deny that he enjoyed that. There was not a more powerful feeling than that of having given a woman pleasure, he decided.

Yes, his own felt good. That could not be denied. But his own pleasure was easy enough to come by—the pleasure she gave him because she desired him, the pleasure that he was able to give to her, that was the sort of alchemy that created pure gold. And that was something far beyond sexual gratification.

He did not take it or her for granted.

Another thing she had taught him, he supposed.

He looked at her, and tried to imagine another woman in her place. It didn't matter what he wanted. Not really. Ariel would be the appropriate symbol. Brianna was nobody. From nowhere.

Except that she was the sun.

There was that. But the sun would always shine. One did not have to keep it locked in the palace in order for that to be true.

"This was a good lesson," he said.

She went stiff in his arms. And he realized that this was a case when honesty had not been the right choice.

"A lesson," she said.

"Yes," he responded. "Skills I will need…"

"I understood what you meant," she said. "It is only that I found it offensive. I don't need to be your lesson. And I don't understand… How you could even say that. After what we shared with one another. Doesn't that feel intimate to you?"

He wanted her. He could not imagine wanting anyone else. But she did not fit into his life, and could not.

Perhaps you could keep her. A concubine. A second wife.

He imagined showering her in gems. Wrapping her in beautiful silks. Making her the most beautiful room in the palace. He liked that.

But no matter what had passed between them…it did

not change what he was. That he could hurt her. That he could hurt others around him.

She'd already had a life filled with pain. Lived in a home with a man she feared. He could not subject her to that.

"I just thought..." She got out of bed and turned to him, her expression pained. "Look, I understand that you're marrying someone else. But I didn't think that I was a *lesson* for *her*."

"You were not only that. I'm only saying that it is perhaps valuable..."

"Don't try to dig yourself out. You're only going to make it worse. I feel... I feel like an idiot. I feel like an idiot for having trusted you with my body. I thought that it meant something to you because it was a first for you. I didn't realize that it was just... A lesson."

"You were happy for the night," he said.

"Yes. But I'm not happy now."

She dressed, quickly. And he knew that he should probably say something, but he was too captivated by the sight of her body to speak.

She turned away from him, and began to walk toward the door.

"Brianna..."

"No. You and I are through. If this is only me training you, then I cannot give you my body as part of your training. I'm not prepared to do it. I was never with a man before you. I thought that it meant something. I thought that..."

How could it mean any more than it did? He would have stayed in this bed with her gladly forever. But he *couldn't.* That was clear to him and it should be clear to her as well. He didn't know what she wanted.

And it... It enraged him. He was tired of not understanding.

He followed her out without bothering to dress. "What is your game?" he said. "You came to my bed knowing that I was to marry someone else. You know that I am the Sheikh. You know..."

"It's what you *said*," she said. "Can't you keep it separate?"

"I'm sorry," he said. "I was trying to compliment you."

"Well, it was a terrible compliment. You shouldn't try that. Just be broody and hot and good in bed. But don't try to make me feel good. You aren't good at it."

It felt just a little like she'd lodged a knife in his chest. "Am I allowed to be hurt by that?"

"That depends," she said. "*Are* you hurt by that? Are you just asking because now you want to pretend that it's even somehow?" She looked away from him. "You are naked."

"I don't care. I'm the Sheikh. Everyone should be so honored as to see the entirety of my royal visage. And if not, they can avert their gaze. It is not my job to make anyone more comfortable. They are supposed to make me comfortable."

"All those years in the dungeon, you're out for just a little while and you think that you're the only person who matters?"

"I was the only person that mattered in the dungeon. I was more free there then I am here. I had nothing and no one else to consider. Brianna, I am sorry that what I said hurt you. I have read a lot about feelings, but the thing about reading is…you see inside people's heads and I cannot see inside yours."

"Is it that you can't see inside my head, Riyaz, or is it that people in books aren't real?"

"I don't know enough about feelings," he said. "With real people, that is the truth."

"Well, word of wisdom. When you actually do have a wife, don't tell her that you learned interesting ways to pleasure her with another woman. Women don't like to hear about other women in the bedroom. Would you like it if I talked to you about other men? If I told you that it was a great lesson? And the next time that I go down on a man, he's going to benefit from what I learned from you? Maybe it will even be your brother." She turned and began to walk away from him, and he growled, grabbing hold of her arm.

"I would not like to dismember my brother, Brianna, do not tempt me to it."

"It is no less than what you said to me. Sit with it."

And then she stomped away from him down the hall, leaving him alight with fury and rage.

And another feeling that—were he not him—he might have called regret. But he was the Sheikh. Whether he was in the dungeon or not. Whether she was angry at him or not.

Nothing changed that. Nothing.

CHAPTER EIGHT

SHE WAS NUMB. She had been... Foolish. An absolute idiot. She thought about calling Cairo for another update, but what was there to say? She had done something incredibly stupid, and then she had the audacity to get angry at Riyaz for being... Whatever he was.

She had thought that he was tortured because of his time in the dungeon, but she almost wondered if he just was... *This*.

If he didn't connect to people. If he didn't feel anything.

Maybe that was why he had survived.

Maybe he had been like that before, and there was nothing more for him to get back to.

Except... She could remember when he had been all fury that day in the library. She could remember when he had held her last night. When he had made love to her with all the passion that he possessed.

He did have feelings. She knew he did. She just had no idea how it related to... The way that he attached to people. Or didn't. Was she just the same as Ariel? Did it not matter who she was?

Maybe he would just talk the way he did to anyone. Maybe that was the other side of his strange sort of honesty.

That he would simply say those things to anyone. The same that he might make love to any female body.

She had always known that Cairo was a bit like that in his sexual pursuits. The person didn't matter to him. Not in the least. It was simply about pleasure, and how he might find it. Maybe that was just some way that they were. Maybe it was in his blood, just like that right to the throne.

She went to her room, took a shower and scrubbed her skin, cried while she did, because she didn't actually want to rid herself of his touch. She had enjoyed it too much. She cared about him too much. She was angry now, but she was already beginning to question that anger. Maybe he hadn't meant anything by it. She knew that he hadn't. He didn't understand how that would hurt.

Or he didn't care.

Well, he wasn't for her. That was the thing. It was just that she had gotten caught up in the fantasy, and she had told herself that she was okay with it. She had told herself that it was all right that this wasn't going to be forever. She had told herself that she didn't want more from him. But…

She stayed away from him that day. And the next. She didn't bother to go looking for him. When she finally came out of her room the next morning, she was told by the staff that he had not come to any meals the last days.

"Well, where is he?"

"I think he's gone back to the dungeon," one of the men said.

"Oh, for heaven's sake," she muttered.

He was having a tantrum, was what he was doing. He was angry because she was like a toy that had been taken away from him. Nothing more. So he was down in the dungeon being a misery. That was about right. That was in keeping with who he was. The kind of man that would *say* that you had given him a *great lesson*.

She gritted her teeth and before she knew it, her feet were carrying her down to the dungeon. Why couldn't she stay away from him? Why wasn't she angry enough to not care right now? She should only care about herself and her own pain and she was still drawn toward him like a magnet.

He was sitting on the bench. Staring. And then he looked up at her. "Why did you remove yourself from me?"

It was so raw and rough, so real and visceral and did he really not understand?

"Because I was *angry* at you," she said. "You're so fond of honesty, and yet when it's given to you, you don't seem to be able to understand it, and you are not a stupid man, Riyaz, so it begins to seem disingenuous. I was angry at you. *You hurt me.* You shouldn't have said what you did."

He looked her up and down, as if searching for wounds he could see.

"I am sorry," he said.

"Are you sorry because you know that it hurt me? Or sorry that you hurt me? Or are you simply sorry that I *removed myself* from you so you could not play with my body?"

"Of course I'm sorry that I could not have you again. What foolish man would not be? Yes. I want you. For more than one night. Yes, I was furious that you deprived me of your company at meals. What is the point in having them if I'm not sitting with you? I might as well go back to the dungeon."

It was… A declaration of feelings, and nothing could have surprised her more.

"Riyaz…"

"Leave me."

"No," she said. "Not until you explain this. It won't do for the Sheikh to be having tantrums in the dungeon when he is denied what he wants."

"What, then, am I supposed to do?"

"I don't know. But not go back here. This isn't yours. It was never supposed to be for you. This is for your enemies. It isn't for you."

He growled. "I know I'm not supposed to do that. I find that I don't care."

"But you care about my feelings."

"Yes, I do," he said. "I also care that if you're angry at me you won't sleep with me. But I care about your feelings."

"Riyaz… Some of this is my fault. I wanted you to be something that you can't be. It's pointless. You can't give me what I want."

"Your normal family."

That was just the tip of the iceberg. But she wasn't going to say that to him. She wasn't going to get soft and needy now.

"Exactly. This is not the life that I want. It isn't ever going to be the life that I want. And so… Wanting you to give me something… Something more. Something romantic, I guess… It isn't especially fair. But I didn't want to think about you with her."

"Jealousy."

"Yes. Remember what I said to you about me using my skills on another man?"

He growled again.

"Exactly. It makes me want to growl too. So maybe we both know that's ahead of us. But it isn't something I wanted to hear when we were in bed."

He cupped her cheek, and without any sort of warning or preamble, he kissed her. Deep and hard and passionate. His tongue delved to the recesses of her mouth, slid against hers.

And she was powerless to do anything but return the kiss.

Because he was glorious.

Because she wanted him, no matter that he had infuriated her. Because she cared for him.

Because her chest was a tangled-up mess, and she didn't want anyone or anything else.

"Have me here," he growled. "You had me in a bed. That is your world. Have me in this world. This is why. This is why I am *me*."

Because no matter that he was the Sheikh in either place, it had affected him. She heard that. Unspoken in that hoarse plea. And she was powerless to resist.

She stripped his shirt off, just as he did the same to hers. She had on a skirt, thank God, so while she was undoing the closure on his pants, he had swept her underwear to the side, and when she rose up on his lap, and down onto his hardened arousal, she gasped as he filled her.

It didn't matter that there was no foreplay. She was wet. From his kiss. From the ever-present need for him that she carried around with her at all times.

She began to ride him. And each thrust of her hips over his was a declaration. Was possessive. Possession.

She claimed him, over and over again, and when he gripped the back of her head and tugged her hair tight, fastening his mouth to hers, she was claimed yet again.

How could there ever be anyone else?

Except there had to be. Because they were from two different worlds. And she didn't want his.

And he had someone else in mind for him.

She shuddered out her climax, and he roared his own. And they clung together in the aftermath, in the dark, in the dungeon.

He rested his head against her collarbone. "That is good," he said. "That I was able to have you in this place. It healed something in me."

"What if we went to the garden?" she whispered. "Have you been outside yet?"

He kissed her neck. "Not yet."

She nodded. She understood. There were certain things that were going to take time.

Of course, what she did not expect was for that time to be dramatically shortened when a holy man from the country arrived at the palace.

"I have just come from the desert. And I have no wish to cause anyone harm or distress, but I am compelled to give you honesty. Your brother, Cairo, has married your fiancée."

She could see a black rage come over Riyaz. And her heart broke in two.

Ariel had married someone else. And that choice had been taken from him. It was only a few moments later that it registered to her that... Cairo was married. Cairo, whom she had fancied herself in love with before the beginning of all of this.

It was a moment of brutal clarity. She wasn't in love with Cairo anymore. The hurt here was that… Riyaz would never be able to choose her over Ariel. Because Ariel had been taken from him.

You idiot girl. You don't want him to choose you. You don't want to stay here. What kind of a life is this? With a man like him.

"Brianna," he said. "We must go to the desert."

"Riyaz, you haven't even been outside yet," she said.

"It is of no consequence," he said. "I decree that we shall, and therefore we shall. The desert will bend to my will."

And that was how she found herself in a helicopter, clinging to the seat for all she was worth. She didn't like this. Not at all. Her breath was coming in short, sharp gasps, panic making itself known in every facet of her body. Completely uncontrollable.

And there was something about the way he was right now. Wild. Untamed. And she didn't know what to make of any of it.

He was clearly in a jealous rage, over his brother marrying a woman that he hadn't even seen for sixteen years. It made it obviously how little what had happened between herself and Riyaz mattered to him at all.

But also, she had a vague concern that Riyaz meant to shed Cairo's blood. Cairo was supposed to be the one that she was in love with. That was the thing. Cairo was supposed to be the one who mattered.

He was the one who had saved her. He was the one that she had thought herself to be in love with. And she had no idea what any of that meant now. When her body still ached with the memory of Riyaz's touch.

Well, her body did not ache now. It was trembling.

Helicopters really were terrible.

Riyaz, for his part, was stone. Motionless. Showing no emotion as they flew quickly over the desert. As he experienced this sort of freedom for the first time in all those years.

It was like he had shut all that off. Like none of it mattered.

And maybe the way that he compartmentalized all these things with such brutal efficiency was part of how he had survived, but she found it... Jarring. Painful. And then, even with her eyes partway closed, she saw beneath the helicopter, a tent. Out in the middle of the golden desert sand.

"Here," Riyaz said to the pilot. The helicopter lowered suddenly, and in spite of herself, Brianna clung to Riyaz's arm. Her anxiety had no pride.

And when the helicopter touched down, Riyaz stepped out onto the desert sand. And she couldn't help but feel something momentous well inside of her. Because there he was, out on the sands as he was meant to be. As he had not been all this time. And he strode toward the tent, with Brianna scrambling after him. "Riyaz," she said. "Please don't do anything..."

And then he opened the flap of the tent, and Brianna saw Cairo in the flesh for the first time in weeks. He was standing there looking ready to do battle himself. And she waited. To feel something. For Cairo.

Instead, all she felt was terror.

"And here I find you. With my woman," said Riyaz.

"My apologies," said Cairo. "She is no longer yours. I have married her. And we have consummated it. Quite thoroughly. You will find."

"So I see." He looked around the tent, his gaze assessing. And she worried… She could feel the energy vibrating off of him and remembered the way that he had come apart in the library. Brianna touched his arm, and he stiffened beneath her fingers, then…he came back to himself. "What is it?" he asked, looking at her.

"You don't want to kill your brother," she said.

He took her chin in his hand, the hold possessive, his dark gaze intense. "I know that, *habibti*. I don't intend to." Then he turned back to Cairo, and she could feel his rage again. "The dungeon might be suitable."

"The dungeon. Is that what you think?" she asked, her heart pounding wildly.

"And will you throw Ariel there as well?" Cairo asked.

"I am the Sheikh. I could marry her if I chose, regardless of whether or not she is bound to you." He paused. "Or I could throw her in there with you. Or… Take two wives."

"Two wives?" Cairo asked.

"Yes," he said. "For I have already decided who I will marry."

Brianna felt the tent tilt.

"You said that you wanted to marry her," Cairo said, gesturing to Ariel.

"I said for you to bring her to me. I said it was what I required. I did not say why. I had thought that I might marry her. But I have decided on another course of action."

"What is that?" Cairo asked.

"I'm marrying Brianna."

And the world became nothing more than shattered glass.

"Riyaz…"

"It will be no argument," he said. "You are mine. Or have I not made you so these last days?"

Brianna's face went hot and she knew Cairo would know, immediately, what had happened between herself and Riyaz.

Their passion was incendiary, but marriage? He had never once acted like he wanted anything but sex from her.

"The situation is complicated, I see," Cairo said. "How dare you burst into my wedding tent given that you already decided what you plan to do?"

"I have not said yes," said Brianna, and then she rounded on Riyaz. "I'm not yours. I don't live here. I'm not a citizen of this country I don't…"

"You're mine now," he said. "Our bodies do not lie. You have lain with me, and you will be my wife."

Brianna's whole body felt like it was on fire. "Can you please not announce…?"

"You have stormed into the aftermath of my wedding night," Cairo said directly to her. "Why should you be embarrassed to have your own activities commented upon?"

"Cairo," she said. "I'm sorry. I…"

"You know, both of you could ask the women around you what they want," Ariel said. "Just because a woman sleeps with you it does not mean she wishes to marry you. Just because she is born doesn't mean she wishes to marry you. Just because her father says."

"Yes," said Brianna. "Exactly that."

"It is done," said Cairo. "You are my wife."

"I'm not *his* wife," said Brianna.

Riyaz looked her up and down. "You will be. Perhaps we might find someone our here to do the deed."

Panic rolled through her.

"You cannot get married in a desert," said Cairo. "You must have a wedding that is symbolic for the people."

"You do not get to order me around. I have spent enough time in captivity."

"But are not concerned at all about putting others in captivity," said Ariel. "I'm pleased that you're alive, Riyaz," she said. "But it doesn't give you license to act like a monster."

"Monster or not. You're both coming with me. Back to Nazul. These games have gone on long enough. It is time I begin my rule."

And that was how they all ended up back in the helicopter. And Brianna felt absolutely shamefaced sitting next to Cairo, with Riyaz across from her, and the very delicate and beautiful Ariel by him.

She couldn't even bring herself to feel anxious about the helicopter ride this time. There was too much else that was going on.

Marriage.

She would lose everything. Her dreams for a normal life. She had loved Cairo all this time and never made a move toward him because she'd known he couldn't give her what she wanted.

Her sweet little family home. Her sweet little family life.

And now Riyaz thought she could marry him? Live in a palace? Be...royalty? How?

You did touch him. You never really wanted Cairo. Not like this. Not like you want him.

But why was Riyaz even doing this? To save face after Cairo had taken his fiancée from him?

What was worse? Being forced into marriage and losing her last grasp on her idyllic, simple-life fantasy?

Or being forced to marry a man who was only doing it to get back at his brother?

It didn't take long for them to get back to Nazul. For them to get back to the palace.

"Go into the palace," Riyaz said. "I will follow you there."

The helicopter went away, and Brianna stood beside him as he simply lingered, there in the desert. She watched as the sun touched his face, and even in her fury at him, she recognized the moment. His freedom. This first time just being. Outside. In the light.

"Riyaz... You cannot demand that I marry you."

"Certainly I can. You are here. And I am the Sheikh."

"Riyaz... You were held prisoner in a dungeon. You would do the same thing to me?"

"The whole world makes demands of you that you do not wish. And this... It is not a dungeon."

And then he turned and walked back into the palace, leaving her there to marinate on her fate.

"How dare you make war with me when you have taken my friend—who I told you was fragile, and you have..."

Riyaz waved a hand, cutting his brother off. "Do not speak to me in such a way. You seem to think that because you lived on the outside for all of these years that you know more than I do. That you get to make commands. Dictating what you believe to be the right thing from your position. You have pulled the strings on all of this, as you have sought to pull the strings on me."

"That is a lie. Everything that I have done has been for your benefit. Except for this. I want her. And I have wanted her from the beginning." Cairo's voice went rough. "I have... I have cared for her since I was a child. And it is... It felt a betrayal to me then. And a folly. And I could not control that which I wanted from her. When she was with me I... I found that I could not give her to you. She could only ever be mine."

And Riyaz did not want her. He did not want two wives. He wanted Brianna, and there was no scope for anything else. No scope for anyone else. And he did not know why he hadn't made that declaration in the first place.

It was only her. Only Brianna.

Would you do the same thing to me?

It wasn't the same. And anyway. Had he not been denied enough? He would have her. He would keep her. He would give her more than she had ever been given. And perhaps... Perhaps this had been a big disappointment to her. Cairo marrying another woman. He would keep her from disappointment.

"Are you going to kill me?" Cairo asked.

"No. Enough blood has been shed in these halls. I am deeply uninterested in killing you over a woman that I do not want. I want Brianna."

"Does Brianna want you?"

"She seems to want me well enough when she is naked with me."

Cairo seemed to dislike that statement.

"She did not seem particularly like she wishes to marry you, though."

He waved his hand. "Neither did Ariel. Did she wish to marry you?"

"That's different."

"Why? Because Brianna is your friend, and you feel possessive of her?" Riyaz asked.

"Did you only decide to have her to get at me? Was she collateral?"

"Do you love her?"

"No," said Cairo, frowning. "Not like you mean."

"She loves you."

He hated that she did, but she'd said it herself, and why should Cairo not know it?

"She doesn't really. She idolizes me because I rescued her. It is not the same."

"It is. She would've chosen you. Though… She cannot resist me. These are inconvenient things. Bodies. I have had no prior experience with it. It is… Intoxicating."

"Marry her then," Cairo said. "But you must have a ceremony that gives the country hope. And you cannot have a bride that looks as though she is being forced."

"I will handle it. And there will be no consequence for you and Ariel. It is also a good thing, I think," he said slowly. "Yes. It is a good thing. Her marrying you or me… The end result is the same. It puts to right something that was wrong. It does not allow her father to have the final say, and it… It may heal something. For our people."

"You are not quite so far gone as you allowed me to believe."

"I was," he said. "Brianna is remarkable."

It was no less than the truth.

"We will announce your marriage, and my upcoming nuptials before the people. I will appear before them for the first time." He nodded. "Yes. This is the way. It will be an excellent first appearance."

"You should get a haircut," said Cairo.

"No. There are certain things about my experience that I cannot erase. And there are certain things that I choose to keep. I will never be the king that our father was. After what I've been through, it's impossible. But I will work to win back every single year that I lost. Every single year we all lost. I will be the ruler this country needs. On that you can trust me. Now. There are apartments set aside for you and your wife. Apartments fitting the new head of the military. We all have our responsibilities."

Cairo looked at him, hard. "Do you love her?"

Everything inside of Riyaz rejected that. Rejected anything like it. He had to keep his emotions more stable than that. He was a potential danger, he knew.

That was why.

He had to protect her. So he had to be in control of himself.

"I don't love," said Riyaz. "But I want her. And I will have her. And you... You won't stop me."

"You're right," said Cairo. "I won't. Because I have the woman that I want... You should have the woman you want."

"So cheaply you sell your friend. The woman who loves you."

"Do you intend to hurt her?"

Riyaz thought about it. He knew that he didn't want to, but he had to consider the possibility that he could. He had very nearly done so in the library.

"No," he said. The idea of hurting her was anathema to him.

"Very well," said Cairo. "But my conscience is clear. As long as you will care for her. Keep her safe..."

"I swear my life on it. I will do whatever needs doing in order to make her happy."

"Good."

"There is a room prepared for you in the back of the palace. It will be your quarters. And you will remember your place."

"It would probably do you well to remember yours," said Cairo. "You are a figurehead, and an imperfect one. And we will need to announce my marriage and yours, and you will have to be ready to face the nation."

"I am ready," said Riyaz.

"Are you?"

"Brianna will make sure that I am. Whenever you say I should."

"You put a lot on your fiancée."

Riyaz nodded. He couldn't deny that he did. "Because she is strong."

And that was the truest thing of all.

CHAPTER NINE

THE NEXT DAY was a whirlwind. They made plans to make the announcement of his engagement, and of Cairo's marriage to Ariel.

Brianna had spent Ariel's first moments of the palace with her, and over the next few days, she found herself with the other woman quite a bit. She wasn't jealous. But she also wasn't fully resigned to the idea of marrying Riyaz either. But then... She wasn't sure she knew what she wanted. At all. She couldn't imagine leaving Riyaz altogether. But at the same time... She had wanted a normal life.

This would be the furthest thing from that. She wasn't certain she could handle that.

"Apparently we're announcing my marriage to Cairo today," said Ariel.

"You've been prepared to marry one of them your whole life. I guess that must feel... Like it was coming this whole time?"

Ariel shook her head. "I wouldn't say that. No. I wouldn't say that. I have loved Cairo since I was a girl. But I spent a long while thinking that he was dead. I didn't think that he had survived, and even if he had, I didn't think I would ever see him again. Much less be married to him. I knew that I didn't want Riyaz. Not ever. We met and there was just no… Connection. I was miserable here at the palace except when I was with Cairo. But you know, the years passed, and things become complicated. He was different when he was a boy."

"But you love him still."

"And you?"

"Yes," said Brianna, honestly. "But as a friend. I thought for a time that I might want him. Because he was the kindest, most wonderful man I had ever known. Because he was a man who cared for me without wanting anything in return. Because that felt revolutionary for a very long time in my life. Especially considering where I come from. I wanted him to love me, because I thought maybe we could heal each other. Maybe we could find something normal and wonderful and special together. But we can't. And I recognize that now. Because… Because he's my friend. He's not the love of my life."

"Is Riyaz?"

That question terrified her. She genuinely didn't want to answer to it. Because if he was the love of her life then… What did that mean for anything? For her life, for her own sanity.

How could she want this? A life in this palace, with that man, who she felt was fundamentally broken in some way.

And even as she thought that, she had an image of wanting to hold him together. Wanting to keep him from shattering into more pieces.

Did anyone know her as well as he did? In just these few days, had anyone ever gotten to know her in a way that was any deeper? Any more real?

She already knew the answer to that.

"Riyaz is complicated. It's like he… Imprinted on me. For lack of a better word. I was the first woman that he saw when he came out of the dungeon. I don't know if he knows what he wants."

"If he is anything like Cairo, then he absolutely knows what he wants. He's already decided. And woe to the rest of us."

"Yes. I believe that to be true in terms of what he wants to possess. But whether or not he has any idea what he feels? Or if it's all just… Well. Stockholm syndrome."

"You think he has it with you?" Ariel laughed. "I was a bit worried that I had it with Cairo. But if so, then I've had it since I was fourteen. Is it Stockholm syndrome? Or is it just powerful feelings expanded by close proximity, by the intensity of the situation? Maybe it makes it faster, but maybe they would've been there regardless."

There was something oddly comforting about Ariel's words. But then, Ariel wasn't in a situation that was any more conventional than Brianna's. So maybe it was just what the other woman had to think in order to feel comforted about her own marriage.

Why aren't you allowed to be comforted? Maybe you should be allowed to feel all right about the situation you're in. Because you wanted it. Regardless of what you've ever told yourself about wanting a normal life, you want this.

That made her want to wail in anger. That maybe she was just too messed up, too broken, to actually even want something normal. She had an image in her mind, but maybe she couldn't even actually aspire to that because of everything that she was.

Her connection to Cairo hadn't fixed her. And it had led right here. And maybe that was the real issue.

"There are worse things, you know," Ariel said, "than having a beautiful, powerful man be a little bit obsessed with you."

"Yes, but this beautiful, powerful man is so intense sometimes I think he might burn me alive. And he says things that... He says things that hurt sometimes."

"Well. That's not ideal. And I guess him not caring about your choice isn't particularly ideal either."

He knows what I want.

That truth echoed in her chest.

And it made her feel horrifically uncomfortable.

He did know what she wanted. And deep down, she did too. She wanted him. She wanted for this to be something more than it was.

And she was willing to live with whatever that looked like.

She wasn't sure if she should call herself a fool, or praise her determination.

She really wasn't sure at all.

And yet she knew, that whatever she said or did, her marriage was being announced today, without her being present for that announcement.

And she had to decide what she was going to do in response to that. She had to find a way to exert her own will.

Because Riyaz actually wouldn't even respect her otherwise.

They had done it. That stereotypical balcony announcement. Riyaz had managed to make a speech promising to bring the country together. And Cairo had announced his marriage to Ariel, and declared it a unifying marriage, that would heal the past betrayals of the country.

It had been a masterful expression of public relations, if Riyaz said so himself.

And it was quite different than anything he had ever done before. And really, everything he believed in. Hadn't he told Brianna multiple times that he didn't understand why people were so dishonest? About what they wanted and who they were. And yet, here he was playing a part of his first official act as ruler of the country. But maybe that was the point of all of this.

Except, when he had chosen Brianna to be his wife, it had nothing to do with the public face of anything. It had to do with what he wanted. In his room. In his bed. But, of course, he was now in this role, and he had to learn to play it.

Even if the entire exercise seemed pointless to him.

He had spent these last days preparing for this announcement with his brother. He had not had Brianna in his bed.

In part because... He was not entirely certain that she would have him. Not after the way his proposal had been received.

Perhaps it had been less a proposal and more of a demand. And yet, he wanted her. But wanting her felt so separate to this new phase he found himself in. This one where he did have to strive to put on a face for the public sometimes. Because now they knew... Now they knew he was back.

They knew that he was not dead.

And again, in some strange way, he felt his freedom slipping away from him.

Because now he was owned by a nation.

When before he had only had to answer to himself.

He had only ever stepped outside that one day into the desert. And then again onto the balcony.

But he had not gone out... Just for himself.

And that was how he found himself, in the late afternoon, stepping out into the beautiful courtyard garden. All white walls and mosaic. It was fragrant, just like he remembered from his childhood. Jasmine, orange blossoms and gardenia.

The air was thick with it.

And right by the fountain at the center, he saw Brianna. She was sitting there wearing a white dress, her shoulders exposed, her red hair like a copper curtain flowing over her shoulders, covering her face.

"Brianna," he said. She looked up at him, and his heart stopped. And all he could think about was how he wanted her. Was that even surrounded by all of this beauty, like that which he had not seen for years, she was still the most beautiful, the rarest site of all. The most stunning beauty.

"What are you doing out here?"

"I came to see the courtyard, but that you are here too feels... Right. We are to be married in eight days," he said.

"Oh, are we? You know, normally, you have to check the bride's availability for the wedding."

"You know how it is between us."

"How what is? That you need a wife, and I happened

to be standing there, not married to your brother, so it seemed like I was a decent option?"

"No," he said. "You know that what we feel for one another is undeniable."

"You're talking about sex. Attraction."

"Yes. I am. But as you and I have both never given in to that attraction with anyone else, it is significant."

"Slightly more significant for the person who hasn't spent the last sixteen years in a dungeon," she said.

He looked at her. Honestly trying to figure out why she was pushing at him. Pushing against him and this. Was it that sitcom family she wanted? She was a smart enough woman to know that whatever a person wanted from their life, they were not guaranteed to get it. That did not mean all was lost. And he should know.

"I lived sixteen years in a dungeon. You lived fifteen with a man who did not care for you at all. We have both experienced long stretches of life that were unfair. That were not what we had would've chosen. Is it not good enough to feel this desire?"

"I don't know," she said, feeling choked. "I don't know what I'm supposed to want anymore."

"Who cares what we are supposed to do?" And in fact, he didn't want to think about supposed to.

He wanted to get back to elemental. Back to what felt right. Back to what made sense. He wanted to get back to that space where there was honesty. Where that was what mattered.

And here he was, out in the sun, free to be for the first time in so many years.

"Do you not know," he said. "All that matters is this feeling. This is real. You would trade it for something you may never be able to have? For a man in khaki pants who complains to you about his job, who leaves the dishes for you to do, who makes you feel as if you must do unequal work caring for your children? That is this *normal* that you want? It is what you crave?"

"No. Of course not."

"What we have found, it is something other than normal. It is honest, at least. Honest in its intensity. In all that we are. It is the truth. And can we at least live in truth if we cannot live in the reality that we have chosen? All of that... All that I must be when standing on a balcony giving a speech to my people, it is not the truth. It is what they need to see. A marriage to Ariel would have been what they needed to see. But I wish to marry you for all that we are when we are not in front of people."

And he would keep her safe. From himself. He would keep himself under control, and keep her with him.

He could do both.

He was resolved.

And he had not yet failed when he was resolved.

"Really?"

"Yes," he said. "You make me feel like there is no end to the heat that we can create. And that... That is simply ours. It does not belong to anyone else. For so many years my life was only mine. Well, with the exception that I could not choose to leave the dungeon. But within that dungeon, it was mine. Ever since leaving, it has been so much more about what others want from me. And this is a hazard of being born the Sheikh. But it has been a change. If I am to survive all of this, it is not simply about you teaching me how to behave. It is about you giving me a space where I do not have to. And what about you,

Brianna? Who are you apart from all of this? Who are you apart from all these demands you place on yourself? You teach people to be civilized. Perhaps I should teach you how to be wild."

He could see conflict in her eyes. He hated that these moments between them were all conflict.

He crossed the space to her, and pulled her up into his arms. "I am outside. Beneath the sky and the sun, because I can be. And I would have you naked. Out here. Because we can. And damn everyone else. Damn everything else. Yes, there is much twisting and contorting for all of this. For all the people in there. For all the people out there. But here we are, just the two of us. What will we make it? Will you allow yourself to be wild? Will you allow this fire to burn your skin?"

"To what end?" She sounded sad, desperate.

"To feel," he said. "To feel all of the things that we weren't allowed to."

And that seemed to spark something in her. Desire. Madness. Something. Because then she wrapped her arms around his neck, and kissed him. Deep and hard, the desert sun exacerbating the heat between them.

Bringing it to a raging inferno.

"You will be my wife," he said.

"Yes," she whispered, sounding broken.

"We do not need to be a sitcom, Brianna. We are wild. And we have already been held captive. Why should we continue to hold ourselves prisoner?"

And then she began to tear at his clothes. As if she was desperate to remove any barriers between them. Or remove the last vestiges of civility. He knew that he was.

For this was freedom. Here in the blazing sun. This

was perhaps who they might've been if they had not been forced to be anything else.

"Habibti," he said, his voice harsher as she reached down and wrapped her fingers around his raging arousal. He wanted this. Wanted her more than anything.

And he knew that things were not settled between them. That while she might marry him, there was work yet to be done. Miles to be traveled on a road where they could find something companionable between them.

There would always be a wall up within him. There would have to be.

For her own good.

But they both wanted this, now. But she felt that desire to be with him now. But he had been right when he had said she needed to release hold on those chains. And she was expressing that freedom in the same way that he wished to. Which meant that he was right about more than he was wrong about. And with her, that was all that mattered.

"Show me," he said, his voice hoarse. "Show me what you would do if there were no bonds. If there were no restraints. You are that wild thing that survived a childhood with a crime lord for a father. Be that wild thing. Show me what you are."

She grabbed his face, and kissed him, and then she raked her nails down his chest, the pain searing and arousing all at once.

"Yes," he growled. "Give me everything."

She moved her hips against his, her desire as insistent as his own. And he put his hand there, and found her slick and wet with wanting.

She gasped out his name but it wasn't enough. He wanted more. He wanted everything.

Because they had been in chains. Not just during their time when they were held captive, but in this time when they were trying to rejoin the world. They had muzzled themselves. And they had... They had it difficult. Figuring out what was real, what was wrong and what was innately part of what they were.

And so now... Now... They were owed freedom.

He pushed two fingers inside of her. "Come for me," he growled.

She ground her hips against his hand, and she shattered.

And he didn't see the point in holding back. The point in pretending that the roar that was building inside of him wasn't there. He was not civilized. And he never would be.

Not with her. She was his, his.

And maybe that did make him as bad as the people who had held him captive. Just maybe.

But it was worth it. To have her.

For the stolen moment in the garden. All blistering heat and sunlight, and all the things that he had been denied.

Why should he be denied? Why should he experience self-denial ever again?

He shouldn't. He should have all that he wanted and more.

Everything.

He should have her. And she wanted it too, whether she could admit that or not. She claimed she wanted normal, but she didn't know what normal was.

Neither did he.

They had no metric for that. No instruction manual. They only had what they were. And what he was, was broken.

But she made him feel like shattered might not be the worst thing a man could be. He laid her back on the edge of the fountain. He reached the side and let his palm capture some of the cool water coming from the spout. And he let it drip over her breasts, watched as her nipples tightened into impossibly glorious pink beads.

"Raspberry," he growled. He leaned forward and captured her nipple between his lips. Sucked deep and hard.

Yes. She was everything he had imagined from that first moment. Tart and sweet and her. All that he needed. Everything.

His body throbbed with the need to possess her, but he did not want this to go too quickly. He wanted to savor this. To savor her. He wanted...

She was panting, begging, her hips shifting restlessly, as if she was seeking something only he could give her.

It was true.

"You might want a normal life," he said, his voice rough. "But where will you get this? Maybe we are lucky to not have normal. Maybe we are meant to have more. Maybe we are meant to be everything. The sun. The desert. The extreme. Why be a cul-de-sac when you can be the wilderness?"

"Are you going to keep talking," she panted. "Because I'm desperate for you."

"I knew that you were," he said. His need was ferocious. It had him at the edge of sanity. But then, maybe he already was. And maybe there was no fixing that, but she wanted him. And if she wanted him, it wasn't so bad.

If she wanted him, then maybe it would be all right.

Maybe he would trash the library and she would bring him cupcakes. Maybe he would create terror in the middle of the night, and she would soothe him with a movie.

And what would he give to her?

This.

This. And it would have to be enough.

He took another palm full of water and left droplets over her skin. Her breasts, her stomach. She gasped as the cold water rolled down between her legs.

She groaned, moving her hips restlessly, because he knew that she was hungry for more. More than a tease. She wanted his touch.

But this was what he had to offer her, and he had to prove that it was something beyond that which she could achieve on her own or with any other man.

This was what he had.

And he would give it to her with both hands. But he would also withhold. Because that would make it all the sweeter.

"Monster," she panted.

"When did I ever give you the impression I was anything but a monster? I think you know this to be true about me."

"Riyaz…"

"They call me the Mad Sheikh. Do you not think it's for a reason?"

"This is too calculated for you to be mad."

"Maybe. Maybe I'm just a beast."

And that was when he lowered his head between her thighs, devouring her. She gripped his head, holding him there as he feasted on her like she was a delicacy. Like she was all he could ever hope to have and more.

She dug her heels into his flanks as he did. Short, sharp sounds of need escaping her.

"Yes," he growled against her tender flesh.

She had come for him once, but he would demand that she do it again and again before he was satisfied.

He pushed two fingers inside of her again, joining with his teeth and lips and tongue, driving them both to the brink. To the edge of sanity.

And then he felt her break. Shatter. Her cries echoing off the walls in the garden.

He lifted his head and licked his lips. "Better than chocolate," he said.

She shivered. "Riyaz. Please."

He thrust inside of her finally. And she let out a hoarse cry. He moved slowly at first, doing his best to keep himself reined in. Under tight control.

He would pleasure her again. He would pleasure her again before taking his own.

She was shivering, shaking as he drew out each and every thrust. Luxuriating in the feel of it. The feel of her. And then his own control fractured. Shattered. Just as she cried out her pleasure.

And his movements became harsh, erratic. He thrust into her, again and again. As need grabbed him by the throat and shook him around. He was no longer in control. It was this. Only this. He wanted her. Needed her. Craved her beyond all else.

He gripped her hips and thrust hard, pouring himself inside of her on one last roar.

And then she came again too, her internal muscles pulsing around his arousal.

"Mine," he said. And he leaned in and kissed her lips. "You need me," he said. "You need this. For without me... Who will make you feel this way? No one. You cannot trade this for suburban despair."

"I already said I'm not leaving," she said, putting her palm flat on his chest. "I won't."

But there was a strange note in her voice, and it felt like something beginning to unravel.

He could not put his finger on it. He could not say what it was or why.

All he knew was that this moment was a temporary fix.

This moment was a Band-Aid.

It had not been the decisive thing that he had wanted it to be.

He felt disquiet in his soul, there beneath the burning sun.

"How does it feel to be out here?" she asked, sitting up slowly, drawing her knees to her chest.

He didn't know why she was asking him that. Why she was looking at him as if she felt worried.

"It is fine. When I'm with you."

"I'm glad."

"How was it for you?" He gripped her chin and forced her to look at him. She did that. Asked him how he felt. Said it was good. Said she was glad. He didn't understand. She seemed to say such bland things. In these moments. Turn them around to him. And he didn't know what the alternative was. He only knew there was something else that should be happening.

What are you to her?

And maybe that was the problem. That even he knew that this… As much as he wanted it to be, might not be enough.

He would figure it out. He would find a way to make this enough for her.

"Will we sleep in the same bed tonight?"

He considered that. "Probably not."

And she looked sad.

But he was keeping her safe. He was keeping himself on a leash, he would have to. It was the only way they could be together.

He was what he was.

He could have her. But he could only give her so much.

CHAPTER TEN

THE PREPARATION FOR a royal wedding was intense. And they were trying to make a gesture, a statement, to the entire nation, and indeed the entire world. Which made the preparations even more intense than they would have been if circumstances were normal. Not that Brianna could quite figure out what would constitute as normal for a royal wedding. All she saw was extravagance. Extravagance on a grand scale.

The dresses that were brought in for her were glorious. Made of fabrics that were so rich and luxurious she didn't think she had ever touched anything like them. Much less had them resting against her skin.

The menu that they were working on was enough to make any foodie stand up and cheer. And she couldn't deny that she was looking forward to it.

The decorations and flowers promised to be a spectacle, and looking at beautiful arrangements had been a lovely way to pass one of the days.

If only things with Riyaz were quite as straightforward as the wedding planning. They didn't share a room or a bed. He was still a part-time dungeon dweller, and given what had happened the time he had tried to sleep in a bed, she wasn't entirely sure how to convince him that it would be okay.

She wasn't even sure if it would be okay. That made it all difficult.

To make matters worse, Ariel, who had become a friend, was clearly going through some things with Cairo, and that made her a bit distant in ways that Brianna could definitely understand. "He's withdrawn," she said. "He won't sleep with me."

"Neither will Riyaz," Brianna said.

"It's this place," said Ariel. "He was different. At the house we married at. I think being here is destructive. There are too many ghosts."

But Brianna understood that there was nothing to be done about that. How could there be? They were the rulers of these ghosts. Of the people in this country. Of all that was good, and all that was dangerous, all that was sad and all that was brilliant. This place, the site of their trauma, was a place that they had to stay.

And as much she appreciated that it was difficult for Cairo, she also found herself having a difficult time being sympathetic to him. Considering that Riyaz had been here the entire time. In a dungeon. This might be Cairo's first time facing these sorts of demons, but Riyaz had been trapped in them.

And now sometimes she felt trapped in them as well. In that sense, she could well relate to Ariel.

But Riyaz was not distant. In fact, he was as attentive as could be expected. During the day, he was being given a million administrative tasks to do, things that were very unlike his life for the past sixteen years, and he was taking them all on admirably.

She imagined that he was extremely grateful that he had made it his goal to keep his mind sharp while he was imprisoned. Because there was definitely a heavy demand on his intellect now.

Thankfully, there was not yet a heavy demand on his diplomacy.

There would be eventually. Eventually, there would be meetings with dignitaries from around the world. Ambassadors and other leaders.

And he would have her.

She tried to imagine that. She had never really wanted a life like this. She had wanted something smaller.

But...

Now it was difficult to imagine a life that didn't revolve around him. So maybe it wasn't so bad. Maybe different was okay.

She walked into the ballroom, which was beginning to be set for the wedding party. The ceremony would take place outside in one of the courtyards. In the ballroom there would be dancing. Various banquet halls feasts, and outside there would be tables laden with food as well.

It would be a time of celebration for everybody.

And she couldn't help but wonder how Riyaz would feel about that.

He seemed determined to go forward with all of this and not feel anything.

The thought stopped her cold.

Maybe that was part of her own disquiet.

Riyaz handled everything much better than she ever could've imagined. But he also seemed... Cold. Distant in a way. As if he was cut off from everything. And maybe that was the only way he could get through it. Maybe it wasn't fair to think that it might be a problem.

After all, when his emotions had gotten close to the surface she had seen what happened.

His PTSD episodes had come when he was pushed too far. And maybe to protect himself from that he had to stay extra detached during these first weeks of his official rule.

Maybe that was all it was.

That thought carried her toward his study. Where she knew that he would be working now.

The throne room was ceremonial. He liked the library for certain things. But for heavy paperwork, she knew that he did like the desk that his father had once done his work at.

She wandered through the glittering palace, looking around at all of the beauty.

Yes. There were ghosts here. But more than that, there was history. There was something beautiful about this place, even if there was darkness here as well.

There was something special about it. Even if it was challenging.

All was contained here. The good and the bad.

The betrayal, the tragedy, but the love that had been here as well.

She could feel it all right then.

She wished that she had known his mother. He could barely speak about her. And she knew that meant that he had loved her very much. Because it hurt too bad to talk about her.

She could understand that.

I care about your son. Very much. I just want you to know.

She said that silent thought, that near prayer out into the universe. And then she looked at him.

"How is everything?"

"Good," he said.

"You're not working too hard, are you?"

"I don't think so."

"Would you have any idea what working too hard was?"

"I might. Are you playing the part of nagging wife in a sitcom?"

He asked it with humor, and she took it that way.

"Maybe. Is that so bad if my nagging is about your well-being?"

He shrugged. "Perhaps not."

She looked around the office and she saw that in the corner, there was one of his spy novels that he liked. She picked it up and sat in the chair next to the desk.

"What are you doing?"

"I thought I might read. While you work."

"Did you?"

"I don't really have anything to do. And you know, I'm going to need something to do."

"We will have children," he said.

Of course they would. And of course he would expect that, and it wasn't as if they had been having protected sex, but the idea made something slam hard into her chest. Probably her heart. Or maybe every single one of her internal organs, really.

She'd wanted children, of course. It was part of that fantasy. Of picket fences and of neighborhood evenings where kids rode their bikes around until the porch lights came on.

But they didn't live in a neighborhood, and they didn't have a picket fence.

They were in the desert, with great stone walls surrounding a palace.

He was a sheikh. She was a woman whose father hadn't cared about her at all. He was a man who'd basically raised himself in a dungeon.

She wanted it, but she felt sad.

That they weren't what she'd dreamed.

She wondered if she even could be.

Children. She wanted them. Wanted his children. She wondered what that meant for them both, but didn't want to dissolve right now.

"Of course. But that… Surely I'll have responsibilities other than the children?"

"Yes," he relented. "I suppose so."

"One thing that is quite important to me is that I have something to do with myself. Something that's my own. Having lived the kind of life that I did before I left my father's house… You can understand."

"What was it like?"

He was looking at her with intent, interest. "Well," she said, frowning slightly. "It was a huge house, often full of his cronies. It was organized crime, but I'm not sure what all… I don't want to know, I never have."

"I can understand. I understand what it's like to…to need to curate your world. Your thoughts. I had to do that in the dungeon."

She nodded slowly. "Well, I wasn't in a dungeon. I was in a big, beautiful house, with no love at all. A big, beautiful house where all of the men were monsters. I had a room, but I slept with the door locked. I had to... make myself a prisoner, in many ways."

"That's a terrible way for anyone to live. Before...before all of this. Before the takeover of the country, I had a family. A real family."

She looked away. "I never did."

"You can have one here." He cleared his throat.

"And what is family to you, Riyaz?"

"A distant memory. But I will keep you safe."

"Do you...your feelings..."

"I have to keep my control. You understand." And though neither of them said anything about love, she could tell that it had been the topic. She'd asked. He'd said no. "I thought you were going to read."

"I thought it was a good opportunity to...to talk about expectations." Her heart was thundering hard. "Because, of course, I have decided to marry you."

A small smile lifted the corner of his mouth. "It would be awkward if not, considering the wedding is fast approaching."

"Yes," she said. "I suppose that's true."

"You know as the Sheikha, you can be in charge of any number of things. Just tell me what would make you happy. You can head up any cause that you would like. That is a common thing, is it not? For the spouses of those ruling the country."

"Yes," she agreed. "It is. So, I will find something that matters to me and set up a foundation."

"Yes," he said.

Something ached inside of her chest, but she opted to ignore it. Because she had to hope that this would help with her restlessness. That it would give her something to pin her desires onto.

And children.

She looked at him hard.

"Even when you were in the dungeon, did you know that you would get out? Did you believe in it?"

"No," he said. "I didn't. I never let myself wonder about that, I never let myself carry concern about it. I simply took the next breath." He paused for a moment. "Do you want children?"

"What would you do if I told you I didn't?"

"We both know that it might be too late for you to make such proclamations anyway. Given that we have not been careful."

"I know." She was silent for a breath. "I do want them. But I was just wondering… Since you never asked."

"But you do. And that's a good thing. Something that I can give you."

She thought it was strange, the way that he phrased that. Something that he could give her. She wondered what he meant by that. She wondered what exactly that meant to him.

"A foundation. And children."

And she was happy sitting there by his desk. Even though for some reason she hesitated to say it to him.

She didn't know why that was so difficult.

Maybe because this was nothing like she had thought. It certainly wasn't a sitcom life.

Except…

Maybe she had never wanted that classic two-story house. With a staircase that had a bend in it so the kids could run down the stairs and then jump over the railing at the end.

Maybe she had never wanted family dinners and big misunderstandings, and hijinks with pets.

Maybe what she had really wanted was to live in a house full of love.

Maybe that was what she really, really craved most of all.

That realization made her feel like something was pressing down on her chest.

Made her feel like she was carrying the weight of something impossible on her shoulders.

Because she was beginning to believe that she loved Riyaz. But as to whether or not he loved her, as to whether or not he could ever love anything. She simply didn't know. And she was too afraid to ask.

Then suddenly a man came through the door. A servant looked wide-eyed and terrified to be entering the Sheikh's domain.

"Ariel Hart has left. Cairo sent her away."

Riyaz went down into the dungeon. And there was his brother, laid out like it was his.

"What the hell are you doing?" he asked.

The voice came from the shadow. "I am seeing what it was like for you."

"Well. I still sleep down here. So you might ask before you enter."

"Why do you sleep down here?"

"Because you don't change immediately," said Riyaz. "I hate it here. And yet for many years it was the only place I saw. There is a safety to it. But it is captivity."

He could hear his brother move toward him, sit down on the bench beside him. "But then. Everything is a cage of some kind. None of us are truly free."

"No," he said.

"I know that Ariel left. Why?"

"Because I told her to."

"I see. And why would you do that? You want to keep her."

"Look at where we are, Riyaz. We are in a dungeon. Do you really think it appropriate to keep a woman in the palace against her will? Even if it is in my bed and not a dungeon?"

"Did she say she didn't want to be with you?"

"No. But, she didn't have the choice to come here in the first place. Not now, and not all those years ago. She doesn't even know what she wants."

He laughed. "Is it her that doesn't know what she wants? Or is it you?"

"And what about you? You are keeping a woman prisoner as well."

"Have I expressed a moral difficulty with this?"

"I would think that you of all people would."

"Why?"

He had nothing to say to that. His brother simply didn't know... What was there to be said?

"Do you want her?" Riyaz asked him.

"Ariel? Of course. I have done everything to have her. I betrayed you. Again."

"What do you mean again?"

"You said that we should keep our demons to ourselves, Riyaz. But I think you should know about mine. I was in love with Ariel when we were children. And I used to sneak out with her. When we were fourteen we went out into the desert. And we were caught. I was. By her father. And he asked me a question... And I answered it. To keep myself from being in trouble. I gave him an easier way to get into the palace. I did not feel as if I could tell him no. Or he would... He would reveal what happened between myself and Ariel."

"So you're the reason they came into the palace."

"Yes," he said.

"That was a very stupid thing to do," said Riyaz.

His words were cold. His heart was cold. Everything in him was cold. Cairo had been the one. He'd been responsible. He'd let his guard down, and he'd been...out with Ariel. Betraying Riyaz, betraying Nazul.

And yet....

What could be done?

If Cairo had been wrong, so had their father been. To let that man into their home in the first place. To trust him, to make an alliance with him.

He felt...angry. He felt enraged, even. And yet... He would not react. What purpose would there be in it? He would lose his temper and he might harm his brother. He could not afford to let himself fully engage with this revelation.

And anyway, what good would it do? Nothing.

"It was," Cairo agreed.

"Fourteen-year-old boys are stupid," Riyaz said.

"Yes. And you were sixteen. And suffered greatly for my stupidity."

Years of stone walls flashed before his eyes. And yet he knew no matter what Cairo had or hadn't done, that would have been the outcome. He was a convenient scapegoat even now for the real villains, and while Riyaz had sharp and jagged feelings about all of this, he could not blame his brother.

Not wholly.

He might feel something angry or twisted up inside his chest, but in his mind he knew the truth.

"They were intent on killing the royal family, they would've done it somehow. Even if it'd been exploding a motorcade. It would've occurred. This was a neat and clean way to do it, but… They would've found a way."

"Are you trying to absolve me?"

He did not have that power. He couldn't pull the blood back from the stones of the palace. He could not offer absolution.

"No. Your actions led to that event. But you cannot control the intent of others. So yes, something that you did played a part in the way they were able to kill our parents and take me prisoner. But… I believe it would've happened either way. And perhaps we all would have been blown up."

"You can't know that."

"No. But you can't know otherwise."

"I don't understand," Cairo said. "Are you blaming me? Forgiving me?"

"I can do either. Here is one thing you learn with only yourself for company for a great number of years. The world turns regardless of your involvement in it. In the dark of night, you only have yourself. And the only way you can be rescued is if there someone out there who cares enough to do it. I can't absolve you. You have to absolve yourself. But you are the person who came for me. Whether you are blameless or not… That is something."

It wasn't a rousing speech of forgiveness. It was something deeper than that. It was something that Cairo could actually... Accept.

Neither of them was perfect. But they were here together in the dark. He had come for Riyaz when Riyaz needed him. And now Riyaz had come for him. And perhaps they could never make fair the things that were unfair. And perhaps they could never make whole the things that were broken.

And perhaps he could never be redeemed.

But maybe... Maybe he could be loved. Just as he was anyway. Because wasn't that what Riyaz was giving him? Not absolution, and not blame. Just acceptance.

"I have to go to her," he said.

"Of course you do," said Riyaz.

"I'm not taking her prisoner."

"I wouldn't care if you were."

"Yes. I know."

He wouldn't care if Cairo was taking her prisoner, because he supposed that was what he had done to Brianna. He had to be honest about that. He had not initially given her a choice, and while she had said yes eventually, he still felt...

He still knew that he was denying her that dream she'd always had.

That normal life.

He had claimed her in the desert, whether she'd wanted to be claimed or not. He had not asked. Though in the end, she had said yes. And he had offered her a foundation. So there was that.

He didn't know what he felt about what Cairo had said. That he was the one who had given the men the keys to the palace. But he was the reason Riyaz had been locked away. That their mother was dead.

But he didn't have it in him to demonize his brother. Not in the least. He simply didn't have the will.

But it left him feeling something he couldn't quite put a finger on. There was something burning inside of him. Some rage. But it was a fruitless rage.

Cairo was his last living family member. There was nothing... There was nothing.

"Get your woman," said Riyaz.

And Cairo did. He left.

As it should be.

But Riyaz simply had his feelings. His own flashbacks to that time.

Riyaz had loved his mother.

His father.

Cairo had loved Ariel. And it had made him make a foolish mistake, but he had been just a boy.

He had only been a boy. What was there to condemn?

He felt like something violent had grabbed a hold of him and shaken him.

He felt numb. Or perhaps it wasn't numbness, but a dawning realization. A peeling back of all the pain and grief that echoed in his soul.

Grim acceptance had kept him alive. Brianna did say he was grim.

The belief he was keeping himself alive all those years by holding it at bay.

The belief he was protecting Brianna by holding his emotions back. That he could not love, because he could not open up the depths of himself in that way and put her at risk.

But there, with his soul scraped raw, and his anger, his pain, at Cairo, at his father, at the men who had done these things...

The memory of his mother.

It was not blind anger that drove him now, but grief. For the way his family had been destroyed and the burden they all carried as a result and it was too heavy.

He could not hold any more.

He could not care for anyone. It would be too costly.

He was not protecting her.

He was protecting him.

He was not a hero.

He was a prisoner.

He did not leave the dungeon.

CHAPTER ELEVEN

BRIANNA LOOKED EVERYWHERE for Riyaz. Except the dungeon. He didn't normally go down there at this time. And yet... There was something that had made her want to check. So she crept down there. And there he was. Sitting in the darkness.

"Riyaz? What's going on?"

"I found Cairo down here. I sent him after Ariel."

"That was very good of you."

"Why?"

Brianna looked away. "I know it was complicated because she was your..."

He gripped her chin and turned her head to face him, forcing her to meet his eyes. "I don't want her." The flame she saw there burned, and it took him a full minute to release his hold on her. "I do not want her in the least. It was not hard at all. It was nothing."

"What's the matter?"

"Cairo... He told me something. He is the reason that those men were able to get into the palace. He gave information to Ariel's father, because he trusted the man. And he was afraid that he and Ariel would get in trouble for being outside the palace. They were children."

"Oh, Riyaz. That must be... Devastating."

He looked up at her. "Why should it be? My brother was a child. He meant nothing by it. He was no more wrong for trusting that man than my father was."

But there was tension there. Something that he wasn't quite telling her.

"Riyaz... Speak to me."

"There is nothing to say."

"Well, would you at least come upstairs for dinner?"

"I... I could."

"Come with me. I don't think you should be alone. I'm also happy to bring something down here. If that's what you want."

"No. We will go upstairs."

She could feel erratic energy coming off of him. And she didn't know what it was. She couldn't quite put a finger on it. She wasn't sure what he was thinking or how... Black his mood was. There was a roast turkey for dinner. And the spread on the table was lovely. Riyaz did not observe any of his learned manners when he sat down, throwing the chair out behind him, and sitting heavily.

"It's all right if you're angry," she said, dishing herself some turkey, and adding some jeweled couscous to her plate.

"I'm not angry. Everybody trusted Ariel's father. All of the men in my family. Why should that make me angry? It simply is. Cairo is no less than my father."

"Is that honestly how you feel?"

"It doesn't matter what I feel. Feelings are not the facts of the situation."

"Or maybe it does matter what you feel, Riyaz. Maybe it does."

"He is my brother," he said. "He is my brother, and I will not condemn him."

"You don't have to condemn him to feel something."

"Enough," he said. He began to put food on his plate. "I am the Sheikh. Cairo is my brother. There is no scope..."

"Who cares about the scope? You're right. Why don't we have honesty between us for a moment. Wildness. Who cares if you're the Sheikh? Who cares if I'm supposed to civilize you?" She wanted love. She recognized that now. She understood it. For what it was.

"Be honest about what you feel. Because it's the only way that you're actually going to move forward from any of this."

"Moving forward. This is not pop psychology. This is my life. This is a kingdom."

"Right here, with me, this is just... Real. This is just feelings. Please. Riyaz, tell me what that made you feel."

"It makes me feel... Makes me feel as if my mother's blood is on his hands. And he... He went free. He ran away, didn't he?" Riyaz looked up at her, his dark eyes blazing. "He ran away from this. From us. He's been free. All this time. Earning money and making the life that he wanted, and... Hell. He's had whatever he's wanted. All the women he's wanted."

Pain lanced her chest. "Is that what you need? Do you need more women...? Do you need...?"

"No," he said darkly. "I don't need more women. I can have a harem if I want to. I am the Sheikh. I can do whatever I want. I... It doesn't matter."

"What is it that's upsetting you?"

"I was in a dungeon. In the darkness. I'm not the one

who caused it. Why was I the one who was punished? Why were we punished?"

"I don't know," she said. "I don't know I..."

"This is when you tell me that Cairo would feel terrible about all of this. Because he's a good man. He's your friend."

"He is my friend. But you're my fiancé. And I don't need to defend him. He's your brother. You love him. That doesn't mean that you can't be angry. That doesn't mean that you can't feel something about the fact that... That his mistake led to this. He has had sixteen years to have feelings about it. You can have feelings. Why shouldn't you? Why shouldn't you have feelings?"

"They mean nothing. They mean nothing. All you can do when you're prisoner is simply survive. It is all you have."

"Do you feel like a prisoner? Are you still just a prisoner here?"

He looked away. "None of it matters."

Oh, how she hated this. The way that they were both bound up here. In duty. In love. Duty for him. Love for her.

"I do not need other women," he said, his voice suddenly hard. "I need you."

And she wanted to be enough for him. She wanted to be everything.

She wanted to find a way to restore everything that they had lost. "Then you can have me."

"Do you not wish to have your dinner?" he asked. There was a vague sneer in his voice, and it surprised her. Riyaz was many things, but rarely unkind. Not to her. And she thought that perhaps this was a reflection of something else.

He's in pain.

"I don't need anything but you," she said. "Believe me. All I need is you."

He growled, and reached across the space, pulling her from her chair and bringing her over onto his. "Why would I need any other woman when I have you? Most beautiful of women. Whenever I desire. Because you are mine. You are going to be my wife."

"Yes," she said. "The wedding is being planned."

"Yes," he said, his voice rough.

There was something fractured in him now. Something on the verge of shattering entirely.

And she wanted to hold them together. Desperately.

And she would show him that she was strong enough. She was.

She was not the girl that she had been, afraid. Forced into a life she didn't want. She was not the woman who had escaped. Who had sought to fit in to her surroundings. Who had tried to blend in seamlessly. This woman who had been so afraid that people would identify that she was different.

But she was happy to be different. She was happy to be herself. Brianna Whitman. A woman strong enough for this man. A woman who could help him navigate the world as he needed to, but let him be who he was when they were together.

"There need be no rules between us," she said. "Those rules are for dignitaries. Sit how you want. Eat how you want. Be how you want. Be angry if you want to be angry. You never have to hide yourself for me," she said.

It was an echo of the time they had shared out of the fountain. When passion had welled up between them and he had demanded that they embrace their wildness. But this was something more. Something deeper.

They did not need to perform for one another. Not ever. They did not need to play parts. She was not a foreign diplomat, and he was not a teacher at a boarding school that she was trying to impress. They were for each other. And yes, maybe parts of the world were a prison. Performances that you had to engage in. But the two of them never would be. Not ever.

She tore his shirt open.

"In the dining room?"

"Don't tell me that's not what you were thinking," she said.

He tore her top from her head, and then began to push her skirt up to her hips. And then he swept her panties to the side and began to stroke her there, between her thighs. She put her hand over his cloth-covered arousal, and he groaned. Then she began to open up the closure on his pants. She freed him, arching her hips forward and sinking down slowly onto his arousal. He filled her. Perfectly. Absolutely. They weren't generally fast like this. He preferred to take their time and feast on one another.

She loved that about him.

She knew that he took exceptional care with her body because there had been no other women before her, so he was never riding on empty experience. Never enacting moves that he had done before. It was all about her. It was all about what it made her feel. All about what she wanted. And that made her feel… Exceptionally good. It made her feel special. But this was something she needed. Fast. Furious. Him. Always him.

She cried out with pleasure as she began to ride him. As he clutched her hips, hard and strong, bringing her up and down over his body. She let her head fall back, a scream escaping her lips. "I love you," she said.

And that was when everything stopped. Everything. At first she thought he meant to leave her body, but then he roared, his climax shaking them both. And he clung to her, his heart pounding in his chest as he stroked her hair.

"I love you," she whispered.

"No," he said. "You do not say that."

But he didn't release his hold on her. "Why not?"

"Because. It is not for me. I do not like the words."

"Riyaz..."

"Let us go to bed."

And that was when he picked her up, and much to her great surprise, he propelled them both not to the dungeon, but upstairs. He laid her down on the bed and he kissed her. And it reminded her so much of their first time together. Something sweet. Something for the two of them. But inside she was breaking.

It wasn't even that he hadn't said he loved her in return. It was his outright rejection of her love.

It was that he wouldn't even let her say it. That he wouldn't accept it. It just felt wrong. Why wouldn't he let her love him?

But then he was kissing her again. Trailing a path of fire down her neck, down to her breast, and she found it difficult to think. Because he was too much. And not enough all at once. Because she was caught in the reality of the situation. Of this life that she was choosing.

Because love was what made the family, and if he couldn't say it... If he couldn't even accept it... Then what did that mean?

Except she couldn't think, because the alternative was a life without this. A life without him.

And it wasn't as if you were given the option anyway.

No. She supposed that she hadn't been given that option.

But then he was in her again, and she just wanted to exist in that moment. In that space. Where they were together. Where they were one. Where she hadn't said that she loved him and he hadn't rejected it. Because it felt better to not know. It felt better to leave it as an open and wonderful possibility, rather than have it closed down as something that could never be.

In the end she wondered what did it matter. If she could say that she loved him, if he could accept it. So long as she did. Wasn't that the most right thing? Wasn't that the most real? Wasn't that the most important thing?

And he took her to the heights again. And she decided that maybe that was the thing. They had these heights. And it didn't matter what they were called.

There was no laugh track on this. No canned responses from the audience to let her know how to feel. There was simply... There was simply all of this.

And it was good.

It was good.

This was the life she chose.

It might not be normal or perfect.

But it was hers.

And much to her surprise, he held her against his body, and they went to sleep.

CHAPTER TWELVE

WHEN HE WOKE UP, there was violence coursing through his veins. Black heat and fire, and the terror of what was to come.

And somewhere, in all of that, something cut through.

I love you.

I love you.

And he looked down and saw his mother, broken and bleeding on the floor.

I love you.

That was the last time he had heard those words. That was the last time. And it tore at him. It made him feel like his chest was nothing more than a bloody wound. It made him feel like nothing in his body was his own.

Except for the pain. The pain was his.

The loss was his.

And in that vision he saw his brother, he saw his father.

And he turned on them.

How dare you!

How dare you trust the wrong people. Look at what you've done. Look at what you've done to her.

There was pain in his chest and there was nowhere for it to go. There was nothing. Because then he was in a dungeon, and he could not afford to show weakness to his captors. He could give them nothing. He could show no pain. He could never let them know.

No. He could never let them know. And so he pushed everything down. The grief. The pain. The rage.

But it didn't work. The rage still bubbled over.

He was not in control at all anymore. The years of it melting away as if it had never been.

It was as he'd always known.

Love made him so very weak. Love made it so he could not hold back the tide of pain that lived in his soul.

And he grabbed something, something heavy, and he threw it toward the part of the room he saw his father and brother in.

But then dimly, he heard a voice. The same voice that had said I love you. Not his mother's.

"Riyaz. Please. Please."

And he realized it was her. And he wasn't back with his parents. He wasn't back in that day. In that space. He was with Brianna.

She had said that she loved him.

His father had failed a woman who loved him. His brother had likewise failed a woman who loved him.

Riyaz had not. Not yet. But it was in his blood, his DNA.

You already have failed her.

You've taken her prisoner.

He was holding her in that cell with him, for he had concluded he was still a prisoner. Of all that had come before. Of all the pain and grief and death, and now she was here with him, instead of in that normal, beautiful house she wanted.

He had proven that in fact he was his brother.

He had felt all that simmering rage at Cairo for his weakness. For the lie that he had bought into. For his cowardice.

He was keeping her prisoner. He was no better than Cairo. He was no better than the men who held him captive.

How was he any different? He might not have spilled any blood, but he was failing a woman who loved him. A woman who should not love him.

For he had given her no reason to. He had done nothing but treat her with disrespect. He had done nothing but treat her as if she was a coup.

And somewhere in the darkness, the haze cleared.

And he was fully in the moment. And Brianna's hands were on him. She was comforting him. She was comforting him as she had done all these times.

And what had he given her?

He had sought to give her pleasure. He had known it would not be enough.

He had sought to give her...

He had not tried very hard.

Normal.

She wanted normal. She had told him exactly what she wanted, and he had not listened.

She had told him that what she wanted was to have that life that she saw on TV. Those family dinners, and what had he given her? Cold meals at a banquet table, and then he had brought her onto his lap and had her right there where anyone could've walked in. It was not what he had promised.

And he would release her now. He had to.

He could not see a way to let himself out of this cell, for he could not endure all of this…feeling.

But he did not have to keep her in it as well.

But in that moment, he faltered. In that moment, he reached for the light, because he wished to see her clearly.

She was naked, standing before him unashamed and unafraid. She had given him her body. She had given him some measure of peace.

And he had done what? Grown her character? Tested her strength? She did not deserve that.

"Brianna," he said. "I want you to go."

"Riyaz, we've been through this. I'm not afraid of you. And I can handle this."

"I don't mean out of my room. I mean away from the palace. I want you to go back to New York. Go back to your town house. Sell it. Buy a house in a neighborhood. I told you that your dreams were not enough. But that was wrong. What you want… It matters. I took it from you. Your choice. I will not do that. Not anymore. I cannot do that."

"Riyaz," she said. "Didn't you hear me when I said that I loved you?"

"Yes. But I am not able to receive it. And loving me denies you of the very thing you want most."

"No," she said. "It's just… It's what I thought I wanted. But I realized something. Normal doesn't mean anything. What I was missing in my family home was love." She shook her head. "That's what I want. I just want love."

"And I cannot give it to you. Don't you see? I grew up in a home where there was plenty of love. It didn't keep her safe. Remember? It doesn't keep you safe. Beth can still die. Remember *Little Women*?"

"This isn't Civil War–era America. And you aren't going to get scarlet fever."

"But it won't protect you. That's what I'm telling you. It will not protect you from what might befall you. But that normal life? That will protect you."

"Tell me why. Tell me why you don't think you can love me."

"Aside from the sixteen years spent in a dungeon? Many reasons. But I cannot… it's my mother's face I see. Dying. Bleeding. They are not good words for me. And I can't…" The pain was too much, and the closer he got to her…

The closer he got to losing every last shred of protection he'd placed around his soul.

"Riyaz…"

"I will fail you. I have failed you. But I won't again. You will go. And you will not come back."

"Riyaz," she said, looking shocked.

And he felt a shard of glass work its way up through his chest.

"I'm the Sheikh. And I have spoken."

CHAPTER THIRTEEN

SHE WAS FROZEN. Ashamedly paralyzed. And it lasted until the sleek private jet touched down in New York. Until she was back on American soil, feeling like a foreigner in her own country. In her own skin. In every way.

Every time she breathed it was like shards of glass being ground deeper and deeper into her chest. And she had to ask herself… Why? Why had she gone so easily? Why had she walked away from the life that she had chosen?

She had been rescued before. This wasn't the same. She didn't need to be rescued from Riyaz, and yet…

She knew why she had gone. Right then, she knew why. She had gone because he needed her to.

He needed to set her free. Or maybe he needed to set himself free. And in the end, the thing that made her laugh was… She was willing to do that. To walk away because he might need a reprieve.

She would not become his dungeon. Even though that might be his motivation for letting her go… She wouldn't be that for him either. She refused.

He had precious little choice in his life.

And if he asked her to go… If he said he didn't want to hear that she loved him…

There were two things, she knew it. There was something in him that was afraid to be too strong, afraid that he might be overwhelming her with force. And something else in him that scared him perhaps even more. Something that he thought might be too weak. The kind of weakness that he saw in his brother, even though he loved him. The kind of weakness he saw in his father, even though he loved him.

And it was all twisted up in that haunting last thing his mother had said to him. He was a man who simply didn't trust. Not the world. Not himself. And how could she ask him to?

She didn't have an answer. So she just stumbled into her town house and looked around. It was a nice place, because of course Cairo would never have bought her a home that wasn't nice. But there was also something incredibly... Normal about it. It was one of the things that she had liked. Right away. The lightly flowered wallpaper, the little breakfast nook in the corner.

It usually made her happy.

But unfortunately, she had been right. The thing that made those families enviable was their love. The thing that made those lovely, normal houses an object of desire was the love within the walls, not the walls themselves.

She had been totally cut off from her family.

She'd had to cut herself off from them, and she had to conform to the outside world. And only with Riyaz had she really felt free.

Maybe there was another lesson in there as well. That you could be normal, or you could be free. But you couldn't be both.

Her chest ached. And she wished she had a friend. One other than Cairo. And then she remembered that she did.

Hesitantly, she decided to call Ariel, whose number she had put in her phone a week or so ago.

"Hello?" She breathed out heavily. "Thank God, Brianna. I was worried."

"I just made it back to New York."

"We're trying to keep word from spreading about the canceled wedding. Just... Just in case."

Brianna looked at the clock on the wall. A very normal-looking clock. Except for who had clocks on the wall anymore? But she had thought that it made a nice accessory. It was a set, this place. She had never really noticed it before.

And owed to the kind of normalcy that she had long thought she needed in order to feel whole.

"I don't think he wants me to come back. He... He set me free. And he told me that I wasn't supposed to come back."

"Cairo tried that with me," said Ariel. "He told me that I hadn't chosen to be married to him. He told me that I needed to be free. To make my own choices."

"So they're the same man, just in a slightly different configuration of trauma."

"Yes. And they did both take us without permission."

She waved a hand even though Ariel wasn't there to see it. "Semantics. I think it's pretty apparent we both want to stay."

"Riyaz was a man in a dungeon, Brianna. I think he couldn't stand the thought of you feeling locked away also."

"I think he's a man afraid of being locked in the dungeon by his feelings for me. That's what I think."

There was a long pause. "Maybe you have a point."

"Did Cairo talk to you? About the fact that he feels responsible for what happened at the palace?"

"Yes. He said Riyaz was very calm."

"He was. He almost didn't react at all. But he's broken by it. And I'm afraid… Actually, I'm afraid the real issue is he doesn't want to step outside the dungeon. He doesn't want to be too angry. He doesn't want to want too much. He doesn't want to feel too much. He doesn't want to ever love anything that can be taken from him." And for a moment, she just felt overwhelmed. By everything that he needed. By everything she wanted to do for him.

And the limits of what she would be able to.

She was just a girl who had been playing the part of somebody who understood normal.

You understand him. You want to. Maybe that's what matters.

"What should I do? I love him. But he already has to do so much for so many people. He has to be the ruler of his country. And where does that leave him? Where does that leave him and what choice does he have in anything?"

"He's going to have to step out of the dungeon," she said. "The dungeon in his mind. More than anything else. He's going to have to… He has to decide."

"And if he can't?" Brianna asked.

"He will," said Ariel.

"Why do you think that?"

"Because I know his brother very well. And because I know how those men love. He might not be able to tell you that he loves you, Brianna, but he does. I'm certain of it."

"Should I come back?"

"Give it a few days," said Ariel. "I think my husband is going to return the favor that he owes your fiancée."

"What favor is that?"

"You know, even when Cairo confessed to Riyaz that it was his fault the palace had been taken… He encouraged Cairo to go back to me. To have me. He could recognize when something is good for someone else. I just think he's having difficulty accepting it for himself. Let Cairo help. And trust… Trust that Riyaz is strong enough to break the chains."

CHAPTER FOURTEEN

RIYAZ HAD NOT felt pain like this since his parents' deaths. On the nights when he had flashed back to their deaths, it was the closest. That was what it was to wake up without Brianna in the palace. Pain. Like a death. It was he who was standing at the top of the stairs, looking down into the dungeon, when he heard footsteps behind him.

"So here we are in a very similar position to what we were in only a couple of weeks ago," said his brother, Cairo, from behind.

"Yes."

"You sent her away."

"I had to. I was forcing her to stay with me when I knew that she wanted something else. You know what you saved Brianna from. You know that her father was going to traffic her. He was a criminal. How can I hold her captive?"

"Well, you could. But you aren't. Because you're a decent person."

"Yes, I am. At least, I am trying to be."

"The thing is, though, eventually, you have to listen to what she wants. She's in love with you?"

"She said she was. But I…"

"You're angry with me, aren't you?"

"Of course not. What you told me has nothing to do with this."

"I think you're lying, my brother. I think you're angry with me. You were very calm. When I told you."

"What is the alternative?"

"Throw some fists. Rage. For God's sake. You're a monster that has been kept in a dungeon for sixteen years, and you can't pull together a little bit of barbarian fury?"

"I don't want to," he said. "What is the point of it? I never raged. I never… I never cried. Nothing. Because what would the point be? Everyone was dead and I was in chains."

"Yes," he said. "Everyone was dead and you were in chains, so what was the point? And yet you have feelings about it. You are not in a dungeon anymore. You're allowed to have feelings."

And suddenly, a nameless rage inside of him boiled over and he grabbed his brother by the throat and pinned him to the wall. "Well, why did you tell him? Why did you tell them how to get into the palace?"

"Because I was foolish. I made a mistake."

"Yes, you did," said Riyaz. "Yes, you did."

"You're allowed to be angry."

"I am," said Riyaz, pounding his fist hard against the stone wall. "I am furious. But Father… He should've known. He should never have trusted him. He should never have put you in that position. Or me. And Mother… He was supposed to protect her."

"Yes," Cairo said. "He was. He didn't. She paid the consequences for that. So did you."

"So did he," said Riyaz. "And this rage is pointless. Because it solves nothing and it brings no one back. Because... The only blame that is to be laid is on the people who... The people who destroyed us. The people who destroyed our family. Our country. Me."

"You're not destroyed," said Cairo. "If I'm not destroyed, then neither are you. I tried. In the back of my mind I knew I needed to come back, I needed to save you. And in the meantime, I tried to self-destruct with excess. I figured even if I limped back here, freed you, but was little more than a shadow of myself, it would all be fine. But I found something better. I found something better than self-destruction. I found love."

Riyaz closed his eyes. "But..." Everything felt painful. Sharp. But suddenly, just suddenly, he realized he didn't hate the words *I love you*. He craved them. It was just that his heart, which had been frozen solid out of the need to survive, hadn't been able to tell the difference. Between a desperate desire and a deeper unrelenting fear. Because they were the same. Because wanting anything had been his enemy. And he felt... It was as if truth was pouring from his chest like blood. And he could scarcely manage it all. He could scarcely understand himself. "I need to go," he said.

"All right. If you need to hit me..."

"I don't," said Riyaz.

Because it was as if that blockade of emotions was suddenly becoming clear. What started as anger, the kind that sent him on blind rages when he had those flashbacks, the kind that had overtaken him just now... They were deeper. And they were more. It was grief. The grief he had never been allowed to have.

And he knew he could have no good thing without allowing the pain out as well.

And because he could, he opened the doors to the palace and he ran. Into the desert, he ran as far as his legs would take him. Because he was free. And then he sank to his knees and he cried out at the unfeeling sky. And a sob tore itself free from his chest, tears falling from his eyes. The tears he had never allowed himself to shed. Sixteen years of them. For the loss of his mother. The loss of his father. The loss of sixteen years of his life.

For all that had been taken from him, all of it. Until he had poured out the unrelenting grief onto the sand.

Until he was emptied of it. These years of pain. All of them.

But there was still something there, a restlessness. A memory.

The love he used to have for his family. And now that the rawness of grief had been removed... That love was still there. But where would it go? And that created a deep sadness within him.

For her. For them.

He wanted to hear that he was loved again. He looked at the sky again, and a hawk sliced through the pale blue. And he did not think the sky was so unfeeling after all.

She was trying to do what Ariel said. She was trying to wait. And wait well.

But it was difficult. But she had to trust... She knew what had passed between them. What had passed between their bodies, whether or not he had been ready to admit what had passed between their souls. And she believed that it was love.

Still, she had put the town house up for sale. And where she would go after, she didn't know. Would it be a cul-de-sac? She hoped not. She would try the palace first. But there was no way to know for sure.

She shut the door behind her one last time and turned the lock. And then she put her hands in her coat pockets and began to walk down the street.

"Brianna."

It was his voice. He said her name in a way only he could. As if he was tasting it. As if it was something special and new. Something he had never tried before.

"You're here," she said.

She looked at him, backed by the city. By skyscrapers, all concrete and glass.

He was in New York. He was out of the dungeon.

"Riyaz…"

"Cairo is managing things in my stead. And I am… I am here."

"You are."

"Maybe I should play tourist."

"You? A tourist?"

"Why not?" he asked. "I'm here."

"Well, I can't invite you over. I did just…sell the town house. I have a room at a hotel until I decide where to go next. I got rid of all my things."

"And why is that?"

"I was really hoping that you would come. That's why."

"I also have a hotel reservation. It might be nicer than yours."

"Probably. Though, hotels have beds, not jail cells."

"I would think that in New York you could find one with a jail cell."

She laughed. "Was that a joke?"

"It was. I read about many of these places. I can't wait

186 A VIRGIN FOR THE DESERT KING

to see them. With you. I hope you understand I mean with you. Because you're why I'm here. I love you, *habibti*. Brianna. And it is not because you are the first woman. It is that you are the only woman. The only one for me. I had to... Feel. Everything. The anger. The grief. Sorrow. So that I could begin to feel the joy. I had to trust that it would not be taken away from me, and only then was I able to see. I did not hate love. I craved it. But when you're in a place of deprivation, wanting is the enemy. So I trained myself not to want. And eventually trained myself to believe all of that was bad. But I want cake. And sunshine and you. I said that my destiny was to rule Nazul. That it was part of me. My blood. But I realize now you are entangled in that destiny. If it took a coup, imprisonment, your awful father, and Cairo, for the two of us to meet, then I will call it all filled with meaning. You take tragedy that could be pointless and make it into something... It in and of itself is not beautiful, you understand, but it has made me into a man who has you. And for that I will be grateful. For that, I can leave the past behind."

"I understand. I thought that I wanted normal. I just wanted to be loved. I wanted to love someone. And I do."

"And I love you."

"And I have my dream. Exactly the way that I always wanted."

He frowned. "I'm not living in a cul-de-sac."

She had to laugh at the expression his face. "I don't dream of cul-de-sacs," she said. "I only dream of you."

The slow grin that cut across his taciturn face was like seeing the sun for the first time. "Good. Then let's go sightseeing."

He took her hand in his, like he was her boyfriend and they were about to set out on a very normal date. Not like he was a sheikh, and she his future sheikha. Not like she had been a prisoner in her own home growing up, and he had been a literal prisoner of a dungeon.

But just as they were.

Just whole, and together.

"What do you want to see?" she asked.

He thought for a moment. "Whatever we want."

And so they did. Because they were free. And they were in love.

EPILOGUE

THE GRAND AFFAIR of their wedding was storied. Written about in publications all over the world. A fairy tale. And on their wedding night, she got to give her husband another surprise.

"Where else would you like to go?" he said. "The wonderful thing about technology is so much ruling of a country can be done from other locations."

She had created a monster. Riyaz did not just like to go outside. He liked to hike. He liked to see the world. Everything that he had ever read about. They had stayed in the rather run-down diner in New York City for longer than she would've liked because he was so entranced by the atmosphere, and how it was exactly as described in a spy novel he'd read.

He was a menace. And she loved him. And she realized that... She was actually getting to live many lives with him. Because they both got to live their dreams with each other.

"Well, that would be a good idea. And we do need to get more flying in before..."

"Before what?"

"They don't like you to fly too late in your pregnancy."

He stood up off the bed. "Really?"

"Yes."

And then he dropped to his knees, and put his hand on her stomach. He looked up at her, his dark eyes filled with emotion. "Brianna, there was a time in my life when I had nothing but darkness. Nothing but despair. And a dungeon. And you have given me the world. You made me the Sheikh. A man. Husband. Now father. What have I given you?"

She leaned in and kissed him. "Everything that I ever wanted."

* * * * *

PREGNANT WITH HER ROYAL BOSS'S BABY

JACKIE ASHENDEN

MILLS & BOON

For the OG Ashendens, Wendy and Richard.

CHAPTER ONE

WINIFRED SCOTT PAUSED and squinted down yet another echoing, deserted palace hallway. She'd been given precise instructions about where her room was by one of the palace staff, but it was one in the morning, and she'd just come off a late-night flight from London and she was tired. So very tired. Getting turned around a few hallways back hadn't helped, especially now that she wasn't quite sure where she was. The hallways all looked the same, that was the problem, and she'd been half asleep when the staff member had given her directions, and now she couldn't remember where she was supposed to go.

Getting lost in the royal palace in Al Da'ira—a small desert kingdom near the Red Sea, currently ruled by King Khalil ibn Amir al Nazari, one of her boss's best friends— was embarrassing, especially when she'd been here before many times. Then again her sense of direction had never been that great.

Really, she should have worked out where her room was *before* she'd landed, but she'd had a number of last-minute loose ends to tie up in London; then her plane had been delayed for three hours, which had meant she'd missed the ball she was supposed to have attended with her boss.

Given that said boss was Augustine Solari, king of the small, mountainous European kingdom of Isavere, and given to tetchiness if she wasn't around when he needed her, she knew he'd be unhappy about her nonattendance.

She hadn't been happy about it herself. Her entire professional life was dedicated to making sure the business of being a king was as easy as possible for him, and her not being at the ball would have complicated things.

Having to go to London in the first place had been a pain, but Augustine was due to arrive on an official visit after he'd finished in Al Da'ira, and there had been a few things she'd had to deal with in order to smooth the way. He did have a very specific set of needs. Then when the time had come to return to Al Da'ira, she'd had to fly commercial because Isavere's royal jet was unavailable, and the plane had been delayed twice, meaning she hadn't arrived until *well* after the ball had ended.

It couldn't be helped, but Augustine had sounded annoyed when she'd called him about the delay, which was going to make dealing with him the next morning fun.

She didn't like it when he was annoyed. His life was hard enough as it was and it was her job to make it easier for him, and when she couldn't she always felt as if she was failing in some way. Which she also didn't like. But some things were out of her hands and plane delays was one of them.

She frowned at the hallway again. She'd just passed some Isaveran security staff so obviously she was at least sort of in the right place.

Perhaps her room was down this hallway.

She tightened her grip on her briefcase and went cautiously along it, pulling the small wheeled case that was the rest of her luggage behind her, before stopping before an intricately carved wooden door.

This must be it. In fact, it had better be it, because she was about ready to drop with exhaustion.

She put her briefcase down and tried the door handle, which opened silently.

Thank God.

Winifred went in, dumped her bags and shut the door. Then she fumbled around for the light switch, which, much to her annoyance, she didn't find.

She muttered a curse under her breath, but as her eyes adjusted, she could see the room wasn't totally dark. Dim light from what she assumed was an outside courtyard was coming through a gap in the curtains, showing her where the bed was.

Bed. That's all she needed. That's all she wanted. The difficulties of having to deal with Augustine she'd figure out in the morning, once she was rested. First a shower though, which meant finding out where the bathroom was.

That at least wasn't a drama, and after shedding the crumpled clothing she'd been wearing for nearly twelve hours straight, she spent a blissful ten minutes standing under the hot water, washing off the travel grime.

Annoyingly, she was just drying herself off when the bathroom light flickered and went out, plunging her into yet more darkness. Irritated, she flicked the switch on and off a couple of times, but the light appeared to be well and truly dead.

Ah well, that didn't matter right now either. She'd stumble into bed and deal with it later, like she would with Augustine. She could manage him. She'd been doing that for five years now and had been very successful. The best personal assistant he'd ever had—or so he'd told her at her last performance review. He never gave out compliments, at least he didn't give her any, so she'd treasured that one. Even thinking about it gave her a little glow.

Pathetic. He doesn't even see *you as a person yet you*

regularly lie down on the floor like a rug and let him walk all over you.

Winifred hung her towel carefully on the rail and walked back into the bedroom, squinting in the dark for the bed.

Ridiculous. She wasn't a rug. She'd set out to be the best personal assistant he'd ever had, and that's exactly what she'd become. Yes, she tried to anticipate his every need, and sometimes that was difficult, but the bottom line was that this job was important. She needed the money it earned her, which she was steadily saving for the express purpose of sending to her two sisters. They'd be coming out of foster care soon and she wanted them to have something, money for a house or college, or whatever else they wanted to do.

Anyway, she loved working for him. She never wanted to leave.

Correction: you love him.

That was also true. An unfortunate side effect of the job. But when you worked for the most charismatic, charming, handsome king in the entire world, falling in love with him almost wasn't a choice. She was his right-hand woman, the first person he went to with a problem, the one he could count on to get him whatever he needed. The only person in the world who knew him better than he knew himself, and that was intoxicating.

So yes, she loved him. But she knew too, that nothing would ever happen between them. He was an inveterate playboy, yet he had strict rules when it came to his employees and he never broke them. So even if he *had* been attracted her—and he wasn't, she was certain—he'd never have done anything about it.

It was fine. Her job was more important than any sleazy affair anyway and not something she'd ever put at risk just for sex.

She put out a hand and found the bed, then slipped into it, nearly moaning in relief at the feeling of cool, crisp sheets against her skin.

After the plane journey from hell, a hot shower, a comfortable bed and clean sheets were bliss.

She burrowed into the softness of the pillow and closed her eyes.

Then just as she was about to drift off, a large, warm hand settled on her hip.

'Hmmm,' a deep, masculine melted-honey voice murmured in her ear. 'There you are. I thought you'd never come.' There was movement in the bed and the heat of another body behind her. Warm breath against her neck. 'Though I have to say, not coming is something you'll never have to worry about with me.'

Winifred froze, utterly still with shock.

She knew that voice. She knew it like she knew her own name. She heard it every day at work, though at work it didn't usually sound so...warm and husky and sexy.

Yet the undeniable truth was that Augustine Solari, King of Isavere, had the most beautiful voice in creation.

Augustine Solari, King of Isavere, who was also apparently in her bed.

Her mind reeled. That was impossible; he shouldn't be here. He couldn't be here. Yet there was no denying the warm pressure of that hand on her hip.

What on earth was he doing in her bed?

He wouldn't be. So are you sure you're in your bed?

Winifred took a long, slow breath, staring into the darkness of the room. Perhaps she wasn't. Perhaps she'd got so lost that she'd somehow stumbled into this room, *his* room. And that hand on her hip, that note of welcome in his voice... He must have been expecting someone. Someone he'd met at the ball, maybe? Someone who clearly wasn't her.

At that moment, his hand on her hip slid down to her stomach, long fingers spreading out over her bare skin, the powerful length of his body shifting and then pressing against hers.

Every inch of her came alive.

Her breath caught, her heartbeat accelerating.

She'd been in love with him for years. The instant she'd met him, she'd fallen under his spell, and as those years had gone by, the spell had only deepened.

She wasn't sure why, because he'd never given her the slightest bit of encouragement and so feeling the way she did about him meant she had to be very careful with her emotions. She'd become very good at hiding them.

It was only that he had a persona that he projected to the world, the charming, dissolute, disreputable Playboy King, but she knew that wasn't him. Because he wasn't like that in private. He was…serious. Intelligent. Sharper than a knife. He had difficulties that he hid, and only she out of everyone in Isavere, knew that about him.

Only she, out of everyone in Isavere, was permitted to know.

Yet she wasn't an idiot about her feelings. She'd known right from the start that kings didn't love women like her. Kings barely even noticed women like her. Also, he was her boss and not only would he not cross that line, neither would she.

For all that he was a playboy, he'd never flirted with her. Not even once. Though that might have been because she'd turned herself from a person into a mere extension of his will. A voice recorder he could murmur notes into. A computer who would send all his emails. A secretary to arrange his diary. A coffee machine who would bring him his coffee. All of which had been her goal. Him treating her that way only reinforced how well she did her job, a seamless transition between his will and action.

But this was not him treating her as an extension of his will. She'd become a person, a woman he noticed. This was *his* hand on her hip, *his* magnificent body up against hers, and he was naked. She could feel the warmth of his bare skin...

Her mouth dried, her heartbeat deafening.

She'd had so many fantasies about him. In the darkest part of the night, when old fears stalked her, reminders of the life she'd left behind, the life she'd run away from, along with the terrible thing she'd done, she'd allow herself to think about him instead. Of his hand on her the way it was now, and his voice murmuring in her ear. Him touching her, caressing her, doing all the things with her that she'd never done with anyone else because she'd had too many demons to outrun.

And now, right this very minute, all those hot, desperate fantasies were coming true.

His hand slid further down, warm and slow, the tips of his fingers brushing the curls between her thighs. She shut her eyes, a prickling heat washing over her, an aching, throbbing pressure gathering just below where his hand was.

He didn't know who she was, she was sure of it. She was absolutely positive. This would never happen if he did, and of course the moment he realised her identity, he'd be furious. And he'd stop.

You don't want him to stop.

She took a silent breath, shivering with desire. No, she didn't want him to stop. She wanted him to keep going, to keep touching her, do whatever he wanted with her. Give her the pleasure she'd missed out on all her life.

So...what if he didn't find out? What if you let him believe you're whoever he's waiting for?

The thought seemed ludicrous. His taste in women was wide and varied—she knew because she was also the keeper of his little black book. He liked them experienced and single-night affairs only. If he was particularly enamoured that could extend to two, possibly three, but never more.

She herself wasn't his type, not at all. She wasn't curvy or beautiful or witty or rich. She was bland. A professional blank space where he could direct his thoughts without ever seeing her, not *her*. Which was exactly how she'd wanted it. If he looked at her too closely, he might see beneath the veneer she'd cultivated, see the scaffold of lies she'd built around herself. Lies such as the fact that her name wasn't even her own, that she wasn't as English as she sounded, and that sometimes she was sure the crime she'd committed years ago had been branded into her forehead and everyone could see it.

If he saw it, it might shatter the precarious little life she'd found for herself.

That couldn't happen. It couldn't. She'd never get another job that paid as well, and she needed the money for her sisters.

Yet now, here, in the dark, she wasn't his PA. He thought she was a woman and a woman he wanted, and she hadn't been wanted for a very, *very* long time, if ever.

His hand slid lower so very slowly and her inner thigh muscles relaxed, allowing his fingers to brush through her curls and cup the heat between her legs gently.

A quiver ran through her, all the remaining breath in her lungs escaping. She couldn't move. Could barely even think. His thumb shifted, caressing, sliding over her slick flesh, and pleasure curled through her in a dizzying rush.

No one had ever touched her there before, no one ever, and it felt *so* good...

Because it's him.

She closed her eyes, trembling. Yes, it *was* because it was him. Because she loved him. Because of all those fantasies she'd had, all that pent-up need.

You should tell him it's you. Stop this before it goes too far.

But it had already gone too far. His thumb was circling, pressing, teasing that sensitive little bundle of nerves between her thighs, and now she could feel his mouth brushing her nape, nuzzling in the vulnerable hollow between her shoulder and neck.

His scent was all around her, a warm, woody smell, like cedar and sandalwood, and she could feel the hard press of every masculine inch of him, and suddenly hunger was all there was. She was made of it.

Keep going. Please, keep going.

Except he stopped, the caressing thumb pausing, the body behind her stilling, and a silence fell.

'I thought you wanted this,' he said in her ear, his voice hard. 'So if you don't, you'd better tell me now. I don't take unwilling women to my bed.'

Oh. He'd clearly mistaken her shock for unwillingness. Which it was not. In any shape or form.

You should tell him who you are. You can't let him believe you're someone you're not.

She almost laughed at that. She only had the life she had now because she'd let him believe she was something she wasn't.

So how would doing this hurt? Her job—everything—

revolved around keeping his secret and that meant doing whatever he wanted when he wanted it, and making sure he was happy, and he paid her astonishingly well for the privilege. But why couldn't she take a little something extra for herself? A chance to live out her wildest fantasies?

If she was careful, he wouldn't know. Surely, he wouldn't. She'd had a shower and she didn't wear perfume anyway, and she had her hair loose, which she never did in his presence. And she'd stay quiet. She'd try not to speak.

He never cared about names when he slept with women anyway, which she was very aware of, and he slept with strangers all the time. In fact, he'd often told her that all he required was a warm, willing body, so why couldn't she be that body now?

One thing was certain, though. If she didn't decide now, he was going to get up and leave the bed, and she'd be discovered, and she'd end up with nothing.

She'd had nothing before. She couldn't bear the thought of having it again.

So, she put her hand over his where it lay between her thighs and pressed down. Then turned her head to where his mouth was beside her ear, his warm breath on her neck. And she didn't need any light to know where his lips were; she found them and covered them with her own.

Augustine Solari, King of Isavere, knew something wasn't right. But he couldn't quite put his finger—so to speak— on what.

He'd been in a foul temper earlier, because Freddie had called him to tell him she'd be late due to her plane being delayed out of London, and then she hadn't turned up at the ball *at all*.

He was here to help celebrate the marriage of an old Ox-

ford friend—Khalil ibn Amir al Nazari, King of Al Da'ira—
and while he ostensibly loved a party, the reality was that
they were only bearable when Freddie was there, and official parties in particular.

He had trouble with remembering people's names and
Freddie was invaluable when it came to murmuring them
in his ear, or dropping them into conversation, letting him
know subtly who he was talking to without any embarrassing errors.

Tonight though, because of Freddie's absence, he'd had to
stand there as if he didn't have the usual headache that had
come on an hour earlier, the one that clouded his thinking.
Covering it, as he always did, by pretending to be mildly
the worse for wear alcohol-wise, all the while trying to remember the speech he had to give and what he had to do at
various points in the evening so he didn't embarrass either
his friend or his country in the process.

Luckily he'd managed, but it was only a decade's worth
of control that had enabled him to do it, and the effort had
left him fatigued and short-tempered by the end of the evening. Not an unfamiliar state of affairs.

He'd retired to a corner with a drink to deal with himself, only to be joined by a lovely woman with whom he'd
exchanged extensive eye contact earlier, and since sex always improved his mood, he'd decided that she was just the
thing he needed. She'd been very willing when he'd suggested she come to his room, though she'd taken her time
about arriving. The evening had taken it out of him, so he'd
fallen asleep, only to wake up the moment a warm female
body had slipped into bed with him.

She was naked and must have had a shower since she
smelled of soap and shampoo, and her long hair was damp.
But the woman he'd been flirting with had been a talker

and enthusiastic, and this woman hadn't said one word, or moved, or even given an indication of encouragement when he'd touched her.

That had scraped against his already foul mood, since he never took a woman to bed who didn't want to be there and if she'd changed her mind, she needed to tell him as quickly as possible. Certainly there'd been a whole lot of mixed signals going on and while he might only be an adequate king, he was a world-class playboy and he knew when women did and didn't want him.

This one did. Her breathing had changed the moment he'd put his hand on her stomach, and her legs had spread for him when he'd slid his fingers between her thighs. And when he'd stroked her, she'd got all slippery and slick, a quiver running through her body.

She had a scent to her beneath the soap, something delicate and musky and feminine, that had somehow hooked into everything male in him, making him hard. And it wasn't just her scent.

He knew all about the physical electricity that occurred between men and women, and he could feel that electricity now, crackling over his skin like a live wire. Making him want to push her onto her back and slide inside her immediately, which was something he almost never did.

Ever since the accident that had taken everything from him, control ruled his life. Even in the bedroom. And he didn't like feeling as if he wasn't in full command of himself. So maybe it was the sense that he wasn't that had given him pause. Or maybe it was that electricity he could feel in the air, an electricity he was sure hadn't been there when they'd been flirting earlier.

Whatever it had been, he'd needed to know if she wanted

this, and he'd been expecting her to say she'd had a change of heart.

Except then she'd held his hand down on her and turned to find his mouth instead.

A soft, hot, sweet kiss. Hesitant at first, yet he could taste her hunger. It was there along with the flavour of the minty toothpaste she'd used to brush her teeth. Was that why he couldn't taste any alcohol? Because she'd been drinking champagne with him before and he couldn't get even a hint of that.

Her lips were warm and satiny, and though there was still something 'off' about this, he couldn't think what it was. Soon, he didn't want to. The feel of her slick flesh beneath his fingers and the scent of feminine arousal, the electricity in the air, the heat between them, were all making it difficult to think of anything at all.

She made a soft noise as he stroked her, and when he took charge of the kiss, easing his tongue into her mouth to explore her deeper, she made it again.

Her hand pressed down harder on his, holding his fingers against her, and she kissed him back with more confidence now, hot and hungry.

There was a familiarity to the sounds she made and to the delicate scent that wound around him, a maddening sense of familiarity. It nagged at him.

Does it matter?

He was starting to think that it didn't. All bodies were the same in the dark and if everyone was enjoying themselves, who cared about a nagging familiarity?

She gave the softest little moan against his mouth, her hips lifting beneath his hand, and both the sound and the way she moved against him were unspeakably erotic. Without thought, he pulled his hand from under hers and slid it down her thigh, gripping behind her knee and lifting her leg, hooking it up and behind his. Opening her up to him.

She shuddered, gasping, and he was abruptly desperate in a way he couldn't remember ever being before. She was slight and there was a fragility to her that he hadn't expected, yet she had the most delicious curves. The softness of her bottom pressed against his groin felt so good, fitting him to perfection.

He buried his face in her neck, inhaling that tantalising, familiar scent, as he slid his hand back between her thighs again, parting the soft slick folds of her sex.

She trembled.

His own heart was beating far too fast and he didn't know why. This was…a great deal more erotic than he'd anticipated.

Lifting his mouth from her neck, he flexed his hips, pressing himself against her soft, wet heat.

She'd tensed.

'Yes?' he murmured. 'Tell me, sweetheart. I need to hear the words.'

She took the longest time to answer, still shaking like a leaf and it wasn't with fear, not given the way she'd moved against him and the slickness against his fingertips. But he didn't move. He kept himself very still.

'Yes,' she breathed eventually.

It was only one word, but her voice was different to that of the woman he'd been talking to earlier. That woman had had an accent, and it didn't sound at all like the murmured 'yes' he'd just heard.

Which meant this woman, the woman in bed with him now, definitely wasn't the one he'd flirted with in the ballroom. She was someone else, someone familiar, and he'd have laid money on the fact that somewhere, somehow, he'd met her. He was also positive that she knew who he was, because why else had she slipped into his bed? Why else let him touch her?

Augustine had never been a man who hesitated. He knew who he was and what he was capable of, and while he might have been a very average king, he was truly excellent at giving pleasure. If a woman was warm and willing, he never said no.

Yet he found himself hesitating now.

But she must have got sick of waiting, because abruptly she pressed her hips back and he felt the hot, slick flesh and then there was no hesitating and indeed, no thinking anymore.

'Wait,' he growled, before reaching for the condoms he had at the ready on the bedside table next to him. It only took him a matter of moments to sheathe himself—he didn't need light—and then he gripped her hip and pushed into her tight, wet heat, feeling her wrap around his aching erection like a homecoming. She gasped, arching against him, shaking.

God, she felt good. So unbelievably good. He liked to go slow, to draw things out as long as he could, precisely because he could. When it came to sex, his control over his own body and its reactions were faultless.

But this... This was different. She was different somehow and he couldn't stop himself from moving, a long, slow glide in and out, holding her firmly. She moved with him, her breathing frantic and gasping, twisting against him, one hand bracing herself, the other gripping his hip the way he was gripping hers, holding him to her.

He shifted, moving without thought, tucking her head into the crook of his braced elbow so he could turn her towards him, his fingers buried in thick, soft hair as he found her mouth. Kissing her deeply, chasing that sweet, delicate flavour.

In the dark there was only the heat between them, getting hotter, the slick grip of her sex around his, the softness of her mouth and the astonishing pleasure that wound tighter and tighter, a spell holding them suspended in this endless moment.

It couldn't last.

Shockingly fast he found himself at the end of his control and when she clutched at him, gasping, he knew she had too. So he took her hand from his hip and guided it down over her stomach, holding her fingers over where they were connected and pressing down. Then he thrust in deep one last time, and she cried out against his mouth, her body stiffening as she came.

Then he was too, an avalanche of intense pleasure rolling over him and dragging him under, crushing him as his own ragged breathing joined hers.

He lost himself for whole minutes—something he hadn't done since he was a teenager seducing one of the palace maids—with his face buried in the warm hollow of her neck, and it was some time before the real world returned.

She was still trembling against him, both of them quiet. And briefly he debated having the conversation about exactly who she was and what she was doing here. Then she turned in his arms, took his face between her hands and kissed him again. And he decided there were more appealing things to be doing in the dark than having a conversation.

He finally fell asleep close to dawn, and when he woke up, he was alone.

She was gone.

CHAPTER TWO

Three months later

THE WRITERS BAR at Raffles hotel, Singapore, had been cleared of the general public as per Winifred's instructions, and now was occupied by only one person. He was sitting at the burnished gold of the bar, chatting easily to the barman. The man had lost his awe at having the King of Isavere seated on one of his bar stools, and was now talking to Augustine enthusiastically about the history of the Singapore Sling cocktail, invented at the beginning of the twentieth century, right here in this hotel.

Winifred didn't want to interrupt, happy to wait until Augustine had finished his conversation.

It gave her time to gather her courage.

It also gave her time to watch him, which was one of her favourite pastimes, and since she wouldn't be able to do that for too much longer, she wanted to indulge herself while she could.

The barman laughed at something he said and it made Winifred want to smile too. Augustine was good with people. He was so charming and always knew the right thing to say to make people forget he was a king and treat him like a friend.

The people of Isavere loved him despite his playboy reputation. Or maybe they loved him because of it.

She loved him too, even though she shouldn't.

She shouldn't be noticing, either, the way the dim lighting of the bar found the gold strands in his dark tawny hair and set them alight. Or how the white cotton of his business shirt fit his wide shoulders, or the dark blue wool of his trousers pulled tight over his powerful thighs and showed off the span of his narrow waist.

She shouldn't be looking at how that light outlined the beautiful lines of his face, the long aquiline nose and high cheekbones. The sensual curve of his gorgeous mouth as he chatted with the barman, giving one of his brilliant, charismatic smiles.

He gave that smile a lot. He was profligate with that smile. It was a lethal weapon, laying waste to his enemies and making slaves of everyone he met.

He never gave it to her, though, and she was glad he didn't. Because that smile was also a mask and he didn't need that mask with her. He didn't need to be anything with her but himself, and she wouldn't have it any other way.

You still shouldn't be noticing any of those things about him.

Her heart clenched tight behind her breastbone.

She'd thought she'd be able to put the night she'd spent in his bed behind her. She'd thought she'd never think of it again. It had been three months after all. Yet, despite everything, that night was all she thought about.

She couldn't get it out of her head.

You have to. Your job, the future you want for your sisters, depends on it.

But that was the problem. The night she'd had with him was the whole reason she was standing here waiting to speak to him, her palms sweaty and nervous tension roiling in her gut.

The reason she was facing having to ask him for six months off. Six months he wasn't going to give her and yet which she absolutely *had* to have.

She'd been putting it off and putting it off, and this morning, when she hadn't been able to get the zip on her skirt even halfway up, she knew she'd couldn't put it off any longer. He was going to notice and that couldn't happen.

He couldn't know she was pregnant with his baby. Everything would be ruined if he did. He'd find out it had been her that night in his bed, and that she hadn't told him who she was. That she'd hidden her pregnancy from him for three months. He'd be so angry and he'd no doubt fire her, and she'd lose her job. She'd lose the potential to save more money for her sisters' future.

And he *definitely* wouldn't be happy at the news he was going to be a father. He'd always been clear that he didn't want children, and while she'd debated telling him she was pregnant anyway, she'd decided in the end not to.

She couldn't bear for her baby to grow up with a parent who didn't want them the way she had. Her own mother hadn't been interested in Winifred's upbringing or in that of her sisters, and she'd often told Winifred that she hadn't wanted children. Certainly, she'd never cared about them because if she had then Aaron, her mother's boyfriend, wouldn't have thought he could simply help himself to them.

Not that Winifred herself would be any better as a parent. She was a criminal just like her mother was, and she wouldn't allow her child to suffer the same fate. She had to break the cycle somehow.

At the bar, Augustine half glanced in her direction, the lights striking yet more gold from his dark hair, while his sharp blue-green gaze swept over her. He wasn't smiling now, his mouth hard and stern, the phenomenal intellect he liked to hide looking out from behind his eyes.

He was...breathtaking.

'What is it, Freddie?' he asked in the deep, melted-honey voice that always made her want to shiver. 'I don't need you tonight, in case you're wondering.'

She'd been going to leave this conversation till they were back in Isavere—Augustine had just completed an official visit to the States—but then he'd decided he had a sudden hankering for Singapore and so they'd made a detour. She wasn't sure how long he wanted to stay here and since there was no telling whether he might want to go someplace else afterwards, she'd thought she'd better ask him now.

The sooner they had this conversation the better.

'Sorry, sir,' she said. 'I need to ask you something. It won't take longer than a couple of minutes.' She paused then added, 'In private.'

Augustine lifted one straight dark brow. 'That sounds portentous.' He stared at her a moment, then gave the barman an apologetic look. 'If you wouldn't mind.'

The man inclined his head, then disappeared out the back, leaving her and Augustine alone.

Winifred resisted the urge to wipe her palms on the stretchy black skirt she'd had to emergency buy that morning. 'Thank you, sir.'

He'd turned on his bar stool, one heel resting on the lower rung, the other on the floor. He had his elbow on the bar itself, his jacket thrown carelessly on the stool next to him.

He was so gorgeous, with his white business shirt open at the neck and no tie, shirtsleeves rolled up. Casual, approachable, effortlessly elegant.

You need to stop mooning over him.

Oh, she did. If the last three months had taught her nothing else it was that.

Gathering her courage, she met his gaze. 'I need six months off, sir,' she said bluntly, since there was no other way to say it.

His expression didn't change. 'Excuse me?'

'I need six months off,' she repeated. 'Six months of annual leave. I believe I'm owed it.'

His gaze narrowed, that sharp, turquoise blue searching her face. 'Six months? You seriously want me to give you six months off?'

Winifred forced aside the nervousness gathering tighter and tighter inside her. This was always going to be a challenge, which was why she'd delayed asking him. And what was also going to be a challenge was her own instinct to acquiesce to his wishes, a habit that she'd spent five years cultivating.

She could feel the words already forming in her mouth: *No, it's fine, sir. I don't need to take six months. I don't need it at all.*

Except she did need it and she couldn't say those words. Instead, she said, 'You make it sound like I'm asking for the moon.'

'The moon would be easier to deliver.' Augustine's tone was flat.

'I've accrued enough leave, sir. The provision for it is all in my contract.' And it was. They both knew that.

He was silent a moment, then he reached for the heavy crystal tumbler that contained the cocktail the barman had made for him. It was a dark, rich red and looked incredibly alcoholic. He took a sip, his gaze still on her and still sharp. There was a tightness around his eyes and a faint crease between his brows, which usually indicated a headache. Hopefully not one of the migraines that would strike sometimes whenever the light was too bright, but it was difficult to tell; he was very good at hiding it when he had one of those.

Still, if he was in the bar, it usually meant he needed darkness and quiet, while at the same time allowing himself to be seen. No one knew he still suffered from the debilitating effects of the head injury he'd sustained nearly ten years ago in the car accident that had killed his father. It was a secret he guarded jealously.

The King of Isavere had to be seen to be strong and in command.

'Why?' he asked, a sharp edge in his voice. 'What could you possibly be doing that you need six months off for?'

Winifred gave a silent curse. She should have ascertained his mood before coming straight out and asking him for something he didn't want to give. When he was in pain, he was difficult, and no doubt he was going to ask her all kinds of questions she didn't want to answer. Though to be fair, he'd have probably asked them anyway.

Six months was a *lot* of time.

'Well,' she said briskly. 'I haven't had a holiday in the five years I've been working for you. And I thought I might take one now, when things are relatively quiet.'

'If you want a holiday, you can take next week off.' He took another sip of his cocktail. 'I can spare you for a week, Freddie, but no more.'

Of course, he couldn't spare her. She'd made herself invaluable, that was the issue, and he needed her. She organised his schedule, liaised with palace staff on his behalf, dealt with his email, wrote his letters, assisted him in reading aloud reports and any other material he needed for his infrequent visits to parliament.

And she did all those things, because he couldn't.

The head injury prevented him from being able to read or write, or concentrate for long periods of time. He also suffered from light sensitivity, fatigue, headaches, and shortness of temper. Complicating all of that was the fact that he'd hidden his symptoms from everyone for years. His father, Piero, had been a great believer in the strength of kings and so naturally Augustine did too.

No one could know the extent of his disabilities. She herself had only found out once she'd accepted the job and had signed the intensely restrictive NDA he'd insisted on. That had been fairly shocking—not so much what he couldn't do as how long he'd successfully managed to hide it—but he hated pity and so they never spoke of it.

She still didn't know the details of the accident, or at least only what had been reported on in the press, and she'd been curious. But it wasn't her place to ask and so she hadn't.

Yet it had made this particular situation even more difficult. She'd lined up a replacement for herself, but the man didn't know the truth about Augustine, and six months was a long time to keep it hidden.

'I'm sorry, sir,' she said, trying for calm. 'But I'm afraid I do need the six months.'

Enough time to go away to the little cottage in the south, where Isavere's vineyards were, where she could spend the remainder of her pregnancy out of sight. She'd already engaged a midwife and there was a hospital nearby in case of any emergencies. Six months would also give her time to review the list of families she'd compiled. Families who would adopt her baby. She already had a few excellent candidates in mind who'd give her child the best start in life.

How can you give your baby up? How?

Pain gripped her, but she ignored that too. She couldn't keep the child, she'd known that the moment the pregnancy

test—against all odds—had come back positive. She'd sat on
the edge of her bath in her apartments in the palace, and allowed herself a small breakdown. Because it shouldn't have
happened, it just shouldn't. He'd had a vasectomy—she'd
booked it herself for God's sake—*and* they'd used a condom.

What were the chances of that kind of failure?

You never think of the consequences, do you?

She hadn't that night, that was for sure. There had only
been him and the pleasure he'd given her. And while it was
true she should never have allowed her own desires to take
over that night, the situation could still be fixed. It was only
a small mistake.

*Some mistakes can't be fixed and you of all people should
know that.*

The pain inside her sank its claws in, but she ignored it.
This was one mistake she *would* fix come hell or high water,
and it if meant giving her child to someone who wanted it,
someone who could care for it better than she could, then
she would.

She couldn't have her family's taint touch her baby. And
as for Augustine, she couldn't put the burden of a child
onto the weight he was already carrying. He had too many
challenges as it was and he didn't need the added stress of
a baby, especially a baby he'd never asked for in the first
place.

Augustine's expression had hardened, the tightness
around his eyes more pronounced now. He *was* in pain.

Her heart twisted. He did so much for his people and
no one knew how it cost him. No one knew how he struggled every day. No one except her. And it made her want
to smooth away that tightness with her fingers, stroke the
tension from his brow, ease him the way she always wanted
to ease him.

Yet she couldn't do that now. She had to dig in, go against her instinct and make his life difficult to save them and their child further anguish.

'Did you not hear me when I said no, Freddie?' His deep voice, textured and soft as cashmere, felt like a stroke over her skin, even if the edge in it was more pronounced now. 'You're not taking six months and that's final.'

You should tell him. Come clean.

But that was impossible. He didn't know that the woman in his bed that night had been her, because if he had, he'd have said something to her the next morning, and he hadn't.

He'd just looked at her impatiently, taking no notice of the dark circles under her eyes and apparently not hearing the mad gallop of her heart, and before she could speak, had told her she was late and then had gone into a rant on how inconvenient her nonattendance at the ball had been.

And all she'd been conscious of was the sick relief that had gripped her when it was clear he hadn't connected her with the woman he'd spent the night with. That her little secret would remain her little secret, and the life she'd built for herself, the life that had nothing to do with the girl who'd grown up in a desert trailer park in California, was safe.

He won't know the baby is his, though.

He wouldn't. Then again, he'd certainly wonder where she found the time to have a lover considering she'd never had one the entire five years she'd been working for him— or indeed ever.

Perhaps she could say she'd met someone while she'd been in England preparing for that last official visit? A one-night stand, since that was more or less the truth. It would make her look careless and irresponsible, and while she hated the thought of that, it would also make him much less likely to ask any awkward questions. Her lies were balanced so finely that anything could set them off.

How can you not tell him? It's his child too.

He'd never explained his reasons for not wanting kids to her, but when he'd asked her to book his vasectomy, he'd told her very clearly that he had no plans for children either now or in the foreseeable future. Where that left his kingship, she didn't know, but again, that was something he hadn't seen fit to share with her. She thought it might have something to do with the challenges he faced due to his brain injury, but that was only an assumption.

Anyway, one thing was clear to her: she never wanted to make things more difficult for him than they were already by confessing that her baby was his.

But she was going to have to give him some truth otherwise she was never going to get the time off that she needed. 'No, sir,' she said, allowing an edge of steel in her voice. 'No, I'm afraid a week won't be sufficient. I need six months.' She paused then added, 'And I need it because I'm pregnant.'

Augustine had another crashing headache. He'd felt it coming on all day—the tour of the Marina Bay Sands observation deck had been wonderful, but standing in the sun all day had its consequences—and while every part of him wanted to go back to his suite where it was dark and cool, he knew he couldn't.

A king had to be seen, so he'd had the bar cleared of patrons and had retired there instead. The barman had been sociable and had mixed him a special cocktail and he'd been looking forward to it since it would help take the edge off the headache.

Then Freddie had turned up.

Freddie, who needed six months off because she was apparently pregnant.

Out of everything that had happened in the last year, Freddie being pregnant was the very last thing he'd have ever predicted.

Shock echoed through him and he found himself giving her a more concentrated survey, something he never did in the usual run of things, mainly because she'd never needed surveying.

She was standing so very still beside his bar stool—she was always so very still—her elegant, long-fingered hands clasped together in front of her. He'd long since stopped noticing her appearance, since she always wore the same thing, day in, day out, varying only in colour.

A knee-length skirt and matching jacket, normally in grey wool, though sometimes in black or navy. A plain blouse in either white, black or dark blue. Tights, usually black. Plain, low-heeled pumps, also usually black.

Her dark brown hair was in its typical neat bun at the nape of her neck, with not a curl out of place. Her face was heart-shaped, her features pleasant yet unremarkable. Everything about her was pleasant yet unremarkable. Except for her eyes, they were very dark, large and liquid, like soft black velvet.

Perhaps she was pretty, but he didn't think of her as such. He barely thought of her as a woman at all. She was his personal assistant, calm and collected and precise, and always available to do whatever he wanted whenever he wanted it.

She never argued. She never protested. She was never difficult. She knew all his secrets, was aware of all his foibles. There were even times when she seemed to know what he wanted before he knew it himself.

She was the perfect assistant in every way.

Except the perfect assistant would never get herself pregnant, not when her presence was vital to the smooth running of his life.

Today, she was in a black skirt of some cheap, stretchy material, and it must have been new since it didn't match her grey jacket. He hadn't noticed it this morning, because he never noticed. And now he was looking directly at her, studying her, he could see why the skirt was necessary. She was definitely thicker around the middle than she had been, though the jacket did hide it.

'Pregnant.' The word come out strangely, as if he'd never heard it before in his life. 'You're pregnant.'

She met his gaze with her usual serene expression. 'Yes. I'm...three months along.'

He found his hand had closed around the cut crystal of his tumbler and he was holding it far more tightly than he should have. The square edges were digging into his palms. Pain throbbed behind his eyes, but he was used to that so he ignored it. 'Three months is a very long time to wait to inform me of this,' he bit out, the only thing he could think of to say.

He'd thought his two Oxford friends, King Galen Kouros of Kalithera and King Khalil ibn Amir al Nazari of Al Da'ira, both getting married within the space of a year had been surprising. He'd never have picked his self-effacing assistant for a shock pregnancy.

'I had to wait three months,' she said in her cut-glass British accent, that made it sound as if she was biting out each word. 'A pregnancy may not be...viable in the early stages.'

Of course, he knew that, though children would never be in his future. Not after the accident. He could barely be a king let alone a father and actually, could he even call himself a king when he couldn't read? When he had to have

Freddie do everything for him? She was the one running the country, not him.

How are you going to do that without her?

He couldn't do without her, that was the thing. Not if he wanted to keep presenting a strong front to the world. His father would have wanted that at least and Augustine would be damned if he let his failings get in the way of his father's wishes.

'So now it's...viable?' There were edges in his voice, edges he didn't mean, but he didn't have the energy to smooth them out. Besides, it was only Freddie. She knew him. She had to know he wouldn't be happy about this.

'Yes. It is.'

He raised his glass and took a sip, letting the alcohol work its soothing magic, while he studied her, a dim part of him still echoing with shock.

If Freddie was pregnant then at some point she must have had a lover. A lover with whom she'd had sex and he couldn't quite reconcile his precise little assistant with sex.

'How did this happen?' he asked, then heard what he'd said and amended, 'I mean, are you married? Or do you have a partner I don't know about? You never said anything about planning for a family, which I would have appreciated by the way.' Yes, he was tired and he needed some painkillers, and he wasn't feeling at all charitable about anything. Especially not the unexpected pregnancy of his highly valued assistant.

You should be congratulating her. That's what normal people do when they learn someone's expecting a child.

Yes, but he wasn't a normal person. He was a king and even apart from that, the thought of her being pregnant sent a strange kind of electric shock through him. Possessive almost, which couldn't be right. He was possessive of her professionally—he'd never allow anyone to poach her, for example—but that was all. If she'd decided to have a baby with a husband or partner, then who was he to argue?

She shifted minutely on her feet and he noticed that her knuckles were white. She was upset, he realised with another little jolt of shock.

She's human. You do know that, don't you? She has feelings.

Of course he knew that. He just didn't often think of her feelings, because he'd never needed to. She never even betrayed that she had them. But she obviously had feelings about this, and it was not the unalloyed joy he often associated with pregnancy announcements.

'I...didn't plan on getting pregnant,' she said carefully and precisely. 'So this came as somewhat of a surprise.' She hesitated. 'You should know I don't have a husband or partner, sir.'

'Well, I didn't know you were pregnant.' He couldn't quite keep the acid from his voice. 'So forgive me if I somehow missed an important man in your life.'

She blushed for some reason and he experienced another jolt of possessiveness. What other man was there? And there had to have been one, because she wasn't the Virgin Mary. So who was it? Had Augustine met him? But how would he know when she never talked about herself?

You never asked her to talk about herself.

No, of course he hadn't. She was his assistant. He didn't have to get to know her. Her only job was to do what he said, help him run the country, and that was all.

'No,' she murmured. 'There is no important man in my life. It was...an unexpected turn of events.'

'An unexpected turn of events,' he repeated, glancing

once again to her white-knuckled hands. 'You didn't want this, did you?'

A twitch of emotion rippled over her face, though it was gone too fast for him to be able to tell what it was. 'Like I said, I didn't plan it. But I'm going to have the baby.'

Something odd was happening inside him, a strange unsettledness. She was upset about this, he was sure. He couldn't read a line of text, but he *was* good at reading people, and those white knuckles told their own story.

'Were you hurt?' he asked sharply. He liked to think he was a decent employer, but if she'd been hurt...

Her dark eyes widened. 'Oh, no. No. It wasn't anything like that. It was...a one-night thing.'

A one-night thing? The words sat oddly with him. Freddie was precise and ordered in everything she did. She was always prepared. And he imagined that any 'one night thing' she embarked on, she'd take the same approach. Which made an unplanned pregnancy *extremely* unlikely.

'A one-night thing when...what? Your partner somehow forgot the most basic approach to birth control?' He knew as soon as he'd said it, that he was letting his headache and his fatigue speak for him, and that the habit of treating Freddie the way he'd treat himself was deeply ingrained. But he didn't take it back, because somewhere inside of him he was angry. Angry with her.

She flushed even deeper, her spine stiffening, her narrow shoulders going back. 'Sir, would you like some painkillers? You have a headache, I think.'

Augustine narrowed his gaze. Was that a...rebuke?

You deserved that, though.

Yes, he did. But she'd never rebuked him before.

There were high spots of colour on her cheeks, but her expression was still serene. Untouchable.

Except someone had touched her.

A deeper shock hit him. Someone had touched her. Someone had wanted her. Someone had taken her to bed.

'Who was it?' he asked, before he could stop himself. 'Tell me. Who's the lucky man?'

Those spots of colour blazed brighter in her cheeks and her expression was not quite so serene any more. 'I'm sorry, sir, but that's my business.' There was a slight husk in her voice, the sound of it hauntingly familiar. He couldn't think where he'd heard echoes of it before, but he was sure he had.

He shook away the feeling. 'Fair enough. I just find it difficult to believe that a woman as organised as you had sex that resulted in an unplanned pregnancy.' He found himself looking at her hands again. She put them behind her back.

Interesting. She was hiding something, some kind of reaction from him. What was it?

Perhaps she's upset she's having an unplanned pregnancy. Just a wild guess...

Once, a long time ago, Augustine had considered other people's feelings. But after the accident, he'd become selfish. His recovery from the head injury had been compounded by grief at losing the father he'd adored, then losing all the things he'd once been able to do that his father had been so proud of, that would make him a worthy heir and his father's successor. Then had come the realisation that he would never get those things back, that he would never be the heir his father wanted or his country deserved.

After that he hadn't had the time or energy to consider other people's feelings as well, and it hadn't bothered him before. He hadn't let it bother him before. Except knowing he'd considered Freddie's feelings least of all bothered him now.

Her face was pale except for those high spots of colour,

her expression giving nothing away, and another realisation hit him. He didn't know a thing about her. Not a single thing. It had just...never seemed important before. But now... curiosity tugged at him. Perhaps he was going to have to dig a little deeper into this pregnancy business, get some answers.

'Well, whether you believe it or not, I'm still pregnant,' she said. 'Sir, if you would, I need to know if you're going to give me that time off or not.'

'No,' he said automatically. 'Of course I can't give you six months off. That's impossible, Freddie, and you know it.'

'I have a replacement lined up and—'

'No,' he repeated. 'I don't want a replacement and you know very well why.' He picked up his tumbler and downed the rest of his cocktail, pain throbbing in his skull. 'There's no reason you can't continue to work for me while you're pregnant. And if it's other people you're worried about, do not. I'll make sure no awkward questions are asked.'

Her mouth compressed and he found himself staring at its shape. It was a perfect, full rosebud.

Someone had kissed that mouth. Someone had tasted it.

Why are you noticing her mouth?

He couldn't think. He shouldn't be noticing Freddie's mouth or wondering who had kissed her, or feeling that strange possessiveness stalk through him. Or even being curious. It didn't matter that she was pregnant. What did he care? As long as she did her job, that was all that mattered.

It's that night three months ago, that's the problem. You haven't been the same since.

Unbidden, the memory of the night in Al Da'ira slipped through his head, the way it had been doing for the past three months, and often at the most inopportune times.

That night and the unknown woman in his bed. The woman who'd gasped and sighed, and twisted against him.

Whose delicate, musky feminine scent had driven him half out of his mind, and whose hot, silky body he'd spent all night exploring.

He was at a loss to explain why he kept thinking about it. He'd had literally hundreds of similar nights, with similar women and sometimes more than one woman. But none of them ever replayed themselves over and over again the way that night did.

Sometimes he indulged the memory, replaying it for his own erotic amusement and quite frankly for some relief— he'd been busy these past three months and hadn't had either the time or the inclination to avail himself of his usual lovers. They all seemed unexciting to him for some reason.

Whatever, that night had nothing to do with Freddie's situation or Freddie herself, and he really needed to stop thinking about it.

'Sir,' Freddie began.

But Augustine was tired of the conversation. His headache required further dealing with and even the dim lighting of the bar was beginning to get too much. He needed darkness and another cocktail, and to be alone.

'We'll discuss it on the plane tomorrow,' he said curtly, getting off the bar stool and picking up his jacket. 'You're dismissed for the night.'

Then he walked past her and out of the bar.

CHAPTER THREE

WINIFRED STARED AT the spreadsheets on her laptop, the tiredness that had been dogging her all day making them blur in front of her. She'd thought that once the first three months were up, the fatigue would get better, but not today. The comforting drone of the plane's engines only made it worse, and the fact that she'd slept poorly the night before didn't help either.

Her brain had been merciless, the scenes with Augustine down in the bar replaying themselves over and over in her head.

She'd thought telling him about her pregnancy would make things easier, would make him less likely to ask awkward questions but it hadn't. In fact, it had been the opposite. She'd stood there, trying not to quail as his relentlessly sharp blue gaze focused on her. He'd never looked at her like that before, not once, and she wasn't used to it, and especially not with the most recent lie burning on her tongue.

She had no idea why he was suddenly so interested in all the ins and outs of the pregnancy—shock, possibly. And no doubt he was concerned about how it would work with her not being around.

She'd been prepared for his anger, but not for all the questions about when and who and how, the answers to which she hadn't given any thought to because she hadn't expected him to be interested.

He *had* been angry, though. She'd seen it flicker in his eyes, heard the edge of it in his voice. Perhaps that's why she'd got all those questions. Because he'd been tired and had a headache and her pregnancy was going to disrupt the smooth running of his rule.

Winifred closed her eyes and rubbed her forehead, the fatigue deepening.

She should have lied more about the 'important man in her life', inventing a boyfriend or even a husband, and how this pregnancy had been completely planned. Augustine might not have been so curious if she had. Except she just hadn't been able to face piling yet more lies onto to the already fragile edifice she'd constructed so far.

Especially not when the child is his.

That had been the real issue though, hadn't it? Standing in front of the man who'd given her the most incredible night of her life as well as the child she now carried, and he didn't even know it. The man she loved, whom she'd had to lie to about all of it, because the truth would bring everything down.

You should have told him right at the beginning.

She leaned back in her seat, her hand going to the curve of her stomach, cradling the small life that was growing inside it.

Children weren't supposed to be part of her future either. They couldn't be, not after how she'd taken that gun and used it in defence of Annie, her sister. She was dangerous when she loved someone. She'd go to any lengths, do anything...

Even kill.

Her throat closed. No, she couldn't think about that. All that mattered was that her child be safe, and they wouldn't be safe with her.

She should have told Augustine, of course she should. But she'd wanted to protect him as much as she wanted to protect their child. He struggled so much day to day, and a child would only add to that burden. She didn't doubt that he'd take responsibility if he knew about the child, and that he'd try his best to be a good father. But she didn't want him to have to try and she didn't want their child to be just another thing he had to deal with.

Giving up her baby wasn't what she wanted, but she had to do what was best for all of them. Even if it hurt.

Anyway, it wouldn't be the first time she'd had to give up something she loved. When she'd run away in the aftermath of Aaron's death, she'd taken her sisters with her because she couldn't bear to leave them in her mother's care, prey for yet another of her mother's disgusting boyfriends. But she'd only been sixteen and had no money, and with them being too young to be left on their own, she hadn't been able to look after them.

She'd had to give them up to social services and while it had ripped her heart out to do it, she knew they'd be better off in a foster family than they would be with her.

'Freddie, we need to have a discussion,' a deep, male voice said from somewhere far too close.

She shook off the memories and opened her eyes to find Augustine already sitting down in the leather seat opposite her, stretching his long, powerful legs out in front of him and crossing them at the ankle. He put his elbows on the arms of the seat and interlaced his fingers, fixing that turquoise gaze of his on her.

She hadn't seen him since they'd boarded that morning in Singapore and taken off. She'd had far too much work to do while he'd been on the phone, talking to some of his advisors. She'd been glad. She knew they needed to talk, but she hadn't felt like she could face him quite yet. However, it seemed as if her brief reprieve was now over.

He looked less tired today and it was clear his headache had gone, so that was something at least.

'Of course, sir.' She sat up, pushing her laptop closed.

His dark brows twitched, his gaze assessing. 'You look tired.'

A little shock ran down her spine. He never noticed whether she was tired or otherwise, and he definitely never made any observations about how she looked. That was new. She wasn't quite sure how to deal with it.

'I'm fine,' she said at last. 'Just didn't sleep well last night.'

He frowned. 'Do you have a doctor? A midwife?'

'Yes.'

'And when the baby is born, what then? Am I right in assuming you'll be coming back to work?'

Something twisted inside her chest, a kind of ache. She didn't want to tell him that she was giving the baby up for adoption. She didn't want to have to explain her reasons for doing so either. That would mean uncovering deeper truths, the extent to which she'd lied to him. She couldn't bear that. The shame would suffocate her.

'Yes, I'll be coming back to work,' she said carefully.

'But what about childcare? Have you got something in place for when you return?'

So many questions. Why was he asking them? He'd never been interested in anything to do with her before, so why now?

'Of course I do.' There was an edge in her voice she couldn't quite mask. 'The baby won't impact my job, sir. If that's what you're worried about.' She took a silent, steadying breath, trying to hold on to her patience. 'Do you have any other questions?'

His gaze had narrowed still further and he looked...focused. As if yes, he had many more questions. As if she was a puzzle he was trying to work out.

'Who is the father?'

Another shock rippled through her. 'Excuse me?'

'I think you heard.' He tilted his head, examining her. 'I'm asking you who the father of your child is.'

Perhaps it was the fatigue or perhaps it was the pregnancy hormones, but before she could think better of it—and she always thought better of it usually—her patience cracked and she snapped, 'That's none of your business.'

His eyes widened in surprise. Because of course she never talked back to him, never raised her voice, never showed him anything but calm. Initially it was because she hadn't wanted to lose her job and she hadn't wanted to give him any cause for complaint. Then it became something more. She wanted to be a soothing presence in his life, someone who would always be on his side, whom he never needed to fight.

Except she was giving him a fight now.

It was the shock affecting her and all these lies piling on top of one another. So many lies, about everything. The only truth she'd been able to give him had been the fact that she was pregnant, and now it was looking like that had been yet another mistake.

You keep making them.

When it came to him, she did. Falling in love with him had been the worst thing she could have done, yet she'd done it anyway, because she was a fool. Because the past five years of safety had made her forget the lengths a person went to for love. Lengths she'd gone to.

'It's very much my business,' Augustine said, his momentary surprise the only sign he'd even noticed her tone. 'You're my employee and I need to know if the father of your child will be arriving at some point and whether you might change your mind about working for me.'

Winifred clasped her hands in her lap, holding them very

tightly. She didn't want to answer these questions. She didn't want him looking at her as if she was a puzzle. He'd never asked her any questions about herself before, not one. Not even when she'd come down with the flu last year. He'd merely sent her a doctor and told her not to return to work until she was well.

She'd returned to work before then, of course, because he'd needed her, yet he hadn't asked her how she was feeling. He'd simply accepted her presence and handed her the latest batch of reports to read.

She didn't understand why he was so interested now. It didn't make any sense.

Perhaps he suspects it was you he slept with after all?

If he did suspect that then he would have said, and he hadn't. He'd never given even the slightest sign he suspected anything. In fact, he'd probably forgotten all about that night.

Winifred held on tight to her patience. Letting her emotions get the better of her was a foolish thing to do—it might even prompt *more* questions. Better to stay in control, to remain cool and calm the way she always did.

'I told you,' she said. 'It was a one-night affair. He won't be arriving anywhere let alone Isavere. If you don't mind, sir, I have a spreadsheet I have to—'

'He must have been quite something,' Augustine interrupted, as if she hadn't spoken, his gaze merciless. 'Tell me, was it good?'

Heat flared inside her, and she could feel her cheeks burning. Yes, it *had* been good. She'd forgotten everything. Even where she was. Even who she was. And now, here he was, forcing her to relive it for reasons she couldn't even begin to guess at. How dare he?

Anger stirred and before she could think better of it, she said, 'What kind of question is that? But yes, as it happens, it *was* good. And he *was* something. In fact, he was the best night of my life. Would you like a diagram perhaps? An in-depth report on everything we did together? Sadly we didn't take a video, but if we had one, I'd gladly play it for you.'

If her tone bothered him, Augustine didn't show it. He simply stared at her a moment more, then shifted, drawing his legs in, leaning forward and putting his elbows on his knees. 'You trusted him,' he said.

Yet more shock jolted her. She stared back, abruptly struggling to catch her breath, the simple statement driving all the air from her lungs.

'You trusted him,' Augustine repeated as if she hadn't heard him. 'And if you trusted him, you knew him.'

Something shook inside her, the fear she'd finally let go of as more time had passed between that night and the present. The fear that he'd recognise her. The fear that had returned full force when she realised she was pregnant.

If he discovered that he was the father of her baby...

Perhaps it wouldn't be so bad. Perhaps he'll claim the child for himself, and you wouldn't have to give him or her up for adoption.

Perhaps. Her child was a prince or princess after all, the heir to the throne, and she knew how he felt about his kingdom. It was important to him. Maintaining the legacy his father had left was important to him.

Yet...he'd been so certain he didn't want children that he'd had a vasectomy. His life was difficult and she had a ringside seat as to just how difficult. Also, if she told him she was pregnant, he'd have to contend with the fact that they'd slept together. That he hadn't known who she was and then that she hadn't told him. He might not actually fire her, but he wouldn't want her being his assistant again.

Everything would change. Everything.

The only thing that matters is that your baby is loved. And is brought up far away from you.

Winifred felt tears prickle in her eyes, which was unacceptable. She didn't deserve to indulge herself like this. She had to be practical. Giving her baby up was the only way.

Blinking back the tears fiercely, she leaned forward, opening up her laptop again. 'I have work to do, sir,' she said. 'If you want these spreadsheets done on time, you need to let me do them.'

There was a long moment of silence.

Abruptly she heard him move, pushing himself out of the chair and getting to his feet. She expected him to return to his position at the back of the plane, but he didn't. Instead, one large, long-fingered hand gently but surely pushed her laptop closed again.

She looked up at him in surprise.

The expression on his beautiful face was hard to read as was the look in his eyes. 'You're tired,' he said quietly. 'And I have upset you.'

Yet more shock rippled through her. 'What? No, I—'

'The spreadsheets can wait while you rest and catch up on some sleep.' He lifted his hand, at his most commanding. 'Come, Freddie. I won't be using the bedroom on the flight so you might as well.'

She had seen him in all his moods and she knew them all well. When he was angry, or tired, or in pain. When he was satisfied. When he was pleased. Happiness was something he didn't seem to feel and that grieved her, and really, that was at the heart of why she didn't let his occasional snappishness and impatience get to her. The moments where he struggled with the effects of his brain injury. He could be difficult, yet he always apologised afterwards when he was, and really, she only wanted to make him happy.

But she couldn't tell what his mood was now, because when he was being the King, he hid everything. And he was definitely being the King now, every inch of him royal.

She couldn't resist him—no one could—and so she found herself taking his hand and letting him draw her to her feet.

A mistake.

He didn't touch her. Ever. So she wasn't prepared for the electricity that crackled over her skin as their fingers touched and she had to bite down on a gasp to hide it. He betrayed no reaction, though she thought she saw something flicker through his gaze. It was gone the next minute however, as his hand opened and he let her go almost as soon as she was on her feet.

'The spreadsheets,' she began, wanting to say something to cover her own awkwardness at the moment.

'I don't need them right now.' He gestured to the aisle that led down the back of the plane. 'You need some rest, so please go and take some.'

Her mouth opened to protest.

'That's an order,' he said before she could get the words out. 'Go now, please.'

She didn't really want to argue, because he was right, she *was* tired. And he said please, which he almost never did. Plus she didn't particularly want to prolong this conversation so she only closed her mouth, nodded, and went.

Augustine watched her go, an unfamiliar restlessness coiling through him. He could still feel the light, cool pressure of her fingertips in his, as well as the unexpected jolt of electricity that had hit him as soon as he'd touched her.

He'd hidden his reaction almost instantly but he hadn't missed the flare in her dark eyes in response.

He knew what that electricity was. He knew it very well.

Physical chemistry.

He moved down the aisle until he was back in the lounge area of the plane, and flung himself down on one of the comfortable white leather seats. Through another doorway he could see the plane's bedroom door, now shut.

A stewardess approached him, smiling, but he waved her away.

The restlessness wouldn't leave him alone, his brain going ninety miles an hour. Freddie hadn't been the only one who hadn't been able to sleep the night before. While his headache had dissipated in the darkness of the hotel room and the fatigue hadn't yet dug its claws in, his brain had raced, going over and over Freddie's little announcement.

As a child, he'd always loved puzzles and there was one in particular his father made up for him, one with numbers, and he'd loved it. The puzzle started off easy, drawing him in, only to get more difficult making each solution hard won yet triumphant. Sometimes it would take him days to solve, especially when it came to solving the last problem. He'd examine it from every angle, unable to leave it alone, coming back to it again and again. And every time, he'd solve it. His father had always been particularly proud of him for that. Perhaps his mother might have been too, but she'd died a year after he was born, killed by the cancer she refused to get treatment for because she was pregnant with him, and he'd never known her.

Of course, these days he couldn't do puzzles like that, but still. He couldn't stop thinking of the puzzle that was Freddie. Freddie, who'd never been puzzling before in any way.

Freddie, whom he'd never felt any electricity from before either. And yet…that crackle had been unmistakable.

Why now, though? He'd never touched her before, it was true, so there had never been any opportunity to find out.

But he generally knew straightaway if he had chemistry with a woman. It didn't usually take him five years to be aware of it.

Was it the fact of her pregnancy? That got him thinking about who'd been touching her and when and why. That had got him feeling...territorial about her almost. Possessive, even. He couldn't think why he felt that, though, since she wasn't leaving him to work with someone else. In fact, as she'd said, she was intending to come back.

Not that he'd do anything about it, even so. He had few boundaries, but those he maintained with his staff were strict ones.

Leaning back in the chair, he shut the blinds on the window next to him to stop the sun's glare from getting in his eyes. Then he stared straight ahead of him, turning things over in his head.

His questioning of her earlier had upset her and yes, he knew his questions were intrusive. It really was none of his business who'd fathered her child. Yet he hadn't been able to stop himself from pushing her about it.

The man had to have been someone she trusted, because he didn't think she would have had sex with a stranger.

When he'd mentioned that, he'd seen something flicker across her face. A face that had grown pale and then flushed with what he thought had been anger. That had fascinated him. First that she'd let her usual self-possession slip enough to reveal what she was feeling, and secondly that he'd managed to provoke her to anger at all. Sometimes she'd seemed so impervious to him that every so often he caught himself wanting to ruffle her. Startle her.

Everyone else found him so very affecting so why not her?

Of course, he couldn't do that. That would cross that boundary he'd drawn and again, he didn't cross those boundaries.

Still…

It was true that sometimes protection didn't work and there was a failure rate. Maybe that had happened.

Predictably, his thoughts turned to that night again, and how he'd reached for the condoms in the bedside table. He'd come close to forgetting about protection himself, and he still couldn't believe he had. But the doctor had been very clear that there was a vasectomy failure rate in the first three months, so he had to be careful.

As usual, the mere thought of that night made his body wake into full, aching life. Making him shift irritably in his seat.

He needed to get himself a lover. Wipe the memory from his brain once and for all. Sex always relaxed him, eased some of the tension from his muscles and that helped him sleep. He couldn't think why he hadn't found a woman sooner, but he hadn't.

It was only that there had been something about the mystery woman that had got to him on a fundamental level. She'd responded to him so honestly, so passionately. She hadn't hidden how much she'd wanted him. Hadn't been self-conscious the way some women were, too busy worrying about how they looked or the sounds they made. No, it was as if she hadn't cared about any of that, giving herself so utterly to him and to the pleasure they created between them that all self-consciousness had fallen away. There had only been him. Only them. Together.

They'd been so in sync with each other it was almost as if they knew each other. She definitely knew who he was, and maybe… maybe he'd known who she was too, deep down in some distant part of him.

But who she could be, he still had no idea.

What would you do even if you did know who she was?

Oh, if he knew, he'd track her down. Find her and get her to agree to another night, that was indisputable. He'd enjoy another night with her, he'd enjoy it very much.

Eventually, after another fifteen minutes of staring pointlessly into the distance, he decided that flogging his brain about the puzzle of his PA wasn't a good use of his time or energy, so he got out his phone and made the calls he had to make.

He couldn't read, so emails or texts were out, he had to talk to people instead, but luckily that was one of his strengths and so he was able to use the time profitably. It took time to manoeuvre a change of king.

What he was planning wasn't something he'd ever told anyone explicitly, but it was something that had to be done nonetheless.

He couldn't be the king his father had wanted him to be, not after the accident, and so he'd decided, years ago, that the only decent thing to do was to hand the crown to someone who could.

That someone was his cousin, Philippe. He'd had to wait until Philippe was of age, but he'd turned twenty-one a month ago and so now it was time to begin the preparations he'd laid in place years earlier. He hadn't told Philippe himself yet, but he needed to. The boy was at Oxford, reading law, and no doubt he'd need some time to adjust, so Augustine needed to tell him and soon.

Philippe was doing well, getting good marks, and he'd make a fine king. A better king than Augustine, that was for certain.

Philippe at least could read his own emails.

Philippe at least could read, full stop.

Augustine spent a couple of hours dealing with calls and then tried to rest on one of the couches in the lounge area.

He knew he'd suffer for it later if he didn't. But his rest was disturbed and full of dreams that made him ache with a longing he couldn't articulate, and he woke a few hours after that, feeling as if he hadn't rested at all.

It didn't matter. They'd be arriving in Isavere very soon and since it looked as if Freddie hadn't emerged yet, he was going to need to go in and wake her.

Getting someone else to wake her didn't occur to him. He simply went to the door of the bedroom and opened it, stepping inside.

She was curled up in the very centre of the bed, still in her clothes, and for some reason he found himself shocked by how that stretchy black skirt she wore had hiked up to midthigh, and that her white shirt had become untucked. She was normally so put together that the untidiness of her clothes was even more arresting than it would have been with someone else.

It was intimate somehow, watching someone sleep. They were vulnerable and unguarded in a way they never were while awake. Not that he was in the habit of watching a woman sleep, yet in this moment he was oddly fascinated.

She was less his perfect PA now, the mere extension of his will that he noticed no more than he'd notice a shoe he put on, and more...a woman.

He came around the side of the bed, staring down at her, unable to help himself. Transfixed by where her shirt had come untucked, revealing the smooth olive skin of her hip and the curve of her stomach, already getting round with the new life growing inside her.

A couple of buttons on the shirt had also come undone, giving him a glimpse of the shadowed valley between her breasts.

Her dark hair, usually so smooth, was slipping out of her

neat bun and unfurling across the pillows. He'd had no idea it was so long, or so glossy. Or so...silky-looking.

His gaze dropped to her face. It was peaceful and still in sleep, her lashes long and dark and silky as her hair, resting on her cheeks.

An interesting face, he realised with a certain deep surprise. Not pretty maybe, but...arresting. Straight, dark brows. A wonderfully proud nose. A mouth that was the perfect rosebud. A mouth made for—

No. No, that was not where his thoughts should be heading. Not about her. She worked for him. She was totally off-limits.

He sat down carefully on the side of the bed, putting a leash on his recalcitrant thoughts. All he was going to do was wake her. That's all. Staring down at her, studying her like this was a gross invasion of her privacy, and he should stop.

Yet...

Her body was warm and he could smell the sweet scent of her skin.

She made a little sound as the mattress dipped under him, like a sigh, and for some reason that sound felt as if it had nailed him to the floor.

He knew it. He'd heard it before.

He stared at her, his heartbeat accelerating, and obeying without question an instinct that gripped him by the throat and wouldn't let go, he leaned down so his mouth was almost brushing the exposed skin of her neck, just below her ear. He didn't kiss her, he inhaled instead, and that scent hit him like a gut punch.

Sweet. Feminine. Musky.

He knew that scent. He *knew* it.

But he had to be certain, so he closed the distance, his

lips brushing over her skin. And she made that sound again, deeper and husky. A sound of pleasure.

The knowledge hit him like a bullet, and he couldn't move, staring at the woman lying on the bed.

It was her. The woman he'd spent the night with three months ago.

It was his Freddie.

Then hard on its heels, came another bullet, hitting him equally hard.

His gaze slid down to the soft curve of her stomach.

He must have been something, he'd said to her.

He was... she'd replied. *In fact, he was the best night of my life.*

If she had been the woman in his bed that night, then the child she carried was his.

Augustine stared at her for one long minute and then it hit him, a surge of desire so intense he couldn't breathe.

The room careened around him, adrenaline pouring through his bloodstream, making him feel dizzy. Increasing the sudden and intense pressure in his head.

He wanted to turn her over onto her back, bury his face in her neck and the hard length of his sex between her thighs. He wanted to taste her, make her scream. Find again the erotic connection they'd forged that night in his room.

But he couldn't.

Because this was Freddie.

Freddie who was now pregnant with his child.

And who hadn't told him. Not one word.

Abruptly, Augustine got to his feet and got himself out of there before he lost his goddamn mind.

CHAPTER FOUR

WINIFRED WOKE FROM the loveliest dream. She'd been with him again, his breath against her neck, his warmth so close. He'd been about to kiss her, she just knew it. About to put his arms around her and draw her to him, and she wanted it more than she wanted her next breath.

Except then her eyes had opened and she'd realised she actually wasn't in bed with him, but in the bedroom of the jet and that she was alone.

Her heart was still beating fast, electric shivers crackling over her skin.

Augustine.

She let out a shaken breath and closed her eyes, trying to pull herself together. Having one of *those* dreams about him while in his bedroom on the jet was a stupid thing to do. Especially given the grilling he'd put her through just before. She had to be better than that. She had to not let him get under her skin so easily.

Slowly, she eased herself off the bed and went into the tiny bathroom to freshen up. She smoothed the wrinkles from her clothes, put her hair back into its bun, put on her shoes, opened the door and stepped out into the lounge area.

Augustine was sitting on one of the couches, talking on his phone. He didn't look at her as she came out, obviously engrossed in his conversation, so she headed past him and into her usual work area.

She'd slept for longer than she'd thought and there was only an hour until they landed in Isavere, so she busied herself with work.

Augustine didn't bother her and he was still on the phone every time she time she tried to approach him to discuss something, waving her away with a peremptory gesture.

It was annoying. There were a couple of things she needed to speak to him about, not the least being what maternity leave she'd be given. Then again, she'd have a chance later, after they landed. Usually after a trip there would be a whole lot of communication she'd have to go through with him, so she could ask him then.

The plane came in to land on the royal airstrip, and Winifred sat in her seat, staring out the window, because she loved the approach to the palace. The palace and the airstrip were set high in the mountains, and it was a narrow flight path, making it seem as if the sharp white-capped peaks of the mountains were just inches from the plane's wings. Isavere was so different from the LA desert she'd grown up in and she loved living here. Another reason, as if she needed another, why she had to keep this job. She couldn't bear the thought of leaving this country she'd come to love.

Ten minutes later, the plane landed and Winifred gathered up her things. Augustine strode past her to the doorway and went out without a second glance, leaving her to stumble along in his wake.

Out on the tarmac, he ignored the various palace officials that had come to greet them, heading straight to the car that would ferry them back to the palace. He didn't wait for her, the car pulling away as soon as he got in, leaving her standing on the tarmac gaping after him.

Sometimes he'd do this, ignore her as if she didn't exist, especially if he was absorbed in something. Normally it didn't bother her—that was just Augustine. But after the way he'd looked at her on the plane, so sharp and focused, and then the dream she'd had, his dismissal felt oddly painful.

She always rode with him. Always.

She shook away the sensation, because really, she was only his PA and had no claim on his attention, and when he came back from a trip, there was always a lot of work to do. He was probably dealing with that and had forgotten about her. Which was fine. It had nothing to do with *her* in particular.

She joined the other palace officials in a second car, arriving at the turreted stone castle that was the seat of the Kings and Queens of Isavere.

It was a literal fairy-tale castle, with ivy climbing up the ancient stone walls and flags fluttering from the turrets, the golden oak of Isavere already flying to indicate the King was back in residence.

She always got a thrill when she arrived back at the palace. That she, oldest daughter of Cassie-Lynne Jones, petty drug dealer, brought up in a run-down trailer park in the desert, should live in this gorgeous fairy-tale castle and be a PA to the ruler of an ancient and fabulously rich European country.

Sometimes it felt like a dream and she had to pinch herself to make sure it was real.

No need to pinch yourself. Just remember what you did to get here.

Winifred ignored the thought and the icy thread of guilt and shame that came along with it. As if she'd ever forget all the lies she'd had to tell to get this job and the constant pretence of trying to be someone she wasn't.

Not that she had to pretend these days. Ellie Jones with her hard American r's was long gone. Now she was Winifred Scott—all poise and a cut-glass English accent—so completely she never thought of herself as Ellie at all.

Her apartments were in the royal wing, a small, but neat set of rooms not far from the royal apartments themselves. She loved them. It was still a thrill to have not just her own bedroom, but a little lounge/receiving room and a bathroom, all nicely appointed. She'd once thought the rooms almost indecently lavish, but after the years spent in Augustine's orbit, her ideas on what constituted 'lavish' had changed.

Now she knew that her apartments weren't particularly lavish at all, but she didn't care. The run-down trailer she'd grown up in had no privacy, not with her mom and two sisters, so even having her own bed was a luxury.

Her rooms were tidy and cosy, and she'd added little personal touches over the years that made it feel even more like home. A small rug in front of the fire. A few bright silk cushions on the plain blue sofa. A beautifully finished wooden bookcase from a local wood turner in the corner, full of her favourite books, plus souvenirs from the trips she went on with Augustine: snow globes and glass figurines and little dolls and sculptures. Treasures she'd collected that she looked at often to remind herself of how far she'd come.

You killed a man, you gave up your sisters, and now you're giving up your child. What makes you think you deserve any of this?

The thought was an icy one and Winifred shoved it away, requesting some tea be brought up and once she was ensconced in her rooms, she unpacked then sat in her little living room with her tea, going through Augustine's schedule for the next day. No doubt he'd want to talk to her about it immediately.

Yet there was no summons as the minutes passed, and

soon hours had gone by and Augustine still hadn't requested her presence.

It was odd and unlike him. Perhaps he was tired—he was often fatigued after a long journey—and maybe she wouldn't be needed tonight. Still, he normally told her if that was the case. This silence wasn't usual.

After another hour had passed, she called him, but there was no reply.

Puzzled, she then called one of the palace staff in charge of his apartments and asked him if the king needed her this evening. No, the man said. The king didn't.

And a little kernel of ice settled inside her.

Something is wrong.

No, it was nothing. Augustine was tired, that's all it was. He'd ask for her tomorrow, no doubt.

She didn't sleep well that night, though that was probably to do with the fact that she'd slept on the plane too. Nothing more. It certainly had nothing to do with her brain going over and over why he might not have called for her to go over his schedule and what he might do about her pregnancy.

Nothing to do with that at all.

The next morning she woke feeling groggy, as if she hadn't slept, but she had a shower and dressed, and had her breakfast in her room the way she always did.

Then she went to her desk in Augustine's office as was customary, to have a debrief with him about the day, but the big airy room with the stained-glass window behind his desk was empty.

Her desk was down the other end of the room, near the bookcases, and she sat there for a good ten minutes wondering where on earth he was, because he was normally very punctual. And she was starting to get a little worried, until another staff member arrived to tell her that the king was in the stables, and he would meet with her at 10:00 a.m. sharp.

Winifred nodded, then frowned at her computer screen after the staff member had gone.

Augustine loved horses and he spent a lot of time in the stables. He said it was calming. Horses didn't require anything of him but a rub down and some hay, the odd pat on the nose and an apple or two. They were undemanding company and they didn't stand on ceremony, or so he said.

But he'd never asked her to meet at the stables. It wasn't where they usually worked together, and anyway, he always preferred to visit the horses alone. She wasn't sure why he wanted to meet there now. Though really, it didn't matter where he wanted to meet her. She went wherever he requested and if he wanted to meet her at the stables, that's where she'd go.

They weren't far from the castle itself, down through the long, beautiful set of terraced gardens that led into rolling fields and the royal wood where generations of the Isaveran kings and queens had gone hunting. There was no hunting now; the wood had been left to regenerate.

The stables were a set of long wooden buildings and Winifred walked briskly along the path beside them, wondering where on earth Augustine could be. Though she could guess. He'd be with one of his favourites, a spirited mare called Honey.

She stepped inside the stables and approached Honey's stall, and sure enough, Augustine was there, grooming her glossy chestnut coat with long, practised strokes.

He wasn't in his usual suit today, but worn jeans that sat low on his hips and a simple black T-shirt that clung to his muscled shoulders, arms and chest.

Her mouth went dry and she had to look away, every

part of her so physically aware of him it was almost painful. Lord, it was ridiculous. She'd seen him in casual clothes before and hadn't had this reaction.

Maybe it's the small fact that you're in love with him?

Yes, but she'd been in love with him for years and hadn't felt quite this strongly…physical about him. It was that night with him that was the problem. Something had flicked on inside her, making her responses to him even more intense. Nothing else could explain it.

'Sir?' she said after a moment. 'I'm here.'

He didn't turn, not immediately, but there was something taut about his posture that set her on high alert.

After a moment, he put down the curry comb, gave the mare's nose a long stroke, then dug into the pocket of his jeans and brought out an apple. He held it in his palm and presented it to the mare whose soft mouth closed around it, crunching as she ate.

Augustine still didn't turn. 'Come, Freddie,' he said. 'We'll talk outside.'

She tensed. There was a note in his voice that made her catch her breath. She knew him; she knew him better than she knew herself and she couldn't shake the feeling that something was wrong.

Her heartbeat hammering, she followed him outside and over to where a wooden seat sat beneath a shady oak. His face was absolutely impassive, his blue-green eyes betraying nothing at all as he gestured to her to sit.

'No, thank you,' she said, her voice hoarse. A feeling of trepidation had collected inside her and sitting was the last thing she felt like doing. 'What is it, sir?'

He was staring at her, his gaze scalpel sharp.

Her heartbeat grew even louder, her mouth dry as the desert that had surrounded her family's trailer.

He knows the baby is his.

No, that was impossible. He hadn't known it was her that night. He couldn't have, because he'd never said anything to her about it.

Slowly Augustine folded his arms, his gaze pinning her to the spot.

'So, just out of interest,' he said. 'When were you going to tell me your baby is mine?'

He watched the colour drain from her face, her eyes going even wider, the dark velvet of her irises deepening into black, almost becoming one with her pupils. And he felt something catch hard inside him in response.

She didn't need to say anything. The truth was written all over her face.

That night in Al Da'ira, that night with that passionate, silky little woman, the woman he'd lost his mind with, that woman was her.

And she hadn't told him. She hadn't said a word.

He could feel it now, the surge of hot desire already building inside him, Remembering that night and the feel of her around him, holding him tight, the taste of her mouth and her skin and her sex. The way she'd put her arms around him, the sounds she'd made…

Didn't some part of you know? Didn't some part of you realise who she was?

Perhaps he had. Perhaps all this time some part of him had wanted her. Yet that didn't explain the rush of intense desire as he stared at her. He'd never felt it before, not with her.

Maybe you did and you ignored it.

Did he? He couldn't remember. His memory was as shot full of holes as the rest of his faculties. She had always been just… Freddie. As ubiquitous in his life as a favourite chair, or a picture he passed by every day, noting its presence, but never really looking at it.

She just was and he never thought about her.

Except…she wasn't just Freddie any more. She was the woman he'd had that unspeakably erotic night with in Al Da'ira, and he was at a loss to explain his reaction to her. Was it because she was forbidden? Was that what it was? Or did it have something to do with her pregnancy?

The thoughts had gone around and around in his head the day before, and he hadn't been able to come to any conclusions. For hours he'd simply been incandescently angry. Firstly at himself for not realising it had been her to start off with and then at her for not saying anything. There were so many questions, and he knew that he was going to have to confront her, but he'd been too furious.

He had to be careful with his emotions. He couldn't afford to indulge in anger, for example, because his control wasn't as good as it once had been, and he didn't want to hurt her by saying something he didn't mean in the heat of the moment.

So he'd waited until today, when he was calmer.

Of course, sleeping poorly the night before hadn't helped, but a few hours in the stables with the horses had. Their undemanding presence had soothed the jagged edges of his emotions and now he could face her. Face her and discuss the things that needed to be discussed because there were decisions to be made.

She was wearing that same cheap black stretchy skirt that she'd worn the day before, since she obviously hadn't bought herself any maternity clothes, and one of her plain blouses—a pale blue one this morning.

Her dark brown hair was pulled back in its usual tidy bun, and there wasn't anything else about her that was different to any other day.

Yet everything—*everything*—had changed.

The pulse at the base of her throat was beating very fast, and he couldn't stop looking at it. He'd put his mouth right there and tasted it. As he'd tasted the shadowed valley where her blouse gaped slightly, revealing the full curves of her breasts. He'd tasted those too and the heat between her thighs. He'd made her scream, hoarse ragged cries of ecstasy...

And there, right there, is the consequence.

The gentle swell of her stomach, where her child lay.

No. *His* child. *Their* child.

There was a pressure in his head, the start of a headache pressing down, and the glare of the sun didn't help. Neither did the hot simmer of anger in his gut that combined with the raw pull of desire into something vicious and aching.

He gripped tight to his control, refusing the tug of his emotions. He could be cruel when he let himself have free rein, and she didn't deserve that, no matter what she'd done.

Her mouth opened, but nothing came out, shock evident in every line of her.

'Well?' he demanded, all of this rubbing him raw in every conceivable way, fraying the grip he had on his anger. 'When were you going to tell me, Freddie? At what point were you going to inform me that I was going to be a father? Were you even going to tell me at all? Presumably since you're now visibly pregnant, you decided to keep it, so what then? Were you going to have my child in some secret little hospital and then discretely get rid of it? Sell it, perhaps, on the dark web? Or were you going to be a single mother, have my child running around in the palace never knowing he or she was the heir to the throne?' His anger twisted inside him, dark and toxic, yet no matter how hard he tried to claw back his control over it, the words kept on coming out. 'Did you think it was funny, perhaps? That the King of Isavere didn't know he had a child? Did you laugh when you realised that I didn't know who you were that night? Did it amuse you the next morning? Or did you know that I wouldn't remember, perhaps? Did you think you could blackmail me even? Use the child against me to—'

'*No!*' The word was hoarse and full of anguish. She was shaking, her hands at her sides. 'No. None of those things are true. None of them.'

Some lost, forgotten part of him tightened at the raw note in her voice and the pallor of her skin, at the dark circles under her eyes. She clearly hadn't slept either.

She's pregnant with your child and she's exhausted, and you're shouting at her. Get a grip.

He tried to corral his recalcitrant emotions, get a leash on the anger that burned inside him. Yet it was difficult. He didn't want to feel sorry for her. He didn't. She'd lied to him, no matter that it had been a lie of omission. She'd known about this for months and hadn't told him, and despite all his good intentions, he was furious about it.

'Explain,' he snapped, unable to keep the sharpness from his voice. 'Explain to me why you didn't tell me it was you that night. Or then inform me that I was the father of your child.'

She was still trembling, her hands now clasping themselves in front of her. She looked as if she was trying to hold herself together to keep from flying apart, and beneath the hot churn of anger, protectiveness stirred.

But he didn't move. He was on a knife edge already and her explanation for this whole farce of a situation might send him over at any minute.

'I didn't know I was in your bed,' she said desperately. 'It was late and I was…tired after the flight, and the palace hallways all looked the same. I thought I was in mine. And then you…touched me. And I—I…'

'You what?'

'I heard you speak.' Her voice was ragged. 'And I knew I was in the wrong place, and I knew it was you, and I...' She took a breath, the colour returning to her cheeks. Her chin lifted a little. 'I wanted you.'

A shock went through him, as if she'd laid a live wire against his skin. She'd never betrayed a hint of that before. 'What do you mean you wanted me?'

She flushed a deeper pink. 'I was attracted to you. And your reputation—'

'Ah, you wanted to see if my reputation was deserved, is that it?' A bitter edge had crept into the words, an edge he couldn't stop. And he wasn't even sure why. There had been an honesty between them that night, an intensity he couldn't put into words, as if they'd stripped away more than just their clothes. It had felt real to him, more real than any other sexual encounter had ever been and yet... All she'd wanted was to test his reputation?

Why does it matter? She is nothing to you.

And yet that night had meant something to him.

Her gaze flickered. 'Yes,' she said.

But she was lying. That was *not* why she'd stayed in his bed that night, no matter what she said.

He was *something,* she'd said to him on the plane when he'd asked. *In fact, he was the best night of my life.*

She hadn't been lying then. *You trusted him,* he'd responded. And she hadn't denied it.

The toxic mess of anger and desire inside him swirled, another feeling winding through it: satisfaction.

'So, why didn't you say anything to me?'

She gave him a slightly defiant look. 'Because I thought you might stop and I didn't want you to.'

And he hadn't stopped. Maybe he wouldn't have even if he'd known who she was, because it had been *that* good.

'What about in the morning? You didn't say anything then.'

'I was going to. I thought you'd know me.' Her eyes were so very dark, even in the sunlight. 'But you said nothing and it was clear that you hadn't realised it was me. I…didn't know what you'd say if I told you and I was…afraid that it would affect my job. I thought you might dismiss me.'

A fair thing to be afraid of. What would he have done? Not that it mattered. She hadn't told him and so he hadn't realised.

How could you not know it was her?

Easily. He'd never thought of her that way, never looked at her that way. She was part of the wallpaper of his life. Mere background noise.

The sun was flickering, the glare making his head throb. He'd been wrong to think he could have this conversation and be completely in control, that none of this would touch him. He was emotionally unstable at the best of times and this was not the best of times.

Still, they were in it now. He had no choice but to keep going.

'And when you found out you were pregnant?' he asked. 'Why didn't you tell me then?'

All the colour in her face had vanished again and she looked down at the ground. Her jaw was tight, the tension in her posture becoming even more pronounced. 'You didn't want children. And I didn't want to make things difficult for you. So I decided to handle it myself.'

That made a certain kind of sense. Her entire job was about making his life easier. And her having his child was the opposite of making his life easier.

No wonder she didn't tell you.

Except all the reasoning in the world didn't change the intensity of his fury. No, he'd never wanted children and he had good reasons for that, but to be cut out of the decision-making process entirely incensed him.

'And how exactly were you going to "handle it" your-self?' he said acidly. 'Please explain to me how this mirac-ulous handling was going to occur.'

She didn't respond straightaway, her gaze firmly on the green grass at her feet. He could feel the distress pouring off her.

Then abruptly she lifted her head and said, 'I'm not feel-ing very well. Excuse me, sir.' And she went to walk past him.

But he'd put out a hand and grabbed her arm before he knew what he was doing, stopping her in her tracks.

She didn't turn, staring fixedly ahead, and he could feel the fine tremor running through her. Her blouse was short-sleeved and he was conscious of the feel of her bare skin beneath his fingers. Warm. Soft. Silky.

But her face was the colour of ashes.

That's it. Totally destroy your pregnant PA because you can't control your anger. Another reason to hand this king-dom on to Philippe as quickly as possible.

Yes, it was true.

Freddie's gaze was even more liquid than normal and he was certain that was due to tears. He'd made her cry. What a bastard he was.

'Come,' he said, gentling his voice and taking his anger in a vice-like grip. 'Let's go inside. The light is too bright, and you need to sit down somewhere comfortable.'

'I'm fine,' she said thickly. 'You don't need to—'

'It was not a request, Freddie.' He released her and turned, then slid his hand beneath her elbow and held her firmly. 'Come with me.'

She stumbled a little as he walked them both along the path past the stables, all her muscles stiff beneath his hand at first. Then she relaxed and matched his stride. Her face remained white, though. As if he was marching her to her doom.

They walked back through the gardens unspeaking, and then into the welcoming dimness of the castle. His office would have been a more appropriate place for this conversation, but it felt overly formal, and this situation had nothing to do with formality, so he headed straight to his private sitting room.

It was on the ground floor, with a walled garden just outside and he preferred it since the room caught no direct sunlight. The walls were panelled in oak, the floor covered in a thick, dark carpet. There was a fireplace, and some battered yet comfortable armchairs and a sofa drawn up in front of it. Shelves stood against the walls, full of books he couldn't read. He'd thought once or twice about getting rid of them, but that would have meant admitting his failures mattered and so he'd left them there.

Propelling Freddie over to the sofa, he sat her down on it, then called one of his house staff for some tea. Then he stood for a moment, staring at her as a thick silence fell.

She was sitting on the very edge of the sofa, looking down at her hands clasped tightly together.

He didn't want to have this conversation, not when his temper was hanging by a thread and she was obviously upset. Yet it had to be done and the sooner the better.

'You'd better tell me, Freddie,' he said into the silence. 'What exactly were you planning to do with my child?'

CHAPTER FIVE

WINIFRED FELT SICK, fear collecting cold and sharp as ice in her gut. Shock was still pulsing through every muscle, and her fingers and toes were starting to go numb. She'd thought she might faint out there by the stables, with Augustine standing there like a beautiful, judgemental god, full of righteous fury.

She'd known what he was going to say before the words had even come out of his mouth; there had been a cold flame in his eyes, anger in his taut posture.

She'd been right. He'd guessed it had been her in his bed and he'd guessed correctly.

It had still been a shock though, and the way he'd hammered at her with those relentless, angry questions. Making it difficult to think through the haze of fear and guilt and shame. She'd wanted to burst into tears. She'd wanted to scream back at him. But as she knew all too well, doing either of those things never helped, so she hadn't.

The worst thing was she could understand his anger. She also knew that he struggled to keep his emotions in check, especially when he was tired or in pain. He sometimes said things he didn't mean during those times and normally she brushed them off, so she'd tried not to let him get to her then.

She'd held it together and answered his questions, and she'd thought she'd been doing so well...

Until he'd asked her how she was planning on 'handling' the child. *Their* child.

She'd felt that tearing pain again inside her in that moment, the pain she'd been telling herself she didn't feel for the past couple of months. That she was fine with the thought of someone else caring for and bringing up her child.

But of course she wasn't fine with it. Yet she had no choice. She was a killer, a murderer. A worse criminal than even her mother. She wasn't a good person, and she knew that down deep inside. So, it was better if someone else should bring her child up. Someone who could give them a good life, someone who didn't have the kind of stain on her soul that she did.

Except, this wasn't just her baby. It was Augustine's too. And with him staring at her like that, with judgement and accusation in his eyes, she hadn't been able to find the words to tell him.

I was going to have our baby adopted by a loving family who would care for it the way I couldn't. That's how I was going to handle it.

She hadn't been able to say that to him. She still couldn't.

Yet now he was standing in front of her, wanting an answer, looming over her, so tall and broad and powerful, and even in jeans and a T-shirt, he looked every inch a king, perfectly in command of himself.

That wasn't the worst part, though. The worst part was how her skin had felt scalded where he'd gripped her arm, and she could still feel the press of his fingers there, like hot coals against her flesh.

She didn't want to tell him. How could she? He'd be so angry and he was already angry enough. She didn't want to make it worse for him. She'd only wanted to protect him and protect their child.

Coward. You're a coward and you always have been.

A shudder worked its way down her spine, the truth like poison in her heart. Of course she was a coward. Fear was why she'd left home all those years ago and not just her home, but her country too. And she was still afraid, even now.

'Well?' he demanded in his rich, melted-honey voice. 'You owe me an explanation, Freddie.'

She couldn't face giving him the truth, yet he wasn't going to let her go without an explanation, that much was clear.

You could distract him.

A wave of heat went through her, warming up her numb extremities, stealing away the pain around her heart, and all she could think about was that he wasn't the only one who needed to be distracted. She did too.

So before she was even conscious of moving, Winifred had got to her feet and had taken a step forward, getting close to him. Then she put a hand on his chest, her palm flat against the warm cotton of his T-shirt, and looked up into his eyes.

His gaze flared, first with surprise and then with an instant and obvious heat, making her breath catch.

Then there was a moment of silence, a moment when the very air around them seem to burn with the force of their attraction.

She shouldn't do this. It was a mistake. Yet she'd made so many mistakes already, what was one more? She wanted him. She wanted his warmth and his touch. She wanted to be close to him in the only way they probably ever would be.

You're still a coward.

'Freddie,' Augustine murmured, his fingers closing around her wrist. 'This is not a good—'

But she didn't let him finish. Instead she closed her fingers into a fist in the material of his T-shirt and pulled him down so her mouth met his, drowning out the voices in her head.

There was a second of stillness, where she felt his whole body tense with surprise, and she knew if she didn't do something more, he'd pull away, continue with his relentless questioning. And she'd have to tell him. She'd be forced to reveal all the lies she'd told him, and then he'd understand what kind of woman she was. A liar. A thief. A murderer.

She couldn't do that. She wasn't ready.

If it hadn't been for that night, she wouldn't have known what to do, because virgin that she was, she'd no experience. But he'd taught her many things that night. Such as what he liked and where to touch him, and how hard. How fast.

So she used what she'd learned, sliding her tongue into the heat of his mouth, tasting him at the same time as she reached down with her free hand to the front of his jeans, cupping him through the denim.

He was hard beneath her hand and hot, and big, pressing against her palm. Her breath caught, the familiar feel of him and his scent igniting her own smouldering need.

It had been so long since that night. Eons. And she was so tired. The last three months had been torture, she could admit that now. Having to guard herself, watch herself. Wondering if now would be the day he'd discover her secret and bring everything crashing down.

Well, now he knew. And it seemed he still remembered that night as well as she, judging from the response of his body.

It *had* been heat in his eyes she'd seen on the plane.

He wanted her. She could feel it.

She kissed him harder, closing her fingers around the

hard length of him behind the denim, pressing her body against his, suddenly desperate. She wanted him to forget all about this; she wanted to forget about it herself. She wanted to give him pleasure to make up for the lies she'd told him.

He deserves better than this. He deserves better than you.

He did. But judging by his body's response, he was quite happy to settle for her.

Yet he didn't move and she was just beginning to feel despair at her own foolish choices, when abruptly his fingers plunged into her hair and closed into a fist, holding her tight. Then his other hand found the small of her back and settled there, pressing her hard against him.

His body was hot, like a furnace, and his mouth turned hungry, his tongue sweeping inside to taste her, explore her. She groaned, melting against him in relief, her fingers still curled in his T-shirt.

Yes, she wanted this. She wanted him. Fear had been with her for so long and now he knew, she could relax.

He kissed her with an intensity that stole her breath, ravaging her mouth as if he was starving, and she could tell, even with her limited experience, that he'd been thinking of that night for three months just as she had. Wanting more, just as she did.

His teeth nipped at her bottom lip, the hand at her back sliding down, curving over her bottom and fitting her hips to his, pressing the hard length of his erection to the hot, desperate place between her thighs.

She gasped, shifting against him, restless and hungry and wanting.

He made a growling sound deep in his throat and then she was down on the floor, on her back, his hands tearing open her blouse, shoving aside the sturdy cotton of her bra, baring her. His dark head bent, the strands of gold in his hair lost in the dimness of the room, and his mouth was at her throat, burning where her pulse beat frantically. Then it moved further down, over the curves of her breasts to her sensitive nipples. His lips closed around one tight peak and he sucked hard, making her groan as sensation sent bolts of lightning throughout her entire body.

All thought had gone. There was only this moment and his hands, his mouth, and the pleasure he gave her. She'd built such a lovely little life for herself here in Isavere. It was safe and secure, but it was also lonely.

She had no friends here. She couldn't allow anyone to get too close, to study the edifice of lies she'd constructed. And she missed having someone. She'd gorged herself on all kinds of romance and love stories, filling the hole inside her with borrowed warmth and vicarious touches.

But this was real. This was a king. This was Augustine touching her, Augustine kissing her. And he made her whole heart catch fire.

She was panting now, trying to reach for him to touch him too, wanting more, but he'd shoved her skirt up to her hips, and then his hand was between her thighs, his fingers stroking through the slick folds of her sex.

She cried out as pleasure rippled through her, becoming more and more intense by the second. Then his hand vanished and her legs were being parted more forcefully. His head was down between them, his mouth on her, his tongue exploring and tasting, and the pleasure wound so tight she almost screamed.

She reached down, burying her fingers convulsively in the rough silk of his hair and holding on tight as he propelled her fast and hard into the most incredible ecstasy. Then she did scream as the orgasm hit, a rush of pleasure so intense she was blinded by it.

He didn't pause.

One minute his head was between her thighs, the next he was there, the rough denim of his jeans scraping her inner thighs. She could feel him move, feel the press of him against her and then she gasped as he pushed inside her, the exquisite stretch of him making her tremble.

'Augustine.' His name escaped like a prayer, her hands splayed against the hard wall of his chest. 'Yes, Augustine.'

He didn't move for one long, aching second, the expression on his beautiful face taut and hungry as he looked down at her. There was no green in his eyes now, they were a deep, dark blue, and they burned.

'Don't think I don't know what you're doing,' he murmured in a rough, ragged voice was that was as unlike his own as it was possible to get. 'And don't think for a moment that I'll forget.' Then he drew his hips back and thrust inside her, and pleasure fractured every single thought in her head. Her hands slid to his shoulders as he drew back once more and he gave another deep thrust. 'There will be consequences for this, Freddie.' Again, his hips flexed and he slid deep. 'And you will bear them.'

Her senses reeled. She could barely take in what he was saying. Then he moved in a relentless, hard rhythm and all thought left her.

There was only him and the exquisite ache he was building once again, the need, the desperate hunger, the fire he stoked inside her.

She gripped him tightly, moving with him, and when he caught her knee and hauled it up around his hip, she called his name again, drunk with ecstasy and with him.

It didn't take long for another climax to hit.

And this time, her name a growl whispered against her throat, he joined her.

* * *

Augustine lay on top of the woman he'd just taken like an animal, his breath coming fast and hard, all his bones molten and liquid inside him.

He was having a hard time holding on to any rational thought, but at least his headache had gone. That stunning, annihilating orgasm had chased it away, taking all his anger and tension along with it.

Freddie was breathing fast too, little puffs of warmth against his neck, the delicious scent of sex and sweetness filling his head. He wanted to peel her out of her clothes, lay her out on his bed, and spend the rest of the day revisiting all the places he remembered from that night, doing all the things he'd done once again. Then maybe trying a few more he hadn't.

But he couldn't.

He hadn't expected this. He hadn't expected her to grab him and kiss him, not his good little Freddie who never did anything he hadn't told her to do.

It had shocked him to his core how he'd gone up in flames the minute her soft, delectable mouth had touched his. How every part of him had roared with hunger as her hand had closed over his hardening sex.

He'd tried to hold back. He'd tried to stop. But it had been three months since he'd last had sex, a long time for a man like him. A long time to be fixated on that one, unknown woman. The woman that had made him lose his mind so completely.

Freddie. That woman had been Freddie.

There had been a fleeting, deep surprise that even knowing who she was now, without the covering darkness and mystery, that he'd responded to her so intensely, when he'd never responded to her in that way before.

But that surprise hadn't been enough for him to stop.

He knew what she was doing though, trying to distract him from his question about what she was going to do with his child, and he'd told her as much.

He hadn't forgotten and he'd told her there would be consequences. And he was starting to get ideas about what those consequences would be.

Children and a wife hadn't been in his future. He'd decided that in the long, terrible months of his recovery after the car accident. Where he'd had to relearn all the most basic functions. Where even a year later he could barely move for the fatigue and even the smallest light was like a knife through his skull. Because how could he? He could barely care for himself and his nation let alone adding a wife and child to the equation.

Even later, after he'd recovered as much as he was ever going to, he hadn't changed his mind. He couldn't be the husband and father he'd wanted to be so he wouldn't be either.

He'd lost his mother so early he had no memory of her. But he knew what it was to have a loving father, a father who was proud of him and everything he did. An exacting father, yes. Who encouraged his intellect and who'd taught him that a king needed to be the best man he could be in order to rule, because how else would his subjects respect him? He had to be the best of the best, the first amongst equals. He had to be worthy of the crown, worthy of the privilege of leading a nation.

Piero had had high standards, but that had only encouraged Augustine to strive for more.

But more was something he couldn't do anymore. All he could do was the bare minimum, and the bare minimum wasn't what he wanted to give his own child. He couldn't. Not knowing what more that child could and should have had.

Except everything had changed now.

Freddie was pregnant and he was going to be a father whether he wanted to be or not. And while he couldn't reach the standards for kingship his father had set him, not these days, he knew what Piero would have wanted him to do now.

He had an heir who needed his protection and so did the child's mother, and marrying her would give them both that protection. It wasn't much, but it was one thing he could do, so do it he would.

Of course, there were other implications to a royal marriage, but he wasn't ready to think about those just yet. It was going to be enough of an adjustment having a wife and child.

What about her? What about what she wants?

Well, she'd forfeited that right when she'd tried to hide his child from him. Now all that mattered was what was best for that child. And what was best for that child was to have its father in its life.

Finally, he shifted his weight so he wasn't lying on her directly, though he didn't move away. He put his hands on either side of her head and looked down at her.

Her face was flushed, making her dark eyes look even more velvety, black almost. There was a shocked expression on her face, the same kind of shock he could feel moving through himself too. This had happened so fast and he'd lost his control so quickly, crossing every single one of the boundaries he'd set, taking his pregnant PA on the floor like a beast.

She was still shaking, making a wave of intense protectiveness wash over him, and that too, was a shock. He couldn't allow himself to be protective of anyone since protecting Isavere took up all his attention and energy. He didn't have any to spare for a person. He'd planned to hand his crown over to someone else who could look after Isavere better than he could, but he couldn't do the same for a wife and child.

Can you do that, though? Can you look after them both?

She looked away, her hands pushing against his chest. 'Sir,' she said huskily. 'Sir, please.'

'Sir?' he murmured, deciding to ignore that thought, bending instead to brush his mouth along the satiny line of her jaw. 'Surely, not. Not after that.' Her sweet, musky scent, the scent that had been chasing his dreams for so long, was beginning to make him hard again, which meant he should really move. Except he didn't. 'Perhaps in some situations, I would definitely appreciate it, but not now, Freddie.'

She stilled at the sound of her name, her hands on his chest, her fingers spread. He could feel each and every fingertip burning through the cotton of his T-shirt.

'Although,' he went on, 'perhaps I shouldn't call you that, either?'

She was staring very fixedly at her hands where they rested on his chest, and he caught himself studying her long lashes. He'd never noticed before how dark and silky they were. So pretty.

A silence fell, and he could feel her tension.

'Look at me,' he ordered softly. 'Now, please.'

Her throat moved as she swallowed, and he could see that frantic pulse. He wanted to press his mouth there and taste her again.

But no, there were still some things they needed to discuss.

Finally, her long, thick lashes lifted and those dark eyes met his. He could see fear in them, yet also a steely determination. It surprised him, though it shouldn't have. She never argued with him and always did what he asked, but she'd never been a pushover.

'I know what you want,' she said. 'You want an answer to your question. You want to know what I was going to do with the baby.'

He didn't deny it. 'Sex was a good distraction, sweetheart. Correction, an excellent distraction, and full marks for trying. But it's not something I'm likely to forget, no matter how good in bed you are.'

The flush in her cheeks deepened, her fear fading as little sparks of anger began to glitter in her eyes.

Fascinated, he stared at them. Freddie never got noticeably angry with him, no matter how short-tempered he was due to fatigue or a headache, or general frustration with his deficiencies. She was always so very patient.

But not now.

'You were going to give the baby up for adoption, weren't you?' he said slowly, watching her, understanding coming to him as he said the words. Because that was it, wasn't it? There was no other reason not to tell him immediately.

The colour left her face, her dark eyes getting even darker. But she didn't look away. 'I couldn't look after a child. I couldn't…give a child what it needs. And you said you didn't want them—you were very clear. So yes, I was. I had a list of families who would give the baby what I couldn't.'

A curious sensation rippled through him, partly his anger pulling against the leash he'd set on it, and partly a curious respect for her courage. Freddie was a compassionate, caring woman and that decision couldn't have been an easy one for her. Still, she'd been going to give his child to someone else without consulting him, and regardless of what he'd said to her about not wanting children, that had been the wrong decision to make.

An intense possessiveness he'd never felt before hardened inside him like granite.

No, she would *not* be giving his child to strangers to be brought up. Not the heir to the throne. He had a duty to his people to provide them with an heir, and while he'd been prepared for that heir to be Philippe, he knew he couldn't do that now. Not in good conscience.

The next heir would be a Solari.

There would be no argument.

Something in his face must have distressed her because abruptly those long lashes swept down, veiling her gaze. There were tears sparkling on the ends of them and he was conscious all of a sudden that they were still on the floor and he could feel the swell of her stomach pressing against him, the little bump where his child lay.

So much for protecting them.

The thought was a bitter one, making his jaw harden. Perhaps he couldn't, but he'd be damned if he wouldn't at least try. He could do that much at least.

He moved, shifting off her before dealing with his clothing. She sat up, trying to smooth her skirt down with shaking hands, but he gently pushed them aside so he could adjust her clothing for her.

'You don't need to do that,' she murmured.

He ignored her, helping her to her feet instead then doing up the tiny buttons of her blouse methodically.

'I can manage,' she protested.

'I'm sure you can,' he said. 'But you will not need to manage today.' He couldn't stop his fingertips from brushing her skin as he did up her buttons, relishing the way she shivered as he did so.

The certainty of his decision was harder than rock now, sitting inside him like the foundation of a castle. For the past five years everything had felt tenuous, precarious. As if he was an imposter in his own life, doing a job he wasn't suited to any longer, and barely scraping by. Hiding his failings every day as he tried and failed to meet the standards his father had set.

But providing an heir, a Solari heir, was one of the prime duties of being a king, and this was one thing he could do. His own reign might be mediocre, but he could ensure that the next one would not be. He could ensure that the next ruler of Isavere would be the one his father had always hoped for.

And as to marrying Freddie, well, there were bonuses. She knew everything about him, at least she knew the extent of his disabilities, so he wouldn't have to hide them from her. Plus, she'd also be a joy to take to bed. *That* he had no problems accepting.

When her buttons were done, he straightened and gestured at her to sit on the couch once more. But, again surprising him, she shook her head, folding her arms across her beautiful breasts. The steely determination was back in her eyes, hiding the fear that lurked beneath it. 'Now what?' she asked before he could say anything.

No, she'd never been a pushover, but she'd certainly never used her teeth on him. Now it seemed she'd had a change of heart. That was going to make things interesting.

Augustine studied her a moment, feeling more relaxed than he had in months. A likely combination of that incredible orgasm and the decision he'd made about his child. He felt as if he had a direction and a purpose now. No longer was he merely waiting and holding on for grim death until Philippe came of age. Now he had a child he could teach, an heir who could be the ruler he couldn't.

'Now what?' he echoed. 'Now, Freddie sweetheart, you are going to put aside your adoption plans.'

'But I—'

'No,' he interrupted, all his certainty and the command of the king in his tone. 'You are having my child. The heir to the throne. You do understand that, don't you?'

'Yes, but—'

'The heir to the throne you were going to adopt out without telling me, I may add.'

Her jaw firmed, her eyes looking black in her pale face. 'That was... I didn't mean...'

'We'll talk about that later,' he said decisively. He didn't like the pale cast to her cheeks, or the traces of fear in her eyes; he didn't want her being afraid of him. 'Sit down. That's an order.'

An oddly mutinous look crossed her face, then abruptly she turned and sat down on the edge of the couch. 'So? I'm sitting. What now?'

'As I said, there will be no adoption. The child is mine and I will claim it.'

'The child is also mine,' she said.

'I realise that.' He paused for effect. 'Which is why I will be claiming you too.'

This time her eyes went wide. 'What? What do you mean?'

'I mean, you will be marrying me, Freddie.' He smiled. 'Welcome to the monarchy.'

CHAPTER SIX

WINIFRED SAT ON the couch, her hands clasped tightly together, conscious of the solid icy ball of fear that had gathered in her stomach. It made for an unsettling companion to the sparks still coursing through her body, little pulses of electricity and flickers of fire, the remnants of his touch.

She'd felt as if every part of her was alive, hyperaware and awake and so achingly conscious of him in a way she hadn't been before.

It was confusing to want him like this and yet to also be so afraid she wanted to run straight out of this room and out of the palace. Run all the way to the next country, put as much distance between herself and him as she could.

Yet she couldn't. She was going to have his child and now he knew, now she'd seen the flare in his turquoise-blue eyes as she'd told him about the adoption, both fury and possessiveness in equal measure; she knew there would be no more running for her.

She'd been caught.

Except that terrified her. He didn't know that nothing about her was real, that everything was fake, a lie she'd told to keep herself safe.

Her name. The accent she'd worked on so diligently. The degree from the Sorbonne. The years of experience working for those *Fortune 500* companies. All those glowing references...

She'd paid an extortionate amount for the best fakes she could buy, yet still had never been able to believe the palace hadn't investigated her and her qualifications more thoroughly. But Augustine had told her at the time that he'd needed someone ASAP, that she was perfect and that he was sure all her details were in order.

Trying to distract him from his relentless questions with her body had clearly been a mistake, though. An act of sheer desperation, because if she'd fully thought it through, she'd never have put a lit match to the smouldering attraction between them. Not when she too had been burned so completely by the flames. What had she been thinking? And now... What? He wanted to marry her?

This was insanity, and she needed to think about her next move, but it was impossible to think of anything in his presence. He made it so very difficult.

There was a knock at the door and Augustine mercifully turned away, dealing with the delivery of tea. The smell of it, a concoction made specially here at the palace, apple and cinnamon with echoes of orange, usually made her mouth water. But today it made her feel sick.

She had to get out of here. She had to find somewhere where he wasn't, so she could think about what to do.

The maid arranged the tea on the coffee table in front of the sofa then withdrew.

'Shall I be mother?' Augustine was already picking up the teapot and pouring.

She couldn't do it. She couldn't sit here sipping tea and discussing *marrying* him. Not after they'd just had sex on the floor.

A king. He was a king. She couldn't marry him. She

couldn't, not with her past. Not with all the terrible things she'd done. He'd find out. He'd know how she'd lied to him, over and over again...

If you're his queen, though, your child would be safe.

Her hand stole to the curve of her stomach before she could stop herself, a complex rush of emotion filling her, everything so tangled she didn't know one emotion from another.

Relief at the thought of her child being safe. Joy at the thought of being his wife. Fear at the thought of actually being a mother. Satisfaction that her child would be heir to the throne...

Why do you deserve any of that, though? After what you've done? You should give him the child and leave, and never come back.

'You're very quiet,' Augustine said, placing the cup of tea in front of her. 'Struck dumb at the thought of being my bride?'

She shoved the insidious thought away and looked up at him.

Even contemplating the idea of marrying him felt dangerous, because if she accepted his proposal, he could never know the truth. That the mother of his child had been deceiving him for years. That the queen of his country had killed someone.

She had dreams sometimes at night, nightmares of Aaron, her mother's boyfriend, trying to drag her little sister into the bedroom of the trailer, and of the gun in her hand, the barrel shaking as she'd pointed it at him. She hadn't meant to kill him. She'd only wanted to stop him from taking Annie. But she'd never fired a gun before, and she hadn't expected the recoil...

'Don't be absurd, sir,' she said, forcing the memories

away and trying to sound even and measured. 'You can't seriously be thinking of marrying me.'

He straightened, folding his arms over his impressive chest, staring down at her.

Her heart twisted. He was beautiful, so very beautiful in his jeans and a T-shirt, with his dark hair mussed from the passion they'd shared not a few minutes earlier. Yet even so, he was still royal, every inch of him commanding.

She still couldn't believe that had happened between them.

She still couldn't believe what he'd just offered her.

'How did you know?' A question she should have asked at least an hour ago, she knew. 'How did you know it was me that night?'

He didn't seem surprised. 'On the plane, I came into the bedroom and you were fast asleep. I went to wake you up and you…smelled familiar. Then you made a sound.' His eyes gleamed, the embers of desire still smouldering in them. 'It reminded me of the sound you made that night, when I made you come.'

Heat crept up her neck, flooding into her cheeks. He was a very observant man, she knew that. It was why she'd been so surprised that he hadn't guessed it had been her before. Then again, she was just part of the furniture to him, wasn't she? At least, that's how he'd always treated her.

'You never suspected—'

'No,' he cut her off flatly. 'But now is not the time to discuss my powers of observation. You're pregnant with my child, Freddie. Which means that we must marry.'

Her heart was beating far too loud in her ears. 'Why? I thought you never wanted to get married.'

'I didn't. But I never meant to have children either and yet here we are.'

'You don't have to do this.' She clasped her hands together tighter, not sure why she was arguing with him when this was a good outcome for her. 'It's not the Victorian era. Probably half the people in the world are born to parents who aren't married.'

'When I said I wasn't going to have children that didn't mean I didn't want them,' he said gently.

A little shock went through her, along with the knife-edge of guilt. She'd been going to keep his child from him…

What other proof do you need that you're a bad person?

'I thought—'

'You probably thought a lot of things. My preferences have nothing to do with the situation we find ourselves in, let alone yours. You are pregnant with the heir to the throne. No, it wasn't my choice, but it is what it is. I have to claim the child, Freddie. An illegitimate heir would cause me all sorts of problems and I can't have that.'

Her fingers were numb. She couldn't believe that he actually thought marrying her was a good idea and that she was actually thinking she'd accept him.

She didn't want to. She couldn't bear to think about all the lies she'd have to tell him, a future unrolling of all the things she couldn't say. A small part of her desperately wished she could confide in him, but she had a horrible feeling it was too late for that. She'd already hurt him enough by not telling him about the baby, and what would he say if he knew she'd been lying to him for years? Not a great way to start a marriage.

Not that she knew anything about marriage. Her parents hadn't been married. She'd never known her father, but she'd assumed he was the same petty criminal as her mother. They'd barely been together for her conception before her mother had moved on to someone else. Then to

Aaron. But she didn't want to think about him or what had happened with him.

The bottom line was that her mother hadn't cared about her father. Then again, her mother hadn't cared about anyone but herself.

Winifred had always thought she was different, but maybe she wasn't. Yes, she loved Augustine, but here she was contemplating telling him yet more lies to protect herself. It made her feel sick.

'You're looking extremely pale,' Augustine said, frowning. 'I know it wasn't the world's most romantic proposal, but there's nothing to be afraid of.'

It was disturbing how he'd somehow spotted her fear.

'I'm not afraid,' she said, trying to sound calm.

But he only kept frowning at her. 'Yes, you are. I know what fear looks like. Your face is white and you're holding your hands clasped together very tightly.'

Instantly she unclasped them, but it was too late. He'd already spotted her trepidation and him being him, he'd want to know why.

She had to say something, distract him again so she wouldn't be faced with yet more questions she couldn't answer.

'It's morning sickness,' she said quickly. 'Nothing to worry about.'

His gaze narrowed. 'I thought morning sickness was only an issue in the first three months?'

'Sometimes it can go on the whole nine months,' she said, forcing her voice to sound steady. 'Stress can add to it sometimes.'

He regarded her silently another moment. 'Drink your tea,' he said at last, finally moving to sit on the sofa next to her.

It was too close. She could feel his heat, feel the urge inside her to lean into him, take some of his strength and certainty for herself, because she felt so weak and power-less and afraid.

She'd been stupid to fall in love with him, but it had happened so slowly, she'd barely noticed. And it hadn't been a lightning strike from the sky or anything. Just an ac-cumulation of small kindnesses. His gentle approach with the organisers of a new network of women's shelters he'd opened. His easy camaraderie with the homeless when he'd toured the country on a fact-finding mission to investigate the current housing situation. The warmth he'd directed to patients while visiting one of the new hospices he'd directed the government to fund.

He was a charming playboy, it was true, but he was also the most genuine, compassionate, caring man she'd ever met.

He was also her boss, and a king and so far out of her league she may as well have tried shooting for the moon. Not only that, she'd slept with him and hadn't told him, had thought she could adopt out his child…

You didn't even have the courage to front up either. You run, the way you always do.

Winifred only just stopped herself from covering her face with her hands. God, was there no end to the mistakes she'd made?

She didn't want the tea, but he was watching her so she reached out and picked up her cup, the teacup rattling on the saucer as she did so. Another betrayal.

And of course he noticed that too.

'This is not nerves, Freddie.' He slid his warm palm be-neath her wrist steadying her. 'This is more. Tell me what the problem is.'

'Seriously?' She didn't want to pull her hand away from the warmth of his, but she made herself do it. 'In the space of half an hour after finding out you're a father, you suddenly decide you want to claim the baby and marry me?'

He eyed her. 'What do you expect? I'm not your normal one-night stand, no matter how much you want me to be. I'm a king, which means that any child I have will be my heir. I don't know whether you know this or not, but succession is the whole point of a monarchy.'

Her jaw set tight, anger collecting inside her. 'I know that. I'm not stupid.'

'Then don't act as if this isn't a surprise to you.'

'I thought you didn't want kids. I thought you—'

'No,' he cut her off with gentle firmness. 'Let's not have the same conversation again. This will be a shock and I understand that. But I'm not a man who avoids his responsibilities and I will not avoid this one.'

'And what about me?' she said, half desperately. 'What about what I want?'

He gave her a look. 'You really want to be a single mother? Having to bring the child up alone? I won't allow you to put the child up for adoption, I'm sorry, but that's final. And I won't allow you to bring the child up away from me either. You may decide you don't want to marry me, in which case you're free to leave Isavere. I'll give you excellent references. You will have no difficulty in finding another job.' There was a certain sharpness in his gaze. 'I'll even find one for you if you prefer.'

The thought of leaving, of finding another position made her feel cold. Even if he found one for her and it was well paid enough for her to keep saving money for her sisters, it would mean not only leaving the life she'd created for herself here, but it would also mean leaving him. Leaving her child too.

You know that's what's best for your baby. Being away from you.

No.

The denial echoed, bone deep and absolute.

No. It didn't matter that she was a criminal. It didn't matter that she didn't know how to be a mother or ever deserve to be one. She couldn't leave her child. It was impossible.

This whole situation was impossible.

If she couldn't run, what could she do?

Stay and face the consequences. The way you failed to do with Aaron.

She looked away, raising her teacup to sip at her tea, trying not to listen to the voice in her head. Her hand was still shaking, but she sipped at the tea anyway. It was lukewarm, the sweetness almost too much for her.

Augustine let out a breath, then he took the saucer and cup from her and put them down on the coffee table. Then he took her hands in his, the warmth of them swallowing up her numb fingers.

She couldn't look at him.

Perhaps it was weak of her to stay. Perhaps it was wrong to not protect her child from herself and the stain of what she'd done, from the taint of her family's name. But she had no choice. The thought of leaving her baby was a pain she just couldn't bear, and if that made her weak then fine, she was weak.

'What is so very distressing?' he murmured. 'It's just marriage I'm offering, Freddie. Not a march to the gallows.'

Her throat closed. 'I'm not… I'm not a queen,' she forced out. 'I'm just your PA. And you don't love me. You don't want me. I've basically forced you into this.'

His thumbs rubbed gently over the back of her hands, causing a cascade of sparks to echo through her and making her breath catch. 'Oh, yes, you've really dragged me kicking and screaming into a proposal.' His rich voice was warm with a very real amusement. 'Let it be known that I, a very powerful and important king, was forced into marrying my pregnant PA.'

She glanced at him, wanting to pull her hands away from his addictive touch and yet not finding the will to do so. 'Don't joke about this, sir.'

'Sir,' he echoed, his voice dropping into the deep, velvety purr she so loved. 'Really, Freddie, what did I say about that? My name is Augustine.' There were such fascinating sparks in his eyes as he looked at her. 'Say it.'

Her mouth dried, her heartbeat getting louder and louder. He was so sexy, and she was so weak when it came to him. Yet she never let herself say his name. It was a luxury she couldn't afford.

You said it just before.

Yes, when he was giving her the most intense pleasure. It was a slip and she couldn't do it again.

'I...can't,' she managed.

'Of course you can. I can hardly have you saying *I, Freddie, take you, sir* during the ceremony, can I?'

He was being so nice to her, so warm. And it wasn't fake. But she didn't deserve this treatment. She didn't deserve his kindness.

'Winifred,' she said coldly, pulling her hands from his. 'My name is Winifred.'

It wasn't of course. But she could never think of herself any other way now.

The warmth died out of his expression and she hated herself for rebuffing his efforts, but she had to distance him somehow. She couldn't let him in, not emotionally. Not even a little.

He didn't reach for her hands again, yet he didn't look away either. 'Winifred,' he repeated, lingering over the consonants in a way that made the name she'd chosen for herself sound unbearably sexy. 'Your turn.'

Damn him. He wasn't going to let her put that distance between them, was he? She knew that look on his face. She'd challenged him and he never let a challenge go. Which meant she'd have to give him something otherwise she'd never get out of here.

She steeled herself. 'Augustine,' she said, hating how much she liked saying it and how badly she wanted to say it again.

Those sparks in his eyes leapt. 'There. That wasn't so hard was it?'

That attraction was starting to build between them again, the electricity that should have been released seeming to spark again without the slightest provocation.

She had to get out of here. Get away from him before she made any more mistakes.

'May I be excused?' she asked woodenly, carefully avoiding the issue of his name. 'I'm not feeling very well.'

For a second she thought he might protest, that he might keep her here, holding her hands and saying her name in that purring, sexy voice of his. Looking at her with those sparks in his eyes and making her hungry, so hungry, yet again.

But after a moment, he nodded. 'You may. In fact, take the rest of the day off.'

'I won't need all day, sir,' she said stiffly, telling herself she wasn't disappointed.

'You might not, but you'll take it anyway. I want you to get some rest today and a good sleep tonight.' The look on his face hardened. 'Tomorrow we will begin planning our future.'

Winifred nodded—what else could she do but agree?—then fled the room before he could say anything else.

Augustine couldn't sleep that night. He was that terrible combination of exhausted and wired. Everything that had happened with Freddie kept replaying in his brain, first the incredible sex on the floor, then her behaviour afterwards. Shocked—which he'd expected—but also afraid. There had been no mistaking her white face and the way her hands had shaken as she'd picked up her teacup. She was afraid, but she was trying to hide it, and it was causing her distress.

He didn't know why. What was she so afraid of? Was it his insistence on marriage? The idea of being a mother? Of being married to him? Or was it the prospect of being queen, because she would be?

It was imperative he find out. Because if he was going to try to be a good father to his child, he needed to try to be a good husband to her. Regardless of what she'd told him and what she hadn't, she wasn't to blame for this.

Yes, having both the vasectomy and the condom fail was bad luck, but they wouldn't be in this situation now if he'd stopped instead of taking the opportunity she'd given him that night.

Anyway, a king always took responsibility for his actions and he would do so here too. He wouldn't allow her to do this on her own.

Look at you, trying to take care of her when you know you can't.

Augustine ignored the thought, eventually hauling himself out of bed and prowling the corridors for a time, making his guards nervous. Then he went up to his office and sat at his desk, with the big stained-glass window featuring the golden oak of Isavere at his back. His guards would be thankful he was in one place instead of roaming around, and he leaned back in his chair, kicking his feet up on the desk and put his mind to pondering the mystery of Freddie.

Her fear was a puzzle. She normally hid her emotions well and the fact that she hadn't been able to disguise that she'd been afraid, meant she must have felt it very strongly.

He had to know why. It wasn't him she was afraid of, which meant it had to be something else. Being his queen shouldn't intimidate her, not when she basically ran the country herself, so maybe it was the issue of being married. He understood, many people didn't want to get married—he'd never planned on it himself.

But that was something they'd discuss. Obviously theirs wasn't a love match, and him being her boss complicated matters, as did the fact that he was a king. Again, though, they could discuss what they wanted their marriage to look like, determine boundaries, etcetera. He didn't want a platonic marriage, that was certain, not with her and not given the chemistry between them. She might not agree however, in which case... Well, again that would be something they'd need to discuss.

What about Philippe?

The electricity in his bloodstream sparked and crackled, making all his muscles tighten. Yes, well, he'd already decided he wasn't going to abdicate. He couldn't, not now. Not given he had an heir.

Your father would have firm views on that anyway.

The old, aching grief that lived inside his heart pulled tight.

Piero would never have countenanced an abdication. He'd

have seen it as a failure, especially after what Augustine's mother had sacrificed for him.

But what has your rule been if not a failure?

Augustine shoved the thought away as his phone buzzed in his pocket. He drew it out, checking the screen. It was his friend Khalil, so he hit the accept button.

'My friend,' he said by way of a greeting. 'If it's late to be calling me, it must be extremely late for you.'

'It is,' Khalil's deep voice responded. 'But I am up anyway, and Galen's asleep, and I have news.'

Augustine grinned. 'If you're calling to tell me you're blissfully happy and Sidonie is the most perfect woman in the history of the world, then maybe you might want to save that for a text.'

'A text you cannot read anyway,' Khalil said dryly, being well aware of what Augustine could and couldn't do. He and Galen were the only ones, apart from Freddie, who knew.

'Which is why you should save it for a text.'

His friend laughed. 'This news isn't for a text. Sidonie is pregnant.'

It was so close to Augustine's own situation that it sent an electric shock straight down his spine. 'What? Already?'

They had only got married four months ago.

'She is sixteen weeks pregnant.' There was a smile in Khalil's voice, his joy obvious. 'We waited to be sure.'

Augustine pushed aside his own reaction. 'Congratulations, Khal. Do you know what you're having?'

'A girl. She will be the most amazing queen Al Da'ira has ever had.'

Despite himself, Augustine smiled. He was pleased for his friend. Happiness wasn't anything he'd thought Khalil would ever find given how much of his humanity he'd had to sacrifice to secure his crown, yet found it he had. With the friend he'd met in his Oxford days, a gorgeous little red-head who'd tempered his darkness with her light.

How will Freddie temper you?

She wouldn't. Because what he and Freddie had was different to Khal and Sidonie's relationship. Khal and Sidonie were in love, while he didn't love Freddie and she didn't love him. Love would never be part of that particular equation.

The urge to tell Khal about his own situation was strong, but he didn't want to take away from his friend's news with his own. This was Khal's moment, not his.

'Of course she will,' he said instead. 'With Sidonie as her mother, how can she fail not to be?'

'That is very true.' There was a slight pause. 'Something is wrong, Gus. What is it?'

Augustine closed his eyes. His friend was too damn sharp, that was the problem. For a moment he debated lying, but then Khal said, 'And do not tell me you are fine. I am not an old friend for nothing.'

'Damn you,' Augustine said with an attempt at lightness. 'I was trying to let you have your moment.'

'I have had my moment. It is your turn now.'

Augustine sighed. 'Freddie is pregnant.'

'Your PA? How is that your problem?'

'The baby is mine.'

There was a very long silence.

'Ah,' Khalil said at last. 'I was going to ask how that happened, but then realised in the time-honoured fashion, I suppose.'

'A case of mistaken identity,' Augustine said. 'You know how it is.'

'No,' Khalil murmured. 'I do not know how it is.'

'You're going to make this difficult for me aren't you?'

'Sounds as if you are already making it difficult for yourself.'

Augustine bit down on a retort. Khalil wasn't being judgmental, he knew that. His reputation as a playboy was one he'd carefully cultivated to cover a multitude of sins, but it did mean everyone would have an opinion on his pregnant PA and that wasn't a good look for him. He didn't care about people's opinion of him, but he did care about their opinion of Freddie. Gossip wasn't what he wanted. Yet another reason, if he needed one, for marrying her.

'It was during your marriage celebration as it happens,' he said finally. 'She somehow ended up in my room and I thought she was someone who was supposed to meet me later. The light was off and when I touched her...' He sighed again. 'She didn't say no.'

There was another long silence.

'And you didn't know it was her?' Khalil asked.

'No.'

'How could you not?' Khalil sounded mystified. 'You see her every day.'

'Because I've never seen her that way. Not once. And in the dark...she was different.' Even to himself it sounded like an excuse. 'Anyway, she's pregnant and the child is mine.'

'You are marrying her?' That it was the first question Khalil would ask said a lot about him and his own opinions. Then again, Augustine supposed Galen would have the same views, especially as Galen was already a father.

They were all of them kings. Responsibility was in their nature as was protectiveness.

'Yes,' he said. 'That's my intention. She's not happy about it, though.'

'Hmmm. That sounds horribly familiar.'

It would. Khalil had had problems convincing Sidonie

to be his bride. In fact, Augustine could still remember the advice he'd given his friend. It made him wince to think of it now.

'As I recall,' Khalil went on, his thoughts obviously following the same track. 'You told me to take her to bed and she would be begging for my ring by morning.'

Astute as ever.

Augustine ignored the thought. 'Was I wrong?'

'No,' Khalil said unexpectedly. 'Though it didn't happen quite like that. Have you thought of trying the same thing?'

But Augustine didn't want to discuss what had happened between him and Freddie. He didn't want to discuss her fear with anyone either. It felt too private to him, a betrayal.

'Perhaps I should,' he said lightly. 'I mean, she certainly wasn't complaining—'

'She matters to you, doesn't she?' Khalil interrupted.

The question brought him up short. 'What makes you say that?'

'You are always very casual about the things that matter to you,' his friend said levelly. 'I presume it is a way to distance yourself. Galen and I have noticed.'

Damn old friends. Damn old friends and their knowledge of you and your secrets.

Is he wrong?

No, he wasn't, that was the thing. Freddie did matter. She was an excellent PA. She was organised, calm and insightful. She knew how to handle him in all his moods. She made things easy, never difficult.

He also had incredible chemistry with her and she was phenomenal in bed.

But does she matter apart from that? Apart from her carrying your child. You don't know a thing about her.

The thought unsettled him. Because no, he didn't know.

She'd never spoken about her personal life, her life outside the job, not a single word. The only reason he knew she liked that tea he'd had delivered this morning to his sitting room was because she had it whenever they were working together and he ordered coffee.

Apart from that, though. Nothing.

'Am I?' He wasn't really paying attention to Khalil now, his brain seizing on the topic of Freddie once again and worrying at it.

Khalil laughed, a soft sound from down the other end of the phone. 'Goodbye, Gus,' he said. 'Sidonie and I will await our wedding invitation.'

After the call had ended, Augustine sat still in the study, staring at the wall opposite, where the formal portrait of his parents hung.

His mother sitting in an armchair in a beautiful blue gown, his father beside her, his hand on her shoulder. They both looked as if they were just about to smile.

He'd often wondered why Piero was so loving towards the son whose birth had essentially signed his mother's death warrant, but Piero had told him that they'd decided together not to get treatment for her cancer, not wanting to risk him. They'd known the consequences and they'd chosen them.

You were loved, Augustine, his father had told him. *And you were very much wanted. You were the heir, and precious, and we didn't know if your mother could conceive again. We couldn't risk it.*

Before the accident, all he'd wanted was to make sure his mother's sacrifice and his father's grief for her hadn't been for nothing. To be the best king, the best son, to make them proud.

His father had told him to make the most of his Oxford days and he had. He'd probably made the most of them a little too much, which his father hadn't been all that happy about. But Augustine had always sworn he'd make up for it.

Then the accident had happened just after he'd left university.

An icy road and the car had slid. They'd hit a tree. Both their chauffeur and his father had died on impact, while he'd been badly injured.

He'd never make it up to his father now, just as he'd never be the king his father would have wanted him to be. A king worthy of his mother's sacrifice.

You won't be a worthy husband either.

His parents had had a wonderful marriage, or so his father had told him, and the grief Piero felt at his wife's death had been intense. Augustine had always told himself that when the time came for him to marry, he too would make sure to be the kind of husband his father had been to his mother.

Except that would be yet another standard he'd never meet.

There was no love in the marriage he'd make with Freddie—they didn't even know each other outside of their professional relationship, apart from sex—and there could be no possibility of love, either, not for him.

Perhaps if the accident hadn't taken everything from him, he might have been able to love her. Yet it had.

Love brought such expectations with it, and it was so heavy to bear. He could barely move under the weight of his father's love and the love his mother had felt for him too. The love that had ended up killing her.

Loving Freddie might end up crushing him completely.

Still, while he might not be a worthy husband in terms of loving her, he could try to be the kind of husband who'd never give her a moment's regret. Who'd try to make her happy. That was at least one thing he could do.

Reaching into his desk and pulling out the bottle of fifty-year-old Scotch he kept in it, he found a glass on the desk-top and poured himself a nip.

Then he lifted the glass towards the portrait in a toast.

'You'll get your perfect ruler eventually, Papa,' he said softly. 'You might just have to wait longer than you'd hoped.'

Then he drank the Scotch down in one go.

CHAPTER SEVEN

WINIFRED BARELY SLEPT that night. Ignoring Augustine's advice to rest, she'd spent the rest of that day pacing around her little sitting room, going over and over her options, looking for a way out despite herself.

But there wasn't one and she knew it.

She'd gone to bed eventually, falling into an exhausted sleep for a couple of hours, only to wake before dawn, her brain still racing.

There was no point trying to go back to sleep, so she pulled on the pale pink silk dressing gown she'd treated herself to, the one covered in chrysanthemums, and went out into the castle.

Sometimes when everything got too much for her, she'd wend her way up the ancient stone stairs of one of the castle turrets to the battlements, and walk along them, letting the wind blow away all her doubts.

The view was spectacular, over sharp mountains covered with snow even in midsummer, and the dark, deep forests. The beautiful terraced gardens that led onto rolling alpine meadows, that in turn led into the valley where Isavere's capital city was located. The castle stood sentinel, guarding it, protecting it.

Every time she had doubts about what she was doing, she

only had to take one look at the fabulous view and what it meant to her.

Yet the view didn't work its magic on her today.

She put her hand down on the curve of her stomach, ignoring the weight of the sleepless night that pulled at her.

Running was no longer an option, she knew that down deep inside. She couldn't leave her child and she couldn't leave him, even though she knew she should. And while that would mean telling yet more lies and constructing yet more fictions, she would have to bear it. This was about protecting Augustine and their baby, and the throne of Isavere, her child's legacy.

If the truth came out about her past, about who she was and what she'd done, no one would want her on any kind of throne. Her very presence would stain it, not to mention the man who held it. And as for that man, well, protectiveness was in his nature, especially of his country. If he knew what she'd done she'd be lucky if he let her stay in Isavere itself, let alone the castle. He might not even want her anywhere near their child.

It's no less than what you deserve.

Her heart ached, the truth eating away at her like acid.

It was true. She didn't deserve to be here, in this beautiful place, doing a job she loved with the man she adored. What she should be doing was putting in place plans to leave once the child was born, so they'd never have to know what a coward and a liar their mother was. But she was weak. She had to stay.

The wind whipped her hair about her face, lifting her silk robe and making it billow. She shivered. It was cold on the battlements, despite the dawn creeping over the horizon and painting the snow on the mountains glorious golds and pinks and oranges.

Yet she couldn't take any pleasure in the view today, not with the ice that sat in her gut.

'How very gothic of you, Freddie,' a deep, warm male voice said from behind her. 'Wandering about my battlements in your dressing gown.'

She froze. Oh, God, what was *he* doing out here?

'You're cold,' he went on. 'Silk is a great insulator, but you really need something over the top of it. Did no one ever tell you that?' Then much to her shock, a pair of powerful arms came around her, pulling her against the hard body and intense heat of the man behind her.

She stiffened, her heartbeat instantly racing, her mouth dry. 'What are you doing here?'

'I couldn't sleep. Coming up here blows the cobwebs away. No,' he added softly. 'Relax. You're cold and I'm not, and I'm only going to warm you up, nothing more.'

Relax? How could she relax when all she wanted was to melt into his warmth, take his heat. Let his strength carry her, because she was so tired of doing this all on her own.

The weight of her secrets felt abruptly so heavy, a mountain she'd been carrying for so long she'd forgotten the weight of it all. A mountain that was crushing her. And she had no one to help her. No one to take the weight for her, even for a moment.

She'd been alone for a few years before she'd come to Isavere, running all the time. And now she'd finally found a place to rest...

You ruined it. You ruined it for him and yourself. You always ruin everything.

She shut her eyes, trying to ignore the thought, but it was lodged too firmly deep in her heart.

As if he could sense her distress, Augustine's arms tightened around her, and she couldn't help it, she did what he said, relaxing against him, into the astonishing heat of his powerful body, letting the delicious scent of him surround her. Taking a moment to give in to the weakness, to let someone else hold her up.

Only a moment, though. Not long. She was allowed that wasn't she?

'You don't have to be scared,' Augustine rumbled at her back. 'It'll all be okay. We're going to do this together, understand?'

Tears prickled against her closed lids. He was the one who didn't understand. He didn't know the kind of woman he held in his arms, the kind of woman who'd be his child's mother. A killer.

No. Your moment is over.

She tensed and tried to pull away, to get some distance, but those strong arms only tightened still further, keeping her against him.

'Don't.' There was a soft growl of warning in his voice. 'I want to know what's going on, Freddie. Because something is. Something you're not telling me.'

'There's nothing—'

'You were afraid yesterday. I could see it in your eyes. And it's not just about the prospect of marrying me, is it?'

'I don't—'

'Winifred.' Her name was a soft command. 'I'm not going to let this go, so you might as well tell me.'

He was right. There wasn't any point fighting him. He was relentless when he wanted to know something and she couldn't face yet another brutal enquiry.

You can't escape. You have to face the consequences of your actions.

A shudder went down her spine. It was true, she did. She had to give him the truth and hope he wouldn't summarily dismiss her from his and their child's lives. And if he did, well… It was no less than what she deserved.

Swallowing, Winifred steeled herself. 'I've been lying to you, sir,' she said. 'I'm not who you think I am.'

He didn't move. 'How very mysterious of you.' There was the slightest thread of amusement in his voice. 'So are you going to tell me who you really are? And if so, do I need to be afraid?'

Winifred jerked herself out of his arms, and turned around, shivering in the cold dawn air. 'It's not funny. I'm being serious.'

The expression on his face betrayed nothing, his gaze cool. 'Then you'd better explain, hadn't you?'

She took a little breath. 'Winifred Scott isn't my real name and I'm not from England. My name real is Ellie Jones, and I was brought up in the desert near LA, in a trailer park. My mother was a small-time drug dealer, and I… I did something very bad, which resulted in me having to leave.'

He was silent, continuing to study her.

'I've been on the run for years,' she went on doggedly, because she had to now. 'I got a forged passport, left the States, found my way to England. I spent some time doing jobs for cash and scraping a living, but I knew that if I wanted any kind of life, I was going to have to do better than that. So I…got a forged degree and some more fake qualifications, some fake references, and I…'

'Got a job here with me?' he finished lightly, his voice betraying absolutely nothing.

She met his gaze squarely. 'Yes. Someone I knew, a cleaner at the Isaveran embassy in London told me about the position and so I applied.'

'I see.' He folded his arms. 'Well, my security team did

tell me that there were some red flags coming up in your CV, but I told them to disregard them. I needed a PA urgently and you were perfect for the job. Perhaps I shouldn't have.'

'Sir, I—'

'So, what was the bad thing you did, Freddie? Or should that be, Ellie?'

Her eyes filled with tears again. Because there was no running from it, no escaping it. She'd tried to put it behind her for years, but you couldn't put a murder behind you. You couldn't.

'I'm not Ellie anymore,' she said huskily. 'I shot someone. And he died.'

Augustine stilled, looking so deeply into her it felt as if he could see everything she was, every dark and terrible thought she'd had. Every moment she lost her temper and that fury of hers got out. The fury that had killed Aaron.

'And why did you shoot him?' Augustine asked.

'He was… He…' She swallowed, trying to go on, but she hated the memory of it. Of her sisters crying as the door of the trailer had been wrenched open and Aaron had sauntered in. Their mother had been having one of her parties in the scraggly, dusty yard outside, and the music had thumped. No one would hear them if they screamed and Aaron knew that.

He'd been her mother's boyfriend for years, and he'd been a constant source of anxiety for her and her sisters. The way he looked at them, the way he spoke to them, was just… wrong. He was a threat, a constant threat.

That night he'd come into the trailer, that horrible creepy smile on his face and he'd reached for little Annie because Winifred was too old for him.

Winifred had screamed at him to leave, but he'd laughed in her face, told her not to be stupid. He wasn't going to hurt Annie, he just wanted five minutes alone with her, but Winifred knew he was lying.

She'd been so angry. Angry with her mother for not seeing what Aaron truly was, for not believing her when she told her about the way Aaron looked at her and her sisters. Angry with Aaron too, so angry.

So when he'd reached for Annie, Winifred had dashed into her mother's bedroom and grabbed the gun she knew was in the top drawer, because she was tired of being under threat. Tired of not being able to protect the little ones. Tired of feeling so powerless.

She'd waved the gun at him and told him to let Annie go, but he'd only laughed again. So she'd shot him. She hadn't known the gun would have a kick and since she'd been aiming at his legs, it had veered. Getting him right between the eyes.

Still lost in the memories, she didn't see Augustine move until he'd pulled her into his arms again, his large, warm hands cradling her face. 'What did he do, Winifred?' he asked gently.

She was trembling. 'He was my mother's boyfriend. He'd keep looking at my sisters and me, and it made us all feel…dirty somehow. I hated it. I tried telling Mom, but she wouldn't listen. She didn't believe me. And one night he tried to drag my little sister away and so I grabbed my mother's gun and… I stopped him.'

Gently, Augustine slid his hands down her neck to rest on her shoulders, his warm thumbs caressing the hollows of her collarbones in a soothing movement.

His presence was so immensely reassuring. She'd noticed before how he radiated calm strength, as if he could solve any problem, smooth over any difficulty. There had been a terrible accident a couple of years ago, a building collapse and several people had lost their lives while dozens of others had been injured. He'd come to the site to pay his respects and to give his sympathies to the families of the victims, and she'd witnessed firsthand the effect his presence had had, how his steady compassion had calmed everyone, allowing them room to grieve.

'Sounds to me as if you did the right thing,' he said.

'I was so angry,' she said desperately. 'I shouldn't have grabbed the gun. I shouldn't have sh-shot him. I should have done something else, *anything* else.'

'How old were you?' Augustine asked.

'Sixteen.'

'And he was bigger than you, yes?' His voice was very gentle.

She gave a jerky nod, because it was true. Aaron had been a big man.

'So, you were a very young girl,' Augustine went on, 'trying to protect your sister from a much bigger, much older man.'

'I know, but—'

'But what?'

'I killed him,' she burst out, making herself say the words. 'I shot him. I should have—'

'Could anyone else have stopped him?' Augustine interrupted softly. 'Was there another adult who could have helped you?'

Her throat closed and all she could do was shake her head, because no, there hadn't been. Only her mother and her mother hadn't cared about anyone but herself. 'There was only me,' she forced out.

Augustine nodded as if this was completely understandable. 'So you did what was necessary in order to protect your sisters,' he said calmly. 'They were younger and more vulnerable than you. They couldn't protect themselves and so you did what you had to do.'

He made it sound so logical, and yet the aftermath kept replaying in her brain, the horror of it. Her mother not even mourning Aaron's death, only screaming at her about how she certainly wasn't going to take the fall for her daughter's mistakes, and that Winifred had to turn herself in immediately.

Except she hadn't.

'I ran away.' The unshed tears kept coming, prickling and hurting. 'I... I was so afraid, and I didn't want to go to prison. Because if I did, that would leave my sisters unprotected and I just couldn't do it. So, when I left, I took them with me, and I... I tried to take care of them myself, but I had no money, and I couldn't get a job because they were too little to be left on their own. In the end, I had to leave them with social services.' She swallowed, her throat tight and painful, remembering how her sisters had cried as the social workers had taken charge of them, and the tearing sense of loss in her own heart. 'It was best for them, and they were fostered together eventually. I tried to get in contact with them after a while, but I couldn't reveal who I was so I wasn't allowed any information about them. I ended up leaving the country.' It was difficult to hold his gaze, but she made herself do it, letting him see that while she'd lied before, she was telling him the truth now. 'I've been saving money for them, but I... I ruined their lives.' The tears she'd been trying to hold back eventually overflowed, running down her cheeks, and all she could do was cover her face with her hands, drowning in the grief and shame, unable to bear his steady blue gaze any longer. 'I ruined yours too. And I'm so sorry, Augustine. I'm so sorry for all of it.'

* * *

Augustine stared at her slight figure, her long slender fingers covering her face as she wept. Shock was still reverberating through him; he'd had no idea the depth of his little PA's secrets.

He'd come up to the battlements for some fresh air after his sleepless night and seeing Freddie standing there in her pink silk robe, he hadn't been able to resist drawing her into his arms. They needed to talk some more, and he'd thought they could do that *after* he'd thoroughly seduced her and taken her to bed.

Yet…he'd never expected this.

She'd lied to him. She'd been lying to him for years, and he should be angry about that. He should be furious. He should also be extremely doubtful that she was telling the truth now.

Except she was sobbing, the sounds of her distress tearing at something inside him. She wasn't lying now, and this was not an act, that was painfully clear.

He didn't think, reaching instinctively for her and pulling her into his arms. Then he pressed her face to his chest, cupping the back of her silky head in his palm, holding her close while she wept.

It caused him actual physical pain to think of how alone she'd been.

Unlike him, basking in the privilege of being the heir to a throne and having a loving father at his side, she'd had no one. Even her mother, the one parent who should have cared for and protected her, hadn't.

So, she'd had to do it herself. At sixteen.

He didn't care that she'd shot someone—she hadn't meant to kill the bastard who'd attacked her sister, that was obvious. She'd only being trying to protect her. God in heaven, he'd have done the same thing himself if he'd been her.

And maybe another man might have faulted her for giving her sisters into care when it was clear she couldn't look after them, or for leaving the country rather than turning herself in. Or for lying to him the way she had.

But he couldn't. Yes, she'd lied to him, but she'd never put a foot out of line in all the years she'd been working for him. He'd put her in a position of great trust and she'd never betrayed that trust, not once. She could easily have let slip some of his secrets for her own gain, for example, and she hadn't.

She'd protected her sisters. She'd wanted to take care of them. Yes, she could have stayed and dealt with the consequences of the shooting, and she might have got off on a lesser charge, but how would that have helped anyone?

As for the lying, there was no point being angry with her for that. He'd already been angry yesterday and that hadn't helped either. He didn't want to be angry anymore anyway. That wasn't an emotion that was safe for him.

Her sobs had quieted, her breath warm against his chest.

He stroked her hair back from her forehead. 'You didn't ruin their lives, Freddie. You saved them. And you haven't ruined mine.'

She looked up at him, her cheeks wet with tears. 'I lied to you, Augustine. I just…needed the job. I needed the money. And I couldn't tell you. I couldn't. I'm going to be the worst mother, I just know—'

Gently he pressed a finger against her mouth, silencing her. 'You lied to me, it's true, and we'll need to discuss that. But not now. Also, you're not going to be the worst mother—don't be ridiculous.'

Her lips were unbearably soft, and he couldn't stop himself from stroking them gently. She was lovely in the dawn, wearing the prettiest dusty pink silk robe, the light and the colour of the silk making her loose dark hair look glossy and her dark eyes even more lustrous if a little red.

'You don't know that,' she said huskily.

'I do know that. You'll be amazing.'

'But I—'

'Hush,' he murmured gently. 'Don't argue with your King.'

Her scent was all around him, clouding his senses, and he could feel the familiar hunger rise.

It was wrong to feel this while she was upset, but he wanted to comfort her, offer her some distraction, and he didn't know what else to do. The only thing he was any good at was giving physical pleasure.

'You're cold, sweetheart,' he went on quietly, looking down into her eyes. 'Let me take you downstairs. Let me warm you up.'

'How can you want me? After I've lied to you? After everything—'

He bent and this time he silenced her with the gentle press of his mouth.

She didn't move, tense for a long moment. Then abruptly, her resistance melted away and she leaned into him, all soft warmth and sweetness.

He slid his arms around her. 'None of that matters, Freddie. Not right now. Come downstairs with me. Let me make you feel good.'

She shivered and let out a breath. 'Okay.'

So, he took her hand, threading his fingers through hers and he led her down from the battlements.

His bedroom was still dim, the way he preferred it, and as soon as they were inside, he kicked the door shut. Then he pulled her against him and covered her mouth with his, relishing how her arms went straight around his neck and how she arched up to meet his kiss, just as hungry as he was.

He got rid of her robe in seconds flat, as well as the pale cotton nightie she wore underneath it, then he swept her into his arms and carried her over to his bed and set her down on the mattress.

He got rid of the T-shirt he'd put on and began with the buttons of his jeans. But unexpectedly Freddie moved, slipping off the mattress and going to her knees at his feet.

She was naked and stunningly lovely in the half-light. How had he never noticed how beautiful she was? It seemed inconceivable somehow.

'What are you doing?' he asked, even though as she pushed his hands away from his buttons it was perfectly obvious what she was doing. 'I'm supposed to be the one comforting you, sweetheart, not the other way around.'

'I know. But I want to do this for you, sir. Please let me.'

He let his hands drop away, his body already so hard he could barely think. 'I feel "sir" in this context is acceptable.'

She glanced up at him then and the fierce light in her eyes stole his breath. There were no tears now, no distress either. Just hunger, blazing high, shocking him with its intensity.

His Freddie seemed to do nothing these days but shock him.

'Tell me what to do,' she whispered, the same intensity in her voice too. 'Tell me how to please you, sir. You make me feel good and I want to do the same for you.'

Something shifted in his chest, a tight, painful feeling. He reached down and cupped her chin, her skin soft and warm against his. 'You already do so much for me. This is supposed to be for you.'

The fierce light in her eyes didn't change, but her lovely mouth curved. 'But this is for me, too, don't you see? Giving you pleasure makes me feel good. As if I can do something more than tell lies and ruin lives and run away.'

He understood then. Pleasure was the one thing he could do well himself, which was why he indulged himself so often. A chance to prove to himself he was more than merely a collection of failings. So how could he deny her? Especially when he wanted this as badly as she did.

Letting go her chin, he held out his hands and when she put hers in them, he guided them to the buttons of his jeans. 'Then give me pleasure, Winifred,' he murmured. 'Or would you prefer Ellie?'

'No. Please, not Ellie. I'm Winifred now.' Her gaze turned darker. 'But I think I like Freddie best of all.'

It was amazing how much that little statement pleased him.

He smiled. 'In that case, Freddie. Shall I tell you how to do it?'

A flush had crept into her cheeks, and it stained her chest, her lovely breasts and her hard, pink nipples. 'Yes,' she said simply. 'Please, sir.'

He was a man not a statue, and he couldn't deny her anything. So after she'd got his buttons undone, he gave her the orders she wanted to hear. To take him out slowly and touch him, run those cool fingers of hers along his length. Then to grip him, harder please, and touch him with her tongue, explore him slowly, as long as she wanted to. Then when she was ready, to take him in her mouth, as deep as she wanted, and then suck him. No, she couldn't hurt him. Yes, hard was good. Hard was very good indeed.

She approached the task as if it was the most important thing she'd ever done, which was how his Freddie approached everything. She took her time, causing havoc and making him crazy, and the obvious pleasure she took in pleasuring him shattered his control completely.

He'd wanted to make it last, with her on her knees in front of him, making soft sounds of satisfaction as she sucked him, yet there was no way he could keep himself in command.

Eventually, he had to pull her mouth away, get rid of his jeans and underwear, and scoop her up from the floor, lay her down on the mattress and settle himself between her thighs. He slid a hand between them, finding hot, slick flesh and she trembled and gasped as he used his fingers to make her wetter, to make her more desperate.

Then when he was finally satisfied and she was twisting on the bed, he positioned himself and slid deep inside her, the sensation making them both groan with the pleasure of it.

He put his hands on either side of her head, staying where he was, buried deep in the tight, slick heat of her sex. 'Say my name,' he said roughly, an edge of demand in his voice. He wanted to hear her say it, right now, as he was buried inside her. The first time, he hadn't known who she was, the second, he'd been too desperate to savour her. But now he was fully conscious of who this was. Freddie. Winifred. The woman who would be his wife. Be his queen.

'Say it.' He stared down at her pale face in the dim room, noting the vulnerable curve of her bottom lip, the strong line of her nose. Her high forehead and straight, dark brows. Her eyes were black, yet they were full of lights, full of stars.

She was beautiful and he couldn't stop staring.

'Augustine,' she murmured, his name sounding like a prayer. 'My Augustine.'

The possessive 'my' sent a bolt of jagged lightning straight through him, though he couldn't quite catch hold of why. Because it also made him want to pin her to the mattress, thrust hard into her until they were both fully aware of who belonged to who. *She* belonged to him. She was pregnant with his child, she was his PA. He'd known her for five years and she was constantly at his side. That made her his. Completely.

She lied to you, though. You have no idea who she is.

No, that was wrong. He *did* know who she was. Not the details of her life, but he knew the woman she was deep inside, the woman he'd worked beside for five years. Meticulous, steady and calm. And beneath that, passionate. Caring. Protective. Vulnerable. And brave. *His* Freddie, was brave.

'Again,' he growled, beginning to move, slow at first then faster, harder, and her nails dug into his back, passion lighting her up.

There were so many things he couldn't do. So many.

But he could do this. He could give her pleasure and he could protect her. She needed someone to look out for her, someone who'd stand between her and the rest of the world. She'd been doing that for him for so long so why couldn't he return the favour? She was the mother of his child, of course that was his job.

He'd be that someone. He'd be the one to protect her.

How can you? When you can barely even rule a country adequately?

He thrust hard, deeper, ignoring the voice in his head. 'Again, sweetheart. I want to hear my name.'

'Augustine,' she gasped.

He gripped her hips, tilting her slightly, angling her so he could go even deeper, the sound of his name in her soft, husky voice making him feel possessive and raw. 'And who do you belong to?'

She was shaking now, so very close to the edge. 'You.' The word escaped on a moan. 'I belong to you.'

He liked that, he liked that far too much. It felt right, as if it was something that had always been right.

He'd never been a man to get possessive of a woman. He'd never wanted to be. But Freddie was different and maybe she'd always been different. And maybe she'd always been his, too, he'd just never recognised it.

Whatever, he couldn't take his eyes off her so he didn't, watching as the orgasm came for her and she screamed in his arms, his name echoing off the walls.

Then he let himself go too and joined her in the ecstasy.

CHAPTER EIGHT

WINIFRED WOKE TO the sound of Augustine's deep voice talking quietly to someone, and it took her a moment to orient herself, not quite sure where she was or what was happening.

Then she remembered.

She'd woken early and gone wandering on the battlements and she'd met him. And...

Oh, no. She'd told him *everything*.

It was enough to make her want to go straight back to sleep again and let unconsciousness take it all away, but of course that was impossible.

She'd fallen asleep in his bed after they'd made love for the third time—or possibly the fourth?—and she hadn't meant to. She'd been so wrung out after the emotional storm that had taken her up on the battlements, and he'd wrapped his arms around her, drawing her in close to the reassuring heat of his body and she'd just...fallen fast asleep. As if some part of her knew she was finally safe.

Are you sure about that?

Winifred shoved the thought away and opened her eyes.

Augustine had just shut the door behind one of the palace servants, and now he turned, coming over to a tray that had been put on a low table near the window. A breakfast tray by the looks and smell of things. Coffee. Bacon. Eggs. Pastries and... Was that waffles? Oh, how she loved waffles.

She swallowed, suddenly starving.

Cautiously, she sat up, holding the sheet up around her, which was a little like closing the stable door after the horse had bolted, but still. She felt exposed and a bit vulnerable.

She'd said a lot to him up on the battlements and she'd wept, and then she'd let him take her to bed...

A wave of heat went through her. *My Augustine*, she'd whispered, when he'd made her say his name. What on earth had possessed her to say that? To his face? He'd been above her, inside her, looking down at her with the most incredible intensity, and she'd felt suddenly possessive.

He is yours, though.

She did think of him that way, it was true. She worked for him, but she hadn't considered it work for some time, more like helping him and caring for him. Yes, she was a lovesick idiot in love with a king, but she was making his life easier and that's exactly what she wanted.

But she should never have said it to his face. She'd rather die than have him know how she felt about him. Her love had to be kept secret, because it put him at a safe distance. Safe from her.

Augustine turned from his contemplation of the breakfast on the table and turned, smiling at her. It was one of his wonderful warm smiles, making her heart squeeze tight in her chest.

'Good morning, beautiful.' He came over to the bed and sat down on it next to her. He was wearing the same jeans and T-shirt combination he'd been wearing before and he was the one who was beautiful. Not her. 'Are you hungry? I had the staff bring some breakfast to us. We need to talk about the wedding.'

She blinked, unconsciously wrapping the sheet around her a bit tighter. 'A wedding? You mean you still want to marry me? After what I told you?'

'Are you still pregnant?' He looked down at the curve of her bump. 'Yes, you are. Which means this marriage is still on.'

'But I lied to you, Augustine. I lied about so many things. And I shot someone. What about—'

Augustine took her face between his hands and brushed a kiss over her mouth, effectively silencing her. 'Come and have breakfast, Freddie,' he murmured. 'Then we'll discuss it.'

He wasn't going to let her get away with *not* discussing it, that was obvious, and even though she quailed at the thought, she had to stop avoiding her past. He knew all about it now anyway, and he didn't appear to be angry. She had no idea why he wasn't, but maybe it would be all right. And anyway, apart from anything else, she was hungry and the breakfast did smell very, *very* good.

'Okay,' she said, giving in.

He smiled again, making everything inside her bask in the glory of it, then he got off the bed, picked her silk robe up off the floor and held it up, obviously intending to put it on her himself.

Her heart beat faster at the thought of him looking at her naked body. She wasn't the most amazingly curvaceous woman in the world, certainly not compared to his usual lovers, but he hadn't complained when he'd been making love to her this morning. In fact, he'd spent a long time tracing each and every one of her curves with his hands and then his mouth, making his enjoyment of her clear.

She'd never thought too much about her looks before. When she'd been on the run, she'd tried to be careful about being too obviously female because she knew that would make her a target. And when she'd got the job with Augustine, she'd dressed to draw attention away from herself not to it. She wasn't supposed to draw notice.

But him standing there, holding her robe, with heat in his eyes, obviously wanting to look at her... She couldn't help feeling a little thrill.

Dropping the sheet, she slipped out of bed and went over to him, enjoying the way the heat flared in his gaze as he looked over her naked body. She smiled as she came close then turned around, sliding her arms into the sleeves.

'I think I should forbid you to dress yourself,' he murmured as he wrapped the fabric around her, enclosing her in his arms. 'I think in future you should only be dressed by me.'

'That could make things difficult.' She shivered as he tied the sash around her waist, then held her tight against him. 'Weren't we going to have breakfast?'

'Hmmm.' His mouth brushed the side of her neck. 'Perhaps breakfast could wait a few minutes?'

She was tempted, so very tempted. It would be a nice distraction, but he was right, they did need to discuss things. 'No,' she said quietly. 'We need to talk.'

'Hold that thought, then.' He didn't sound disappointed. 'Also, you need food.' He released her, then took her hand and led her over to the table where breakfast had been set up. He pulled out a chair for her in a courtly gesture and sat her down in it before moving to take the chair opposite. Then he began pouring orange juice and putting food on a plate, and since it was all the things she liked to eat, he obviously meant it for her.

She hadn't thought he'd noticed her preferences and it made her feel good in a way she probably shouldn't to watch him put the waffles on a plate, with strawberries and cream and some maple syrup. And then some of the crispy bacon because she did like it extra crispy.

'I can do it,' she said. 'I'm not completely helpless, you know.'

'I know.' His blue gaze caught hers. 'But you need to let me look after you, Freddie. As your husband that will be my job.'

There was something intense in his eyes that she didn't understand, as if looking after her was important to him, which was odd. He'd never looked after her so explicitly before. Was it because she was pregnant?

'But you're not my husband,' she pointed out.

'Yet.' He pushed the orange juice in her direction. 'But I will be.'

She shook her head. 'You can't want someone like me on the throne, sir. Not with my past. I'm a…a murderer.'

He handed her plate over to her. 'Firstly, we're not in bed now, Freddie, so you can stop it with the sir. Secondly, someone like you will be perfect for the throne. And thirdly, you're not a murderer. There was no intent to kill that bastard, you were just protecting your sister. I told you that.'

'But I… The law could be after me.'

'Is the law, in fact, after you?'

Taking the plate, she put it down, feeling stupid. 'I…don't know. I couldn't bear to find out.'

'Well, I'll find out and then I'll handle it.' Amusement glittered in his eyes, yet there was an edge to his voice. 'What's the point of being a king otherwise?'

He did tend to make light of things that he secretly took seriously.

'But I—'

'You're not going to jail, Freddie. I won't have it.'

Heat crept up her neck.

You should go to jail. You must answer for your crimes.

A strange, almost despairing feeling wound through her. Did admitting to not wanting to go to jail amount to self-ishness? Did that mean she was really like her mother deep down?

Cassie-Lynn had never wanted kids, or so she'd often told Winifred. She'd only had Winifred and her two sisters because their fathers had wanted them. But then the fathers had left, leaving Cassie-Lynn to look after the kids, which was a usual bitter complaint.

Though really, it was Winifred who looked after the children, so Cassie-Lynn could lie around on the sofa all day watching TV or having parties in her yard, or doing the few little drug deals that paid for her expenses. She'd been a dis-interested mother, and when Aaron had come along, she'd been even more disinterested, especially when he started paying her bills for her.

'I should,' she said, looking down at her plate. 'I have to answer for my crime.'

'For the crime of defending yourself? And defending your sister?'

Winifred knew she should eat, but abruptly she wasn't hungry. 'My mother never took responsibility for anything,' she said after a moment. 'It was all about her and what she wanted, and if things didn't go her way, it wasn't her fault. It was someone else's.' She swallowed and looked at him. 'She didn't believe me about Aaron when I told her he made me and my sisters uncomfortable. She said I was making things up, that I was a liar. And I was so...angry with her.' Winifred could still remember the hot boil of rage that had gripped her with Aaron looming over her as he held little Annie's wrist. And along with it, a terrible sense of betrayal, that the one person who should have protected her, who should have believed her, hadn't. 'I can't blame her for this, though. She didn't pull the trigger. I did. Then I had to take my sisters away. I couldn't leave them with her, not after that. I thought I could take care of them, but I couldn't.' There was another lump in her throat, but she wasn't going to weep again so she forced it away. 'They cried when the social workers came to get them.'

There was a long silence and when she looked at him again, she found something hot burning in his eyes that stole her breath. 'She should have been there for you,' he said flatly. 'She was your mother. It was her job to protect you, you do understand that, don't you? You might have pulled the trigger, but you shouldn't have been in that position in the first place.'

'Yes,' she said, her voice hoarse. 'It's just...sometimes it feels as if I'm doing the same thing, running away from something I should have taken responsibility for. And maybe I gave my sisters up just because I didn't want to take care of them.'

'If you hadn't wanted to take care of them, you could have left them with your mother and you didn't. You wanted to make sure they were safe.' His gaze was relentless. 'And if you hadn't run away, you might have been put in jail and that wouldn't have helped anything, Freddie.' All the amusement had died out of his eyes now, leaving behind a fierce intensity she didn't quite understand. 'You also might have been acquitted, but it really doesn't matter, because either way you wouldn't have been here, helping me. You've been basically running this country for five years... You do understand that, don't you?'

A little shock went through her. 'No, I haven't. I'm just your PA. I help you do the things you need to do, that's all.'

'Are we just going to ignore the fact that without you,

all I could do is make nice at balls and be charming to the media?'

It was another light, casual comment, but there was an undercurrent to the words that was not light or casual.

He was a man of such opposites sometimes. He seemed so easygoing and relaxed on the outside, so charming and approachable. And yet…while that charm wasn't practised or pretend, he used it to hide another part of himself. A deeper part, that she'd glimpse when he was tired or frustrated, or there was something difficult he had to deal with.

He'd get dark and brooding and angry, and it made her ache to see that part of him. It made her want to know what he was so angry about and what he brooded on, and to tell him that he didn't have to pretend he didn't feel those things with her, that she knew all his frustrations, and his angers. He could be himself with her, he didn't need to hide all the time.

But she could see that part of him now, the deep, emotional part of him, the empathic protector she knew he was.

He is going to make the best father for your child.

A part of her shifted and settled at the thought. He would. Her child could not be in better hands than his when they eventually made it into the world.

'You are the king,' she corrected him gently. 'It's more than parties and being a media sensation, and you know it. Your people love you… Augustine.' It was such a thrill to say his name like that, so casually.

'They don't know me.' The words were almost dismissive. 'Don't forget I have as many secrets as you.'   .

He did. The fact that he couldn't read or write being the main one. He treated it so casually that she knew without a doubt that it bothered him, frustrated him. That sometimes it made him send her away when he was in one of his darker moods.

A traumatic brain injury, that's what he'd told her when she first came to work for him. Since then she'd done a lot of her own research about it, reading about personality changes, fatigue, clouded thinking, aphasia, and other symptoms.

She'd asked him once why he had to keep his symptoms secret, and he'd said that no one wanted an incompetent king. She'd told him that he wasn't incompetent, that there were some things he couldn't do, but his brain was working just as well as hers and why would his people care anyway?

He hadn't answered her and she hadn't brought up the subject since. What was the point? Besides, she was just his PA. Who was she to question him?

You're not just his PA now.

It was true. She would be his wife.

She had no idea what actually being a wife entailed, but she'd read widely from the books in the palace library and she'd watched a lot of movies.

Love was the reason you married someone, but obviously that wouldn't apply here. She loved him, but he didn't love her back, and she'd been fine with that for years.

Are you still fine with it now?

She ignored the thought. She'd lived without love for most of her life, and she'd survived so far. It didn't matter that he didn't feel the same way.

Still, she wanted to know exactly where she stood with him, and how *he* saw a marriage between them.

Winifred put down her fork. 'So, about this marriage. How do you see it working between us then?'

Augustine picked up the coffee pot and poured some of the rich black liquid into his coffee cup. The smell was so good and he was feeling pleased with himself.

Despite not sleeping much the night before, he'd had the

most excellent sex and now there was coffee, and Freddie was sitting opposite him, looking gorgeous in her pretty pink robe, the distress that had been in her eyes the day before completely gone. Her hair was loose in glossy dark waves over her shoulders and he could see a few darkening marks on her neck. Marks he'd made himself. Looking at them satisfied him on a fundamental level he couldn't quite explain.

He leaned back in his chair and sipped his coffee, regarding her for a moment.

She'd asked him the question in her usual calm, professional voice, the soft vulnerability she'd shown as she'd sat down for breakfast, all worried about whether she was selfish or not for giving up her sisters, for running away, gone.

She wasn't selfish, and he believed that, and he hoped she'd believed him when he'd told her that too. Because she wasn't selfish. She'd been a child who hadn't been protected by the one person who was supposed to protect her: a parent.

How could she blame herself for running away? For giving up her sisters when she hadn't been able to look after them? She'd been scared and only sixteen, far too young for that kind of responsibility.

Anyway, regardless of whether she should have or not, she had, and that had brought her to him, and he couldn't regret that, even with the lies she'd told him, not for one second.

In fact, it made him want more. He liked her professionalism, he always had, but that wasn't what he wanted from her now. Because she wouldn't be his employee any longer, but his wife and the mother of his child, and he liked her confiding in him. He liked her telling him her secrets.

'For a start, you won't be my employee,' he said slowly. 'Which means you don't need to be all professional with me.'

'But if I'm not your employee then who will be your PA?'

That was a good question and one he hadn't considered, not given how tumultuous the past twenty-four hours had been.

'I can get someone to deal with the day-to-day donkey work. But it would be better if you could still help me with the…more personal requirements.' He hadn't meant it to sound like a double entendre, but it came out sounding like one all the same.

Pink tinged her cheekbones, but that calm look didn't budge. 'I'm serious.'

'So am I. You can still read my correspondence and delegate the rest. That way no one else need know anything.'

She frowned, but didn't say anything for a moment, slowly eating the rest of her waffle. 'And what about us? Do we live as husband and wife?'

'Of course.' He took another sip of his coffee. 'You'll share my bed, my apartments, and once you're crowned, you'll obviously be sharing in any royal duties.'

She put her fork down, a crease between her brows. 'Augustine,' she said softly, the sound of his name in her husky voice sending a pulse of desire through him. 'Your queen… I can't. I was brought up in a trailer park. My mother was a petty criminal and small-time drug dealer.'

'So?' He met her dark gaze and held it. 'You're not your mother, Freddie, I told you that.'

'That doesn't change the fact that I killed someone,' she said starkly. 'And I lied to you.'

'You shot someone who was going to hurt a child. And then you were trying to rebuild your life.'

'But—'

'Have you indulged in any petty thievery while you've been here?'

She frowned at him. 'No.'

'Dealt any drugs?'

'No, of course not.'

'No,' he agreed, 'you haven't. You've been a thorough professional for the last five years, even though you have more access than most to the royal coffers and expense accounts, not to mention the crown jewels.' He put his cup down and leaned his elbows on the table. 'Nothing's gone missing since you've been here and no one else has turned up shot, have they?'

'You don't know that for certain.'

'Okay, have you stolen anything since you've been here? Shot anyone?'

She let out a breath. 'No.'

He smiled, very much enjoying outplaying her. 'Freddie, sweetheart, the facts are staring you in the face. You're not a criminal, no matter what you think.'

She was sitting very still, her gaze dropping to her food, the colour fading slowly from her face. He didn't like that at all, so he reached over the table and took her fingers in his. The tips of them were cold so he lifted them and brought them to his mouth, brushing kisses over them.

'You need to tell me about your life in the trailer park,' he said. 'I want to know everything.'

'It's awful.' But she didn't pull away. 'You don't want to hear it, not really.'

'Why wouldn't I?'

'Because it's...dull.'

'Freddie, nothing about you is dull.' He searched her face. 'Unless there's something else you're not telling me?'

For some reason she blushed. 'No. No, there's nothing.'

'Are you sure? Seems like there's something.'

She pulled her hands away and he let her go, watching

her, half of him wondering what else she was keeping from him, the other half wondering whether to let this conversation lie and go straight back to bed, where things were simpler. Where there was just his naked body and hers, and there wasn't this barrier between them. Because there was one, he could feel it. A distance she was putting him at.

'I've told you something already,' she said. 'What about you? This can't be all one way, sir.'

She'd slipped back into work mode, that was obvious.

He didn't like that. Not at all.

'You know all about me. Head injury. Can't read. Can't write. Emotionally unstable. What else is there to say?'

Her eyes were very dark as she pushed her plate away and then leaned her elbows on the table too, mirroring him. 'I don't know anything about your childhood.'

The statement jolted him, though he wasn't sure why. His childhood had been ideal, so there was no reason to feel as if he'd just put his hand on a live wire. 'I was brought up at the palace,' he said lightly. 'Groomed from an early age to be King. My father was a good man and a wonderful ruler. There's no hidden trauma, I can assure you.'

'You don't talk about your mother much,' she said carefully.

Again that electric jolt. He ignored it.

'No, because there's nothing much to say. She died when I was a year old, so I don't remember her.'

'Did your father ever speak of her?'

'Bits and pieces. A lovely woman, by all accounts. And he loved her very much.' He reached for his coffee and lifted it, taking another sip. 'Next question.'

But Freddie only looked at him, as if she could see inside his head. See what lay at the heart of him, not the King his father had wanted or that his mother had given her life for, but the broken man he was inside.

'I'm sorry,' she said quietly. 'That's awful for you.'

'Is it?' He couldn't quite keep the edge out of his voice. 'You don't miss what you never had.'

There was a pause.

She was still looking at him, a slight frown on her face, her dark eyes full of a compassion that made his chest feel tight. 'I heard she had cancer.'

You might as well tell her. There are too many secrets as it is.

That was true. And what did it matter anyway? It was ancient history and a matter of public record. He'd never known his mother so there was no reason for this reluctance.

'Yes, she did.' This time he made sure there was no edge at all in his voice. 'They discovered it quite early on in her pregnancy with me. Breast cancer. The treatments would have meant losing her baby, so she chose not to have treatment until after I was born.' He could feel himself smiling, which was just strange because it was nothing to smile about. 'But sadly by then it was too late. The cancer had progressed and she was terminal. There was nothing to be done for her.'

Freddie's gaze had turned soft and something glowed in it, something he didn't like. Something that looked like pain or sympathy, neither of which he needed or wanted.

His mother had given her life for him. He hadn't had a choice about it. He'd planned to be the best damn king he could be so her sacrifice wouldn't be in vain, but then his father had died and the young man he'd been back then had died along with him.

He was different now; the brain injury had seen to that. Oh, he pretended he was the same man—he remembered

enough of who he'd once been to keep the veneer in place—
but he wasn't.

He was darker, more impatient, the grip on his temper
less certain. When he'd been in hospital, he'd experienced
waves of frustration and rage he hadn't been able to control.
He'd destroyed one hospital room and scared the daylights
out of the staff. He'd done it in the palace too, once he was
king, frequently breaking things in a fit of rage.

You haven't done it since Freddie came.

No, it was true, he hadn't. She calmed him, steadied him.
But that didn't mean the anger and frustration had gone away.
They were still there and were still overwhelming sometimes.

He was aware that there was a sudden ache behind his
eyes, a headache starting up. Instantly Freddie pushed back
her chair and came around the table to him; she seemed to
have a sixth sense when it came to his headaches and always knew when he was experiencing one. No doubt she
was heading to give him one of those neck massages that
really did lessen the pain. Except he didn't want that from
her now. That wasn't her job, not anymore. *He* was going
to take care of her, not the other way around, because that's
the one thing he could do, dammit.

So he shoved his own chair back and stood just as she
approached. Her eyes widened and she took a quick step
back. 'Sir, I was just—'

'No,' he said flatly. 'I don't want you doing that anymore.
It's my job to take care of you, not vice versa.'

'But I want to help you.'

'I don't care,' he snapped, then took a breath, because
he didn't want to get angry and this was a silly thing to get
angry about. 'Look,' he went on, more quietly. 'There aren't
many things I can do well these days, but taking care of you
is one of them. So, please. Let me do it.'

She stared at him a moment longer, her hands at her sides, half closed into fists. Then she let out a breath and nodded.

So he led her back to her seat, pulled out her chair for her to sit, then once she had, he came back to his seat and sat down. 'Now,' he said. 'Tell me about your childhood. Tell me everything.'

CHAPTER NINE

WINIFRED SOON FOUND herself at the centre of a whirlwind. First there was the announcement to parliament about the King of Isavere's upcoming marriage, and then came the press release announcing it to the rest of Isavere.

Augustine had asked her if she wanted to change her name legally to Winifred and since she couldn't bear the thought of not being his Freddie any longer, she decided she would.

She was nervous, though. The King of Isavere was a well-known playboy, which meant any woman he eventually chose to be his wife would be under scrutiny. Luckily, the palace PR machine was excellent and they spun it as an epic love story with a Cinderella element: the woman who'd been at the King's side for so long, who'd eventually captured his heart, would now be his queen.

They'd discussed what they wanted to say about Winifred's past and while she was nervous, she was determined it couldn't stay secret. Someone would unearth her background eventually and it was better to confront it head on. The truth would allow the palace to control the story and pre-empt any media storm.

Augustine did some investigation into the circumstances around Aaron's death and found that the police investigation into it had been lacklustre at best. No one was very interested in the death of a small-time drug dealer who already had a rap sheet littered with sex offenses, not to mention that the statute of limitations had run out. As for Winifred's mother, she'd been sent to jail for dealing meth and wouldn't be getting out anytime soon.

So, the press release included the details of her past, reiterating that the King had known the truth for years but had been protecting her. She had his full support, not to mention that of the American embassy, and he hoped she would also have the support of Isavere as a whole. And, oh, yes, she was expecting his heir.

To Winifred's own surprise, everyone loved it. The people of Isavere had always taken a certain amount of pride in the fact that their king was a media star, and now their prospective queen had the most scandalous and delicious background; they were thrilled. They also loved the idea that the right woman for the king had been at his side for so many years and he'd just never noticed. The story was picked up by the press and soon the web and print newspapers were running the story of the king and his PA. A Cinderella story for the ages, one newspaper trumpeted.

Augustine also calmly set about finding her sisters and contact was soon made. Winifred had a video call with them, getting all weepy when they told her they had the most wonderful foster family, who'd given them the loving childhood they'd missed out on in the trailer park.

Annie was in the process of applying for colleges while the youngest had just started high school, but both girls were thrilled when Winifred asked them if they wanted to be her bridesmaids, because obviously they had to be.

Augustine was making good on his promise to take care of her, and while she wasn't used to having someone look after her that way, she let him. She couldn't forget the way he'd said, *There aren't many things I can do well these days, but taking care of you is one of them. So, please. Let me do it.*

As if being a king and ruling a country for the past five years had been the 'many things' he couldn't do. Which was ridiculous. She knew he struggled with the limitations the brain injury had given him, but he'd managed to rule very well. She helped him, it was true, but every decision was his. And it was because he couldn't read that he preferred talking to people rather than relying on reports or other information, playing to his strengths, whether he was aware of it or not.

No, he couldn't read a press release, but he certainly knew what to say. And he knew what his people wanted because he talked to them. Exhaustively.

But she'd never liked the way he talked about his own limitations. He was casual about them, dismissive almost, which was a clear sign that they bothered him.

It made her wonder why. Made her want to know what his thoughts and feelings were about the situation, because she wasn't just his PA anymore. She would be his wife. And while it was true that she didn't know what being a wife meant, she did know that she was supposed to support her husband. He'd already stated that their marriage would be a real one in every sense of the word, so in order to support him, she had to know him.

And while she might know him as a boss and a king, and the object of her fantasies, she didn't know the man. The person he was behind all those things. He'd never revealed his vulnerabilities to her, apart from the headaches he got. But that was it.

It wasn't enough.

Over the next week, after the press release had been is-

sued, Augustine set about organising everything. He set to
it with a purpose, getting his events team to start planning a
royal wedding and a celebratory ball, then organising medi-
cal care for her pregnancy. He sat down with her to consult
about refurbishing the queen's apartments, then the royal
nursery. He contacted designers for her wedding gown, and
then other designers for a new wardrobe for her for state oc-
casions. He also put together a schedule for her coronation.

It was clear he was going all out, no expense spared.

He also went all out privately.

She was in his bed every night, which she had no problem
with whatsoever, and he insisted on having all their meals
together, where he asked a lot of questions about what she
wanted for the future and what her opinions were on what
seemed like everything under the sun.

Clearly she was his current obsession, and while she
basked in his attention after so many years of not having
it, there was also an underlying worry she couldn't quite
get rid of.

Because he didn't talk about himself and whenever she
asked, he'd deflect, or say something lightly, or dismiss it
entirely. She didn't know why that was, but she suspected.

Since that day when they'd shared breakfast and he'd told
her about his mother and how she'd refused treatment for
the cancer that would kill her in order to have him, she'd
read what she could about his parents. Because no matter
what he'd said about not missing what he'd never known,
and not having known his mother, she knew it meant something to him. Why else would he talk about it so casually?

King Piero Solari had been an excellent ruler. An in-
tellectual, he'd believed very firmly in the importance of
a good education, had very high standards for both himself and his employees, and worked long hours. He'd put

through parliament several measures that had improved his people's lives, but it was also clear that his people had found him slightly distant and unapproachable. They'd loved his Queen, though, and so had he, judging from the fact that he'd refused to marry again after her death.

A good man, Winifred learned, and one Augustine loved very much. Yet, she couldn't help wondering how those high standards of his had affected his son, and they must have. Why else would he be so very hard on himself?

She was in Augustine's office, reading a press release relating to the accident that had killed Piero and injured Augustine so badly, when he suddenly came in, his phone stuck to his ear.

'Freddie,' he said peremptorily. 'Next week for your scan. In the morning, yes?'

A little shock went through her. She'd almost forgotten that was due. 'Yes, that's fine.'

'Yes, perfect,' Augustine said to his phone before disconnecting the call. Slipping the phone into his pocket, he came over to his desk where she was sitting, and smiled down at her. 'What have you been doing this afternoon, sweetheart? Something restful I hope.'

The endearment gave her a thrill, which she hid. He looked tired, though. She could see the lines of strain around his eyes, and it made concern tighten inside her. He'd been pushing himself too hard with all this wedding stuff, and she didn't like it.

She didn't want to remind him about his father and all the things he wasn't telling her, not when he was tired like this, so she only shook her head and pushed the laptop closed. 'Oh, nothing much. Just looking at spreadsheets.'

'No, you weren't.' He was still smiling, but there was an edge to it. 'I saw the royal crest on your screen.'

'It's nothing, Augustine.' She smiled back. 'Truly.'

His expression darkened. 'Don't placate me. You know I don't like it.'

There was an edge in his voice now, too.

You're going to have to push him, even if you don't want to. Even if he's tired and you want to protect him. Because if you don't, what will your marriage look like? He'll be the one calling all the shots, because if you give him an inch, he'll take the whole damn country.

It was true, he would. Yet she couldn't stop thinking about the real question: What *did* she want their marriage to look like? It couldn't be a mere extension of her job, where she did what he said and everything was all about making his life easier.

Because he wouldn't be her boss anymore. He wouldn't be her king either. He'd be her husband, her equal, and she wouldn't be his PA, but his wife.

Perhaps it was time he started seeing her that way.

So, on second thoughts, maybe it *was* time to push him. Because if she didn't the rest of their marriage would be her being his PA except with sex. Oh, he'd said he wanted to take care of her, and she had no issue with that. Except that was *still* him calling the shots. Especially when he refused her taking care of him.

'I was trying to find out more about your father,' she said after a moment.

Augustine raised a brow. 'Oh? And why, pray?'

'Because you won't talk about him.' She met his gaze steadily. 'And you won't talk to me about the car accident. Or your childhood. You keep deflecting or dismissing every question I ask.'

He shrugged. 'It's not important.'

'It *is* important,' she disagreed. 'You know everything

about me and my horrible mother, and growing up in that trailer. But I know nothing about you. How is that fair?'

His expression was impossible to read, which was a sign that he did not like this line of enquiry. 'Fine. What do you want to know?'

She blinked, not expecting him to give in. 'I just... You don't talk about your childhood much and you...never talk about the accident.'

A burst of what looked like pain flared in his eyes, and she half rose to her feet to go to him, but his expression hardened. 'No,' he snapped. 'I'm not a child. I don't need comforting. It was years ago. It's fine.'

She stiffened. 'I'm sorry. I didn't mean to offend you.'

His blue gaze was cool, his expression unyielding for a second. Then it softened a little and he lifted a hand, rubbing at his temple. 'Sorry, I don't mean to snap. I've had a busy day and I'm tired.'

Her own hands itched, wanting to massage the tight muscles around his neck and shoulders, ease the physical pain that was obviously troubling him. But again, that would be what Freddie, his PA, would do, and she wasn't his PA any more. She didn't *want* to be his PA any more, she suddenly realised.

She wanted to be his wife.

'Augustine,' she said steadily. 'You can't expect me to take whatever you give me and be happy with it. I'm not your PA anymore. You wanted a full marriage and a full marriage involves give and take. And I'm not going to be the one doing all the taking, do you understand?'

A muscle leapt in his strong jaw. 'So, what? I presume you were reading about the accident? Well, the car slid on a snowy road. There was black ice and the driver lost control of the car. It was no one's fault. My father and the driver were killed instantly and I was injured.'

She took a silent breath, masking her own concern and hurt for him. That clearly wasn't what he wanted and if she was going to get information out of him, they'd have to do it his way. That was fine. 'Badly injured, right?'

'I guess if you term taking a year to relearn even the most basic of bodily functions badly injured then yes, I was badly injured.'

'Why do you do that?' She couldn't help it, the question just came out. 'Why do you make light of everything that's important to you?'

Again, his expression was like granite. 'I don't.'

'Yes, you do. Everything terrible, that's obviously painful to you, you joke about. Why? Is it easier? Do you need distance? What?'

That muscle leapt again. 'Do we have to talk about this now?'

Her heart squeezed tight behind her breastbone. No, she didn't want to. She didn't want to make things harder for him, that was never what she'd wanted to do. But…she had no choice. If she was going to be his wife rather than his PA, she couldn't let him call all the shots.

'Yes,' she said flatly. 'Yes, I think we do.'

He didn't want to talk about this. It was the last thing in the world he wanted to discuss. He'd spent a very productive week organising his wedding and dealing with announcing her as his chosen bride, and managing the refurbishment of the various parts of the castle that needed it, and he didn't want to be distracted. Not when it felt as if he was finally accomplishing something worthwhile.

He just hadn't expected her to be interested in his childhood or the accident, or anything really, mainly because she'd never expressed interest before. Then again, she'd been his PA before and their relationship had been purely professional.

It was nothing like professional now.

He shouldn't have snapped at her, that was unfair, but he'd been caught off guard and the flare of grief when she'd mentioned it had also been unexpected. Then she'd moved to comfort him, and he hadn't wanted that either. He'd already felt too vulnerable.

She always saw too much, that was the problem. She was attuned to him in a way no other person ever had been and he wasn't sure he liked it.

She's not wrong, though. It's not fair to keep asking her for information when you won't volunteer any of your own.

No, it wasn't fair. But he didn't want to talk about it, not with her. She affected him in ways he wasn't prepared for and he didn't have the capacity to deal with her affecting him any further.

Like her, in many ways, he'd been alone a long time, keeping people at a distance so his secret would stay his. It was automatic by now to keep that distance and Freddie had always respected it.

Yet she wasn't now and he didn't know why.

What he did know was that he was tired, and he had a headache, and this was a difficult conversation that he didn't want to have, but maybe it was better to get it over and done with now. Surely if she knew all about the accident and his childhood, she'd eventually stop asking questions.

He shoved his hands in his pockets. 'Yes, I do make light of things. Because you either laugh or you cry, isn't that what they say?'

Her dark eyes held his. 'And you'd rather laugh?'

'Naturally. Crying would be unbecoming in a king.'

'Doing unbecoming things as a king has never bothered you before.'

Another statement that he wasn't expecting. Another observation that caught him off guard. He gritted his teeth. 'No. Because the press loves the unbecoming things I do. You know this, Freddie.'

'You do other things as well, though. It's not all about scandals. What about the network of shelters you set up last year for the homeless? Or the new women's hospital you funded from your own private coffers?'

He wanted to shrug, as if neither of those things mattered, wanted to make a joke, because those projects were small things. Drops in the bucket of his father's expectations. Expectations that he would never meet.

But he knew that if he said something casual or dismissive, she'd again know exactly how much those things had mattered to him.

'What about them?' he asked instead.

'You don't make a big deal of those.'

'No, I don't. Because they weren't a big deal.'

She frowned. 'Of course they were. They were a big deal to the people affected by them? Why do you keep dismissing them?'

His chest tightened. 'My father overhauled the entire public health system so that good healthcare could be accessed by anyone,' he said. '*That* was a big deal.'

She was silent, her dark eyes surveying him. Then she said, 'He had such high standards, didn't he?'

Something in him froze solid. 'What makes you say that?'

'Just from what I've read.'

'He had high standards because he was the king and he wanted what was best for people.'

'I didn't say that was a bad thing,' she said quietly.

Augustine found himself biting back all the defensive statements he wanted to say, that of course his father had high standards. Kings had to be the most responsible since they were leaders of entire nations. They held lives in their hands, so naturally they had to be held to high standards.

And you don't measure up. Not anymore.

'Yes, well.' He forced the thought away. 'It's not.'

There was a small crease between her brows as she looked at him, as if she was trying to figure something out, and it made him want to stroke it away with his thumb, perhaps distract her from this conversation with something that would make them feel so much better.

Except then she said, 'You hold yourself to those high standards too, don't you?'

He laughed, the sound coming out bitter and forced. 'Me? You're joking. Of course I don't have those high standards. I don't have any standards at all.'

'Don't do that. Don't pretend with me.' She rose, coming around the side of the desk and he found he'd taken a couple of steps back before he could stop himself.

She halted, the crease between her brows deepening. 'You don't trust me do you?'

The question somehow cut him somewhere deep inside and he didn't know what to say. Because of anyone in his life, she was the one he could trust and yet…something in him didn't want her near him or want to talk to her about his father, still less his mother.

She already knows how broken you are.

No, she didn't. She saw a king who couldn't do things but who was ultimately in charge. A king who dealt with everything that came his way without a problem. Who was charming and laid-back, whom everyone loved.

She didn't see the man who had no patience and whose grip on his temper was thin. Who was short with people and terse, who scared people, who could barely control himself.

A man who was barely surviving.

A man who was going to struggle to be a father let alone a husband, no matter how many times he told himself that he was going try.

How could he show her that man? She might refuse to marry him, and he couldn't bear that.

'Freddie,' he began, not knowing what he was even going to say to her.

'I'm tired. And I am…not a nice man when I'm tired, as you should know by now. Perhaps we should have this conversation when I am less so.'

'I don't need you to be nice.' Her dark gaze looked into him, seeing him. 'Because I'm not very nice either. I killed a man, remember?'

'Freddie…'

One corner of her mouth quirked in a charming half smile that nearly stopped his breath. 'You don't need to be afraid of me, Augustine. I'm not that scary.'

Something twisted in his chest, something that made him want to pull her close, kiss that adorable mouth, crush it beneath his and then take her so that the only words she'd be saying were 'more' and 'please' and 'harder, sir'.

But that would be dishonest of him and unfair. She wasn't asking for much, only the truth.

He let out a breath. 'You're right, I don't trust you. I don't trust anyone, but you…'

Her hand landed on his chest, a gentle touch. 'Me what?'

He met her dark gaze. 'You are going to be my wife. You are going to be the mother of my child. And you both…deserve better than what I can give you.'

'You're making me a queen, Augustine. I'm not sure how much better you could give me.'

'A whole man,' he said starkly. 'That's what you deserve. And I am very far from whole.'

Her expression softened and somehow it hurt. 'Ah,' she murmured softly. 'So that's what this is about. I wondered.'

'You don't know what the injury did to me.' He lifted his hand over hers and held it on his chest, needing her touch despite everything he told himself about distance. 'I had to learn how to do even the most basic tasks all over again. I had to learn to walk, learn to talk, to feed myself. And... I was not the same man I'd been. I have no patience now. I lose my temper easily. I'm much...darker than I was.'

'But I didn't know the man you were back then. I only know you now. And I don't find that man dark or angry. Impatient, yes, and unhappy, maybe, but not dark.'

He smiled, but it was more a baring of teeth than anything else. 'That's because I try to hide those parts of myself from you, Freddie.'

Her palm was warm against his chest. 'You don't hide them as well as you think you do. In fact, if I'm going to be your wife, you shouldn't hide them at all. I don't want you to.' Her eyes were so dark, like warm black velvet. 'You know the worst parts of me. I have a temper too. I was angry when I pulled the trigger on Aaron. I was furious with him and I was furious with my mother. I was furious at both of them for putting me in that position.'

He let out a breath and shook his head. 'I know. But you're not the king. Those parts of myself have to stay hidden precisely because of who I am. No one wants a king who can't control his emotions.'

'Is that what your father said?'

Irritation coiled inside him. Why did she keep bringing

his father into it? Very conscious of staying gentle, he lifted her hand off his chest and took a few steps back, needing some distance. 'He's got nothing to do with this. It's self-evident.'

She didn't move. 'He does have something to do with this. He set some very high standards for you, Augustine.'

'What? Being able to read and write and stay in command of myself?' He couldn't stop the words from spilling out, burning like acid. 'What's so high about that? A child could do it.' He left unsaid the fact that he couldn't, but he could hear the words echoing between them as if he actually had said them.

Freddie just stood there, and no doubt she could hear those unsaid words as loud as he, and suddenly he didn't want to be here anymore. He didn't want to be in this room with her, because his temper was so short and there was a pressure in his head. He didn't want to be here while she was looking at him, seeing exactly the kind of broken man he was deep inside.

'What are you so afraid of?' she asked. 'You're a good king, Augustine. You know that, don't you?'

All his muscles were tight, his shoulders, his neck, his spine. He ached. 'I'm a mediocre king doing the bare minimum, which is all I'll ever manage.' He knew he sounded harsh, but he didn't bother to moderate his tone. 'Which is all I'll be able to spare for you and the child too.'

Her expression softened, her eyes full of an awful, painful compassion. 'Augustine, no. You can't believe that—'

'I told you I don't want to talk about this anymore,' he snapped and then, because he was angry and he wanted some of the power back, he took a step towards her. Then another, and another. Slowly backing her up to the desk, until she was pressed against it.

Her expression didn't change, still so full of compassion and sympathy, he wanted to shout. But she was also warm and her scent was all around him, and there was only one way he knew of to wipe it off her face, and to get rid of that terrible vulnerability he was feeling.

He put his hands on her hips and gripped her tight, pressing his rapidly hardening groin against her. 'I'd much rather do this instead.'

CHAPTER TEN

AUGUSTINE WAS PRESSED against her, all raw masculine heat and explosive temper. Yet she could see that beneath that temper was fear. And she didn't need to ask him what he was afraid of. She knew.

He was afraid of himself, of what he termed his failings. Of actually being the mediocre king he told himself he was, and that the bare minimum was all he could do.

It hurt that he thought those things about himself. Because mediocre was the last thing he was. What he *actually* was, was wonderful. Warm and empathic and caring. Protective. And while there were some things he couldn't do, there were also some amazing things he could, such as connecting with his people in a way she'd seen no one else do.

And as for those emotions of his, well, while he might think himself impatient and angry and dark, he was no more so than anyone else. Besides, she'd never seen him take his frustrations out on anyone, not even once.

Yet the worst thing was, it wasn't his fault he thought those things of himself. It wasn't even his father's. It was a combination of circumstances and the kind of man he was that had driven him to believe that. A perfectionist nature combined with grief, and a powerful love. Because he'd loved his father, that was clear. Just as he must have felt powerfully about his mother, too, since he never talked about her. But she'd given her life to have him.

And now that was just another burden he had to bear.

She could see the fear and anguish in his burning blue-green eyes, could see the rage too. He was trying to frighten her away, she also knew that, as well as deflecting from what was obviously a painful conversation.

Well, she'd allow him the distraction. She didn't want to hurt him. But if he thought him being angry would frighten her, he had another think coming.

He clearly thought that the man he was now was something terrible, but he was wrong. She hadn't known him before the accident. All she knew was the man he was now, and she'd fallen in love with that man. There was nothing terrible about him. He said he'd hidden those darker parts of himself, but she'd caught glimpses of them over the years. When he was tired, he got short and snappy, but he wasn't ever cruel and he always apologised. Also, shouldering the burden of a country would make anyone short-tempered sometimes.

He brooded a lot sometimes too, sitting there in the darkness of a room some nights, sipping Scotch. A serious man, and tortured, but not dark.

She put her hands on his chest, looking up into his eyes, feeling the heat of him soak through the dress she was wearing. 'I'm not afraid of you,' she said. 'So if you're thinking of doing some grand reveal of the terrible monster you are deep down, I'm telling you now that it's not going to work.'

'Perhaps you'll think differently in a minute,' he growled then bent his head and covered her mouth with his.

She didn't flinch away. She met his kiss with her own, a feverish, explosive kiss that had desire igniting in the air around them like a blowtorch lit with a flame. Because while he had a temper, so did she, as well as a hunger to match, and if he was going to unleash himself on her, she would unleash herself on him in return.

He'd been so careful with her this past week in his bed, all soft kisses and caresses. Gentle touches, lovemaking long and slow.

But this was nothing like that.

He growled deep in his throat and shoved his hand beneath her dress, sliding it between her thighs, fingers curling beneath the lace of her knickers and tearing them. She bit his lower lip and widened her stance so he could touch her the way they both wanted him to.

Pleasure flared as he stroked the folds of her sex, finding the most sensitive part of her and sliding his fingertip around and around, firm strokes that made her pant and writhe. Then he pushed a finger inside her and then another, and she groaned into his mouth, because it was so good.

She loved this side of him, the demanding side. She loved every side of him.

He pressed against her harder, another growl escaping him as she bit him again, the kiss getting deeper, hotter. The edge of the desk was digging into the curve of her bottom, but all she was conscious of was the thrust of his fingers inside her and how good they felt. And how she wanted more.

As if he read her mind, he said in a low, guttural voice. 'You really want me like this? You don't know what I'll do to you.'

'Yes, I want you like this,' she panted back. 'I always want you, any way I can get you. And as for what you'll do to me… Do it. You can't do anything to me that I wouldn't want.'

For a second, he lifted his head, staring down into her

eyes, and she could see the ferocity burning there, so she let him see the ferocity burning in hers. Showing him the truth.

He cursed and then before she could move, he'd taken his hand from between her thighs, and had turned her around, bending her over the desk. He shoved her dress up over her hips. She heard him unzip his trousers; her breath was coming in short, hard pants.

She had never wanted him so badly. She liked him when he was gentle, touching her as if she was precious, but she liked this too. Him touching her roughly as if she was as hard as he was. As if she was as strong as he was.

She braced herself and then she felt him thrust inside her, hard. Pushing her against the edge of the desk.

It was glorious and she cried out in ecstasy. It felt so good. *He* felt so good. She loved how he'd unleashed himself, and she wanted to be equal to that, so she shoved herself back against him, letting him know that she was finding this every bit as intense as he was.

He thrust even harder, deeper, his breathing as wild as hers, and she noted dimly, that even as he was moving inside her without any restraint, she felt the little touches brushing against her abdomen, and how he adjusted himself so she wasn't pressed too hard against the wood. Protecting her and protecting their child even as he released his anger and his fear into her.

She moaned against the desktop, letting him move as hard as he wanted, the pleasure inside her pulling tighter and tighter until she thought she couldn't bear it.

'Touch yourself,' he ordered, low and dark. 'Put your hand between your thighs and make yourself come.'

So she did, and he moved even harder, thrusting deeply enough that she felt him everywhere. Behind her, inside her, around her. A wild, dark energy that called to something wild and dark in herself.

His movements became faster and suddenly the tension inside her pulled apart, unrestrained pleasure flooding through every part of her being, making her shudder and shake against the desk.

He put one hand on the desk beside her head, thrusting faster and faster before he fell out of rhythm, stiffening. Then his mouth was on her shoulder, biting down as the orgasm came for him too.

His other hand came down on the desk then as he braced himself, clearly not wanting to rest his whole weight against her, another sign of how he took care of her even when he was furious. And for a minute both of them were still, the room full of the sound of their ragged breathing. Then he pulled away, smoothing down her dress and adjusting the rest of her clothing.

As the aftershocks began to recede, she straightened and turned around.

He'd just finished doing up his fly, the rest of his clothing back in place again. But the look in his eyes was still fierce. 'Did I hurt you?'

'No, of course you didn't.' She held his gaze. 'I told you that you didn't frighten me. Was that supposed to be an example of why you're such a terrible person? Because if so, you're going to have to try harder.'

He swore. 'You really think that's how a king should act? Taking his pregnant fiancée over the—'

'You're not a king with me, Augustine,' she interrupted sharply. 'You're a man. A man who's had some awful things happen to him, and is still struggling with the effects of an injury, not to mention dealing not only with the grief of losing his father, but also of losing the person you once were.

A man who has distanced himself from everyone in order to do this alone. But the problem is, you can't do it alone.' She stared steadily into his eyes. 'I tried to do that myself, to deal with my secret by myself, to deal with this pregnancy all alone, and look where that got me? I couldn't do it. And now I know that actually I didn't want to. You need someone, Augustine. You need someone you trust, and you can trust me.'

His expression hardened, his blue eyes suspicious. 'Why should I?'

'Because I'm going to be your wife.' She took a small breath. He should know. He should know that the man he was now wasn't terrible and he wasn't broken. That he was a good man, a man who was going to make an excellent husband and an even better father; she just knew it. 'And because I love you.'

Freddie was standing there, her pretty dress all wrinkled from where he'd shoved it up above her hips. Her eyes were so dark and her hair was falling down around her shoulders, the flush of her orgasm still staining her cheeks.

She was so beautiful.

And he didn't understand how a woman so beautiful, so intelligent and passionate and honest, and caring, was telling him that she loved him.

Him. Who'd taken her over the desk like an animal.

What the hell was she thinking?

'What do you mean you love me?' he demanded, abruptly furious for reasons he couldn't have articulated.

Her chin lifted, as if she was preparing to do battle. 'Exactly what I said. I love you, Augustine. I have loved you for a long time. Years in fact.'

He could see the truth in her eyes, but suddenly couldn't

bear it. He couldn't bear the thought of the impossible burden love exacted being placed on his shoulders along with everything else.

His father had loved him, had expected great things from him, and he'd failed to live up to those expectations.

His mother had loved him and she'd chosen him at the expense of her own life.

All these people loving him and all he'd given them in return was disappointment. He couldn't bear to do the same with Freddie.

'I don't want you to love me,' he said roughly. 'I didn't ask for it.'

'Too late. That's the way it is.'

The pressure that the sex had relieved somewhat was building again. A pressure he didn't know what to do with. The pressure of his painful emotions, his grief for his father, for the King he was supposed to be and couldn't, for his mother's sacrifice all in vain, and for his child. Because his child would be stuck with him, a man who wasn't even really a man, not fully.

'I'm not in love with you,' he said. 'You know that, don't you?'

'Yes.' She didn't flinch. 'I know.'

'And if you're hoping my feelings will change, you'll be hoping forever. Because they're not going to. Marriage won't change anything.' It couldn't. He could barely rein in the emotions he had, let alone compound the burden by adding love to it. And love was so heavy. Heavier than the crown.

Her dark eyes didn't flicker. 'I understand that too. I wanted you to know, because while you might not like the man you are now, I do. He's stronger than he thinks he is, and is an excellent king. I've always thought so. He knows his people like no one else, and he's so good with them.

They love him so very much. He doesn't let what he can't do limit him, and the fact that he cares deeply about their welfare is what makes him so amazing.'

He didn't understand it. Didn't she know that was all an act? Something he tried hard to maintain, because his father had told him that a king knew what was going on in his country and that talking to people was the best way to do that.

'It's all pretend,' he said acidly. 'All of that is just an act, Freddie. Because if I didn't, all the people would see is a rabid dog snarling and pulling at the chain around his neck.'

She sniffed. 'Don't be so dramatic. It's hard for you, I know. But none of how you connect with people is an act. You might feel that way, but it isn't, Augustine. Neither is the way you care about people.'

This was an impossible conversation. He could see that now. She saw him through rose-coloured glasses. She didn't see him how he *actually* was.

'No, you're—'

'You're very committed to this idea that you're terrible somehow,' she interrupted, steamrolling over him as if he wasn't the King of the entire country. 'That you're mediocre and do a bad job. But you're wrong.' She stepped up to him suddenly, the lights in her dark eyes burning hotter now, the signs of her own anger flickering. 'You're just wrong. And I don't know why you want to believe that so badly about yourself. I can only assume it's because you're afraid. You don't actually think you're mediocre and a bad king. You're just afraid that you might be.'

She's not wrong.

No, she wasn't. Except he wasn't afraid. He'd accepted the truth of his own failure long ago. Failure to measure up to being the King his father wanted him to be. Failure to make good his mother's sacrifice in having him.

Failure to bear the burden of love placed on him by so many people, including that of his own country.

'I don't believe it,' he said. 'And I'm not afraid, because it's true and I've accepted what I am. And the quicker you accept it too, the better it will be for all of us.'

He couldn't stand being in the same room with her all of a sudden. With her liquid dark eyes, and her compassion. Her sympathy. Her insistence on him being better than he was. Her love.

He didn't want it. He couldn't bear it. Already the weight of everything he had to carry was too heavy. He couldn't carry anything more.

So, before she could say anything else, he turned and walked out.

He walked blindly, without direction. Several people approached him, no doubt with things they wanted him to do, but he gave them a look and they soon kept their distance. Of course they did. No one wanted to deal with him when he was in this mood.

After a time he found himself in the familiarity of the stables, the smell of horse and hay easing something inside him. He went to Honey's stall, and there she was, a glossy chestnut with a white blaze on her forehead.

She put her nose over the gate and he stroked it, all warmth and silky hair. Then she began to nose for a treat.

That was the thing with horses, they were undemanding. All they wanted was an apple or a stroke or a comb. They didn't require anything else. It was soothing.

You shouldn't have treated Freddie that way.

He picked up the curry comb and began to stroke it over

the horse's glossy coat, getting rid of the splashes of dirt on her legs and sides. She waited placidly beneath the comb.

He shouldn't have treated Freddie that way at all. But love? What could he do about that? She'd been in love with him for years, she'd said...

How are you going to face this marriage?

He'd face it the way he faced everything else. He'd grit his teeth and do the best that he could. He couldn't love her—at least he'd made that clear—but he could be a husband to her in all other ways. The only alternative was not marrying her, and he couldn't—wouldn't—do that. His child needed a father and while his best wasn't what it should be, it was better than nothing.

She deserves better than that, and so does your child.

Augustine gritted his teeth. She did. They both did. But unfortunately for all concerned, they only had him, and he wasn't a man who shirked his responsibilities. That wasn't the way he'd been brought up. Yes, his father had high standards, but the standard that kings held themselves to *had* to be high, and higher than that of other men, because the fate of a nation was involved.

As to husbands, his father had been an exemplary husband too. Which gave him an example to follow, even if he'd never measure up to that either.

Augustine ran his hand over the mare's glossy haunch, examining his work critically. This was something he could do well too. He could groom a horse so she shone.

He would do the same with Freddie.

He had a special evening planned tomorrow, a picnic in her favourite place in the palace, the little apple orchard that had been there for centuries, full of gnarled old apple trees that produced the sweetest apples.

He wanted to formally propose and give her his mother's engagement ring. The forms had to be observed. He'd thought about an engagement ball, but he wanted to marry her before their child was born and he wanted a formal occasion, which would take a bit of time to organise.

So no engagement ball. But that didn't matter, they'd have a wonderful wedding in the ancient cathedral in the middle of Isavere's capital, and then there would be a formal celebration. The invitations to the various heads of state had already gone out.

Satisfied and more settled, Augustine stepped back, put down the curry comb, put a blanket over the mare and then let himself back out of the stall.

Tomorrow night he'd make it up to Freddie. He'd give her a wonderful picnic and a beautiful ring, and then he'd take her back to his bedroom and he'd make them both feel good.

That would surely be enough for her.

It would have to be.

CHAPTER ELEVEN

THE MOMENT WINIFRED walked into her new rooms in the Queen's apartments and saw the garment bag lying on the bed, she somehow knew Augustine was involved.

There was a white envelope sitting on the bag, and when she picked it up and opened it, taking out the small white card inside, she saw someone had written on it in elegant, cursive hand:

Meet me in the apple orchard at seven p.m. Wear the dress.

It wasn't his handwriting, of course. She didn't know what his handwriting was like since she'd never seen it, and now he couldn't write anyway, but it was from him, nevertheless.

Last night he hadn't come to bed until after she was asleep, and when she'd woken up that morning, he wasn't there. He'd been absent all day.

She'd gone through his correspondence the way she normally did, annoyed when she couldn't find him to ask him a few things.

But maybe after their confrontation of the day before that was a good thing. Perhaps they both needed some distance.

You shouldn't have told him you loved him.

Her heart tightened in her chest, pain arrowing through her. He hadn't taken it well, but she should have foreseen that. She'd only wanted him to know that she didn't see him as broken the way he seemed to think he was, or that he was a lesser man now than he'd once been.

But perhaps that hadn't been the right thing to do. He'd been furious about it, and maybe he had a right to be. They'd never talked about love, after all, and she was the one who'd brought it into the conversation. Plus, he seemed to think her declaration a demand, which wasn't at all the case. She knew he didn't love her, and she didn't expect him to.

But don't you want him to?

The thought was uncomfortable. Love was something she'd never thought about after she'd left the States, not when she'd been too busy surviving. Then there had been the years in Europe, moving from place to place and trying to make ends meet. She hadn't thought about love then either.

Her mother hadn't loved her, though she knew her sisters did.

Regardless, it wasn't something she thought she needed, and after all, she'd survived well enough without it so far. Even meeting Augustine and falling in love with him, hadn't changed her mind.

Love was something she gave. She didn't expect anything back.

Sometimes she'd look at couples and wonder what it would be like to be loved by someone. To be important to someone. Then again, she'd been important to her sisters and so they'd always looked to her to protect them.

Love could be demanding. Love could ask you to do terrible things.

She didn't want that, and she especially didn't want it from someone who didn't want to give it to her anyway. She didn't want to be a burden to him, not when he was carrying so many already.

Pushing aside the thoughts, Winifred put down the card and picked up the garment bag, opening the zip.

Inside was the most beautiful ombré gown. It was the same dusty pale pink silk as her dressing gown at the neck and bodice, then gradually deepening into lilac at the hem. There were also sequins scattered everywhere like a constellation in the sky.

Her heart squeezed even tighter. Whatever he'd planned tonight, it was something wonderful, she could only assume since the gown was so beautiful.

Are you sure you want to go through with his whole charade?

Winifred let out a breath. Of course she had to go through with it. She said she'd marry him and she would. Because fundamentally, no matter what she thought about love, this wasn't for her sake but her child's. She'd grown up without a father and while she wasn't sure what kind of mother she was going to be since she had nothing but a bad example herself, she did know that their child would need Augustine. He'd had a father he'd loved, and whether he knew it or not, he was going to make a great father himself.

She couldn't do her child out of that, even despite the throne.

Winifred took her time getting ready that evening. She showered and dried her hair, letting it hang loose over her shoulders in glossy waves because she knew Augustine liked it that way. Then she put on the beautiful dress.

It fitted perfectly, even over her little bump, the pale dusty pink darkening into a swirl of deep lilac around her knees to her ankles.

When she was finally ready, a staff member came for

her, leading her through the castle and out into the walled orchard.

It was dark, the stars glittering in the sky like jewels, the grass soft beneath her feet. The air was warm and spiced with the scent of the apple trees.

But it wasn't that that made her catch her breath.

There were fairy lights giving off a soft white glow in the darkness, wound around the branches of the apple trees, shining down on the thick blanket that had been laid beneath them. And on the blanket was laid the most delicious-looking food, from pregnancy-safe cheeses to fruit and delicious little savouries. There were also small cakes and chocolate truffles, and in a silver ice bucket, a bottle of her favourite sparkling water.

But that wasn't even the best part.

The best part was Augustine standing beneath the apple trees in the glow of the lights, the gold strands in his dark hair gleaming. He wore a plain white shirt and dark trousers…simple clothing that only served to highlight the beauty of the man himself.

Her heart tightened.

He's not here for romance, remember. He doesn't love you and he never will, that's what he said.

No, she knew that. He'd been very clear. So there shouldn't be any reason why the loveliness of the scene should make her vision swim and her breath catch. Why the thought of him doing this for her because he loved her made her ache.

He was marrying her for the child's sake, nothing more. None of this was for *her*.

And why would it be? You don't deserve his love even if he was going to give it to you.

No, that was true. She didn't. But it would be nice to

think that maybe, one day, she did deserve it. And that one day, maybe, she could have this, could have him and his love too. But that was always going to be too much to ask for, wasn't it?

Winifred walked slowly under the apple trees and over to the blanket where he stood, trying very hard to not let even a hint of what she was feeling escape. She didn't want to ruin the evening by bursting into tears.

'This is beautiful,' she murmured. 'What's the occasion?'

His gaze swept over her, intensity burning deep in the turquoise depths. 'It's an apology,' he said. 'For yesterday, and also...' He took his hand out of his pocket, his fingers curled around a small black velvet box. 'I wanted to do this properly.'

Everything tightened, her heartbeat accelerating. Because she knew what he was going to do. He was going to get down on one knee and propose, as if this was an engagement between two people who loved each other, and not a simple marriage of convenience.

She didn't want him to all of a sudden. Because why? Why bother with the pretence? Why bother with the lights and the lovely dress and the food? She'd already agreed to marry him. There was no need for this performance.

'It's fine,' she said quickly. 'You don't need to do this, Augustine.'

His dark brows lowered. 'I don't need to do what?'

'Get down on one knee. Propose.' She took a little breath. 'Do all the lights and picnic. I don't even need a ring. I've already agreed to marry you, so what is the point of all of this?'

An expression she didn't understand rippled across his handsome face. 'Why do you think? I want to be a good husband to you, Freddie. And that starts with a formal proposal.'

'Does it?' It felt threatening, all this romance with no substance, no feeling. A show. Just more lies. God, she was tired of lies. 'I don't need a formal proposal—I told you that already.' She couldn't seem to temper the edge in her voice. 'I mean, I appreciate it, don't get me wrong. And I love the dress and the effort you've gone to for this. But...'

He'd gone very still. 'But what?'

Perhaps she shouldn't push this, ruin what would probably be a lovely night. But it felt wrong. It felt like buying into something dishonest and she was tired of the dishonesty. Tired of pretending to be someone she wasn't. Tired of pretending she didn't feel what she felt. And she was tired of him pretending too.

'You don't love me, Augustine,' she said flatly. 'You're marrying me because I'm pregnant. And all of this...' She gestured. 'Is just a show. It's a performance. Except I don't know who you're performing for because I already know you don't love me and that our marriage is just for our baby.' And then understanding abruptly hit her. 'Oh, I know. You're doing this for your father, aren't you?'

Augustine's expression hardened. 'He's got nothing to do with it. I'm doing this because I want to.'

But of course his father had something to do with it. He had everything to do with it. This was about Augustine trying to live up to his example, to do the things that were expected of him, even if that wasn't what he wanted for himself.

And that was another question. What did he want for himself? Did he even know?

'Do you? Do you really?' She stared up at him. 'Is this what you really want? To get down on one knee and propose to a woman you don't love, so you can have a wife you don't want? All for a child you never planned on having in the first place?'

His fingers curled suddenly around the velvet box, a muscle jumping in the side of his strong jaw. 'I never said I didn't want any of those things. I said I couldn't. There's a difference. I only want to make you happy, Freddie.'

He meant it; she could see that. He *did* want to make her happy. And while part of her loved that he did, she also knew that it wasn't enough. She wanted him to do all of this because it was something he wanted, too. Because he felt the same way she did. Except, he didn't. So what was the point?

You want him to love you as you love him.

Everything inside her curled up tight as the truth settled down inside her. A truth that she didn't want to examine too closely, because it wasn't anything she could ever have.

He'd been very clear that he didn't love her. Very clear. And she'd thought she was fine with that. Except...she wasn't fine with that.

She wasn't fine with that at all.

She wanted more. She wanted all the things she thought she could never have, all the things she thought she didn't deserve. And she wanted them with him.

'You know what would make me happy?' she said. 'Me, taking care of you. Me, supporting you. Me, loving you. And you doing those things for me too. And not because you think that's what a good husband does, or because of some impossible standard you're trying to live up to for your father's sake. I want you to do them because you want to. Because you love me.'

That muscle in his jaw leapt again. 'My father's standards are not part of this conversation. I care about you. But love isn't something I can give, Freddie. I told you that.'

Something died a little inside her, a hope she didn't know she'd been nursing. It was very clear he meant it, and she had no idea why she should feel the pain of it so acutely when he'd always been honest with her about what he could and couldn't give. She only knew that it hurt. It hurt very much.

'I see,' she said, her voice getting husky. 'And when our child is born? Are you going to tell them that you can't love them either?'

The angry sparks in his eyes glittered sharper, brighter. 'That's different. A child is—'

'It's fine,' she interrupted before he could go on, because one thing was becoming increasingly clear to her. 'You're going to be a good father, I know. But...' She took a ragged breath. 'I'm sorry. I think I've changed my mind. I just don't think I can marry you.'

Shock stole his breath and for a minute he had no idea what to say.

He'd done everything he could to make this night special, organising the picnic in her favourite place and buying her a dress he knew she'd love. The ring in the box was a sapphire, a historic piece of Solari history and his own mother's engagement ring. He knew she'd love that too.

And he'd been expecting to go down on one knee, to propose and have her smile at him, to slide that ring on her finger and then they'd have a lovely picnic. Then he'd been thinking obsessively about how he'd strip that dress off her and feast on her instead, under the apple trees, in the soft glowing light of the fairy lights.

The last thing he'd expected her to do was refuse.

'What do you mean you can't marry me?' The words came out even harsher than he'd intended. 'You said you would. You promised, Freddie.'

Her eyes were very dark, the glow of the fairy lights making them look even darker. 'I know. And I'm sorry.' Her hands were at her sides, closed into little fists. 'I thought it didn't matter that you don't feel the same way about me that I feel about you. I've been in love with you for so long, I got used to not having it reciprocated. But the baby... You... Everything's changed.'

The pressure was starting up inside him again, a growing desperation that he didn't understand. She *had* to marry him. He'd decided. He would be the caretaker of his own throne until his child was of age to take it, and he needed her at his side.

'What do you mean everything's changed,' he demanded. 'Changed how?'

'You doing this for me.' She gestured at the lights and the picnic. 'You holding me at night. You protecting me. You supporting me. I like it, Augustine. No, more than that, I *love* it. But I can't help thinking about how much better it would be if you actually meant it. If you wanted me the way I want you, if you let me take care of you. If you let me make *you* happy.' Her dark eyes were soft as black velvet. 'But you don't. You keep holding me at a distance. And you're so focused on what you think you should be doing, on what a good king does, a good husband does, that you don't think about what *you* want.'

She's right. Have you ever *thought about that?*

Of course he'd thought about it. And this *was* what he wanted. How many times did he have to say it?

'You know what I want. You to marry me. You as my wife and my queen. Our child to have a family.'

'But where does love feature in all of that?'

His anger built, a fire that burned inside him that he could never seem to put out. Why did she keep talking about love? Hadn't she been listening to him?

'It doesn't feature,' he snapped. 'I thought I made myself clear about that.'

'You did. But I don't think that's what you want, not deep down.' She searched his face. 'You're so hard on yourself, Augustine. You expect so much of yourself and I don't understand why.'

His grip on his anger began to loosen. She didn't understand; that was clear. Of course he was hard on himself. He had to be. He'd never be the king his father had hoped for, but he kept trying. It was the trying that mattered. Because what else would he be if he stopped?

You'd be broken. You'd be nothing.

'Someone has to expect more,' he said roughly. 'How else can I be the king that Isavere was promised? That was the king that my father brought me up to be. That my mother *gave her life* for. If I'm not hard on myself, if I stop trying...' He tried to keep hold of the anger that kept welling up inside him, a hot, depthless rage he couldn't contain. 'Then what good am I?'

Freddie took an abrupt step forward and put her hands on his chest, a deep compassion in her eyes. 'You don't need to be good. You don't need to be anything at all. You just need to be you, Augustine.'

'Yes, me.' He gave a mirthless laugh. 'A man who can't do what a six-year-old child can do. A king who can't read or write. Who can't even control his own emotions. My father would be spinning in his grave if he knew what I'd become, and my mother—' He stopped, biting down hard on the words so they wouldn't reveal the depths of his own self-loathing.

'Your mother loved you. She gave up her life for you

because she loved you.' Freddie's eyes glowed with a sudden, fierce light. 'And she'd love you no matter what you are. Don't you understand that? And so would your father.'

'How would you know?' he said harshly. 'You never met either of them.'

'No, but I'm going to be a mother soon and I know that all I care about is that my child grows up happy. That's *all*.' She stared up at him, the force of her conviction burning in her expression. 'Tell me. If you were your father or your mother, would you be disappointed with the man you've become? Or would they think that you were brave and strong, and amazing for battling such terrible things and coming out the end still alive. Still a king. Still a man to be proud of.'

No, he couldn't think of those things. He couldn't. Because how would they be proud of the man he'd become when he wasn't? And he wasn't.

He had nothing but the dogged intent to try and keep trying.

'It doesn't matter,' he said. 'None of it matters. And none of it changes anything. I'm still the man that I am and that's all I'll ever be.'

'Yes,' she said insistently. 'And that's the man I fell in love with, don't you see? I don't want you to be another man. I want the one standing in front of me.'

He didn't understand what more she wanted from him. He'd told her what he could give her and that was it. There was nothing more. 'And you have him,' he said roughly. 'It's not my fault you want more than I can give.'

A bright, sharp ripple of pain crossed her features, and he could feel it in himself too. As if he'd stabbed a knife into his own heart.

Her hands dropped from his chest and she took a step back from him. Her chin lifted, a steely determination hardening her expression. 'It's not your fault, no. But I still want it. And I'm tired of pretending. I'm tired of pretending I don't feel what I feel. That I don't love you with every part of me. And I'm tired of pretending that I don't want more too.' There was no softness in her dark eyes now, they were sharp as obsidian. 'Which means I can't marry you, Augustine. I don't want that to be my life. And I don't want that to be yours either.'

The pressure inside him mounted, a crushing, agonising weight. 'What does my life matter? Surely what matters is that our child has their mother and their father. You can't deny them that, Freddie.'

'I'm not denying them that. You'll still have your child, Augustine, I promise. But I can't marry you. I don't want a marriage where you end up resenting me and I end up resenting you, because that's what will happen. And I don't want a marriage based on a lie either. That's not good for us and it's not good for our child.'

Every part of him was tense, his muscles aching, the pressure in his head getting worse.

She's right. You know she is.

She was. And he couldn't force her to marry him if she didn't want to. He was supposed to make her happy, after all. Except…it felt as if he was losing something he didn't know he wanted, and he didn't know how to hold on to it.

He couldn't love her back. He couldn't.

Love was the burden he couldn't bear, not when he was carrying so many other things already. It would crush him. It would make his anger more intense, his fear even more extreme. His emotions were already in as tight a grip as he could have on them, and love… Love made everything worse.

'I can't,' he forced out, because she deserved the truth

from him at least. Even if it was a truth she didn't want. 'I can't give you what you want. My emotions are already hard for me to contain and love... It would make everything a thousand times harder. The mood swings, the expectations... Everything, Freddie. I can't do it. I just can't.'

Her gaze was sharp and yet there were tears in her eyes, too, he could see them gleaming, and one escaped, sliding down her cheek, glittering like a tiny diamond. 'I know,' she said. 'I know.' She half lifted a hand as if to touch him, then dropped it back at her side. 'I'm sorry, Augustine. I didn't want to put this on you. But I just don't see how we can make each other happy. And more than anything, I want happiness for you.'

There was a tight feeling in his chest. So tight it was as if he couldn't breathe. 'Marrying you would make me happy,' he forced out.

'Not like this it wouldn't.' She stepped forward abruptly, went up on her toes and brushed her mouth over his. And he knew it was goodbye. He knew it. His hands almost went to her hips to hold her, grip her tightly against him and never let her go.

But he didn't. Because she was right, wasn't she?

She loved him and he wouldn't love her back, and that would only make her unhappy. And she'd had so much unhappiness in her life already, she didn't need any more.

So he didn't reach for her.

He let her step back and slowly turn and walk away.

And he kept on standing there under the lights as the food on the blanket slowly went cold, the ice in the bucket turning to water.

As his heart went cold inside his chest, and eventually froze over entirely.

CHAPTER TWELVE

THREE DAYS LATER, Winifred had moved out of Augustine's bedroom and was back in her own private apartments. She felt as if she'd had part of her soul cut out and the rest of her was merely going through the motions.

She looked into moving out of the castle altogether, perhaps finding a nice little apartment in Isavere's capital, or maybe a cottage somewhere in the castle grounds. She wanted to be in her child's life, that much was certain, and had been working on a shared custody arrangement that she could bring to Augustine when he was ready. She wouldn't give her child up, but she'd never deny them their father either.

Augustine hadn't contacted her since the night she'd left him in the orchard, and she didn't expect him to. It hurt. It hurt a lot, even though she'd had to do it. She'd had to leave him for both of their sakes.

She was looking at some apartments online when her phone went off and when she looked at the screen, a little shock went through her.

It was King Galen Kouros of Kalithera, one of Augustine's closest friends.

Instantly, she hit the answer button. 'Your Majesty. What can I do for you?'

'None of that,' Galen said sharply. 'It's Galen, Freddie, and you know it. What's happening with Augustine? I haven't heard from him and he's not answering his phone. He won't answer it when Khal calls him either.'

She swallowed. 'You know about...'

'You and him and the baby?' Galen said. 'Of course. I read the palace announcement like everyone else in the entire world.'

Winifred sighed. At least that was one thing she didn't have to explain. 'I refused to marry him. He didn't like it.'

There was a silence.

'Well,' Galen said at last. 'Of course he didn't like it. Why did you refuse?'

There was a lump in her throat, making her voice sound tight. 'I... I love him. I love him so much, but he keeps holding me at a distance. He says he wants to make me happy, but I know it's because he thinks he should, not because it's actually what he wants. And I think... I think we'll just make each other miserable.'

There was another long silence.

'This is a very personal question, I know,' Galen murmured. 'But...does he love you?'

'No,' she said starkly. 'No, he told me he can't love me. It's to do with the accident and his emotional instability, or at least that's what he said to me. He said love makes everything worse, which is why I had to call it off. He'll only end up resenting me and feeling like my love is an emotional burden, and that's not what I want for him.'

'Clearly not.' There was another silence. 'He deserves better than that.'

'I know. He deserves everything. But he won't let me give it to him.' She hesitated. 'He thinks...he's broken. And he just can't accept it when I tell him he isn't.'

'Sounds like he's being a stubborn horse's ass,' Galen muttered. 'Let me talk to him. Khal and me.'

The tight band around her heart loosened. 'I think you should. He won't listen to me. But he might listen to you.'

'Leave it with me. We'll handle it.'

And for the first time in days, Winifred felt a little bit of hope.

Augustine sat in his dim sitting room. He'd been there for three days with the curtains closed, everything in darkness. Just how he liked it.

In the three days he'd been there, cutting himself off from everyone, he'd worked his way through two bottles of very good Scotch and he had big plans for the rest of the palace's cellar.

He didn't see why he shouldn't. If he was going to be in torment, he might as well blunt the edges with some very good alcohol.

He was in the process of getting into his third bottle, when there was a loud commotion from outside the door. His guards sounded as if they were arguing with someone, and then, quite suddenly, the door was kicked open and two men came in.

Two very familiar, very unwelcome men.

Augustine scowled as the tall figures of Galen and Khalil approached. 'What do you want?' he snapped gracelessly.

The pair of them came over, Galen dropping into the armchair opposite, while Khalil leaned against the mantelpiece.

'That is a fine welcome,' Khalil said. 'I left my pregnant wife because you are sulking like a child. I hope you are happy.'

'I didn't ask you to come,' Augustine growled.

'No,' Galen said. 'Freddie did.'

Instantly everything inside him went taut with pain. 'Well, you can go home again. She's got nothing to do with either of you.'

'Actually, she has,' Galen said. 'I'm fully intending to be godfather to your child, and Khal is too. Also, I was promised a wedding and your stubbornness is going to do us out of one, and quite frankly, I'm annoyed. Solace was looking forward to it.'

'So was Sidonie,' Khal added. 'I do not want to upset my pregnant wife.'

'Too bad,' Augustine said. 'Freddie said no. She doesn't want to marry me.'

'Because you're being an idiot.' Galen kicked his feet up onto the coffee table and sent him a hard glare. 'She loves you and you love her. You've been in love with her for years—don't lie to yourself.'

Augustine's heart contracted in his chest, the pressure, the relentless pressure inside him gathering. 'No, I'm not. I can't. You don't understand.'

'Of course, we understand,' Khalil said.

'We know that you think you're broken and a terrible king, etcetera.' Galen waved a hand. 'It's all very boring, Gus. Because you're not broken, and you know it.'

Augustine sat forward. 'But you—'

'So, there are some things you cannot do,' Kahlil interrupted. 'And you have some difficulties. Everyone has difficulties. You are not that different.'

'Except I—'

'You're a damn good king,' Galen said, taking up the thread. 'You play to your strengths and you have a gift with people. Your country and your people are thriving, and that is all down to you.'

The taut things inside him tightened still further, the urge to deny it so strong his jaw ached with the effort of biting down on the words.

Your friends don't see you as broken, and neither do your people. And neither does Freddie. Why can't you accept it?

'And also, Freddie has loved you for years,' Galen went on. 'All she wants is to make you happy and you won't let her. Why the hell not?'

'You know my moods are…difficult,' Augustine said through gritted teeth. 'I get angry easily, I have little patience. I have—'

'Do not be any more stupid than you are already,' Khalil cut him off. 'I did not take you for a man who relies on excuses and those are excuses.'

He's right. That's exactly what they are.

Augustine tried to ignore the thought. 'I don't want to make things difficult for her,' he said roughly. 'And she shouldn't have to put up with a moody bastard of a husband. She deserves better than that.'

'But don't you deserve better too?' Galen asked. 'Don't you deserve to have happiness?'

Something inside him twisted. 'This isn't about me.'

'Isn't it though?' Galen's blue gaze was uncompromising. 'Aren't you making it all about you right now? You and your terrible 'failings'?'

Anger gathered inside him, a hot ball of it sitting in his gut, and he opened his mouth, ready to spill all the furious, defensive words he wanted to say.

'Is she not more important?' Khalil asked quietly before he could get a word out. 'Is her happiness not more important than your feelings of brokenness? Does she not deserve more than a man who thinks his pain is more important than hers?'

Something in his friend's voice echoed inside him, hitting a deep truth he hadn't wanted to face.

She is more important; you know that.

'It is only love that she wants, Augustine,' Khalil went on, still quiet. 'And you might not think that you can give her that, but you can. It is a choice and you have to choose. And what is more important? Her happiness or your fear?'

The words were an arrow and they pierced his heart clean through.

His friends were right, he *was* making this all about him and his failings. About all the things he couldn't do, and all the things he was afraid to do. Because that was it, wasn't it? It was all about fear.

Fear of not being what she wanted, of not being a good husband, a good father. Fear of not being worthy. Fear of the burden that love had always placed on him.

Her happiness or your fear. What was more important?

It is a choice and you have to choose, that was what Khalil had said.

But Augustine knew in that moment, that there was no choice to be made. Because he'd already chosen. And perhaps he'd chosen that night in the palace, when he'd put his hand on the satiny skin of a woman he wasn't expecting. A woman who'd first set his body on fire and then his soul.

Winifred. His Freddie. She was more important. She would *always* be more important.

If you were your father or your mother, would you be disappointed with the man you've become? she'd asked him that night in the orchard. *Or would they think that you were brave and strong, and amazing for battling such terrible things and coming out the end still alive. Still a king. Still a man to be proud of.*

He didn't know if that was true, but in that moment he suddenly knew exactly what it was that he wanted.

He wanted to be a man that *she* could be proud of. A man who could make her happy because he wanted to. Because he loved her. And he did love her. He loved her so much. It hurt that love, it was too sharp and too bright, and so very hungry. But she loved him in return and her love was strong and steady, a rock he could ground himself on. She was the anchor in the stormy sea he floated in and she wouldn't let him drown. She would keep him close.

God, what had he been thinking? Wasting three days drinking when he could have spent three days showing Winifred Scott exactly how much he loved her.

Without a word, he launched himself out of his chair.

'You have to go and see a woman about a broken heart?' Galen inquired.

But Augustine was already gone.

Winifred was in her apartments, sitting on the sofa and looking at houses for rent on her laptop, when Augustine came bursting in through the door.

She looked up, her heart contracting in her chest when she saw who it was. 'Augustine? What are you—'

But he'd crossed the room, taken the laptop off her lap and tossed it heedlessly down on the floor, then hauled her straight up off the couch and into his arms before she could finish the sentence.

The look in his blue-green gaze burned as he looked down at her, the intensity in it stealing the breath from her lungs.

'Winifred,' he said, and there was nothing but rough gravel in his beautiful voice. 'My darling Freddie. I'm sorry.

I'm so sorry about the last few days. About that night in the orchard. About everything.'

She was trembling all of a sudden, her eyes full of tears. She didn't understand what was happening. 'I don't know... what...'

'I've just had a talking to from two friends who know me better than I know myself.' His arms tightened around her. 'And they delivered a few home truths. Firstly, that I'm a selfish bastard who made all of this about me and my issues. And secondly, that there's another person whose happiness is more important to me than anything else on this earth.'

Her throat tightened and she couldn't speak.

'It's you, sweetheart,' Augustine went on, the flames in his eyes making her nearly catch alight too. 'It's your happiness that's important to me. *You* are important to me. And I should have been listening to you all along. I'm sorry I didn't. I was...afraid. Afraid of not being able to be the husband you want, the husband you deserve. And you deserve so much. You deserve everything that's in my power to give.'

'You already *are* the husband I deserve,' she said, her voice thick with emotion. 'You don't have to be anything at all but you. You never did.'

Impossibly, the look in his eyes grew even more intense. 'Oh, sweetheart... You have no idea how much you mean to me. I was wrong when I said that love wasn't something I could give you. Turns out, I loved you anyway. I think I loved you the moment I found you in my bed. Possibly even before that.'

There was a lump in her throat, a prickling of tears behind her eyes, and her chest felt so tight she could hardly breathe. This couldn't be real, could it? Was he really saying what she thought he was saying?

'But…' she said hoarsely. 'You didn't know it was me.'

Augustine smiled, a smile so warm and full of tenderness that she couldn't keep the tears back no matter how hard she tried. 'My heart did.'

'Augustine…' His name came out as a plea or a prayer, she didn't know which. She just wanted the pleasure of saying it.

He bent and kissed away the tears that were sliding down her cheeks, gathering her even closer. 'I was wrong about something else too. As it turns out, love doesn't make everything worse. Certainly your love doesn't. It grounds me, Freddie. It steadies me. It anchors me. And I don't think I can live without it.'

She swallowed, pressing her hands to his chest so she could feel his heat and his strength. 'Isn't it lucky then that you won't have to?'

His smile deepened. 'Does this mean you're going to marry me after all?'

Winifred's heart just about burst for joy. 'Perhaps I could be persuaded.'

She didn't need persuading, but Augustine took it for a challenge, and set about doing so anyway.

Turned out he was very good at it.

Augustine Solari was very good at a lot of things, a king, a lover, a father.

But he was best of all at being her husband.

EPILOGUE

'HE'S BEAUTIFUL,' GALEN SAID, after inspecting the small bundle Augustine had held out to him. 'He definitely takes after Freddie.'

'He does,' Khalil agreed. 'A perfect little boy.'

Augustine had left his sleeping wife for a moment in order to show off his new son to his friends, and was already glowing with pride and a fierce, protective love so strong he could hardly bear it.

Khalil and Galen had arrived not long after Freddie had gone into labour, there to offer their support at the birth of Augustine's first child. They'd brought Solace and Sidonie respectively, along with Leo, Solace and Galen's toddler son, and Khalil and Sidonie's baby girl, Zahra.

Augustine hadn't known how much it meant to him to have his friends here until now. He was also pleased that Freddie's sisters were coming, because she needed her family here too. Both girls had fallen in love with Isavere when they'd been bridesmaids for his and Freddie's wedding, and they were desperate to see their new nephew.

He chatted with his friends for a couple of moments, before retreating back into the bedroom, to find Freddie awake and sitting up in bed. She held her hands out for their son and he came over, tucking the small bundle back into her arms. Then he sat on the bed beside her, his arm around her shoulders so he was holding them both.

'Khal and Galen think he looks like you,' Augustine said.

Freddie leaned against him, tired but radiant with joy. 'He has your eyes, I think.' She kissed their son's forehead, then glanced at him. 'You still want to call him Piero?'

He knew what she was asking. Did he want to name their son after his father? Before the birth, he'd been uncertain, a part of him still unsure. But now he knew something he hadn't known before his son's birth. A truth that had settled deep inside him, easing a wound that had been with him a long time.

'You know you told me that my parents would be proud of the man I am now?' he said. 'I didn't believe you.'

She settled against him. 'I know you didn't.'

'I do now, though.'

Her head shifted on his shoulder and she looked up. 'Because you're a father?'

He smiled. 'Yes, because I'm a father.' Gently, he reached out to stroke his new son's downy forehead. 'And I know there's nothing that this little boy can do to make me love him any less. Nothing to make him any less worthy in my eyes than he already is.'

Freddie smiled back and he could feel the warmth of that smile in his soul. 'Piero definitely takes after you.'

Augustine didn't think it was possible for his life to become any richer, any more full of joy, any more full of love than it already was.

He was wrong.

* * * * *

COMING SOON!

We really hope you enjoyed reading this book. If you're looking for more romance be sure to head to the shops when new books are available on

Thursday 26th October

To see which titles are coming soon, please visit

millsandboon.co.uk/nextmonth

MILLS & BOON

MILLS & BOON ®

Coming next month

PREGNANT AND STOLEN BY THE TYCOON
Maya Blake

One night. It was only meant to be one night.

Genie only realized she'd said it out loud when Seve's whole body tightened, turning even more marble-like than before.

"Why are you doing this? You don't want even want a child. You said as much when we had dinner."

His eyes glinted, his incisive gaze tracking her as she paced in the small cabin. "What I felt a few weeks ago no longer matters."

"That's absurd. Of course it does."

He gritted his teeth. "Let me rephrase. The child you're carrying—*my* child—is now my number one priority. I'm not taking my eyes off you until he or she is born."

Continue reading
PREGNANT AND STOLEN BY THE TYCOON
Maya Blake

Available next month
www.millsandboon.co.uk

LET'S TALK

Romance

For exclusive extracts, competitions and special offers, find us online:

MillsandBoon

@MillsandBoon

@MillsandBoonUK

@MillsandBoonUK

Get in touch on 01413 063 232